Desert
Lily

Desert
Lily

~

A Novel

Peter A. Pascaris

iUniverse, Inc.
New York Lincoln Shanghai

Desert Lily

iUniverse books may be ordered through booksellers or by contacting:

iUniverse
2021 Pine Lake Road, Suite 100
Lincoln, NE 68512
www.iuniverse.com
1-800-Authors (1-800-288-4677)

Because of the dynamic nature of the Internet, any Web addresses or links contained in this book may have changed since publication and may no longer be valid.

This is a work of fiction. All of the characters, names, incidents, organizations, and dialogue in this novel are either the products of the author's imagination or are used fictitiously.

"Fall" by Hans W. Cohn appears in *With All Five Senses*, translated by Frederick G. Cohn, published by Menard Press, and is reprinted with permission by Mr. Anthony Rudolf, Menard Press, 8 The Oaks, Woodside Avenue, London, United Kingdom.

ISBN: 978-0-595-44120-4 (pbk)
ISBN: 978-0-595-68493-9 (cloth)
ISBN: 978-0-595-88444-5 (ebk)

Printed in the United States of America

Based on a true story.

Dedicated to Donna, whose flower grows in my heart, and to our children, Gail, Matthew, and Amanda, for whom this story was written so they may understand.

I rely on the presence of memory, an imperfect truth at best.

—From *Siblings* by Claire Kemp

ACKNOWLEDGMENTS

I wish to acknowledge and express my heartfelt gratitude for the support of the following people: My wife, Merrilee, who brought sunshine and life to my darkened heart and opened my mind to creative thought. My mentor and friend, Margo LaGattuta, whose skill and nurturing spirit guided my writing. Michael Abbott, a friend who came out of the past and into my future. And I thank all those who read and commented on my work-in-progress to help me shape it into a labor of love.

CHAPTER ONE

My memory of that day is like television itself, sharp and clear but unreliable.

—**From *She's Come Undone* by Wally Lamb**

Amy stumbles. I catch her arm and nearly fall with her.

Urging her along, I steer her toward our car in the driveway and worry that her appearance and my clumsy effort will attract attention.

I used to enjoy seeing heads turn when Amy dressed in her stylish outfits. Now she's wearing a simple housedress, the only one I could manage to put on her. It hangs on her frail eighty-pound body like a sheet over a stickback chair.

After settling Amy in the passenger seat, I take a quick look around the neighborhood. It's Sunday-evening quiet. Soft breezes sprinkle dots of sunlight along tree-lined Sorrento Avenue. Long black shadows reach across green yards, stretching endlessly. Normally, it's my favorite time of day, but today's different. I'm taking my wife, Amy, to a place I had promised never to take her.

The radio blares when I start the DeSoto. "Midway along Route 1966," says the DJ, "on Detroit's Top Forty, the Four Tops promise 'Reach Out, I'll Be There.'"

I snap off the radio switch and glance at Amy. She sits in a rag-doll slump and seems not to have heard a thing. I press her overnight bag firmly against her lap, vainly trying to prop her up. Then I frown. Our daughter, Eleni, should be on Amy's lap, but she's at my folks' house. She's too young to understand the reason for the delay of her birthday celebration. Amy's parents, the Millers, know but aren't telling anyone. My mom and pop think Amy's going in for some "neurological tests." They don't ask for details.

Amy's eyes widen at my touch, and she says, "Nicky, please don't."

Her sudden reaction suggests that the medication has yet to take full effect, but she's had other episodes where tranquilizers have taken hours to quiet her.

"Sorry, pumpkin. I'm afraid you'll fall against the dash."

"No. I mean don't take me."

"Honey, I wish there was another way, but—"

"I'm all right now. I've mostly slept since you took Eleni to your mom's house. Nicky, please. I'll be better. I belong with Eleni on her birthday. I promise to be good."

"Amy, don't keep saying that. You're not bad, you're sick. And I'm not punishing you."

"Yes, you are. You don't know what they'll do to me. Please. Give me another chance. I promise not to be bad, and I'll do whatever you say. But, please, not the hospital."

Amy often carries on about punishment for her bad behavior, sometimes flailing her fists while hurling angry accusations, mostly at herself. When exhausted, she settles into protests of innocence and becomes sullen like a scolded child. Then the cycle begins again. Before her emotional episodes, I regarded mental illness, as most of my friends did, as an unfortunate thing that happened to other people. Most of us spoke with concern about victims of emotional breakdowns. Our superiority gave us comfort. The worst of us made shaming comments that encouraged others to laugh as if mental illness was fodder for comic gags.

Now, the few family members who know about Amy's situation don't want to talk about it and have warned me not to mention it to others.

Committing Amy feels like surrendering. The doctor treats her anxiety by dulling her senses so that she sleeps for hours and can't recall her therapy sessions. Maybe he's to blame for her stupor. Maybe Amy's not as ill as he thinks.

Amy begins to cry, a symptom of her depression that I fear has evolved into a tactic. Earlier I gave in to her pleading and took her back to the house. Then, after waking from a nap, she marched into the kitchen and began emptying cupboards and scrubbing everything in sight. Within minutes, her eyes glazed over, and I was powerless to overcome her obsession to make everything perfectly clean.

Our entire house is spotless from Amy's constant attention. Though she's often lethargic, she has bursts of frenzied housekeeping that bewilder me. This morning she was heavily medicated. I thought she'd give the countertops a swipe and quit in exhaustion, but she didn't stop until she had filled a trash bag with "contaminated" packages, rags, and mops. She even insisted on discarding the clothing she wore.

When I called Dr. Florence, he said, "Amy should go immediately to the hospital. She needs to stay two to three weeks, depending on the treatments."

"Treatments?" I said.

"The ECT sessions I mentioned before."

"I don't remember hearing that. ETC?"

"E *C* T, electroconvulsive therapy. We've—"

"Shock therapy?"

"I don't like to call it that. Don't be alarmed. It's proven to be remarkably successful for treating depression."

His assurance was not comforting then, and I still don't like it. Tranquilizers are one thing, but shock treatments scare me. I can take care of Amy. If I try hard enough—if I love her enough—she'll be okay. Sure she's depressed, but we all feel sad now and then. We get over it. Jesus, Amy's not....

"You're right to be concerned," said Dr. Florence, "but Amy's not *insane*, and Lynnwood Hospital is not an *asylum*."

His words clung like prickly briars. I felt chastised and trapped. Have I been wrong to trust modern psychiatry? Shock therapy? It's 1966, for Christ's sake. Amy is only twenty-five years old. Isn't shock therapy for old people confined to prison—or for fictional characters? I remembered once a colleague at school read a passage aloud from the novel *One Flew Over the Cuckoo's Nest*, about a patient made senseless by repeated jolts of electricity.

"Mr. Demetriou," said the doctor. "I've discussed this with Amy. She seems fine about having the procedure."

How can she be "fine"? I thought. *She's so drugged. How can she know what the hell he's talking about?*

Nevertheless, obeying the doctor made me feel like a soldier in a strategic operation. The exercise of plotting my route to the hospital was fortifying, as if the magnitude of my effort would overwhelm Amy's illness. Yet, now I feel vaguely disappointed that Lynnwood Hospital isn't farther away. It's a destination I'd rather not reach.

Next to me, in the car, Amy has stopped crying. Her eyes are closed and her head is resting against the back of the seat. Oh, God, she's deliberately taken too many pills. My breath stops until I see her chest rise and fall in rhythmic motion.

Amy opens her eyes but remains motionless. Her head is tilted back to reveal the contours of her nose, mouth, and chin—sweet aspects that I love, but now her face is dim and pale like moonscape on a cloudy night. I speak to her with little hope that she understands, and I'm afraid to mention the hospital again. Will she be angry? Dear God, does she know my betrayal? For the thousandth time, I pray that I'm doing the right thing.

When she shifts her eyes toward mine, I say, "Amy, I ... I'm taking you to ..."

In a voice that is not her own, she says, "To the hospital. Yes, I know. I'm ready now."

My wife of thirty months looks at me peculiarly as if I'm someone else, some-one familiar, but not me. I want her to tell me that she's not afraid to go and not angry that I'm taking her. What assurance, I wonder, does she want from me?

Anticipating Amy's admission, I drove by Lynnwood Hospital last week while Amy was with Dr. Florence, and Eleni was with Mom. I had arranged for a sub for my classes at James Junior High and was hoping to start summer vacation early. At the time, I felt that Amy would be in good hands and I'd get some relief, but now, as the red brick structure comes into view, I sense something else.

This time the hospital reminds me of the first schoolhouse I had attended as a child, except the hospital is more intimidating. I had once run away from school by jumping out an open window, but unlike the school, the hospital windows are barred. I look for the driveway that leads to the parking lot behind the building. Though I spot it, I drive past and turn at the next street, circling the block to give me another chance to change my mind and take her home.

Suddenly, I have feelings I've never known. *Dammit, Nick, get Amy inside before dark.*

I park near a sign marked "Patient Admitting." Amy lets me help her out of the car and then stands with the overnight bag hanging loosely at her side. I offer to carry it, but she pulls away and shakes her head. I hope the willful gesture is a good sign, evidence of a stubborn strength that'll help her recover. I listen for words of encouragement, hoping for one of her wisecracking responses—another thing I love about her. I still believe in her power to brighten my mood. I want to know that she's all right about entering this place—that she forgives me for bringing her here. However, Amy offers only silence and a hollow stare that makes me feel invisible.

Though dusk's long shadows lay across the pathway, only a few lights appear to be on inside the hospital. Maybe no one's home and we'll have to leave. Brush-ing away that thought, I wipe perspiration from my forehead with an icy hand. A sudden chill threatens to overtake me, but I lead Amy like a Sherpa guide coaxing her up Mount Everest.

When we reach the entrance, I turn the handle and pull, then push hard. The door is locked. A sign beneath a broken lamp reads, "Ring Bell for Entry." I touch the button and am startled by an alarm-like ring. Through a small window in the door, I see movement beyond the wire-imbedded glass. A large, longhaired man dressed in white lumbers toward us. *The man in the white coat is coming to get us.* The stupid joke is not a joke. When the latch reports a loud *clack*, I imagine the door opening like a vault. I hear a gust of air escaping with a *whoosh* and smell disinfectant.

"You the *Demetri* people?" the man asks with what I try to believe is a smile.

"*Demetriou,*" I say, fearful of sounding too corrective.

"This way."

He leads us down a long and dimly lit hallway. An uncertain light creeps out on the left. *Squish, squeak. Squish squeak* go the orderly's crepe soled shoes in time with his side-to-side swagger. The tapping of our hard leather soles follow, out of step and out of tune. He points to the left and says, "Cheryl will take care of you." The way he pronounces the name—with a hard *ch*—makes me feel odd. Then the orderly steps back, leans against the wall, and stands with his arms folded like an Indian at a powwow. My mind warps him to Chief Bromden standing guard over the Cuckoo's Nest.

A single spotlight greets us around the corner. My hand shoots up to shade my eyes. Amy looks into the light without blinking. I move my hand over her eyes, but immediately feel foolish. A woman in a tattered sweater peers curiously from behind a cluttered desk. She smiles, as though amused by my antics. I shrug and point to the light above. The woman nods.

Cheryl is exceedingly thin. Like the odd sound of her name, she appears to be a different sort. In her position behind a tall Pepsi cup and a short stack of papers decorated with wadded candy and gum wrappers, she reminds me of a waitress at my dad's restaurant. Up close, I smell licorice and see a pencil stuck next to a silk flower in her hair. A repeated *snap!* clicks from her mouth as she chews her gum. Her lips are bright red, and her high cheekbones are crowned with silver dollar swatches of dark rouge. Cheryl puts down a magazine I recognize from the barbershop where I get my haircut, a recent issue of *Look* with a photo of a new star named Streisand. Seeing something current and familiar in this strange place makes me feel better. Cheryl looks up, giving each of us equal attention as if to ask, *Which of you is the patient?*

"Hello," she says. "Here to be admitted?"

"Yes. We ... my wife, that is. She's with Dr. Florence. His patient, I mean. Amy Demetriou. I brought her here. I'm Nick Demetriou. I'm her husband."

She offers a syrupy smile. Something black darkens one tooth. "Of course you are," she says.

Pulling the pencil from her hair, she touches the point to her tongue and marks a spot on her magazine before leafing through stacks of papers. Several Black Jack gum wrappers flutter to the floor. When she speaks again, her voice is surprisingly pleasant.

"Here it is. Dr. Florence and Mrs. Amy Lynn Demetriou." She pauses a moment and smiles. "Oh, your middle name is Lynn, like the hospital." Amy stares blankly at no one in particular. "Welcome to Lynnwood Hospital, Amy Lynn," Cheryl says. Her tone suggests that Amy is meant to be here.

She stuffs some papers into two separate folders and says to me, "Bring these forms with you to the third floor. Albert will take you to the elevator." Turning to Amy, she winks and says, "Don't you worry, hon. You'll be safe here."

I lick a bead of sweat from my lip. The salty taste quickly turns sour. I take the forms in one hand and Amy's hand in the other. Hers is cold and dry. Mine is clammy. A moment ago, I was cold. Now, hellfire rises around me. I pull Amy nearer.

Albert leads us to an elevator that appears large enough for two dozen people—fewer if some are on gurneys like those parked in the hall. The elevator is open. Albert motions us in. We step into the box and immediately turn to face forward. Albert reaches inside and punches the "3" button but doesn't join us. Two doors slowly close—one is a solid two-piece sliding door with a lever arm, the other a metal gate that expands to a cage-like grid. The whir of the motor doesn't prepare me for the jolt of the lift or the "Hello" that echoes behind us.

My heart jumps. I turn around sharply. Diagonally across the elevator stands another man, smaller than Albert, but his sudden appearance seems more menacing.

"Name's Jack. Got elevator duty tonight. Ya need ta step over here. Door opens this side for the third floor."

Just another orderly for the disordered.

Amy is still looking the other way. She wears the same non-expression she wore fifty minutes ago. I inch her to the other side of the enormous cell. The silence we ride in is a welcome respite. I hate the drama that my emotions are creating. In the past, I've taken pride in my ability to reason logically, but tonight I seem unable to discern real events from skewed perceptions in a bad dream.

The door opens into a room with a chest-high counter that's a step or two away. A faint light halos the counter. On the ceiling, only every fourth lamp is lit, graying any color that might be present. I draw Amy forward. Jack sticks his head out of the elevator and calls in a raspy whisper, "Thelma, got someone for ya." Then he pistol-points his finger at me and says, "Be waiting for ya."

As he ducks back into the elevator, I imagine him blowing across the tip of his finger as if he has just fired a shot. If I were a gunfighter, I'd have nailed him the instant he pointed at me.

I can see the top of Thelma's cap and cigarette smoke that curls and rises like a snake from a jar. The nurse is an older woman with lacquer-sprayed hair the color of dirty dishwater. When she steps out to greet us, I see that she wears an old-fashioned uniform—stiff white dress, pointy cap with rounded loops, ghost-white hosiery, and chalk-white shoes. She clutches a clipboard protectively to her chest. A fluorescent lamp reflects violet off her cat-eye glasses, concealing the expression behind them. She moves toward us, holding the clipboard shield tightly, one finger strategically placed under its top sheet. A starched smile precedes her singsong greeting.

"Welcome to Lynnwood Hospital, Amy. My name is Thelma. Here, let me have your things. You won't need these now. We'll take good care of everything."

Amy gives up her bag without resistance. I hand the folders to Nurse Thelma. She walks behind the counter while Amy and I approach like accused felons. I feel nauseated and dizzy, and my knee buckles as I step forward. Losing my balance, I let go of Amy's hand. Only my arm bumping the counter keeps me from toppling. Nurse Thelma pushes her pointed-framed eyeglasses back in place and watches me suspiciously. I back off, not daring to rest against the counter.

A small desk lamp faintly spotlights the forms she withdraws from a folder, and Thelma examines them like a customs officer inspecting passports before snapping a single sheet to her clipboard.

"Mr. Demetri—"

"It's 'Demetriou,' with an 'iou.'"

Thelma appears to question what I said, then looks at her clipboard, and then smiles as she says, "Yes. Dr. Florence completed the documents for admission, but I need your signature on this one."

"What is it?"

"A release form. It grants the hospital permission to carry out the treatments Dr. Florence told you about."

"The ... treatments?"

"Yes."

She offers no explanation and smiles again when I say, "Oh. Of course."

As I look over the form, I feel her eyes attack me. My only defense is to play the good soldier. "The treatments," I say. "I guess I should sign, but what about Amy?"

Amy is beside me gripping the counter's edge as if standing at a ship's rail peering mindlessly out to sea. My head swims. The floor moves in a Titanic heave.

Nurse Thelma points her pen at the "X" scratched next to the form's last line and says, "You'll have to sign for her."

I try to read the statement above the mark. There are only a few lines—something about liability, but I can make no sense of it. Is this what Dr. Florence explained earlier?

I draw a breath and hold it like it's my last, not exhaling until I've scribbled my name.

Thelma hands me a thin sheaf. "You can do the yellow forms at home where you'll be more comfortable. No sense in staying here longer than necessary." She nods as if I should know what she means. My Judas feeling returns.

"However, you must complete these *pink* ones before you leave tonight. I'll show you where you can sit."

As she steps from behind her station, another man materializes—a third man—mysteriously, like Orson Welles' *The Third Man*. Thelma takes me by the elbow and moves me like a schoolboy to a small desk near the elevator. The third man escorts Amy down a corridor. I break free from Thelma and call to Amy.

The escort turns, but Amy continues walking without hesitation, showing no sign of the weakness that made her stumble earlier. "Amy," I call again, feeling the space between us stretch like threads about to break. "Amy," I plead. "Sweetheart. I'll be here tomorrow. I'll come every day."

After months of powerless waiting, my shock at surrendering Amy is mixed with relief. I've done the best I could, and now Amy is in the hands of people who know how to help her. Nurse Thelma puts an arm around my shoulders. All at once, the nurse's touch seems comforting. So do the pink forms in my hand. This is something I can do for Amy. She needs me to tell the caregivers what she cannot report. I mustn't let her down.

I take extra time to write carefully. Then I step to the nurse's station and give the papers to Thelma. As she examines them, a gurney carrying Amy comes out of another room. Amy is strapped down flat, with wide black belts around her ankles, her wrists, and over her waist. One binding is across her forehead.

My God. What have I done?

"Amy," I call.

I start toward her.

Nurse Thelma grabs my wrist with a schoolmarm grip. "She can't hear you," she says. "She's been given an injection. Believe me, she'll be all right. It would've been better had you not seen her like that." Then, with what sounds to me like the same conviction she showed toward Amy's overnight bag, she says, "We'll take good care of her."

I jerk my arm away. The nurse reaches out again but hesitates when she sees my clenched teeth and angry eyes. The gurney is moving down the corridor. I go in that direction but Jack, the elevator man, moves in front of me, and steps closer until I back off.

At the far end of the corridor, the last glow of twilight slinks through the doorway of a large room where patients are gathered. A smoky haze hangs in the air further diffusing the orange light of dusk. I see robed figures—silhouettes really, for the only other light comes from a black and white television. Most of the people hunch in chairs or shuffle about with their heads down. It's impossible to tell if any are men. Except for one. In the hallway at the entrance to the big room, a man lurks and casts a gaze in Amy's direction. A cigarette dangles from his mouth; it brightens when he takes a long drag. Breathless moments pass before he exhales. When he does, the cigarette remains in place as billows of smoke mask his face.

CHAPTER TWO

A guilty conscience needs no accuser.

—Philippine proverb

Outside, a gust of wind kicks up just as I reach the car. The nerve-racking ordeal inside the hospital has left me hot and sticky, so I welcome the breeze. Then a more powerful burst nearly blows the hospital forms out of my hand. Cursing, I clutch the papers and look to see if any have gotten away. Satisfied, I opened the door, tossed the crumpled forms on the passenger seat, climb in, and start the car. I drive away, but look back because I can't shake the feeling that I've left something behind.

By the time I shift into third gear, my thoughts have turned to anger and blame. I hate what I've done, yet I confess that I'm glad to be rid of Amy's fearful questions and constant need for reassurance. Then I think, *for Christ's sake, it's not her fault. I can't blame her for being sad.*

Goddamn it. That doesn't help. *Someone's* got to be at fault. Someone's responsible for how Amy's turned out. She wasn't like this before. Something out of the ordinary must have changed her.

Then I recall how I felt minutes earlier in the hospital—how I let my emotions affect my perception. Maybe it wasn't as bad as I made it out to be. My thoughts were irrational—almost like Amy's thoughts. But hers were out of control. Despite all I tried to do, her behavior had gotten worse—bad enough to convince me to … to put her away. *Jesus, maybe I'm to blame.*

All at once, crazy notions swarm through my head. I swing my hand wildly to chase them away and accidentally hit the steering wheel. The car suddenly swerves, sending yellow papers sliding off the seat. I start to reach for them, but a driver in the next lane leans on his horn and startles me.

I pull off the road and stare into the windshield. Cringing at my distorted image reflected off the darkened glass, I rub my face and feel a roughness that surprises me. In the rearview mirror, I see my eyebrows knit together in a single line

10

and a beard that is burly despite a recent shave. I tilt the mirror and see myself as an older man with swarthy skin—not the face that Amy called "Mediterranean charming and Amy-able."

Flipping the mirror back in place, I try to compose myself. I'm a twenty-five-year-old college grad with a degree in science, trained to think logically. I know better than to let emotions get the best of me.

After a moment, I spot the hospital forms that had fluttered to the floor. They're my salvation. My chance to help Amy. I need to do what I teach my students to do—identify cause and effect. Dr. Florence should be told about Amy's parents. They've had a hand in her depression. I'll tell him of Amy's confusion over Andrew's gentle affection on the one hand and his fits of temper on the other. I should say something about her mother, Saundra, about her cold and distant personality, and Amy's reactions to her constant criticism.

At home, before beginning the forms, I call both sets of parents. Mom and Pop agree to keep Eleni overnight when I explain what I need to do. They don't question me, and they ignore how I emphasize *General* when I say Lynnwood *General* Hospital. Amy's parents have never been as helpful as mine have, and I'm glad Eleni's not with them. The Millers *seem* like good people. But what kind of parents could have overlooked their daughter's problems? What did they do to her when she was a child? I had always thought Andy and Saundra an odd pair—so opposite from each other and so different from my mom and pop.

I finish the short-answer form quickly and begin the long one with a simple paragraph about Amy's change from happy-go-lucky confidence to fear and apprehension. I guess at the causes—the Miller's insistence that Amy can't survive the ordeal of college, the mixed messages of Andy's excitability, and Saundra's micro-control. I make assumptions about what went on before I knew Amy, imagining psychological abuse that she probably endured as a child. How else could she have turned out as she has?

Amy's mother is icy and detached, I write. *Her father is emotional and intrusive.* Proudly, I avoid speculating about physical abuse. I have no such evidence. Still, it feels good to indict *someone*, and Amy's parents make fine defendants.

Outside, a storm begins. I close the windows. The house is hot and stifling. I pour myself a Coke and get back to blaming the Millers. Booming thunderclaps seem to punctuate my message.

A sharp crack of thunder rocks the house and rattles the ice in my glass. I take a sip. The Coke tastes good and feels cool. Condensation drips onto the table. I set the glass in the puddle of water. When I take my hand away, the glass begins to slide by itself—as if pushed by unknown forces. What the hell causes that?

I stick my finger in one of the puddles and begin to doodle. I write *Love* and then *Lover* on the table. Sometimes her father, Andy, calls Amy, *Lover*. I like the caring way he says it. He's very demonstrative, and I know he loves Amy very much. Saundra's personality is quite opposite, but she loves Amy, too. I admit all this, but don't write it on the yellow form.

I continue doodling and scrawl *Pumpkin Pookie* with the water. That's my pet name for Amy. It's silly, but our love's been like that. Fun. At least it was in the beginning. God, I love her. I have for a long time. Longer than Amy has loved me. She turned me down time after time, but I never gave up. Why was she so hard to land? Why was I so persistent?

We met in high school but didn't date until I started college and Amy was working full-time. From the very first, I hoped for a serious relationship, but she only wanted to be friends. Heartbroken, I almost flunked my freshman year and had to see a counselor about it. That was six years ago.

I remember him—the shrink—as *Dr. Anthony*. It wasn't his real name, and he wasn't a doctor yet. His general appearance reminded me of Anthony Perkins, the actor in *Psycho*. His Princeton haircut and the way he asked questions about my mother while he sat in his rocking chair cinched his name.

The scholarship office said I had to see him after I bombed my midterm exams. I was obligated to six meetings. The counseling was free. So was my tuition if I kept up my grades. The almost-doctor was working on his doctorate. I'm probably in a textbook someplace.

It was 1960, and I was only nineteen. I considered turning down the counseling, but the scholarship office threatened to drop my stipend. At the time, I wanted it over with, but now I think that I'd have paid better attention had I known what would happen to Amy.

He made a big deal of how I remembered so much about the first time I met Amy in tenth grade biology. I told him that I heard her giggle and then picked her out by looking around the room until I saw her face. As I talked to Anthony, I could see Amy in my mind, but had a hard time describing her the way I wanted. Even now, words fail me, but I'd probably say that everything about her colors the way I feel.

"Whenever I see Amy," I said, "I get … you know, like the song says, smoke gets in my eyes. It's hard to describe her."

"Go ahead," he said. "Give it a try."

I thought for a moment and said, "Well, I'm only five-nine, and she makes me feel tall. I found out later that she's five-two."

"Uh-huh. What else?"

"She reminds me of a movie star."

"Oh? Someone sexy?"

"No," I protested. "Someone like Ann Blyth in *Kismet*."

"*Kismet*? Ah ... so you think fate had something to do with your meeting?"

"What?"

"Do you remember what was she wearing?"

"Yeah, she wore a red and black plaid dress—'jumper' I guess it's called—with a white blouse underneath. Something like what Catholic girls wear. But she didn't wear kneesocks. Anyway, Amy's too cool and has too good a figure to be in an all-girl's school. You know what I mean? She's a very nice girl, but she wouldn't make a good nun."

"I see. You're doing very well. Keep going."

"She wore white bobby socks to go with her white-and-black ... whadayacallum? Saddle shoes. Small ones—like little kid's shoes. And I liked that her blouse was open to the second button. I liked her hair, too. It was cut real short, so you could see the back of her neck. I noticed it when she undid her little scarf. It made me think of *bare neck-ed*."

"Did you tell her you thought of her as *naked*?"

"Are you kidding? Not then I didn't. Not ever, actually. Amy's not that kind of girl. She's not shy, but she's very proper about some things."

"What about you?"

"Me? I turn red just thinking about it."

"So you usually shy away from girls?"

"Yeah, but Amy's different. *I'm* different with Amy. Even that first day I noticed a lot about her. She wore the reddest lipstick I'd ever seen. And she had the straightest, whitest teeth—like a model in a toothpaste ad."

"You like looking at girls in ads?"

"No," I said, defensively. "I notice teeth because mine are crooked. When I smile I keep my lips together. Her smile was like ... wow! Teeth surrounded by red lips that made me think of cinnamon candies that I could almost taste."

"Red Hots?"

"I was thinking about *sweet*."

"But you never told her? Do you always have trouble talking to girls?"

I ignored him and said, "She was talking to some girlfriends. Her hands were weaving the air like she was shaping her words. When her mouth moved, I shivered a little. She looked as if she were acting out a story. The way she bounced and bopped around I imagined her dancing the chicken. Even her face was animated, not cartoonish but … uh … *expressive*. After a while, she leaned down and whispered to someone. All of a sudden, she looked in my direction—you know how girls look at you with their head down and eyes turned? Oh man, I didn't want to, but I looked away and hoped she hadn't caught me staring at her. At the same time, I wished that she had."

Anthony scribbled in his spiral notebook and said, "So did you approach her?"

"No, it sorta happened by chance."

"Did you talk to her?"

I frowned and mumbled, "That was kind of embarrassing."

He stopped writing and waited. When I didn't go on, he clicked his ballpoint pen several times as if to get me to tell more. The clock on his desk showed that I had twenty minutes left. Finally, I said, "It was the first day of class and the teacher assigned seats by drawing names from a big beaker. We sat at the same lab table. Normally a *Miller* wouldn't sit near a *Demetriou* because most teachers give out seats by the alphabet."

"So it was Kismet that you met?" said Anthony.

"Huh?" I said, bewildered by his rhyme.

"Never mind. Go on."

"She was prettier up close, but not like those girls who flip their hair and act snooty. Amy was more like an actual person. The teacher kept calling out names and pointing fingers, and I kept stealing glances at Amy. When she was on the other side of the room, her short hair seemed darker, almost black. Now she was a couple feet across from me, and her curls looked like swirls of chocolate icing. You know how hard it is to resist sneaking a lick of frosting off a cake? I wanted to do that. I mean, I wanted to touch the curls, especially the one on her temple in front of her ear. She had chocolate brown eyes, too. Almond shaped. Small eyes that matched her tiny features. I have dark hair and brown eyes, too. Except that my eyes are sleepy and hers are lively—dancing eyes with light shining through. She smiled almost all the time, and her cheeks made the cutest dimples I'd ever seen—tiny eddies like the loops in her hair. I peeked at her out of the corner of my eye when I thought she wasn't looking, but she caught me and.... Holy crap, I turned away and pretended to study my class schedule. But then, oh man, I couldn't believe it when she said hi and told me her name."

"Oh, hi," I said, feeling about as suave as Soupy Sales.

She smiled at me. I felt my face turn red and said, "Uh, my name's … um...."

"Nick," she said with a laugh. "*Everyone* knows your name."

"Huh?"

She giggled again. "Mr. Dilbock called your name four times before you sat down. Didn't you hear him?"

Anthony clicked his pen again, this time popping me back into his office. "That's a lot of detail to recall about something that happened more than three years ago," he said.

What was that supposed to mean? Yeah, I remembered. Amy was all I thought about. That's why I was flunking. *That's why I'm here, stupid.*

After that, I made the mistake of saying that Amy ignored me for most of high school. He looked at me odd when I said I was grateful that she introduced me to her girlfriends. "Wasn't she steering you away so you wouldn't bother her?" he asked. I said I didn't see it that way. I didn't know any girls … at least not ones I wanted to date. Amy made me feel like I was okay and that I could get over my shyness by hanging out with more people. When she told me that some of the girls thought I could be good looking, I started using Clearasil more often. I even got a brush cut so I wouldn't look like a greaser. It made me feel more confident, but I never fit in with the frats anyway.

At the end of our session, Anthony really got on my case. He acted like I was weird because I was messed up about someone I'd never dated in high school and dated "only a couple of times" since I started college. (It was actually three or four.)

"All this upset in your life," he said, "because you can't get over someone you can't have. Dr. Freud has interesting theories about that."

I hated when he pulled that Freudian stuff. Instead of paying attention to me, he spouted something to show off how smart he was, but he didn't have an idea of his own. Everything he said came out of a textbook.

Why couldn't he see that the moment I met Amy, I felt like I was waking up from a long sleep? She was like sunshine after a rain. Amy was going to change everything I hated about myself, and she was going to show me how to have fun.

Despite my grumbling, I must have taken some of Anthony's criticism to heart because I stopped trying to see Amy for a while. Then, a year or so later, when my grades were better, I got the courage to try again. That lasted a month, but I wasn't through yet.

In 1962, my senior year, I sent Amy a Christmas card and signed it, "Nick. (Remember me?)" A while later she sent me a card that read, "Of course I remember you. Let's get together after Christmas."

CHAPTER THREE

Who would have supposed that maturity
is only a short break in adolescence?

—Jules Feiffer

I take another sip of soda and backwash warm, syrupy goop back into the glass. It's late, but there are more questions on the hospital form, so I get another warm Coke from the cellar steps. A little ice from the fridge rejuvenates the drink, and I mop the puddled condensation on the table with a dry cloth.

Describe early events that might have led to the patient's current diagnosis.

Jesus, I had no idea what was coming. Before we got married, I thought *I* was the worrier and Amy was lighthearted. She had a keen sense of humor that went with what seemed like a perpetual smile. My dream was that she'd pull me out my seriousness and help me have some fun. She said her life was too much like a teeter-totter and that we balanced each other pretty well. I was sure I was the *down* one and she was going to pick me up. Back then, she never seemed down about anything.

I used to call her "Frank" because she was, and I loved how she'd get right to the point. Sometimes her words would bite, but her sarcasm added spice to her sweetness—like chili pepper in salsa.

I remember the night she asked me to be a better kisser. We were in my old VW, parked in front of her house on an unusually cool evening in early June of 1963.

"Nicky, warm me up," she said. "It's cold out tonight."

"This is a Beetle, remember? There is no heater."

She was still not used to my car, and I wasn't used to the idea that we'd been dating since the first of the year.

"That's okay. Daddy says not to sit in a parked car with the heater on. I guess I have to rely on you."

"I was thinking that *you* could warm *me*," I said.

"Not until my motor starts purring," she said.

I put my arms around her and gave her a gentle kiss. After a little cuddling, I said, "I used to worry about parking here. I thought your dad would bang on the car with a baseball bat."

"He has one you know. A little one—like a billy club."

"I'm not worried. We're not doing anything wrong—just keeping each other warm."

It had taken me a while to feel comfortable with Amy. When we first got together after the New Year, I thought she was using me to get rid of an old boy-friend who'd been bothering her. She told me I was a good guy because I was "safe."

That night in June, she snuggled closer and said, "I'm glad that you're so toasty. You're like a little furnace."

"Hot Macedonian-Greek blood," I bragged.

We cuddled some more, touched noses, and kissed again. That was when she said, "Nicky? Don't you like to kiss me?"

Her question was whimsical, but I tend to ponder even the simplest questions before answering. The truth was that I thought about kissing Amy all the time, so that night I answered her quickly with a kiss that was long and wet.

When our lips parted, we fell against the seat, gasping for breath.

"Wow," she said. "If your kisses get any hotter my fillings'll melt."

I laughed, but the kiss triggered serious thoughts that I didn't want to deal with. I considered cracking a joke, but the *funny* feeling I had wasn't at all humorous. Though I had wanted to kiss Amy like that for a long time, I held back because I wasn't ready for a serious relationship.

"Amy," I said, "I can't explain exactly how I feel about you, but you're wrong to think I don't want to kiss you. Every time I kiss you good night, I hate to let you go. I want to kiss you—not softly, but … well, like we just kissed. The problem is that I'm afraid I won't be able to stop."

I slid across the seat and pinned Amy so close to the passenger door that she got concerned about spilling onto her front lawn. So she wiggled closer to me.

"I liked your first answer better," she said. "Now you sound too solemn."

"I promised myself to stop being like that, but I have to be me," I said. Then I made myself take a deep breath because I almost told her that I loved her. "Amy, I … I like you," I stammered. "I like you very much. You bring out something in me that I've never felt free to show anyone else."

She looked at me so warmly that I got scared and backed away. I put my hand on the steering wheel and said, "I'd like to tell you something, and I don't know if it's all right to say it."

Amy touched my cheek and gently turned my face toward her. She gave me a kiss that was unlike any she had ever given me—it was tender, lingering long enough to let me know that she had more kisses to give.

"Nick, I haven't been fair to you. I tease you about being so serious, but the truth is that I like the way you are. Don't try to change on my behalf. A couple of years ago, I thought you were too intense, but I've learned better. I like your thoughtfulness—how you remember special occasions and notice the things I like. It's neat that you sometimes know what I want before I ask for it."

"You mean like kissing you?"

She giggled and said, "Once in a while you need a kick in the ass."

"I was afraid you wouldn't want me to kiss you like that."

"I'll remember to clue you in," she said. "Now, tell me what you're thinking."

"I'm thinking about how much I love … how much I love to hear you laugh. When you giggle my heart jumps. You make me want to forget about serious stuff—bad things that happen everywhere. I used to think I should try to save the world from all that."

"But Nick, I like that part of you. You don't have to be the life of the party. Oh, I admit that I kinda like your corny jokes. In spite of the faces I make, I think some of your silly puns are pretty clever. I only pretend to be annoyed because I like to tease you. But the part of you I like most is that you're an idealist. Don't give up your dreams for me. You want to be the best teacher ever, and I believe you can be."

"Sometimes I'm afraid that you won't want to see me anymore."

"Listen, I have a confession, too. I'm not always the carefree girl you think I am. It's scary to know that you depend on me to have fun. Honestly, I wonder what you think I can give to you. You seem so self-reliant and sure of what you want. I don't know if I can live up to your standards. When I think about what you might expect of me, I get afraid."

"Afraid? Why?"

"Because I don't think you want to know who I really am."

What was she scared of?

"That's not true," I said. "I want to know all about you. I already love your frankness and quick wit, and I know there's more to you than you're willing to show me. Sometimes I think you're doing what I'm doing—keeping part of yourself hidden. You don't have to do that."

"But you won't like that other part of me," she said. "What if I can't be what you want me to be?"

Amy turned away, but not before I saw a tear in her eye. I wanted to say something sweet, but everything I thought of was too syrupy. So I said, "Now you're the serious one. We're just dating, right? We haven't discussed any plans or made any promises to each other. Let's just have some fun. Okay?"

"You're right," she said, and then looked at her watch. "Gosh, look at the time. I should go inside before Daddy starts thinking bad things about you."

Neither of us moved, and it became so quiet I could hear us breathing. Sinking into the driver's seat, I pressed my hands together like I was about to pray. Then I studied the space between my thumbs and tried to close the gap. As my mind drifted, my hands separated. I looked at the window and wiped off the mist that had collected, all the while wondering what was out there for Amy and me.

A sudden gust made the Beetle rock noticeably. Amy didn't stir. I wondered what she was thinking. Was it about me? About us? When our eyes met, she smiled. When I kissed her, the breeze outside seemed to play a strain of "Cast Your Fate to the Wind."

Nestling against me, Amy said, "I'm glad I found out."

"Found out what?"

"That you're much nicer than the cold, logical person you pretend to be."

"Uh … thanks … I think. I guess my moodiness chased you away before?"

"Scared the crap out of me," she said. "You still do, sometimes."

"I do? I thought you said I've changed."

"You have, but now and then you get back into your old self."

"Like tonight, I suppose."

"Yeah, like when you argued civil rights with Daddy. You don't understand him. He might talk tough about Negroes, but if a colored person needed help, he'd be the first to offer it."

"Hmm."

"I'm glad I yanked you away from him before we missed the movie."

"Wonder if he'd approve if he knew the movie was *To Kill a Mockingbird*."

"He would. It's a good movie. You know, you remind me of him."

"I remind you of your father?"

"No. Well … yeah, kind of in an odd sort of way, but I was talking about Gregory Peck's character. He's an idealist and a gentle, sensitive man. It's the gentle, sensitive part that I like most."

"That's the part I like about you, too. You aren't fooling me with your brassy talk. I think it's all a big front."

"You know what they say, 'It's what's up front that counts.'"

"There," I said, raising a finger. "That's what I mean. You're hiding something."

"Bullshit. What you see is what you get. Just what do you think I'm covering up?"

"The same mushy stuff you like about me."

"I didn't say I liked you. I said I liked Atticus Finch."

"What's he got that I haven't?"

"For one thing, he looks like Gregory Peck. And he practices what he preaches."

"You saying I don't?"

"I'm not sure. You talk like you want to save the world, but you haven't done anything yet. Maybe by the time you're as old as Atticus...."

"Hey, I've met James Farmer and other people—people who know Martin Luther King."

"Yeah, you *talked* with them."

"What about you? What do you want out of life? What commitments are you willing to make?"

Amy looked away and did what she does when she's thinking about what to say; she chewed on the inside of her cheek. The way her mouth twists reminds me of Minnie Mouse. That night it was still new to me. I watched her and smiled.

"What are you laughing about?" she said.

"I'm not laughing."

"Look," she said sharply, "maybe I don't have lofty goals, but I think about stuff—important stuff, like being a wife and mother. You'd be out of a job if mothers weren't making kids."

"Hey, take it easy," I said.

Amy sat back and folded her arms across her chest. "I'll tell you one thing," she said. "If I ever get married it'll be forever."

I couldn't believe she brought up marriage.

"Hmm, *It'll be forever*," I said teasingly. "Sounds like a song title."

"S'not funny."

A remnant of my junior high mind urged me to say something about *snot*, but the teacher in me ruled against it.

"Marriage," she said haughtily, "is as important as your 'save the planet' ideas."

"You're right. I agree. Getting married is *once and for all* for me, too."

"I want to have babies and a nice house with a big garden. What's wrong with being a stay-at-home mom and a devoted wife? Helping my husband is as important as anything you've got in mind. I want a house on a hill, a yard full of flowers, a picket fence, a dog, and nine or ten babies."

"Are you kidding me? You *are* kidding me. Aren't you?"

"No, I mean it. I want lots of babies because my mother doesn't think I can handle it. Besides, what's it to ya? You'll have nothing to do with it. I won't marry anyone who doesn't believe in God."

"I believe in God—at least I think I do."

"That's what I mean. You're too ... too...."

"Tentative? Yeah, that's me. Suspend judgment. Look at different ideas."

"Why do you have to question everything? Why are you so against religion? Why can't you just believe and go to church?"

"I did that. I went to a Greek Orthodox Church. The ritual gets in my way. All that folderol stands between me and God and stops me from seeing who he really is."

"I thought you weren't sure there is a God."

"I'm not. I'm still looking for something that'll verify his existence."

"That's stupid. You can't prove there's a God by reason alone. Some things you accept or reject, period. Make up your mind. Like Daddy says, 'Shit or get off the pot.'"

"Well, what about church dogma? I can't accept it. Too many rules get in the way of true worship."

"Worship who, yourself? You either believe in God or you don't—and if you don't, then you believe only in yourself."

"Amy, you make everything too simple."

"No, I don't. The trouble is you make it too complicated."

"There are tons of philosophers who write about this all the time."

"I read stories, not philosophy. Novels tell about truth in word pictures."

"How do you come up with stuff like that? A Frenchman named Camus said nearly the same thing."

"Kamu, Shamu, I never heard of him. I just know it. Intuition I guess. Everyone would be better off relying more on intuition."

"I don't trust intuition. It gets me into trouble. I have to think about my decisions—any decision, even simple things like choosing sweet or dill pickles for my hamburger."

"Pick either one. The worst thing you can do is nothing."

"That's what Teddy Roosevelt said."

"I said it first."

I couldn't tell if she was serious or just needling me. Whatever it was, I couldn't keep it up.

"Amy, why are you getting into this? Tonight of all nights."

"Why, what's wrong with tonight?"

"I've got exams to think about."

She shook her head up and down. "Yeah, you're right. I know you have to study. We should call it a night."

Once again, neither of us made a move to leave.

"Umm ..." I mumbled. "There's something else on my mind."

"What is it?"

"Oh, nothing," I said. Amy squiggled her mouth in that way she does. She was miffed by my silence.

"So," she huffed, "am I supposed to beg you to tell me what's on your mind?"

"It's no big deal. I guess I'm just disappointed."

"In what, me?"

"No, Amy, everything's not about you. In case you haven't noticed, I have a college career, too."

"Career? Don't be stupid. You're graduating. A career starts with a job."

"Yeah, I know, but a special ceremony's coming up for the College of Ed."

"So?"

"Well, I'm the president of the student council, and I thought they'd ask me to give the commencement speech."

"Why?"

"I've done a lot for that school. If it weren't for me, there wouldn't be a student council. It just seems fitting."

"You had a spot last year and introduced Eleanor Roosevelt. Isn't that enough?"

"That was last year. This year, it was my idea to have a separate honor for teachers."

"Sounds like you were looking to 'honor' yourself."

"That's not true. It's just that—"

"It's just that they chose someone else. Who is it?"

"Some single mom who became a teacher after raising six kids or something."

"What do you mean 'or something'? She deserves the honor. You've done nothing compared to the sacrifices she's made. You have a three-point in math and science; she has a four-point in life. I'd say you need to learn a little humility."

"But—"

"But, but. You sound like a motor scooter. Listen, buster, being a martyr doesn't give you permission to act superior. Stop feeling sorry for yourself, and give this woman the credit she's entitled. Your time will come another day—if you earn it."

"I thought I already did."

"That proves you don't deserve it."

God, she was brutal—and probably right, too. I didn't want her to think I was a snob, so I said, "I should never have brought it up. You don't understand."

"What do you mean by that?" she screamed. "Exactly what don't I understand?"

"You never went to college. You don't know about final exams and graduation."

"Oh, you think I'm not smart enough?"

"No, it's not that. I … I don't know. You've got me all confused."

"You'd better figure it out fast or you'll wear your ass in a sling."

"Look, I can't decide."

"Decide what—whether I'm smart enough or not?"

"Amy, don't put words in my mouth. I never said that. It's just … you know … things are closing in on me from all angles. I've got too much on my mind. I can't be thinking about my classes and my career and you, too."

"What are you saying? Aren't I good enough for you?"

"No. I mean, yes. Damnit, you've got me all mixed up."

"Better decide what you mean. I'm not sitting around while you figure it out."

"What I'm trying to say is that I can't deal with making decisions and planning for our future and what's to become of us—not all at once, I can't."

"What exactly are we *becoming?*"

"What I mean is that you probably think I should make up my mind about you and me, but the thing is … like I say, with graduation and final exams and term papers … well, I can't decide what to do about us. I've got a lot of studying to do. I spend too much time with you, and I'm really behind in all my classes. So … so I … I…."

"So you *what?*"

"I don't want to see you for a while. Ten days or so. After that, I'll be free to decide what to do with you—I mean about you. Or us. You understand, don't you?"

"Like I give a shit! Who do you think you are? Let me tell you, Mr. Nicholas Demetriou, you're not the only fish in the open. You've got a lot of nerve accusing me of waiting for you to propose. What makes you think I want you to ask? I'm not some lonely-hearted chick desperately looking for a husband. If you can't make up your mind—fine. Don't! Go ahead. Take your ten days. Take ten years for all I care."

With that, Amy jumped out of the car and slammed the door so hard that my Beetle rocked like it was about to tip over.

She was already up her front steps, and—too late—I was speechless. I should've shut up long before that. By then, I wasn't sure what either of us had said.

CHAPTER FOUR

Most decisions are seat-of-the-pants judgments. You can create a rationale for anything. In the end, most decisions are based on intuition and faith.

—Nathan Myhrvold

My hand shook, and I fumbled my key as Amy disappeared into her house. When I finally turned the ignition, I gunned the engine, popped the clutch, and tried to lay some rubber. But, like Amy, my Beetle was unpredictable. It leaped forward, jumped the curb, and headed toward a tree before I turned the wheel sharply and steered back to the street. Nevertheless, the car grazed the tree trunk before bouncing onto the street, where I shifted over second gear, slammed into third, and roared away. At the stop sign, I hit the breaks hard and did a 180, ending up stalled and facing Amy's house.

My hands were white-knuckled and locked on the steering wheel. I looked at the porch where I'd last seen Amy and wondered if she'd heard the racket I made for her benefit. The light above her front door went out. A chill rushed around me like a draft rising from an empty cellar. Goddamn it, I had lost her again.

I turned the wheel hard and pressed the accelerator, forgetting that the engine had stalled. Opening the door, I set one foot on the pavement and peered at Amy's house. I thought about leaving the car there and running to her to apologize—to ask her not to turn me away and tell her that I couldn't stand to be without her.

A familiar emptiness grew in the middle of my chest, as though someone had reached in and yanked me inside out.

It's what I always feel whenever I'm afraid of losing Amy. It's what I feel every fall when school begins anew. It's what I felt when my mother left me at kindergarten for the first time. It's the feeling that made the six-year-old me dash to a school window, crawl out, and run home.

Amy's words rang inside my head. The worst thing you can do is nothing.

Why was she forcing me to make up my mind? Why now of all times?

I closed my eyes to think more clearly, but could only think of Amy slamming the car door in my face. It felt final—like she had cut me away from a favorite snapshot.

I spent the rest of the night and the entire morning at Metro Airport writing page after page of pros and cons about why I should or shouldn't ask Amy to marry me. In the end, I decided not to ask.

At home, I told Mom I was at the airport not at Amy's house. What I didn't tell her was that I discovered that I have to marry Amy right away. I tried to explain the "have to" part, but Mom wrung her hands and mumbled *Lord have mercy* in the Macedonian language I understood and something else in Greek that was all Greek to me.

Though I wasn't hungry, she made me eat breakfast. (Mom believes that food—lots of it—will cure anything.) Then she insisted I get some sleep. "I'm still your mother," she said. "I know what's best for you. And don't tell me you were in bed because if you were it wasn't for sleeping."

I went to the bathroom instead and stared at myself in the mirror. My face was puffy. A down-turned mouth and dark rings under my sunken eyes made me look like Weary Willie—Emmett Kelly's hobo circus character. The characterization was not without irony. Amy had a keepsake doll of the famous clown in her bedroom.

When I first started to shave, Mom suggested I use the Norelco. I think she worried about sharp razors and me. She was right. My hand shook so badly that I nicked myself several times and left blood lines in the sink that resembled family trees. I couldn't find a styptic pencil, so I used pieces of toilet paper to stop the bleeding, ending up with wads of tissue stuck to my face and neck. The guy looking back at me in the mirror was a clean-shaven Emmett Kelly doll-head with his stuffing coming out. I changed to clean khakis and a pullover shirt, but still looked down-and-out.

It was four o'clock in the afternoon. Amy got out of work at five. I had to talk to her face-to-face before she went home. I was in no shape to see her, but I had to—with or without the shakes.

I drove to the Michigan Bell customer service branch where Amy worked and parked in the lot next to the office. When I peeked in, I saw she was busy—too busy to spot me at the window. There was a long line of customers waiting to see her and the other service reps, so I knew she'd be working late. I thought about hanging around outside until she came out, but a security guard at the door eyed me suspiciously. Amy's office had been robbed a few weeks earlier, and there was increased vigilance for shady-looking characters like me.

So I went to Christel's restaurant on the other side of Woodward and sat at a table by the front window where I could read the "closed" sign that hung on the door a few feet from Amy's desk. After a while, the cluster of customers waiting for service in the telephone office lessened considerably, and I began to worry I wouldn't catch Amy as she left the building. Then I thought that a face-to-face confrontation on the street without warning wouldn't be fair. I also knew that I had lost my chance to call her or ask a colleague to pass her a note. Although the staff had to take care of customers already in the office, they didn't let anyone else inside or answer phone calls after closing.

Consequently, I wrote Amy a note on one of Christel's napkins, ran to the parking lot, found her car, and put the note under the windshield wiper. Just as I snapped the blade down, the parking attendant, an older woman who looked like she rode to work on a broom, charged toward me waving the pointed end of a red umbrella. She and I had met before, and she calmed down as soon as she recognized me. After I shared my plan about meeting Amy over at Christel's, the old witch turned into Mary Poppins and became my ally.

Back at the restaurant, the dinner hour had begun. Someone was sitting at my sentry table. I took a table at the back and ordered a cup of coffee. Now and then, I got up and peeked out the window. The glare of the sun made it hard for me to see into Amy's office, but I noticed her car was still in the lot. I waited, worried, and drank more coffee, and waited and worried some more. While the restaurant filled with hungry patrons, thoughts of how my plan would fail crowded my brain. There were a hundred ways for Amy to say no.

In my reverie, I heard someone say, "You all right, Mister?"

A waitress held a round glass pot in her hand. The stuff inside was black, and the steam coming out was white.

"Maybe you'd rather have Sanka?" she said.

"No, please," I said. "Regular coffee. Keep it coming. And ... uh ... say, you got any change for the jukebox?"

"You kidding? I get nothing but two-bit tips. How much you need?"

I handed her a couple of bills, then clasped my trembling hands in my lap so she wouldn't notice the shaking. She dropped my change on the table and filled my cup. I waited until she left before picking up my coffee, which I did with both hands. Nevertheless, I spilled coffee down my chin. When I set the cup down, it rattled loudly against the saucer.

Sweeping the coins into my hand, I went to the jukebox and put in all of them. Then I searched for "Love Me Do" by the Beatles. It wasn't there, but "I Want to Hold Your Hand" was. I played it and "I Only Want to Be With You," by Dusty Springfield. I looked for others that Amy and I called *our* songs, but ignored "Breaking Up is Hard to Do," "Lonely Boy," "Crying," and all the songs from "West Side Story" because Tony never got Maria. I punched the buttons for "Peggy Sue," "That'll be the Day," "Peppermint Twist," "The Wanderer," "Dream Baby," "Put Your Head On My Shoulder," "Be My Baby," and "Fools Rush In," and still hadn't used up my selections. But my head began to spin when the records went around, so I left the other choices for someone else to pick.

All my tunes played through, and still no Amy. It was nearly six thirty. I was sure she had gone home without me seeing her. Forlorn, I got up to leave, but stopped when another familiar song began to play. It wasn't one that I had selected, but it was a favorite. I sat down again and said the words to myself as the Rooftop Singers sang, *Walk right in, sit right down, Baby let your hair hang down …*

Only a fool would believe this, but only fools fall in love. And the one I was in love with walked into Christel's restaurant at that very moment.

CHAPTER FIVE

Pleasure is very seldom found where it is sought; our brightest blazes of gladness are commonly kindled by unexpected sparks.

—Samuel Johnson

My joy at seeing Amy faded when I saw her frown. Her round face appeared long and dour, and she hesitated before stepping slowly toward me. When she reached my table, she extended her hand tentatively toward a chair and then drew it back when our eyes met. My heart sank when she shifted her weight and appeared to turn away. Unable to speak, I looked down into the cup I was holding and felt helpless until I heard her say, "Nick, what's wrong? You look like death warmed over."

I wrestled my cup to its saucer and fought to find the words I had planned to say. Amy moved closer and touched my hand, calming the cup, but exciting me. A scent of White Shoulders wafted from behind her ear. She was wearing a belted slimline dress with a wide neckline that showed off a string of pearls laying modestly, but charmingly, on her creamy smooth skin. On her head was a Jackie Kennedy pillbox hat, a fashion statement complemented by the short, white gloves that were Amy's trademark.

"Can we talk?" I said.

"About what?" she asked, tilting her head.

"There's only one thing I can't agree to," I said.

She sat down and ran her finger around her bare earlobe in the way that usually meant contemplation. Curiosity seemed to have replaced worry.

"We're not having nine kids," I said. "Two or three are enough."

"Huh?"

"We're getting married," I said.

"We are?"

"I decided."

"All by yourself?"

"No. You and I … both of us. I can't do it alone. I have to marry someone."

"What?"

"Amy, I love you. I'm saying I want to marry you, but I'm not doing it very well."

"Wait a minute. I'm not doing very well either."

"You were right."

"I was?"

"About me making up my mind to marry you."

"I don't remember saying that. I don't remember thinking it either."

"You were confused, so I went to the airport and figured it out for you. You don't have to say yes right now. I just want you to know I love you and I'll wait for you."

"Nicky, I—"

"Here. I want you to wear this."

"What is it?"

"My Mackenzie Honor Society pin."

"From high school?"

"From Wayne State. The honor society and our high school are named after the same guy. I thought it'd be fitting—since we started then and ended now. Know what I mean?"

"No."

"You won't wear it?"

"No—I mean, yes, I'll wear it, but…. Nick, you're not making sense."

"I know. Did I tell you that I haven't slept for two days?"

A week later, Amy and I were sitting in her mom and dad's TV room, but she and I weren't watching the screen. My eyes kept darting from her to her dad and then to Saundra. Andrew, who had recently let me call him "Andy," was only slightly taller than I, but I always felt I had to look up to him, even then as he sat next to me in his rocker. Neither *Andy* nor *Andrew* seemed like fitting names for someone like him. It should have been *Gregory* or *Caesar Gregarious*. Amy's mother, on the other hand, was always *Saundra* with the *auwn* sound strongly emphasized. Saundra was a properly quiet lady who managed to make her presence known despite her small size and Andy's big voice.

It was time to tell them our news. Amy had warned me about her dad's temper and said she should be the first to speak, but I had my doubts about her resolve after watching her alternately yawning, sucking the inside of her cheek, and toying with her earlobe. Meanwhile, my eyes bounced from her to Andy to

Saundra like pinballs in an arcade. Amy had been in and out of the room several times, running off to her bedroom for no apparent reason. Finally, I intercepted her in the hallway.

"You gonna tell him or am I?" I whispered.

"I will as soon as I have a chance," she promised. "Don't worry; I know how to handle Daddy."

When we stepped back into the room, Mr. Miller glowered at me when I bumped his chair and Saundra Miller cleared her throat.

"Excuse me, Mr. Miller."

"*Andy*," he said. "Call me *Andy*."

"Yes, sir."

I sat down, and Amy went upstairs again. She soon returned wearing a different skirt and blouse. My pin was on her collar and a forced smile was on her face.

"Daddy, look what Nick gave me."

"Eh? Where?"

"Here on my blouse."

"Jesus, I can hardly see it. What is it?"

"It's from Nick's honor society. It means that we're pinned."

"What the hell is *pinned*?"

"*Pinned*," I interjected, "like to each other."

He laughed and slapped my knee. I had a simultaneous leg-and-heart knee-jerk reaction. I felt like an idiot until I saw Amy's reassuring nod.

"It's kind of like being engaged to be engaged," said Amy, "but not exactly."

Andy laughed so loud, I could feel a vibration in my chest.

"Andrew," said Saundra, eyeing him sternly.

"I've never heard of such a dumb-ass thing," he said. "Either you are or you aren't. Which is it for Christ's sake?"

"Sir," I said, "I've made up my—ouch." Amy's sharp elbow stopped me short.

"Daddy, don't be mean. We *have* decided. We just haven't set a date."

"What you mean is that Nick can't afford to buy a ring, so he calls me *Andy* instead of *Dad* until he does."

"Mother, tell Daddy to stop teasing."

Saundra made a stuttering noise in her nasal passage. I thought she was laughing, but with her I never knew. "Well," she said with a wry smile, "we've been expecting this. Is it too early to offer congratulations?"

"No," I said.

"Maybe," said Amy.

Amy's answer was more definite in August when I gave her a ring and we set sail for a June wedding. By October, I was regretting the wait. In the summer, it had been easy to spread a blanket on the grass and watch the submarine races. With fall's cold weather, we spent more time in the VW Beetle than anywhere else. Forget what Ralph Nader said about "unsafe at any speed." When Amy and I parked, the Beetle was pretty damn safe. The front seats were separated by a gearshift on the floor—a modern version of the Puritan bundling board. We never got in back—not for lack of interest, but because we were afraid of getting caught by Andrew.

Mr. Miller's edict was that once a week we could stay out until two, but the car had to be parked in front of the house before one. He and Amy had gone toe-to-toe one night after we were out late and out of sight. He wondered why we were hiding. I stayed out of the argument. I was afraid of Andy's temper, but knew he wouldn't let himself hurt Amy—though his language sometimes bordered on verbal combat. Nevertheless, Amy knew the way to his heart wasn't through sweet-talk. She did better with nose-to-nose battle where she could match him cussword-for-cussword. Finally, she negotiated a parking spot for us across the street.

One cold and rainy evening we sat in the car so long that the windows fogged over. We had obediently parked diagonally across from Amy's house, but things were heating up—and I don't mean discussion-wise. Since Amy's provocative question about my kisses, I had thought of other things, including more places to put my hands, but had been frustrated by lack of maneuverability. Constantly bumping into obstacles above and below as well as right and left, I kept hitting my backside on the steering wheel, my front on the gearshift, my head on the ceiling, and my feet on the brake and clutch pedals. It took imagination, but I wiggled around to make the most of space and time before curfew.

Suddenly, two lights appeared in a fogged window. I wiped the glass and saw that the porch lights at Amy's house, which had been off earlier, were shining brightly. Silently, I scrambled to get back to my side of the car, but my hind end fell against the center of the steering wheel resulting in a characteristic Beetle toot that came off like a fart at a prayer meeting.

A couple of minutes passed uneventfully. The lights went out, and Amy and I inched closer together again. I switched the ignition key to *accessories* and tuned in the radio. The Beach Boys were "Surfin' USA." The music was normal, but our evening was not. The cold air that had been both outside and inside the car when the rain began changed to warm and muggy inside. It was pea soup thick, and I couldn't open a window because it was raining too hard, but steamed-up windows curtained us from the world. With that in mind, I was still cautious about steering clear of the brake pedal, but became less guarded about avoiding other *wrong* things. Who was to know?

On the radio, the Beatles were singing "Please Please Me," and I was making out pretty well until I accidentally kicked the gearshift into neutral. Evidently, the street Amy lived on wasn't entirely flat. While she and I dreamed with the English Beatles, my German Beetle rolled out of its parking spot, drifted diagonally across the street, crept up the Miller's driveway, and onto their front lawn. Initially, I attributed the movement to the orbit Amy had sent me into. I didn't notice where we were until I leaned against the steering column and heard a *click*. Alarmed that I had turned something on, I looked up suddenly and saw flashing yellow lights in the windshield. Out the back window, I saw red lights flicker on and off in perfect sync with the yellow.

Amy bolted up, hit her head on the visor, and said, "What's that?"

"Lights," I said.

"I know that, but where are they coming from?"

I cleared a swath across the dew on the windshield and saw that the lights were mine.

"Hazard lights," I said. "I must've turned them on accidentally. Don't worry. There's no emergency."

"There will be if Daddy sees them."

Searching frantically for a button, I cried, "Holy shit, how do you shut them off?"

"I don't know. It's your car for God's sake. Try that thing over there."

"Where?" I spotted a button and leaned across the wheel to press it.

The VW tooted a loud "BeeeeeeeeeeeeeeeP."

"Don't do that!" said Amy.

"Jesus Christ," yelled someone outside. It was Andy Miller, and he was charging off his porch, his dark bathrobe flailing behind him like a caped crusader. In an instant, I saw two red eyes staring into my windshield and heard a roar that would have frightened John the Baptist.

Amy jumped out of the car to prove she was fully clothed, and I hit every switch I could to shut off the commotion. The headlights came on immediately, and the wipers started to swish, but it took forever for the flashers to disengage. By then, Mr. Miller had sunk to his ankles in the muddy yard, and I was in deep shit.

Reluctantly, I climbed out of the car and joined Amy and her dad in the pouring rain. The more I tried to explain, the deeper I sank into the muck—a situation made worse because I was standing in a tire track I had carved into Andrew's rain-soaked lawn.

Finally, I shut up and waited for Mr. Miller to ream me out. He was yelling at the top of his lungs—loud enough to be heard above the storm. Worse. His voice was probably heard in Kalamazoo. He read me the riot act while marching around the car like a drenched mariner inspecting a moored ship. As he passed Amy, he jerked his thumb toward the house, pointing for her to go inside.

Amy ignored him and stepped to my side, where she stood firm—like Guinevere beside her Lancelot. Still pointing, Mr. Miller moved one foot toward her and lost his slipper in the quagmire that was his lawn. His royal blue robe had become shapeless. Overcoming the sucking muck, he stepped toward me. I held my ground, but flinched when he raised his arm as if to strike.

Suddenly, I felt his arm around me and begin to shake in his powerful grip. To my surprise, Andy Miller was laughing. He had put his arms first around me and then around his daughter. In his embrace, my head fell against his chest. The echo of his robust laughter sent tremors throughout my body, and I knew that I'd remember Andy Miller like that for the rest of my life.

CHAPTER SIX

Presentiment—is that long Shadow—on the Lawn
—Indicative that suns go down—
The Notice to the startled Grass
That Darkness—is about to pass.

—Emily Dickinson

A sharp pain at the back of my neck makes me open my eyes, and I stare into an empty glass next to me. Realizing that I had fallen asleep during my reverie, I pick up the hospital forms and frown. The puddle around my soft drink has spread onto the papers, smearing some of my penciled comments. Fatigued, I press my fingertips against my forehead. The pressure feels good. Some of the memories I recalled also felt good, but it's probably the bad experiences—the ones that confuse me most—that'll help me understand what's happening to us.

Setting the papers aside, I think about going to bed, but another memory compels me to go on. There were things that happened just two years ago that I should have seen as warnings.

At Thanksgiving time of 1963, I had much to be thankful for. It was my first year as a full-fledged teacher, and I was getting married right after Christmas. We had moved up the wedding date after we realized that eight months was too many to wait for permission to do what society dictated we couldn't do outside of marriage.

Meanwhile, my students at James Junior High must have sensed my euphoria. A full week before Thanksgiving Day, they began acting as if the holiday had already started. Usually I enjoyed the fun and still had time for the lesson, which always began with a chalkboard message about a scientific discovery that was made on the same date in history. But my November 22 note was erased by someone who wrote "*December 28, 1963. Nick and Mrs. Nick discover birds and bees.*"

Normally, I would've played along with the gag, but that morning Amy and I had argued about her wedding dress. When I walked into my classroom and saw why the students were laughing, I bawled them out and then lost my temper when they didn't take my chiding seriously.

Before class, I had called Amy a second time because I was upset about her fretting over her gown. When she complained about a cold and said she'd stay home from work to get over it, I joked that her cold was a ruse so she could try on her dress while her mother was at work and unable to criticize. Amy had gotten angry but seemed bothered by something else as well. Though her concerns about wedding arrangements weren't uncommon, I expected this one would be resolved by the time I called her at noon. That day I was too busy to call.

Around one thirty, a click on the PA interrupted my lesson. It had happened before when someone in the office accidentally bumped a switch causing the entire school to be distracted by sounds from the office. While I waited for the inevitable second click, I heard muted office voices saying … *Shh, she's trying to turn it on now … No, not that switch, the other one … Here, let me do it.* Another click and music replaced voices. It was band music, military-like, but very solemn. Abruptly the music stopped, and I heard, "… from *CBS News.*" The male voice was familiar, but it wasn't from the school office.

"Ladies and Gentlemen," said Walter Cronkite, "we are still awaiting word from Dallas. At this time, we can confirm that shots were fired, but we have no official report on the condition of the President."

I waited expectantly but heard nothing more. The students began to whisper. Their murmurs grew louder when dirge-like military music began to play. Confused by the lack of information, I prepared to say something when a painful feedback squawked through the PA and quelled everyone's chatter. Someone had turned on the office microphone with the radio or television still on. Input and output clashed, creating more chaos until there was another silence, followed by a throat being cleared in a way that I recognized—the principal's signal that he had an announcement to make.

"Everyone … teachers, boys and girls … this is Mr. Hansen. I'm sorry to have to report this, but the President of the United States has been shot in Dallas, Texas. Please remain calm and stay in your classroom until further notice. I will keep the television on so that you may listen to news reports and immediately learn what has happened."

Some students screamed in confusion. Walter Cronkite came back on the air. His words—caught in mid-sentence—stopped everyone cold. "… F. Kennedy is dead."

The announcement sucked emotion out of the classroom. The moment lasted until music again filled the vacuum. Morbid symphonic movements created visions of dark processions in my mind, and time passed as if marching in stiff, halting steps interrupted by irregular news reports.

At first, my students drew tight at their seats, and many clasped their hands together. Several teens pulled in their breath with short sucking sounds as if desperately trying—as I was—to keep from crying. A few looked around, perhaps ashamed that someone might catch them acting like babies. Some muttered in disbelief. Others couldn't contain their shock and began to wail openly. An instant later, there was laughter—first, in one corner, then in another. Accusations flew at those who laughed, but some of the chortle came from sensitive children I suspected were most affected by the news. It was an odd and offensive response, but perhaps understandable for adolescents whose raw edginess was pushed too far.

Thirteen-year-old Nancy, one of my brightest students, kept repeating, "I don't believe it." Then she said, "Maybe it's a radio story put on by actors." Although fearful that I might frighten her more than she already was, I took Nancy aside and did my best to tell her that it was real. All the while, I was hoping that she was right. I spent the rest of the afternoon calming everyone, trying to explain the unexplainable, but I had no success. I felt weak and pained—as if the assassin's bullet had run through the president and into me.

After the students went home, I had to wait for an office phone to free up before calling Amy. Everyone wanted to know that loved ones were safe and the world was still normal. For the moment, I cared only about Amy.

A TV played loudly in the office. Crowded scenes of hospital people and reporters flashed on the screen. Walter Cronkite's voice echoed in the background. I turned away from the often-repeated scenes. I needed to talk to Amy. I needed to touch her. I needed to feel her heart pulsing with mine, telling me that our life would go on. *Thank God that Amy and I have each other. That matters more now than ever before.*

When I finally heard Amy's phone click after several rings, I said "Hello" and then repeated it when there was no response. "Amy? Is that you? It's Nick."

"Oh, hi. Yeah, it's me," she said roughly. "My cold's made me hoarse, and I can't talk very well."

She wasn't fooling me. She'd been crying. And for the first time that day, I let myself cry, too.

Through the noise and confusion in the office, I heard her say, "Nick, at first I was afraid for you to call, but now I'm glad you did." Amy's voice was raspy, but there were no sobs. Her dry and guttural tone indicated that she had cried away her tears and could only express herself in parched phrases. "I wish you could hold me," she said. "Oh, Nick, I'm so frightened. It's a bad omen for our wedding. For our life together."

"No. No, it's not. It's a terrible thing, but it means nothing like that."

Amy talked on, even as I did, and seemed not to hear me.

"It felt horrible," she said. "When I saw it, I tried to turn away, but I couldn't take my eyes off it. It was like something evil was controlling me, and I couldn't stop staring. I screamed and felt sick, but I couldn't get rid of it. Even though I cried and cried, it didn't go away. I opened my diary and tried to write what I felt, but it made everything worse. Then I got afraid Mother would come home and see me like that."

"Amy," I said, "don't dwell on it. Turn off the damn TV."

"Wha …?" she said. Another moment passed before she added, "What TV?"

"Sweetheart, I know how you feel. I feel it too. I'm scared and sad and mad and … God, I've never felt like this before."

"You…. Nicky, you know? How could you know? You didn't see me, did you? You weren't here, were you? No, that's impossible. Did someone tell you?"

In Amy's voice I heard the cacophony of sounds I had heard in the classroom and continued to hear in the office—the snatched breath, the rapid speech, the fear and confusion.

"I'm at school. I heard the news like you did. It's all over radio and television."

"What? How could that be? What are you talking about?"

"Kennedy. President Kennedy in Dallas. They think they've trapped the assassin in a movie theater."

Silence hung like a moon mysteriously balanced in a cloudless sky. I grew frightened for Amy. She was acting strange. I looked around the office. God, everyone was frightened. Everyone seemed different—different, but not strange.

"Tell me again," she said. "I … I can't believe what you said."

I felt like I was talking to Nancy, the student who was unable to accept the news. I repeated it as gently as I could, and Amy said, "Kennedy is …"

Seconds passed before she started again. "That's what you're talking about? President Kennedy? Kennedy's dead?"

"I know," I said. "It's impossible to imagine. I don't want to believe it either. At any minute I expect to hear that Kennedy's alive and well, but it won't happen. He *is* dead. He died in Dallas. The first bullet probably killed him."

Amy began to cry. Her sobs rushed out as if suddenly released from a spillway that, moments earlier, had been dammed. With it came relief in her voice—a change that calmed me as well.

"Sweetie, I'm coming over right now. I want to—"

"No. No, you can't."

"Why, what is it? What's wrong?"

"Nothing. I ... I have my wedding dress on. It's bad luck for you to see me in my gown before the ceremony. I don't want you to see what I saw in that mirror."

"What mirror? What did you see?"

Then I heard a rustling sound that I didn't recognize. *The movement of her dress?*

"Amy," I said again, "what did you see in the mirror? What frightened you?"

The rustling stopped. I strained to hear more but could not.

"Amy," I said gently.

"What?"

"What's going on?"

"Nothing. My veil caught on my ring and I had to be careful not to tear it."

"What frightened you in the mirror?"

"Mirror? Did I say mirror? I meant TV. The news on TV was so ... so real."

The commotion around me grew and drew my attention to the office TV. A sketch of a man in an overcoat appeared on the screen. *Did Cronkite say there's a Cuban connection? Is an invasion suspected? A plot to assassinate others?* I turned away and covered one ear to hear Amy better.

"Amy, are you all right? Shut off the damn TV and keep it off. Listen, did something else happen? You seem surprised by the news. You did know about Kennedy, didn't you? What else is going on?"

"Nothing. Nick, don't ask any more questions. I'm all mixed up, and I can't talk about it. I don't know what's happening, and I need you to tell me that everything's going to be all right."

"Yes, sweetheart. Absolutely. For us, everything will be all right. I don't know what happened today either, but I know everything will be okay for us because we'll always have each other."

"Yes," she said, dryly. "Till death do us part."

CHAPTER SEVEN

All tragedies are finish'd by a death,
All comedies are ended by a marriage.
The future states of both are left to faith.

—Lord Byron

Later, when I asked Amy about our phone conversation, she was evasive. Her only explanation—that she awoke from a bad dream after taking a decongestant—was plausible, except for her insistence that I never mention it again. Though I was unable to forget it completely, my focus turned to grief over the slain president. As with most Americans, competing emotions complicated our mourning when we attended family Thanksgiving gatherings within the same week as the national funeral. But melancholy media stories about the martyred president and widowed First Lady showed Amy and me how important our relationship was. By Christmas, our spirits had brightened, and we were ready to celebrate. Our holiday season culminated joyously with a candlelight wedding and a four-day stay at ice-crystalled Niagara Falls.

Kicking off our marriage with the New Year gave us a great start at home, but brought little change at work. My classroom control problems were typical for a first-year teacher, while Amy's problems centered on something she had always complained about—phone company managers who demanded that she sell products to people who couldn't afford them. On top of the push for sales, (she had been a top salesperson for two years) Amy also had to handle irate customers with grievances about unpaid bills for products they were talked into buying. Eventually, our homelife was affected as well, mostly when both of us were stressed out at the same time, a tension we hoped to relieve with our first summer vacation trip.

I recall most of the road trip with fondness, particularly the afternoon we headed east toward Albuquerque along old Route 66. We had left Michigan eleven days earlier and traveled west toward the Dakotas and Wyoming. Then we drove southwest across Colorado to Arizona before heading back east. Amy and I had planned a circular route so that our outward and homeward paths would be different. Along the way, I enjoyed the sound of Amy's voice as she read aloud from tour books to give us a flavor of the territory we passed. I especially liked the stories about Route 66—tales I was sure would become legends. New highway construction paralleled the historic two-lane road, and we lamented that the interstate system would soon make Route 66 just a memory.

With that in mind, we enjoyed the landscape and looked for beauty in even the most desert-like areas. "Here's something," said Amy. "'The bulb of the ajo desert lily, a native of the Sonoran desert, can remain dormant under two feet of sand and wait for years until the right conditions allow it to emerge and bloom.' God, I'd hate it if I had to wait that long before I bloomed."

"That's why the desert's a good place to visit, but impossible to live in. We've seen a lot of desert here in the southwest," I said. "Me, I prefer mountains."

"But the desert's fascinating. Think of it, Nick. Barely staying alive for *years* and then flowering into something beautiful. It's horrible and inspiring at the same time."

"Sort of like the death and resurrection of Christ."

"Yeah, but this little bulb is dead for *years*, not just three days. Can you imagine being buried and left for dead? I mean, how does the bulb even know it'll be there when its life begins?"

"Hey," I said, "cheer up. I see mountain peaks ahead. We won't be seeing many more of those after New Mexico, will we?"

"I'm afraid not. Sorry. I know you'll be sad to leave the mountains."

"Sad, but happy to have been there. Driving into Colorado was the first time I'd ever been near a mountain, yet it felt like I'd been there before."

"Maybe in another life you were a mountain person."

"More likely in my father's life in the Macedonian mountains of Greece."

As I talked, I let the car slow to a crawl. The Manzano Range outside of Albuquerque was almost in full view. To the north, reddish brown Sandia Crest loomed above the other peaks. Earlier, I had marveled at how the view of the same mountain shifted with the changing light and our changing perspective.

"Honey," said Amy, "are you all right?"

I wiped a tear from my cheek, and said, "Yeah, I just got some sun in my eyes."

"The sun's behind us, cowboy. Look, it's okay to get emotional, just pull over for a while." She touched my arm and urged me to move off to the shoulder of the road. After we stopped, she said, "Nick, you don't need to explain. Showing your feelings isn't a weakness. The fact that you do is one reason I love you so much. Just be still and let the mountains talk to you."

"It's not sadness that I feel," I said. "It's a sense of power and weakness at the same time."

"Kind of like having sex," she said, sidling up to me and laying her head against my arm. "But since we're not doing that, I think you might be feeling a touch of humility."

"Yeah, the majesty of a mountain and the lowliness of one person on this gigantic earth. Power and submission all at once."

Amy snuggled tightly against me and said, "Oooo, *power and submission*. Now *that* sounds sexy."

"Hey," I said, "I'm being serious here. I have a feeling that this trip's the start of something big, and our journey is just beginning."

"Yeah," she said, "I feel it, too. Kind of like that desert lily, I'm finally ready to start my real life. Until you and I got married up, I wasn't ready to bloom."

"Cool," I said. "I'll help you bloom, and you can lead me to new places."

A pickup approached in the other lane; the sound of its rickety engine changed pitch as it passed at high speed. "I'm not sure where we're going," said Amy, "but I'm sure we're on our way."

"Wouldn't it be great if our life was always an adventure?"

"Sure, as long as we keep having fun."

"It'll get even better," I said. "I guarantee it."

Amy snuggled up close and said, "Nicky, I want to have your baby."

"Huh?"

"I mean it. I want to quit work. I want to stay home and make babies."

"Judas Priest, you pick the oddest times—"

"You said you liked me unpremedicated."

"*Unpremedi TA-ted.*"

"Same thing. Are you still against having nine or ten?"

"Kids? Well, we have to start with one."

"Not necessarily. There are twins in both our families."

"Amy, you know how much I want to have kids. One or two would make me the happiest man on earth."

"What about three or four?"

"We'll cross that bridge when we come to it."

"Hmm," she said, "can we start crossing tonight at the Holiday Inn?"

The motel was in a busy part of Albuquerque, but the mountains in the background gave it an air of serenity. From the pool, we could see winter ski runs on the distant slopes. The enchanting colors of New Mexico were great backdrops for photos and provided just the right suggestion for romance. But the drive had been tiring, so we decided that a swim before dinner would rejuvenate us. I took a few pictures of Amy lounging in her black-and-white swimsuit and then swam in the pool to await the sunset. Amy snapped a few shots from the chaise lounge, shooting me over her toes while I splashed in the water. I laughed at how she aimed the camera over her feet. I was sure that she got all ten of her toes in perfect focus. Unfortunately, I never knew for sure because the film couldn't be developed.

Not knowing that at the time, I finished the roll on a sunset that was to die for and then relaxed on a deck chair beside Amy. When I took her hand and kissed it, I got teary-eyed again.

"Mmm," said Amy, as I held her hand to my chest. "That's a good start."

Then she turned toward me and saw my far-off expression. "What's wrong?" she asked.

"Nothing's wrong, pumpkin. I'm just happy that everything's so right—and I owe it all to you. You're the reason for my happiness. Without you I'd never have become a *minch*."

Minch was a word that Amy made up for the most special people in her life. I'm her minch, and she's mine. Our kids will be little minchkins.

"I knew you were the one the moment we met," she said.

"Oh, is that why you ignored me in high school? Or was that because I wasn't suave enough?"

"Well, you were the guy who thought *panache* was a car company."

"Come on, that was a joke."

"Actually, that's part of what makes you a minch. I wouldn't like you if you were too worldly. This way, I can suggest a trip out West and make you think that *I'm* worldly."

"Yeah, well whatever it is, thanks for talking me into it."

"We had to go on a long trip this time. Our honeymoon was puny."

"*Puny* is not the word a guy wants to hear about his honeymoon."

"Sorry. How about *magnificent*?"

I laughed and said, "This trip's been magnificent. Because of you, I got to see a mountain. When I think how much I need you, I'm thankful that...."

Amy stiffened and pulled her hand away. "Don't say that," she said sharply.

"What?"

"Don't say that you need me."

"But I do. Right now I need you more than anything."

Suddenly, Amy sat up in her chair. "Don't tell me that," she said, nearly screaming. "I hate it when you get this way. You were like that when you were so down about school. All winter you complained and expected me to make it better. I'm not all that happy placating the vultures that come into my office, you know. Sometimes you're so damn self-centered. You think you're the only one with problems? What about me?"

"Sweetheart, I'm sorry. I didn't mean it that way."

"Just what do you expect of me, anyway?" she said. "Whatever I do doesn't seem enough for you."

"Amy, I'm not expecting anything. You're the most important person in my life. I'm trying to give you credit for making me happy."

"And make me feel guilty when you're not happy? No thanks."

"What's wrong with saying that I need you? I thought it was a compliment."

"It scares me."

"Well, I get scared, too. I'm only saying that I need you to—"

"Stop saying that."

She leaped up and snapped her towel off the chaise, knocking the camera into the pool. Still barefoot, she stomped toward the room. I fished the camera out of the water and gathered our stuff before I followed her. By the time I got back to our suite, Amy was in the bathroom, where the sounds of shower spray and splashing water mixed with another sound. When I put my ear to the door, I recognized it as crying.

My throat tightened, and I felt acidy warmth spreading in the middle of my chest—a sensation that has since become familiar—a God-awful feeling I get when I'm afraid that Amy will leave me. Her sobs grew louder, and so did the splashing. I knocked on the door and turned the handle. The door was locked.

"Amy? Amy, are you all right?"

Her crying stopped momentarily, but started again as she said, "Go away. Please leave me alone."

Minutes later, she came out, her face contorted as if in pain. "I'm sorry," she said. "I don't know what came over me."

"Honey, I'm sorry too. Are you all right? You don't look well."

"It's nothing," she said. "My stomach hurts, but it's just hunger pains."

I eyed her skeptically. Amy had acted similarly in February. Her ailment was eventually diagnosed as chronic colitis.

"We can wait a while to go for dinner. Maybe we should eat light tonight?"

"Stop telling me what to do. Go on, take your shower. I'll be better by the time you finish."

I waited until she calmed a bit before I ran the water. Then, just as I stepped into the tub, I heard loud and rapid knocking on the bathroom door.

"Nick, get out of there quick! I need to use the toilet right away."

Amy didn't come out of the bathroom for several minutes. When she did, she looked awful. Her hands pressed against her abdomen, her mouth pinched, her eyes narrowed, and banners of taut lines ran across her forehead.

"Sweetheart, what is it?"

"Colitis. I thought I was over it. I haven't had a problem for a long time, not since we started planning this trip."

"What brought it on?"

"Probably thinking about going back to work. I hate it there. Sometimes I've felt so sick that I've had to stay in the office and skip lunch."

"You didn't tell me. I thought you were better after you saw Dr. Sal."

"She's helped, but there's only so much she can do. The rest is up to me."

"What do you mean?"

"Dr. Sal says I have a spastic colon. Thinks it's my nerves from too much stress at work. She's right. Away from the office, I've felt okay. Nicky, I thought today was a good time to start making babies, but I don't want to try if I'm still sick."

"We can wait. There's no problem with that."

"I don't want to wait. We'll skip tonight, but as soon as I'm better...."

"Honey, you can quit work right now. Don't go back. How are you going to get better if you keep working with all that tension?"

"Willpower," she said. "God knows I've got plenty of that. I can do it. I know how you worry about expenses, and we need the money I make. I want to save enough so I can stay home and take care of babies, but not before I feel better."

Amy's expression softened as she talked. A smile began to form—not her usual broad grin, but the suck-lemon look was gone.

She was right about money and me. I was always anxious about it. With her sales commissions, Amy made more than I did. I had to work during the summer months to make ends meet. Two days before we left for vacation, I agreed to a job in a warehouse that paid less than I'd made as a bagboy at Kroger's three years earlier. I wanted us to have a family and buy a house, but I worried about how we'd pay for everything.

"Nick, I'll be okay. I'm better already. Just thinking about quitting helps me. I'm sorry, honey. I love you, but I'm not in the mood for making love. Do you forgive me?"

"Don't be silly. It's still a long way home, and I want you to be comfortable. We should wait anyway. At least until after you've seen Dr. Sal again."

"There's something else. I think birth control pills make me jittery. I want to stop them, but now I'm thinking it's too risky. I mean, I want babies. I just don't know when. Oh Nick, this is so complicated. Why can't things be simple?"

"Sweetheart, we'll manage. We love each other too much to let the future get us down. Let's take care of *now*. I want to be sure that you're okay."

"I am. I don't have that shakiness in my stomach anymore."

Insisting that we eat in our room, I went out and got something at a nearby carryout. When I returned, my hands were full, and I knocked on the door with my foot. When I heard Amy moan and call my name, I dropped the packages and rushed in. I found Amy sitting on the toilet, bent over so low that her head nearly touched the floor.

"Sweetheart, I'm taking you to the hospital."

"No!" she screamed. "I'm all right. I'll be okay. It'll pass. It always does."

"You need to see a doctor. I can take you to emergency."

"No. No. No. I don't want some stranger looking up my ass. You don't know what they might do. They might—"

"Amy, that's nuts. You're acting like a—"

"I'm not crazy!" she screamed. "I have a stomach ache. It'll go away."

"Jesus, Amy, you're in agony. I can't just watch you double up in pain."

"It'll stop, I promise. Just don't take me to a hospital. Promise me that you won't. Nick, please. I'm not nuts. I just have a bad case of nerves. I worked myself up about going back to the office. I'll get over it. I'll be fine in the morning. You'll see. But please, don't take me to the hospital."

CHAPTER EIGHT

Happiness is like a butterfly, which appears and delights us for one brief moment, but soon flits away.

—Anna Pavlova

By Labor Day, the girl I had fallen in love with had returned. Dr. Sal's new prescription helped, but the real reason for Amy's improvement was Amy herself. After bowing out of sales competitions at Michigan Bell, she took the high-pressure campaigns less seriously and later was able to stop her medication altogether. The change made life easier for me, too. Although I hated my summer work at the warehouse, I never brought the job home. Instead of exchanging complaints across the dinner table, Amy and I traded dreams for our future.

I had marked Labor Day with red letters on my calendar. It was my last vacation day before returning to school, and Amy and I had planned an outing at the beach on Lake St. Clare. I remember it as one of our last truly carefree days before entering parenthood.

We spent the day swimming and playing tag in the water like a couple of teenagers. When Amy pushed my head under, I held my breath and sank to the bottom, intending to sneak up behind her and dump her in the water. But when I came up for air, she had already splashed off toward the shore. I chased after her, but she was sprinting along the water's edge while I was still churning in deep water. Once I reached the sand, I could run faster and was right on her tail when she fell on our blanket. Panting, I collapsed belly first and landed on the transistor radio that was playing Bobby Darin's "Splish, Splash."

"Ouch," I said, panting loudly. "Who ... put ... that ... there?"

"You did, Aquaman," she said.

"Yeah, but ... you ... left ... it ... on," I gasped. "Wasting ... batteries."

"My battery's okay," said Amy. "You're the one who's out of breath."

"It's ... your ... fault."

"Me? What did I do?"

"Threw sand in my eyes ... and dunked me. You don't play fair."

"Says whose rules?"

I laughed. "Jesus, what *are* we talking about?"

"Nothing," laughed Amy. "Isn't it fun?"

I rolled onto my back and looked into the sun through water droplets hanging from my lashes. Circles of light danced around the sun's edge, radiating brilliant colors everywhere. Turning to my side, I watched Amy put on her lipstick. Glistening beads of water kaleidoscoped in rainbow puddles all over her body. Her capless hair was wet and shiny, her lips were red, and her black bathing suit hid too much of her beautiful body.

"You really are something," I said.

"Just *something?*" she said, pressing her lips together to smooth her lipstick.

"No," I said. "You're *everything*. You make me as happy as a pig in mud."

"Ha. That's *pig in shit*. And you make fun of *me* when *I* mess up a phrase."

"I know what it is. I'm just too couth to say it your way."

"Well, couthness never held me back."

Amy reached behind her, undid the strap, and shimmied her body under her suit.

"What are you doing?" I said.

"Getting naked."

"No, you're not."

"I will, if you do. Come on, I dare you to take off your bathing suit."

As she reached for the string at my waistband, I grabbed her hand and playfully threw her down on the sand. Then I kissed her. I kissed her hard and long. I kissed her on the beach in front of everyone, and I didn't care who saw us.

The ten months that followed included nine pregnant ones, and they were the happiest days of our marriage—although Amy's patience began to wane considerably around the end of May. One evening in mid June, with the baby due "at any moment," we passed the time by watching *Bewitched* in the living room. Amy planted herself on the sofa, and I sat on the red rocker I'd gotten her for Christmas. She hadn't been able to use the rocker for a while because once she sat in it she couldn't get up. On TV, Samantha the witch wiggled her nose, and a basket of fruit popped out of a newspaper ad.

"Crap," said Amy. "I wish I could crinkle my nose and make this kid pop out."

"Uh-huh," I said.

"Don't be smug. You don't know what it's like. Look at me. I'm big as a house."

"Hmm."

"You won't even look. Can't stand me anymore. You don't love me 'cuz I'm fat."

Without answering immediately, I got up, gave her a peck on the cheek, and said, "I love you so much, I *made* you fat."

"Thanks, but no thanks."

Though Amy's frustration grew as her due date approached, she remained in good humor, and I remember how elated I was that she felt so well. Her wit, however, had become increasingly sarcastic, an indication that I should be more understanding. Rather than return to the rocker, I sat on the armrest of the sofa and put my hand on the enormous bubble she cradled in her lap.

"It won't be long now," I said. "I can tell."

"You can't tell. Men don't know anything about it. My doctor says, 'The first one could come at any time.' What a jerk. I don't see how men can be gyneco-ol-o-gists."

"Cuz they're *guy*-necologists."

"Shut up."

"I have complete confidence in Dr. Whatshisname," I said. "He's experienced in these things."

"Ha, you don't even know his name. It's Dr. Bowles; and he doesn't know my ass from a hole in—"

"I do. And I knew you were pregnant before he did."

"Yeah, in a pig's fly."

"No, I swear it. I could tell because your mixed metaphors started making sense and you started looking beautiful. Before that, you talked funny and were kind of blah."

"How romantic."

I touched her cheek. "The first thing I noticed was this pretty color you have—sort of a permanent blush. And I felt it in the softness of your skin. One day you were standing beside me at church, and you nuzzled my arm the way you do. I turned to kiss the top of your head and smelled it in your hair. Knowing you were pregnant was like knowing when a peach was ready to pick."

Amy laughed. "What do you know about peaches? You can't stand the fuzz."

"You're right; peach fuzz gives me chills. But I know about ripe peaches. Learned from an old neighbor named Mrs. Lumley when she taught me how to spot the ripe ones so I could pick 'em. I felt sorry for her because she was crippled with arthritis, so I gritted my teeth and tolerated the fuzz. She rewarded me with a sandwich, a pickle, a glass of milk, and a healthy dose of Jesus."

"I thought *I* brought you to Jesus."

"You did. Mrs. Lumley was my John the Baptist. She prepared the way."

Amy sighed, and then smiled ever so slightly when she said, "Thanks, Nicky."

"For what?"

"For reminding me why I love you. I'm sorry for being such a pest. I want this baby, but I'm tired of waiting. I'm so big I can hardly sit down, and when I do, I can't get up."

I smiled and barely contained a laugh. "I know. I wish there was an easier way."

"There is. You can have it for me." Amy sighed and grew reflective. "Things were great at first," she said. "Being the center of attention at Christmas was neat. The whole family treated me like royalty."

"They still do. You have a striking resemblance to Henry VIII, you know."

I dodged Amy's wild swing and nearly fell off the armrest. Her fist sank into the cushion and I retreated to the red rocker. In December, Amy was a picture of Christmas when she sat in the rocker. The colors—her dark hair and that special glow of her complexion on the red cushions made the season bright and made my heart thump like a kid waiting for Santa.

"Nick, I'm worried about being so late."

"Dr. Bowles said you're fine. It's normal for a first delivery."

"I know, but I wonder about that spotting I had early on. Maybe I did something wrong. I don't like having to be so responsible."

"You've done all the right things—followed the doctor's instructions, avoided aspirin, taken vitamins. And you've read Dr. Spock three times, for heaven's sake."

"Don't say *heaven* in anger. God might not like it. Oh, Nick," she sighed. "I don't want anything to hurt my baby. Maybe I haven't taken enough vitamins—or too many."

"Look, you did and are still doing everything you should do. With all the advice you've gotten from my mom and yours, you can't miss."

"Maybe, but I don't always take their advice. I can't please them both. My mother hardly calls and keeps me guessing. Your mom calls every day. I'm caught between Saundra's standoff righteousness and your mom's in-my-face helpfulness. Doesn't anybody besides my daddy know that I like to do things *my* way?"

"Well, *I* sure have noticed."

"You still fuming about dinner? Well, tough shitski. I might not be the world's best cook, but I won't have you telling me what to do. Just 'cause your dad's a chef and you're such a mama's boy doesn't give you the right to boss me around the kitchen."

"I said I was sorry."

"You insinuated that I poisoned you."

"I only said that I'd rather do my experimenting at school."

"So that's what you call a compliment?"

"I was joking. Can't I make a suggestion without you getting bent out of shape?"

"You don't understand. Mother never let me do a thing in her kitchen. She made me feel like a klutz. You do, too, when you take over like that. I need to do things on my own. Thank God I can be pregnant by myself. No one can take that away from me."

"Hey, I'm sorry. I'll be more careful."

"Yeah, I'm sorry, too. It's this constant waiting and waiting and waiting. I wish someone would make this baby arrive. It's been nine months, ten days, and counting."

"Our baby is as stubborn as you are—won't let anyone dictate a timetable."

"Yeah, and after the baby's born, nothing will be the same."

"Things won't change that much."

"For you, maybe. Marriage was a big change for me; I even lost my name. I lost my job and my friends, too. All I've gained is weight. People think I'm having triplets."

"Sweetheart, you're not fat. I like the way you look. Besides, it's only temporary."

"But everything else is permanent. Nick, don't you see? From now on, I'm defined by you and our children. In everyone's eyes, you're the head of the family. You even took away my car."

I cringed. I felt guilty about selling her car, but we needed the cash.

"Honey, you know how hard that was for me, and you agreed that we can't afford two cars without your paycheck coming in."

"Nick, you're a good provider, but try to understand what I have to deal with. You have new things to do, too, but they're *added* to your life. The old Nick Demetriou still exists and goes on with the new one. My old life's been taken away. It'll never be the same for me."

I felt like Scrooge and Blackbeard the Pirate—miser and merciless thief combined.

"Oh, Nick," she said. "I'm sorry. I know how much you love me."

Amy pushed against the cushions to get up but managed only to bury herself deeper. Then she placed both hands on the armrest and made a mighty effort, but was able to raise herself only an inch or so.

"Ooof," she said. "I can't even get up to give you a hug. Come over here and help me. I love you, you big dummy. I love this baby, too. I know I complain a lot, but I really want this baby. It's just that I'm tired of waiting. You'll see. I'm gonna be a good mom and the best damn wife you never had."

Baby Eleni was born a healthy seven-pound-six-ounce, nineteen-inch beauty queen in waiting, and she showed so much spunk and energy that we had to stay up every night to keep up with her. In our sleep-deprived stupor, we wondered if she was truly ours. Oh, she was wonderful, but it took a few weeks for her sweet disposition to emerge and finally allow us a peaceful night. After that, we knew for sure she was ours and we couldn't have done better had we ordered her through a Sears catalog.

Now, as I recall those happier days of just one year ago, I remember how thankful Amy was for my mom's assistance. Together, she and Mom developed the loving bond that means so much today. I don't know what I'd do now without Mom and Pop's help while Amy's in the hospital. At the same time, I remember Amy's mixed feelings about accepting Mom's assistance with Eleni. Amy said then that she didn't want to be dependent on Mom, but there was more to her concern than a simple desire for independence. During those first months, Amy managed to keep her mother away most of the time—not that her wishes mattered, but because Saundra never volunteered anyway. Now a year later, I realize that behind Amy's independent stance was a wish that her own mother had shown her the affection she needed.

Luckily, it was summer when Eleni was born, and I was at home often enough to help. Earlier, I had been awarded a scholarship to complete my master's degree on a part-time basis, so I was able to have a part-time summer job and take a class or two. Mom offered to stay at our house until Amy got used to her new routines, but Amy declined. Nevertheless, everything worked out remarkably well because Mom stopped by regularly.

Meanwhile, I wasn't a useless drone. I had been thirteen when my sister was born, old enough to learn something about what an infant needed. More importantly, I enjoyed being Amy's partner. Diapers weren't a problem, but I hated the cottage-cheesy stuff that Eleni spit up after feeding. Other than that, I couldn't have been happier. It seemed impossible, but I swore that Amy was even more radiant than when she was pregnant. She was delighted to be a mom, and I had never seen her more at ease. I guess I was seeing what I wanted to see, because now I remember things that should have warned me.

Toward the end of the summer, Amy and I began taking Eleni to the park where we enjoyed reading aloud while she lollygagged in her playpen. A day or two before I was to return to teaching, we set up Eleni's playpen in the cool, dry grass of our favorite spot and spread a blanket for ourselves. *The Lion, the Witch and the Wardrobe* from *The Chronicles of Narnia* was our reading selection for the day. Amy selected the story after I had argued about her other choices. I had said that I liked the romance of *Claudia and David*, but prefered to read a classic. She had suggested that children's stories would be a good influence on Eleni. When I balked, she'd offered *Narnia*, claiming that it was for older kids and had an adult subplot. Whatever the story, I enjoyed hearing Amy read and, despite Eleni's lack of comprehension, I suspected she, too, was comforted by the sound and rhythm of her mother's voice. After all, Eleni's chief occupation was sleeping and ours—at least on picnic days—was to imitate her tranquility, which was hard to do with all the packing, lugging, and unpacking we did.

At one point, Eleni began to cry, and I picked her up before Amy set her book down. Eleni stopped crying as soon as I cradled her in my arms, so I laid her between us on our blanket. The little doll kept still until I began to tickle her tummy with a wiggly finger. She giggled and rolled as I poked my fingers in her belly.

"Don't be so rough," said Amy. "She doesn't like to be teased."

"Come on, what baby doesn't like to be tickled?"

"Dr. Spock says too much of it is bad for the nervous system."

"How about you?" I asked, waving a one-finger airplane over Amy's tummy. "I remember making you giggle like that about nine months before Eleni arrived."

I set the baby back in her playpen. When she cooed and drooled onto the plastic padding, I wiped it up and watched as her eyes began to close and her breathing lengthened until she fell asleep. Nearby, Amy was on her back, and her eyes were closing, too. Her face was partially covered by an open book that was resting against her nose.

"Ah, my two sleeping beauties," I bragged.

Amy closed her eyes more tightly and appeared to sleep, but her smile gave away her act. I fell on all fours and paced a circle around her, growling like a lion and eyeing her hungrily. "The lion king, ravenous after many months of famine, stalks his prey."

Amy smirked and opened one eye. "It's the lioness who hunts for food."

"This lion's not after food."

Stealthily, I took the book from Amy and tossed it onto the grass. She didn't resist, and I purred with satisfaction at her obedience. Suddenly, she threw back her arms as if to surrender. Mock fright appeared in her widened eyes. "Please Mr. Lion King, don't hurt me. I will obey you."

Slowly, I positioned myself above her, knees straddling her hips and hands and holding down her wrists. Snarling menacingly through gritted teeth, I bent toward her throat and then, all of a sudden, I released her arms and began to tickle her, making her laugh and rock from side to side. Freeing herself, she rolled from my grasp, and we howled hysterically until Eleni stirred in the playpen.

Little Eleni, bless her heart, had learned to sleep through practically anything. Nevertheless, Amy and I raised a finger to our lips to signal that we needed to be quiet. I, however, saw the signal as a pretense for a surprise attack, and decided to act first.

In a flash, I sprang toward Amy, but I was too late. She had rolled out of the way and, in a speedier instant, managed to throw herself on me and wrestle me down.

"Now, Mr. Kitty Cat," she said, "let's see how *you* like it."

Her tickling fingers were merciless. I couldn't stop laughing and yelping like a vaudeville madman. My laughter grew more exaggerated and burlesque.

Unexpectedly, Amy, still on top of me, stopped tickling, but I continued to laugh like a three-year-old.

After another moment, she screamed, "Stop it! Stop it! Stop it! Stop it!"

Her hands flew up to cover her face and her body quivered. I tried to take her hands in mine, but she shook more violently and began to sob. Try as I did, I couldn't pry her hands from her face. Suddenly, without warning, she climbed off me and stood with her arms flung out and her fingers stretched wide.

Then, in a staccato, creature-like monotone, she said, "Don't touch me! ... Don't.... Touch.... Me.... And Don't.... Ever.... Do That.... To Me.... Again." Her voice was barely a whisper, but her hissing words might as well have been shouted.

The look in her glassy eyes warned me to remain absolutely still, and I fearfully obeyed. What I saw in her eyes I had never seen before—and I hoped to God that I would never see it again.

Suddenly, she retreated and shrank back as if to melt into a puddle. Neither Amy nor I stirred for several moments. Then she began to cry in soft, sad sobs—unlike the frenzied sobs of a moment earlier. Through tears, she began to speak in a voice I recognized from the day Kennedy was shot—another day of mysterious behavior.

"Please, Nicky," she said, "don't act crazy like that. I can't stand to think that you could ever be out of control. I need you to be my rock. I need you to be reliable. Promise that you won't ever do anything foolish—that you will never be reckless or irresponsible."

CHAPTER NINE

In a dark time, the eye begins to see.

—Theodore Roethke

The kitchen clock reads 2:15. I've spent most of the night drifting through years of memories trying to understand what led to Amy's hospitalization, but it's odd, I don't feel tired anymore. The memories are inexhaustible because each thought triggers another one. Even now, the baby bottles that line the counter remind me of the first time I took the warnings seriously.

It was early morning, and Amy was sterilizing baby bottles at the stove while I got ready for work. Though our chatter was light, I remember thinking that she seemed pensive, and I wasn't surprised when our conversation turned somber.

"I'm glad you like being a dad," she said, "and I appreciate your help, but … I … I hope you don't think you have to. I'm not incompetent, you know."

"Are you kidding?" I said. "I'm amazed that you've become such a good mother."

Without turning around, she said, "The fact that you're *amazed* means you didn't think I was capable in the first place."

"No, that's not what I meant."

Amy lifted the lid off the hot sterilizer and immediately dropped it when steam burst into her face.

I jumped to my feet. "You okay? Here, let me give you a hand."

She raised the lid off the floor and held it like a shield. "Will you please stop interfering," she snapped, slamming the lid on the sterilizer. "Leave me alone, and let me do my work."

"Honey, I just thought you could use some help. Honestly, you look worn out."

"God, you're so critical. Now you don't like the way I look. Listen, this is a big job, and it's not always a joy for me. I don't have time to look beautiful."

"Hey, I'm not criticizing. I understand how tough it is to be a wife and mother. I don't expect—"

"*Don't expect*? The hell you don't. You watch over me like a warden. I know what I'm supposed to do. You don't have to remind me all the time."

"Sweetie, I'm not telling you to do more. I want to help. Let me do the bottles once in a while."

"And prove that I'm not capable? No thanks."

"Sweetheart, it's only right that I share the work around here."

"You have your own work," she said, reaching for a box of Pablum. "Anyway, you'd mess things up. By the time I show you where everything is, I might as well do it myself."

"Maybe we should ask my mom to help during the day—or yours if you'd rather."

"Your mom does too much already. I love her dearly, but she drives me nuts with her offers to help. And I'm not going to ask Mother because I know she'll say no."

"There must be some way to make things easier."

"Why? Don't you think I can handle it? Don't you trust me?"

"Of course, I trust you."

"Well, you don't show it. You keep telling me that I need help."

"Look, I care about you—a lot more it seems than you care about me. You never ask how I feel. Maybe I ask about you because I want you to ask about me."

She spun around quickly and sprayed Pablum from the box in her hand. "Why? What's wrong with you?"

"Nothing. I'd just like you to ask me sometime."

Since school had started, I had been feeling low. The dread that I felt every September when school began hadn't gone away as it usually did.

Amy's lips twisted in a snarl. "Well, I'm *sorry* to *neglect* you. There, feel better?"

"No, I don't. Pardon me, but you're not the only one having a hard time."

She stared at me and absently tilted the box, spilling more Pablum onto the floor. Then she looked aghast at the spilled grains—horrified, as if seeing danger.

"Nick, don't scare me like that. You *are* all right, aren't you? Don't get sick on me. I couldn't stand it if something happened to you."

"I'm fine. Nothing's going to happen to me."

She set the box down and moved toward me. Cereal crunched beneath her steps. "Shit, look at what I've done," she said, peering down with a frightened look. Then, without looking up, she said, "I'm sorry I've disappointed you. I've tried to be a good wife. I'll do better. I promise."

"I wish you wouldn't apologize like that."

"You're mad at me, aren't you?"

"Bullshit! I'm not mad. I know it takes time to get used to a baby."

"You keep checking up on me—making sure that I'm a good mother."

"No, I'm not worried about that. I know you can do it, but all new mothers need a little help to get the hang of it."

Amy turned and crunched the cereal under her feet. When she looked again at the spill, I was startled that her expression reminded me of the terrified look I had seen earlier that summer.

"Never satisfied are you?" she charged. "I can't please you no matter what. You're so damn demanding."

"I never demand …"

"You say you don't, but you do. I know you. You think you can do everything better than me. You and your mother. You should've married her. If I don't do it like she does, I'm no good. Don't deny it. I see how you watch me—how you judge me. Sometimes you can be a self-righteous son of a bitch."

Amy raised a clenched fist and appeared ready to strike me, but then jammed her hand into her apron pocket and looked down at her feet. "Look at the mess I've made."

Stooping to one knee, she swept the cereal granules together with her hands, moving slowly and cautiously as if to gather herself as well. I knelt to help, but she waved me away. "It's my fault," she said. "Go on, get to work." Then she went to the broom closet and yanked on the door handle. It came off in her hand and she began to cry. I hugged her and promised to fix it when I got home. I wanted to hold her longer, but I had to get ready to leave. When I pulled away, she drew me in tighter. "Nicky, don't …" Her sentence was left unfinished, broken off like the handle in her hand.

"Honey," I said, "what is it?"

"Don't …" she said. Then she let me go. "Don't be late for work."

A car horn sounded in the driveway, and I gulped the last of my coffee. A couple of weeks earlier I had joined a carpool with Bill and Rudy, good friends who taught with me at James Junior High. I drove every third week, which allowed Amy to use the car two weeks in a row. I had thought that a chance for her to get out would make a difference.

Though the guys were waiting, I stopped at the bathroom—lingering to be sure Amy was all right. When I came out, Amy was waiting with Eleni in her arms. Together, they seemed peaceful, content.

"Don't worry," said Amy. "I'm okay. We're both all right, and no matter how I feel, I won't ever harm my baby."

It was an odd thing to say, but I let it go and went out to the car. My buddies were good guys, but there was no way I'd tell them my worries. Mostly, I talked sports and told corny jokes, anything to pretend things were fine. Anyway, what could I say? I had no idea what was happening.

Amy didn't answer the phone that day when I called at noon. I thought maybe she had gone shopping with Eleni, but then I wondered if she'd gone to Mom's again, the one place where she felt safe. I had learned that the word "safe" had special meaning for Amy when she refused my suggestion that she have lunch at a restaurant with Eleni. She said she was afraid of exposing Eleni to contamination. No place, not even NASA's white room, could match Amy's spotless house. Then, when I suggested leaving Eleni with someone while we went out, she responded, "No, I can't trust a stranger to take care of Eleni. Eleni is *my* baby."

At the end of the day, Bill dropped me off at home. My heart sank when I didn't see Eleni and Amy peering out the front window like they often did when I came home. I made more noise than usual as I trotted up the wooden front steps, but still no one greeted me. As I fished for my key, I recalled how Amy used to tease me about keys when I'd leave the house without them. Back then, all our mistakes were laughable.

I turned the key in the lock and pushed the door. It opened about an inch before the security chain stopped it. The startle annoyed me. Our car was out front. Where the hell was Amy?

"Amy," I called through the crack in the door. "It's me. Open up." Next door, a neighbor started his lawn mower, muffling my call, and I cussed under my breath. If Amy was at the back of the house, she might not have heard me. I went to the little used side door. We avoided that entrance because we needed two keys to get in, one for the outside door leading to the basement, which we shared with the upstairs tenants. A second key opened our kitchen door at the landing. Amy wouldn't expect me to come in that way, so as soon I opened it, I called, "Honey, it's only me."

No one was in the kitchen. I noticed the lid off the sterilizer with baby bottles still inside. The house was quiet until I heard a stirring in the baby's room. I immediately realized that Amy was probably putting Eleni to bed and I needed to be quiet. Here I was, Mr. Klutz, making enough racket to wake the dead, and making a mountain out of a molehill to boot. I tiptoed to Eleni's room and gently pushed the door open.

The sight of Amy on the floor caught my breath. She was sitting cross-legged with an empty box of tissues on her lap. Wads of used Kleenex were strewn around her bare feet. She was in her nightgown, rocking slowly back and forth. The gown was bunched on one side, and one strap was off her shoulder. Dots of teardrops spotted the stretched fabric between her knees. Her hair was rumpled and matted; her eyes were sunken in deep muddy pools and nearly shut by puffed lids.

I rushed to her, "Sweetheart, what's wrong?"

"I don't know," she sobbed. "I start crying for no reason and can't stop. I'm exhausted, and I've hardly done anything all day long."

When I knelt beside her, she stiffened, and then grabbed my arm so tightly I felt her fingernails dig into my flesh. "Nicky, don't be mad at me. I'm not lazy. I didn't sleep during the day like I did yesterday. Honest, I didn't. I wouldn't let myself sleep. I took care of Eleni. She's been fed and diapered. I bathed her too. She's such a good baby. She's not a problem—not a problem at all. I'm not complaining. I haven't done anything bad. I shouldn't be tired, but … Nick.…" Her eyes searched my face for an answer that I didn't have. She pleaded, "Nick, why do I feel this way? Why am I so scared? Why do I worry so? Why do I constantly worry, worry, worry?"

After comforting Amy, I checked on Eleni and called the gynecologist. Earlier, he had told us about new mothers having *baby blues* and advised us to expect the possibility of mood swings. This time, Dr. Bowles said to bring Amy in immediately. I helped her into a housedress and coat and sat her down on the couch while I dressed Eleni. I soon discovered Eleni had a freshly soiled diaper, so I undressed, changed, and redressed her. With the baby in my arms, I went back to the living room to fetch Amy, but she wasn't there.

"Here I am," she said from behind me.

I turned and watched Amy walk in with her head cocked to one side. She was snapping on an earring and wearing one of the stylish dresses she used to wear to work. Her short, naturally curly hair was brushed into place, and she had put on some makeup. Smartly dressed, she looked like a professional woman preparing for an interview.

My mouth dropped open. "Amy, I.…"

"What are you looking at?" she said. "You didn't think I'd go out in a flimsy housedress, did you? My mother would skin me alive. Besides, I feel better already."

Her sudden change in attitude was baffling, but it had happened before. Despite how she was with me, Amy could will herself to put on an act for other people.

Dr. Bowles saw Amy in his office alone for several minutes before calling me in.

"Can you get someone to be with Amy and the baby for a day or two?" he said.

I glanced at Amy and she smiled.

"Well … yes. I think so," I said.

"Don't bother asking my mother," said Amy. "She's working every day. Your mom will come. She always wants to do something."

"I'm sure she'll come. If not, I'll stay home. But, doctor, what's going on?"

Dr. Bowles smiled warmly. "Don't worry, Nick. Amy doesn't have a disease. I've talked with her before about this possibility. It's not uncommon for first deliveries. Sometimes it's called *baby blues*. The new term is *postpartum blues*, but that sounds much worse than it is. It's quite normal after childbirth, and it's usually not treated because it goes away by itself. I'm sure that Amy's situation is a mild discomfort. All she needs is a little rest and permission to relax."

Addressing Amy, Dr. Bowles continued. "Take these prescriptions, young lady, and, for God's sake, follow my orders. Order number one is to stop trying to be a perfect mom. Relax—and don't you dare try to *relax perfectly*. Do something enjoyable. Go to a movie or read a book—something other than Dr. Spock or anything resembling *how to do everything right*."

He laughed and patted her hand. Amy nodded and smiled. Afterward, I wondered if I had imagined the scene in the doctor's office—or exaggerated the one at home.

The following week, my mom stayed at our house Monday, Tuesday, and Wednesday. On Thursday, Pop picked her up on his way home from work. Mom was gone by the time I got home, but she'd left a nice dinner for us to warm up. Amy seemed appreciative, but worried that Mom thought she was lazy. I assured her that my mother wouldn't accuse her of anything like that, and Amy finally dropped it.

We sat together at dinner, but Amy ate only a little, claiming she had nibbled on too many snacks. I was eating off her plate when she said, "I'm tired. Today wasn't very restful because Mom left early when Pop came by. Your mom means well, but she talks a lot. I know she's trying to help, but all that advice tires me out. I'd like to lie down after I take care of Eleni. You don't mind, do you?"

"No, of course not. I'll clean up in here and then read the paper. I'm bushed, too. I could use an early bedtime myself."

I put off doing the dishes until after I sat down with the paper. When I started on the pots and pans, sleepy-eyed Amy came into the kitchen.

"Still at it?" she said through a yawn.

"Late start. Sorry, I won't be long."

"What's this white stuff on the floor?" she said with some alarm.

I turned and looked where she was pointing. "I don't know," I said. "Looks like flour. Did someone make pancakes today?"

Amy's eyes seized upon the white specks. She bent down, picked one up with the tip of her finger, and examined it with a look that resembled fright. Then, in a sudden movement, she licked the speck from her finger. Hardly pausing, she continued to pick up and taste white particles wherever they were. I watched in amazement as she followed a trail of white dots that led to the edge of the sink where she spotted a can of cleanser.

"Where'd that come from?" she said.

"I found it under the sink. You must've put it there."

"I did not. I told you not to use dry soaps and powders. They're dangerous. I got rid of them weeks ago. You put it there against my wishes, didn't you?"

"What are you talking about? I never heard your stupid rule about dry soap."

"Dry chemicals of all kinds can kill you. They don't dissolve. They can't be washed away. Why did you bring ...? Wait ... it's your mother. She brought it with her. I should've known better than to have her stay here."

"Amy, what's this all about? You're making no sense. Maybe you should go back to bed and let me finish the dishes."

"No. Put down the pan and step away from the sink." She spoke slowly, like a cop giving orders to a dangerous criminal. "Now, dust yourself off—Not like that! she yelled. Brush *downward* onto the floor. Okay. Now, without moving your feet, reach over to rinse your hands, but be careful not to touch the cleanser can. No! Don't wipe your hands; let them dry in the air. Just walk over to the edge of the dining room, but don't go in yet. Stay on the linoleum, step out of your shoes, and then step directly on the carpet. No, don't touch your shoes! Just step out of them. Good."

Once I stood on the dining room floor, Amy let out a sigh. Calm settled on her face like a mask she had willed to appear. "I'll take care of it," she said. "Why don't you take a nice long bath? When you finish, I'll take one before I join you in bed." Her words seemed almost cheerful, and something resembling a reassuring smile was pasted on her face. I feared deception but dismissed it, accepting it as one would accept a magician's illusion.

The next morning Amy seemed rested and in control. She was up early caring for Eleni and getting my breakfast. I resisted when she insisted that I go to work, but Bill and Rudy were expecting me to drive that day and I had an important presentation at school. Nevertheless, that God-awful feeling came over me again.

Amy handed me my keys and gave me a kiss. "Honey," I said, "if there's something bothering you, I want to help. Is there anything I can do?"

"Oh, sweetheart, thanks for asking. I'll be fine if you do just one thing for me. Could you take out the big bag of trash I put at the side door?"

I needed both arms to lug the doubled plastic bag to the alley, so I carried my briefcase flat with the bag balanced on top. The bundle was up to my eyes, and I couldn't see where I was going. Tripping on a crack in the pavement, I pitched the bag forward as I fell. The bag landed with a clang and split open, revealing the frying pan, my shoes, pants, shirt, and underclothes from the night before.

On the ride to school with the guys, I didn't let on that I was worried. Before class, I phoned Amy. She seemed okay, so I didn't question her about the trash bag. I gave the students in my first class a reading assignment, and scrounged around for movies to show for the rest of the day. I called home again at lunchtime, and then phoned Mom and asked her to call Amy, too.

"No, I'm not worried," I lied when talking to Mom. "Uh-huh, she appreciated your help the last few days." ... "By the way, does Amy talk with you about things?" ... "You know, *woman type* stuff—mother things." ... "She's worried you might think she's not a good mother—not that you'd really think that, but, you know, getting used to the baby and ..." ... "No, no, don't tell her that." ... "I think she's lonely and needs you to be a good friend."

Before I called Amy's mother, I planned what to say. Saundra was hard to figure. Though she didn't want to be involved with the baby, I thought she'd want to be informed. At the same time, Amy was adamant about not telling her mother anything that hinted of failure, so I kept the conversation light.

"Saundra, can you call Amy to let her know your plans for Thanksgiving? We'll be at my folks for dinner, but we want to see you, too." ... "Uh-huh." ... "Yeah, why don't you call Amy this afternoon before you leave work?" ... "Yes, I'm sure she'd like that."

When I got home, Amy was sitting up in bed. She told me that she'd taken care of Eleni and prepared a casserole for dinner but wanted to take a nap. I told her that I'd take over while she rested.

Eleni was in her crib and apparently perfectly fine. She had on a clean diaper and the nursery was neat and tidy. A sweet scent of baby powder lingered in the room, even the freshly washed diaper pail had a pleasant odor. I wandered through the rest of the flat. I found perfection everywhere—nothing out of place, everything sparkling clean, not a speck of dust anywhere.

Amy stayed in bed that Friday and all the next day. Her crying and tossing and turning interrupted her sleep and mine as well. On Saturday evening, she awakened and began talking rapidly, rattling on about all that needed done to keep the house in order. She got up and moved from room to room, wringing her hands and nervously examining everything in sight with the urgency of a soldier searching for hidden explosives. After a time, she began to shake her head and complain mournfully.

"Oh, no. Oh, no," she repeated until her mantra became frenzied and she escaped to bed. Despite her collapse, she didn't sleep, but fell into fitful crying that repeatedly burst into hysteria. I called Dr. Bowles. He was out of town. His backup physician, Dr. Caldwell, was attending a delivery. The answering service and Dr. Caldwell's nurse recommended I take Amy to emergency, but Amy was nearly convulsive at the mention of "hospital." When I balked at the nurse's suggestion, she got huffy and said, "Well, I guess she's not sick enough then, is she?"

When Dr. Caldwell called, he too was annoyed that we'd rejected emergency care. Reluctantly, he prescribed a tranquilizer and offered to call a 24-hour pharmacy.

Amy refused the medication, preferring to wait for Dr. Bowles, but it was noon on Sunday before he called. By then, I was practiced at describing Amy's condition, but Dr. Bowles didn't wait for me to finish. "I'll be at your house as soon as possible," he said. "Stay by her side. Whatever you do, don't leave Amy alone for a second."

After a short time alone with Amy, the doctor asked me to sit on the bed beside her. Dr. Bowles sat on the opposite side holding her hand. While he spoke gently and reassuringly to Amy, his eyes darted repeatedly to mine. "It's nothing serious, Amy. You're going to be all right in no time."

I felt his expression indicated that he wasn't telling her what he really believed.

"Don't worry about a thing. You're safe with Nick, and I'll see that you get the best care to chase away your scary feelings. I promise that you'll be well before you know it. I saw how tough you were when baby Eleni was born. You showed us that you have the stuff to get through anything. Right now, let yourself rest."

Amy's sobs, which hadn't stopped for hours, began to soften. Dr. Bowles stroked her hand lightly and kept repeating, "There, there, darling child. There, there, now."

When he and I stepped into the living room, out of earshot from Amy, he said, "I've given your wife a tranquilizer. She should sleep for several hours. I'm going to find a doctor for her. You'll hear from—"

"She wants *you*. You're the only doctor she'll see."

"I'm a gynecologist and postnatal physician. This is not related to childbirth. Her illness is way beyond anything I can treat. I've seen postpartum neurosis before, and this is something else. Amy needs a psychiatrist and may need to be in a hospital."

"My God. What kind of hospital?"

"Try to calm down. You have to stay in control. She needs you, and so does Eleni. They're depending on you now. You've got to be their rock."

"Of course," I said, still not knowing what to do.

"Nick, I'm sure you never expected to be tested like this, but you and Amy can overcome it. I'm confident of that."

"Doctor, what are you saying? What exactly is Amy's condition?"

"Amy has an emotional illness and needs a specialist, a psychiatrist who's experienced with such matters. None of us can predict what might happen. Some patients are cured immediately, spontaneously responding to minimal treatment. I can't tell you how Amy will do, but I believe her chances for a quick recovery are better than most. In the meantime, you'll need to take on a bigger share of responsibility for your family."

Suddenly, I realized that I hadn't checked on Eleni for several minutes. "Doctor, before you go, will you please look in on the baby? I want to be sure she's okay."

"I'll be happy to, but I don't think you have to worry about your little girl. Amy has taken good care of her. She loves you both, and she's done a marvelous job as a new mother. I have every reason to believe that she'll soon be back to normal."

When Dr. Bowles went to the nursery, I sat on the couch opposite Amy's red rocking chair, but I was unable to look at its emptiness. Turning away, I glanced at the Sunday *Free Press* and saw a headline that read, "Despondent Mother Charged in Child's Death."

CHAPTER TEN

What difference do it make if the thing you scared of is real or not?

—**Toni Morrison**

A day had passed without word from Dr. Bowles, and I was beside myself when I spoke to his receptionist.

"Doctor advises that he is not able to set up the appointment you requested," she said stiffly. "He wants to assure you that he will provide a referral as soon as possible."

"I don't understand. How can you put us off like this?"

"I'm sorry. Doctor is doing his best. A wait of a week or so is typical for—"

"But my wife is very ill. I'm losing time from work, and my daughter is—"

"Is your daughter ill, also? Doctor didn't tell me you needed two appointments."

The receptionist went on in her perfunctory manner. *Doctor … this, and Doctor … that.* I hated her calm condescension … hated the way she said *Doctor* without a definite article.

"Tell THE goddamn doctor I want to talk to him immediately!"

There was a long silence. When she replied, her disdain was more pronounced. "That would be impossible, sir. Doctor is with patients. I will give him your message."

When Dr. Bowles finally called, his voice was barely discernable over rumbles of background voices. Someone near him interrupted with a question. At my end of the line, I began pacing back and forth, stretching the spiral phone cord while I walked.

"Mr. Demetriou," he finally whispered, "please excuse my receptionist. I didn't tell her the nature of Amy's problem. You understand. No need to let the world know the details. It's best to keep this sort of thing confidential."

"What's that noise? Why are you talking so low? I can hardly hear you."

"I'm calling from the hospital. It's crowded here, and I'm trying to be discreet."

"Why are you calling from the street?"

"I'll have someone for Amy very soon. Let me assure you, I've personally tried to arrange for a good...." He paused. His hesitation was puzzling. I never knew a doctor to hunt for words. I wrapped the cord around myself once more before he started again. "... for a ... *specialist* ... to see your wife. The one I have in mind is not immediately available, and I think an emergency hospital admission would be too frightening for Amy."

What sort of code was this? Why couldn't he say psychiatrist without gagging? Why did he suggest hospitalization? Amy wasn't crazy, for God's sake.

"Doctor Bowles, there must be a psy—" I bit off the word. I couldn't say it either.

God almighty, this is nuts.

"Mr. Demetriou, Amy might snap out of it spontaneously. She has a very strong will and could surprise us all. Even now, she recognizes that her fears are not rational. That's a good start. I have in mind a young man named Dr. Florence. He's in Europe now, but will see her when he returns next week. Amy's medication will get her through until then."

I wanted to say *not the way she's taking it*, but my throat had tightened and I could hardly speak. "Doctor ... a psychiatrist? ... she's not ...?"

"No, she's not ... it's not what you're thinking, but keep your voice down. Amy mustn't suspect that you're overly concerned."

"What about Eleni?" I asked. "I can't stay away from work indefinitely. What should I do about my job? How can I ...?" I had reached the end of the phone cord and it had stopped me short. Awkwardly, I tried to untangle, but was suddenly startled by the familiar sound of Amy's giggle. She stood in the hallway dressed in her red robe and wearing slippers. Her short black hair was pushed into place, and her lips had a hint of color. Striking a nymph-like pose, she peered curiously at me, rubbed her eyes, and looked again. Then she stood akimbo, cocked her head to one side, and smiled broadly.

"Oh, Nicholas Demetriou," she laughed, shaking her head from side to side. "What kind of mess did you get yourself into?"

The discord between the doctor's serious tone and Amy's apparent gaiety dumfounded me. I lowered the receiver from my ear and held it at my side, letting the doctor's words tumble from the phone without reaching anyone. I didn't want Dr. Bowles to hear Amy's laughter for fear that he would discount her illness. I wanted him to feel the urgency that I felt. He never really saw her as I did. It seemed no one ever did.

I raised the receiver to my ear, offered an empty *thank you*, and hung up.

"So," said Amy, "is the good doctor going to lock me up?"

"No, of course not."

Amy bowed her head and looked at me through raised eyes. "I'm sorry, I shouldn't have said that. You're worried. I am too, but I can lick this. It's just a feeling that comes over me sometimes. I'm better now. I'm getting a handle on it. You'll see."

"How long were you listening?"

"Not long. I woke up a while ago, though. I washed and went back to bed to think about things. Thought about Scarlett O'Hara and decided to read my favorite passage again. You know the one—at Tara? Where she takes dirt in her hand and says, 'As God is my witness....' Well, I'm a fighter like Scarlett. I won't let this thing get me down."

I felt frightened. I couldn't understand Amy's blend of pledge and apology.

"Sweetheart," I said weakly, "is it time for another pill?"

"No. Maybe I'll take one when we go to bed, but I'm okay now."

Amy helped me twist out of the tangled phone cord wrapped around my body, and I tried to restore the spiral to its original elasticity but quit in frustration. The cord, stretched beyond its limit, would never be the same.

Focusing on the table where the phone rested, Amy narrowed her eyes as she gathered the cuff of her sleeve and dusted the tabletop. With the tip of a finger, she pecked at a white speck and started to put it to her mouth. Then, abruptly, she flicked it away.

"Amy, I'm concerned," I said. "You need help. I'm worried about Eleni, too. She's a handful right now. We could take her to Mom's and let her stay until...."

"I know. Maybe you're right, but first let me try it by myself. I love you and I love our little kid. I would never do anything to harm either of you. Besides, what will we tell Mom and Pop? We can't tell them that I'm a nut case."

"You're not a nut case. And we don't know how they'd react to ... to any news."

"I'm already under suspicion 'cause I'm not Greek and I can't cook. God knows how much stock they put in food. Even my own family believes I'm incompetent."

"Honey, your dad adores you," I said. "In his eyes, you can do no wrong. Your mother loves you, too. She just can't show it like he does."

"Let's not go there, okay? I'm not getting into that right now."

"Okay, but don't be so harsh on my folks. They're not as critical as you think."

Amy's expression softened and I sensed again a quality I had fallen in love with—a childlike insecurity she hid in the skirts of sass and flirtation and revealed only to me. I treasured that little girl within her, yet I felt sad whenever I was allowed to see her.

"Nicky, will you always love me—I mean forever and ever?"

"Of course I will, sweetheart. For ten thousand, thousand forevers."

"I have about that many flaws, most of which you never knew. Aren't you afraid?"

"Sometimes, but I'm not perfect either. I believe in you and me as a team. Together, we can do anything."

The little girl raised her eyes to mine. "Nicky ... please don't send me to a hospital."

"What? Why do you say that?"

Amy trembled and turned away. "When I was twelve years old, Daddy was put in one of those places. I saw him there. It was awful. I have nightmares about it."

"I didn't know."

"No one does. Mother said not to tell anyone."

"Have you told her about your nightmares and talked about how you felt?"

"I used to. She told me to put them out of my mind. She said that talking about them would make them come true, so I stopped telling her."

"Sweetheart, I'm sorry. It's okay to tell me. It might help you—and me—to understand what's going on. Is this the same dream you had when Kennedy—"

"What? No! Nicky, I told you to never bring that up."

"Sorry, I thought...."

"This dream is different, but almost as scary. When I visit Daddy in a hospital like the one he was in, I see *myself* instead of him, and I'm tied down in a bed with wires and things. I watch myself for a long time, staring at the helpless person that has suddenly become me. Then, to the person in the bed that is me, I say, *You will never leave this place.*"

The first time I met Dr. Florence, he gave me a weak handshake that fit the image I had associated with his name. He was about thirty, had straight yellow hair parted on the right, and combed to fall above a left eyebrow darker than his hair. He had an irritating way of flicking at the strands that fell over his eye. Gold rings and diamond studs glittered from his hands and wrists. A bracelet that hung loosely from his right wrist clicked on his desk and against the stud of his French-cuffed shirt. I couldn't make myself believe that one of his many rings meant he was married.

Florence took a long time telling us about himself before asking Amy anything. Finally, he said, "Mrs. Demetriou, tell me how you feel."

Amy, who had spent an hour primping for the appointment, looked as if she were modeling for *Good Housekeeping.* "I ... I don't know how to describe it," she said. "Sometimes I feel sad. It comes and goes."

That's not enough, Amy. You aren't showing the urgency that I've seen. You aren't telling him how bad it really is.

The doctor nodded and waited for her to continue. When she didn't, he said, "Why don't you tell me about yourself. Did you work before the baby was born?"

Slowly, Amy told him about her job at Michigan Bell. Recalling the many sales awards she had received seemed to put her at ease. As she talked, my mind wandered, and I found myself examining Dr. Florence and his paneled office. He reminded me of Peter O'Toole, an actor whose skill I admired.

He sat behind a huge desk—mahogany, I thought. The entire wall behind him was filled with books that seemed coordinated with the judge's-chamber-style of his office. Amy and I sat facing him in oversized leather chairs. His desk was clear of clutter. A lamp rested at one corner, its light dim and nonfunctional. The desk itself was so shiny I could see the overhead lights and our faces darkly reflected in its surface. The ceiling lights were recessed. The bright fluorescence flooded the room, eliminating shadows from everything except the curves and hollows of a miniature sculpture that sat on his desk opposite his lamp. The sculpture was of nude male and female forms locked in intimate embrace. On its base, a brass plate carried the inscription: Rodin, The Kiss. Fascinated by the sculpture, I caught myself staring at it and looked up to see that Dr. Florence had caught me, too.

"It's a motif from Rodin's *Gates of Hell,*" he said. "Are you familiar with it?"

His question startled me and sounded almost accusatory. I hadn't realized my gaze was so obvious. "Uh ... no. No, I'm not."

"The *Gate* is a door at the *Musée des Arts Décoratifs* in Paris. I was there last week. Rodin never finished the door, but he produced several separate sculptures from his original design. Each one represents a scene from Dante's *Inferno.* Intriguing, isn't it?"

"Uh ... yes. Very interesting."

"And you, Mr. Demetriou. How do *you* see Amy's problem?"

Caught off guard for ogling nudes, I tensed at his question. How could I answer without betraying Amy? *She* had to tell him about her weirdness—not me.

"I ... I see her crying all the time—not *all* the time, but a lot. She gets very sad, even when there seems to be no reason for it."

Something stopped me from saying more. Was it my loyalty to Amy? Or was it my reaction to Florence? Amy won't like him, I thought. She's drawn to John Wayne types—men like her dad.

When I fell silent, the doctor told Amy how he would proceed. "... once a week for a while ... a prescription for a mild tranquilizer ... a period of evaluation...." I listened, but heard his voice in an odd way as if he was a radio wearing a slick silk suit. Amy seemed receptive to his instructions, nodding agreeably to his minor queries. When he asked me to return to the waiting room while he visited alone with Amy, I was relieved, but reluctant to go. Florence got up quickly, but I rose slowly, feeling as if the doctor had thrown a weight in my lap. Amy smiled. "It's okay, Nick. I'll be fine."

I was uncertain what I feared most—staying there with him or leaving Amy? The doctor was at my side, ushering me out. I remember how easy it seemed for him to open the huge door, but how difficult it was for me to walk through the portal. I heard the *click* of the latch as the door shut behind me. I turned to face it and, for a long while, studied its elements. The brass strike plate that jutted out at the latch, the wide muntins separating the beveled panels, the wing-like flaps and stout pins of the elaborate butt hinges, the shield-like escutcheon guarding the keyhole, and the broad horizontal crossbar—all of these appeared as barriers designed to block me from caring for Amy.

I will never share this with Amy because I fear what it might do to her recovery, but I've had a recurring dream since she began seeing Florence. In it, I'm on a suspension bridge over a vertical-walled canyon—a place like the thousand-foot Royal Gorge that Amy and I visited in Colorado. The dream-chasm is black and ugly and has no bottom. I'm on one side of a rickety wooden bridge held together with ropes tied to tree roots. Amy has wandered away from me to the center of the bridge. An infant is in her arms. I start toward her. Terrified, I stop after a single step. Amy leans against the rope-rail, the infant dangerously near its edge. Frightened and unable to reach her, I call for help. A tall man, shrouded in silky black robes and flashing glittery gold teeth, appears on the other side of the canyon. He extends a diamond-studded stick toward Amy and beckons her to take it. Stopped in the midst of the swaying bridge, she turns toward me, pauses, and then faces the man again, making no move either way. My head spins, and I totter from side to side causing the bridge to sway. I dare not look down. I'm terrified that my imbalance will topple Amy, the baby, and me over the side. Will this man rescue us? Can Amy go to him on her own? I fear she can't. My lips move to call for the man to go to Amy and bring her to me, but my words either don't form or they fall into the chasm before reaching anyone.

CHAPTER ELEVEN

*Psychiatrists seemed to fear the taint of insanity much as
inquisitors once feared succumbing to the devil.*

—**Robert T. Pirsig**

Though our emotional toll was incalculable, the statements clearly listed our monthly medical expenses. Amy saw Dr. Florence every week. His fee was forty-five dollars per session. My yearly teacher's pay was barely five thousand dollars, and my insurance covered neither outpatient mental health care nor prescriptions. Consequently, as Christmas approached, I pretty much ignored the thought of buying gifts.

Holidays were especially difficult for Amy. The demands of joyful seasons magnified her sorrow. Sometimes she met the challenge with a burst of merriment that seemed to come from nowhere. More often, she found a pretense to avoid gatherings entirely. Other times, she simply placed herself in the midst of the crowd, where she swirled like a stone in a punch bowl, a noticeable presence that never blended in. Sometimes I wondered, however, if we were fooling ourselves into believing that no one but us knew the true character of her mood. I had to admit that I could never be sure who the real Amy was.

When Christmas was only a week away, Amy suddenly got into the holiday spirit. I remember my surprise when she said, "Come on, let's go out and celebrate" after leaving Florence's office one afternoon. "My next appointment is not until January thirtieth," she beamed. "From now on, I'll see him only once a month."

Initially, I wondered if it was just another U-turn. Previous abrupt reversals had led to disappointing setbacks, yet I remained naively hopeful that her recovery would be as quick and unexplainable as the onset of her illness.

"Gee, that's great," I said weakly. "What do you want to do?"

"It's Eleni's first Christmas," she said. "Let's go shopping."

With Eleni safely tucked in at Mom and Pop's, we had a couple of hours to spare. I didn't like traipsing from store to store, but the mall atmosphere was festive and the switch to once-a-month therapy sessions meant more cash was available.

"How about we break up and shop separately for a while?" she said.

My heart quickened when I thought of letting her go off on her own, but she had been alone every day when I went to work, so we agreed to meet in two hours at Hudson's entrance. Time passed quickly, and I found only a couple of gifts that I could afford. The previous year, I had decided to buy Amy a red rocker and drove myself nuts before finding the right one. I'll never forget the look on her face when she saw it. I wanted to make her happy like that again, but lately, nothing I did seemed to be enough.

On my way to the spot where we had agreed to meet, I stopped for a moment to admire a giant Christmas tree in the center of the mall. "Guess who's under the mistletoe?" said someone behind me. I turned. It was Amy, and she waved a sprig of something over my head. She gave me a quick kiss and thumped down several brightly wrapped packages, none as radiant as she.

"Wanna know how many boxes are yours? Wanna know what's in 'em?"

"Holy cow, how many gifts did you buy? I didn't get you that much."

"They're not all for you. Besides, who said anything about an even trade? You and Eleni are my best presents. On the other hand," she said slyly, "I won't object if you give me a Mustang convertible."

A plump Santa and a tall Nutcracker walked by and wished us merry Christmas. Amy giggled at them and said, "Nicky, I have a feeling that this is going to be our best Christmas ever."

In the afternoon of Christmas Eve, Amy asked me to take care of Eleni while she took a nap to rest before our long evening at her folks' house. I never took naps, but I didn't see Amy's request as a problem. Besides, I was too excited about spending Christmas Eve with her folks and the next day with mine. Andy and Saundra put on a great party. The real fun would begin after midnight when only the immediate family remained to see what Santa brought. Despite the Miller's great show, I thought the next day at Mom and Pop's was more *colorful*—though Amy might have said *chaotic*.

Around three o'clock, Amy was still sleeping. Since we were expected at the Miller's at five, I went to the bedroom and shook her awake. Suddenly, she bolted up and screamed, "Don't ever do that to me, you son of a bitch! Don't ever wake me like that."

"What? What did I do? I'm sorry."

"You did that on purpose. I know what you're thinking. 'There she goes again, sleeping the day away.'"

"I had no such thought. I just figured it was time to get ready for the party."

"I would've gotten up by myself, but you don't trust me. It's the same as always. You think I'm lazy. You think I can't take care of things around here. 'Poor Amy's too sick. She can't even keep the house clean. Amy's—'"

"Sweetheart, stop," I pleaded. "What are you talking about? The house is spotless."

Amy was shaking so fitfully that I put my arms around her and held her to make her stop. When she continued to tremble, I held her more tightly.

"Let me go. Let me go," she screamed, wiggling and twisting to get herself free. "You're hurting me. Get away from me. You bastard, let go of me and get out of here!"

With her arms flailing wildly, she spun away. Standing squarely, she raised a hand, extended her arm like a traffic cop, and looked fiercely—challengingly—into my eyes. "I won't let you hurt me," she said, her voice low and severe. "I won't let *anyone* hurt me."

"Amy, please. What is it? What's going on?"

Amy's eyes widened and her face twisted as her fingers slowly curled into tightly clenched fists. When she raised her hands above her head and shrieked, I rocked back against the door, and slammed it shut. Startled, she ran toward me with balled fists and pounded on my chest until I nearly cried out. Then, in an instant, her fists opened, her body suddenly slackened, and she would have collapsed to the floor had she not grabbed hold of my shirt.

"Oh, Nicky, Nicky, Nicky," she sobbed, still holding on to me.

She cried for several minutes. I could do nothing but sit with her on the edge of the bed with my head bowed, staring at the worn rug with such intensity that its exposed threads seemed to unravel. When Amy began to sigh, I faced her and took her hands in mine—gently this time, so as not to frighten her. Her gaze remained fixed on some aspect of the same faded rug.

"Sweetheart, what's going on?" I said. "What happened just now?"

"I don't know. Something is wrong with me. Maybe I'm no good. My mother's right. I can't be a wife. I can't take care of a house. I can't—"

"Amy, that's nonsense. You've done very well. The last few days have been ... they've been ... like before. Something brought this on today. What is it?"

"Nick, I'm scared. I don't want to see your family. They know. They can tell. They don't trust me. They'll take me away from you—from Eleni."

"No one will ever take you away from me. I swear I'll fight for you with every ounce in my body. I'll never give up on you. We can skip my folks if that's what you want. Maybe we should spend both days with your family—talk things over and get their advice."

Amy leaped from the bed and backed into the corner of the room. Her eyes widened larger than before, but this time they showed fear, not anger.

"No. Please, no. We can't do that. Not my father. God, no. Not my mother. I know what she'll say. We can't tell them anything. We can't tell anyone."

Amy cowered and shivered like a cornered mouse. She said she was afraid to go, but worried that it was more frightful to have to explain canceling at the last moment.

The phone rang. Amy's startled eyes indicated I should answer it.

"Hello?" I said. "Oh, hi, Janet." It was my sister-in-law, my brother Gus's wife. "Yeah, Merry Christmas. Yes, I think we're bringing a dessert tomorrow." Amy nodded when I looked her way. "Yeah—pumpkin pie—homemade by our neighbor Sara Lee. Uh-huh, it's dinner rolls for you. Okay, see you at about two. Bye."

"Nicky," Amy said before I hung up, "I can't go. Tell them I have the flu."

I nearly exploded. The *flu* was an excuse we'd given a dozen times before. How long must we use it as a generic equivalent for whatever she really has?

"Look, I'm getting tired of this," I said. "First, you jerk me around and scare the hell out of me. Then all of a sudden, you have a miraculous healing. For a week, you've been telling me everything is hunky-dory. Now you're pulling that *sick* routine again."

"I'm sorry. I don't mean to spoil things. Maybe, you and Eleni can go by yourselves."

"Like hell, we can."

"Nick, don't be angry with me."

"I'm not angry!" I hollered. "You did this to me on Thanksgiving. I can't stand...." I took a breath and tried again. "Sweetie, I'm not angry. I just don't understand."

"Nick, I'm not faking it. Something horrible takes control of me."

"Honey, everybody feels down once in a while. You think *I* don't get scared? You think *I* don't feel like stopping the world and getting off? Jeez, I worry about where the next dollar's coming from. Do you know how often I've felt like running out the door? Your feelings are nothing new. Snap out of it for Christ's sake—everyone else does."

"I'm trying, I really am, and I was doing well. I even stopped my medication. I thought I was fine until today. Then all of a sudden—"

"Well, damnit; it's time to grow up. You're a big girl now. You're my wife and the mother of our child, so start acting your part. When you get that feeling, do what I do. Ignore it. Shake yourself loose from … from whatever it is … whatever you're imagining. You have a life to live, a family to care for. Get on with it, and stop feeling sorry for yourself."

"But everything I do seems hopeless, and I feel like I have nothing to live for," said Amy.

"Shit. What am I, chopped liver? Aren't *I* worth anything to you? What about Eleni? Isn't she worth the little sacrifice you have to make? I work like hell to provide for you and our daughter. I think I do a pretty good job taking care of things. What the hell do you have to be sad about? We might not have a lot, but there are plenty of people who have diddly-squat compared to us. We pay our rent every month. We have a car, a few bucks to spend, and a little bit of savings that might last if you don't squander it on something foolish like … like goddamn psychiatrists."

Mentioning money was like hitting myself with a hammer. If anything could drive me nuts, it was worry about money. It was bad enough when all we had were normal expenses. Then everything went haywire. All because of—God, I don't even know what it was—that … thing … that had gotten into Amy and made her act weird.

"Nicky, I'm sorry. Please stop yelling. Everything you say is true. I have no reason to be depressed, but I am, and I feel so ashamed. Maybe I'm just no good."

Amy looked down and drew her hands together, wringing them like dishcloths. I hated when she did that. I'd seen this submissive pose before. It was so unlike the Amy I thought she was before we married. *Depression? Shit, it's nothing more than a hole she digs herself into because she sets herself up for criticism. She knows she can't bake a cake, but she goes ahead and bakes one anyway—just to prove that she can't. She's her own worst enemy when it comes to proving her shortcomings.*

I didn't know what to do. I left Amy sobbing and walked into the nursery. Little Eleni smiled up from her crib. She's such a sweet baby, so docile and easy to please. I wiggled my fingers above her and made her giggle. When I lightly tickled the palms of her hands, she instantly grabbed my fingers and began to tug, urging me to pull her up. The little monkey loved to play like that. She was so predictable, so unlike her mom.

Amy used to be more predictable. In the past, I was able to rely on things like her sense of humor and sharp wit—things I could count on to chase away my own blues. Now the only certainty was that she would vacillate between vile anger and hangdog shame.

I continued to fuss over Eleni, deliberately spending extra time so I could think through my strategy. That's what it had become—a *strategy*. I couldn't be spontaneous. I had to scope out everything—make a plan before saying or doing anything. Yet, I had to admit that helping Amy had not been my only motive for yelling at her. I had spoken in anger and wanted her to know that I hated what she was doing to me.

After calming myself, I went into the living room. Amy was sitting motionless in the red rocker.

"Nick," she said, "I know you're right, but I can't help it. My insides are knotted up. I'm sorry. I know I cause you—"

"No, I'm the one who should apologize. I acted like a jerk. I lost my head. I know it's hard for you. We shouldn't argue. I'm sure we'll overcome this if we work together."

I knelt before her chair and put my head on her lap. I wished I could've taken back my words, but also thought that maybe they needed to be said. Amy's thinking was irrational; I had to do something to get her back to her senses.

"I'm sorry," we said together. We laughed a nervous laugh. Amy stroked my hair and kissed the top of my head. I yelped when she rocked the chair and caused the runner to pinch my leg. She started to apologize, but I put my finger to her lips and said, "My fault."

She kissed my finger, and then bit it playfully.

"I'm sorry," she said, and then added, "I'm sorry you're such a jerk."

"Me, too."

We sat silently for several moments. Slowly, Amy's expression became pensive again, and she began to chew the inside of her cheek in that way she does.

After a moment, I said, "What's on your mind, pumpkin?"

"Nothing."

"Come on, those are words you're chewing on, not bubble gum."

"I don't want to say anything. You'll get mad at me again."

"Look, I was surprised and lost my head. You've done so well lately, and all of a sudden, you changed. It's not like you to give up without a fight. You're the most willful person I know. Why don't you put that stubbornness to work for you?"

"I'm trying. God, I'm exhausted from trying so hard."

"Honey, don't give in so easily. You used to be a spitfire and never let anyone get you down, not even me. Wouldn't it be idiotic to be beaten by ... by *yourself.*"

Amy nodded, but tears welled in her eyes. "I know," she said. "You're right. I should do better. I can. I will do better."

I took her hand. "Think of all we have. I mean the important things, not the material things. You've got a mother who cares about you and a dad who dotes on you, not to mention a mother-in-law who wants to adopt you, and—"

"They all think I'm not right in the head."

"You are not *not right.* You're just upset or something. Nobody knows about Dr. Florence unless we tell. We won't say a word about ... about anything."

Amy got up and squeezed my hand. "Thank you," she said.

"So ... you'll go? We can have Christmas with the family?"

"Ye ... yeah. I ... I'll give it a try."

"You'll see. You won't regret it."

"I do have a lot to be thankful for, don't I?"

"Sure do. Most important, you have Eleni and me. We love you. In spite of my stupidity, I love you now more than ever."

"Maybe it's *because* of your stupidity."

Amy buried her face in my chest and murmured, "Nicky, do you really love me?"

"Yes, I really love you."

"No matter what?"

"No matter what."

"Forever and ever?"

"For ten thousand, thousand forevers."

Amy's litany of fidelity used to be endearing, but had grown to be annoying. The words had become ceremonial, a recitation that reminded me of her unquenchable need for assurance, yet I knew I would always promise freely and completely. The ritual was a knot in the tie that bound us. The problem was that I felt singularly responsible for securing the knot, and I was afraid it would always be that way. Nonetheless, I still hoped Amy's anxiety was temporary and she'd soon offer me the reliability that I pledged to her.

Amy put on a good show at both Christmas parties and might even have persuaded others that her listlessness was due to a "touch of the flu," but her charade only increased my alarm. Her pale complexion was covered with makeup and her anxiety disguised with Valium, but cover-up didn't erase the effects of her mysterious attack. To deny it, as she tried so hard to do, was a bald-faced lie, but her doctor was unavailable, and Amy wouldn't consider seeing a different one. Even if she had seen another doctor, she would only have put on a deceptive show of composure. Chameleon-like, she had the ability to change her color and appear calm, cute, and charming, and then be sent home with nothing more than an aspirin.

I couldn't reach Dr. Florence until January 18, the day after Amy's twenty-fifth birthday. Once again, Amy's frame of mind had changed. After the holidays passed, her moods leveled out, and she became less anxious, more content, and not as ruffled when things went wrong. The seventeenth, when we celebrated her birthday, she seemed as happy as the day we had gone Christmas shopping. Boasting of another *spontaneous cure*, she claimed her symptoms had disappeared with the holiday tinsel and she was no longer depressed. Unconvinced, I wasn't relieved until I got the doctor on the phone. Unfortunately, my relief was short-lived.

"She's okay right now," I said, "but the holidays were tough for her."

"That's common for my patients," replied Florence. "She'll get better over time."

"But I should tell you what happened. She had an episode where—"

"Does Mrs. Demetriou know you're calling me?"

"Well, no, but we—"

"I'm sorry; I don't want to jeopardize my professional relationship with Amy. If she is able to speak for herself, she should. Can't this wait until her appointment?"

"Uh ... yes. I mean, no. Can you see her before her scheduled time?"

"Is that what she wants?"

"She hasn't said, but I think—"

"I'm afraid I can't see her earlier than the thirtieth, anyway. Is this an emergency?"

"No, not now ... but on Christmas Eve—"

"Mr. Demetriou, unless there's an emergency, I really should have this conversation with Amy, not you. Does she wish to talk to me?"

"Uh ... I don't know. She doesn't know I called you."

"Let me assure you that emotional patients routinely have difficult holiday periods, and I might add, so do their loved ones. Let's see how she is on the thirtieth."

"She'll be there, Doctor, but at Christmastime she—"

"Mr. Demetriou, Mrs. Demetriou and I have established doctor-client confidentiality. I will not violate that. I suggest that you speak with Amy about your concerns. She presents herself to me as perfectly capable of handling her own affairs. Perhaps you're overreacting. That, too, is common for young couples. I'm sure she'll be fine. She may call me if she wishes. Now, I really must go."

I hung up wondering which of us was crazy—Amy ... the doctor ... or me.

CHAPTER TWELVE

For secrets are edged tools,
And must be kept from children and from fools.

—John Dryden

The first three months of 1966 were such a contrast to the end of the previous year that I began to believe Dr. Florence was right; maybe I was overreacting. Amy had become the picture of health. She lost the weight she had gained after Eleni was born, and was prettier than when she was Miss Michigan Bell in the Michigan Week Parade the summer before we were married. The only thing I lamented was that Amy was reluctant to have sex, saying that she thought it was safer to wait until she stopped her medication altogether. Though I often felt frustrated, I figured that sex would come in time because, up to a point, Amy offered affection freely.

Starting in February, we began attending church again and visiting friends more often, especially after Amy stopped seeing Dr. Florence. Our attitudes were upbeat, and we grew so confident in her recovery that we began to shop for a new house.

She was as excited about the house as I was. Even after we realized that we had to pare down our dream, Amy shrugged it off and seemed content to settle on a modestly priced home. Then, when we found a bungalow in Detroit that required a down payment that was out of our reach, she surprised me with a little secret. While she had worked for the phone company, Amy had set aside part of her pay to buy AT&T stock, and the company had matched her contributions dollar for dollar. After some quick calculations, I saw that her shares were valued at more than three thousand dollars, a sum greater than the fifteen percent required for a down payment.

Though I was elated, I also had an uneasy feeling about why Amy hadn't told me about her cache. Her explanation that her parents had warned her to keep it a secret—"just in case things didn't work out in our marriage"—made matters worse for me. *Hadn't I proved myself trustworthy? Surely, I had shown my fidelity during the last two and a half years.* Then, when she volunteered that perhaps her parents' caution had more to do with mistrust for her than for me, I wondered what that meant.

The windfall could easily have turned into a storm had Amy and I not been able to talk about it openly. In the end, our frank discussion drew us closer together. Amy's unemotional but sensitive response was compelling, and I felt we had reached a level of shared responsibility that had been impossible months earlier.

Despite our resolution, however, our bid was submitted late, and we lost the house. I think it was after that that Amy's mood began to change. Little things, like her attention to cleanliness in a prospective home, and her impatient demands that the realtor find a house before Easter, grew into obsessions. At first, I liked her "get the show on the road" attitude, but then she acted as if her life depended on the conditions she had set.

Ironically, her desire to find a home fast was thwarted by her high standards for cleanlines. When she suggested a just-built house that was already spic and span, I countered that new ones were out of our price range. In older homes, she fretted about the stuff that people left behind—not big items, but little things that I hadn't noticed at first. She inspected cupboards, closets, and basement storage areas. She looked under sinks, in tile cracks, and down drains. Though I was uneasy about her meticulous scrutiny, I dismissed it as a symptom of fatigue from house hunting.

In late April, our broker called to tell us that our bid on another bungalow had been accepted. It was in the same neighborhood as the first house we liked. I ran to Amy without hanging up. I was so excited I practically ripped the phone off the kitchen wall.

"Hey, punkin, we got it!" I hollered.

Amy smiled, spreading her lips thinly—not the big Pepsodent smile I expected.

"The house on Piedmont?" she said.

"Yeah, the realtor just called. Sweetheart, aren't you excited? We got ourselves a house!" Amy's blank expression made me ask again, "Punkin, did you hear me? We just bought a house."

Without replying, Amy began to wander from room to room of our rented flat, pausing at each doorway. Her eyes darted from pillar to post, and her expression was as stoical as the face of a Greek sculpture.

"What's up, kiddo?" I said. "Doing a house inspection?"

"Huh? Yeah," she said, peering at the floor. "Nick? At the new house—remember the worn carpet in the room that'll be Eleni's? I want to replace it … but not before we scrub the floor and spray it down with Lysol."

"Shouldn't be a problem," I said, "but we ought to make do with some.…"

She ignored me and continued to walk through our flat like a cat on the prowl. Amy moved slowly and deliberately, but her comments suddenly became rapid and urgent.

"Did you notice the bathtub? I saw scratches. You think they used powdered cleanser? I'll have to wash it carefully to get rid of the residue."

I didn't quite catch what she said about the kitchen because her words ran together in one incessant garble. When she looked into our cupboard, she furrowed her forehead as if recalling the cupboard at the new house. All at once, she stopped talking, stepped to the middle of the kitchen, and took a deep breath.

"Humph," she said, shaking her head. "I have a lot to do before we move in. I have to clean those cupboards and wash everything. We don't know what kind of stuff they kept in there. I'll have to paint, too. And that wallpaper will need—"

"Amy, did you forget about me? Tell me what you want done. I can help with the cleaning, and I'm a pretty good painter, if I say so myself. You won't need to do it all by yourself, and we won't have to do it all at once either."

"I won't let us move in until it's completely redone."

"What? That's unrealistic. We can't do anything at the house until after the closing—and that's weeks away. After that, we should move in right away, otherwise we'll have two payments—one for the house and another for this flat."

"I don't care. I won't live there until I've cleaned it from top to bottom. There are all kinds of contaminants in there."

She moved to the sink, turned on the faucet, and held her hands in the running water. Then she stood and stared, mesmerized by the flow swirling into the drain.

"*Contaminants?*" I said.

Amy turned around sharply. The water continued to run in the sink, and her hands dripped water onto the floor. "Don't," she said. "Don't look at me like that. You know what I mean."

"Listen, summer vacation starts right after the closing. I have a couple of free weeks before my college classes begin. After that, I'll get home by one o'clock and have plenty of extra time."

"I want to start sooner than that."

Though I thought her demand was impossible, I was afraid to say so. Instead, I offered, "Well, in the meantime, we can pack and get things ready to move in.

After we're settled in the new house, we can fix up a little each day. Mom said she'd help."

"No!" she screamed. "Your mother uses cleansers and powdered soap. That stuff is dangerous. I won't allow it. I don't trust your mother. She'll sneak it in without telling me, and if you ever dare to bring any of that in my house, I'll kill you."

"Amy, calm down. You're being irrational."

She responded with a shriek so loud that it caused the door chime to resonate. "*I'm* irrational?" she screamed. "No, you're the crazy one. You're so indifferent that I have to shout to get your attention. Don't you see how dangerous it is to live in someone else's mess?"

"Amy, be reasonable."

"Hey, smart-ass, you're unreasonable, not me. I can't believe you don't see the contamination. Well, I do, and I won't take a chance like that. I won't. I just won't."

Amy beat her fists in the air and shouted, "No. No. No." Suddenly, she began striking herself hard on the top of her head. I rushed to her and grabbed her arms, forcing them to her side. "Amy, please stop. Please, I beg you."

Though I was eight inches taller and seventy pounds heavier than Amy, I was unable to contain her. She fought fiercely until she bounded away like a tight spring that had come undone.

Suddenly, she wrapped her arms around herself and slithered to the floor like a Slinky at the bottom of the stairs. I stood back, uncertain whether to go to her. In another moment, her head drooped, and her body seemed to soften. She began to cry, her sobs mixing eerily with the sound of the water still running in the sink. "Nick. Oh Nick, what's wrong with me? Make it go away. Make it go away."

I was dumbstruck by what had happened. My heart ached, and my body shivered at the sight of her. Was her cry a child's plea or a madwoman's rant?

Several weeks after we had signed the purchase agreement, Andy, Saundra, Amy, and I were sitting around the TV at Andy and Saundra's house. Amy was between Saundra and me on the small couch facing the TV. I was on Amy's right, holding her hand. Andy was in his swivel rocker to my right. On TV, Dick Van Dyke walked into a wastebasket and fell head over heels. Our silence in the room was louder than the canned laughter on the TV.

We were together in close quarters because I had something to say, and everyone's anticipation of my announcement seemed to be crowding against us. Glaring at the television, we avoided eye contact like mourners around a coffin. I focused on a starburst clock on the wall. Its motor whirred periodically as if rewinding. Its regularity provided a semblance of normalcy that I needed in an otherwise odd moment.

Amy had finally agreed to tell her folks what I believed they already knew. Nevertheless, she had made me promise not to tell my mom and pop. Although our parents had wondered for weeks about Amy's behavior, no one had pried us with questions. Everyone, it seemed, wanted to avoid an uncomfortable situation. Eleni was with my mother that night, as she was so often. When Mom asked about why we needed her to care for Eleni, I lied and said that Andy and Saundra were helping us sort out details of our home purchase.

Weeks earlier, I had stopped carpooling with my buddies to save face at school. Lying wasn't necessary if I didn't talk to anybody. We hadn't been to church in weeks because Amy felt judged rather than welcomed. Though she needed the promise of redemption, she heard only the certainty of damnation. I prayed alone whenever I could, but my prayers were aimed at a different God than the one I had believed in before.

The TV show broke for a commercial, and I said to the center of the room, "Uh … can we turn off the TV? Amy and I need to tell you something."

"Huh? Yeah, sure," said Andy. "Nothing but a damn commercial anyway."

Andy watched the Alka-Seltzer tablets plop into a water glass on the screen and waited for the *Plop, plop … Fizz, fizz* jingle. Then he laughed nervously and clicked off the set. For several moments, only the clock's annoying whir spoke. I slid to the edge of my seat and cleared my throat. Avoiding Saundra, I glanced at Andy, hoping for encouragement. Andy looked at his hands. The wall clock was the only audience to face me.

"Uh … you know, we've kept this hidden too long," I began. "Amy's doctor is a psychiatrist not a neurologist like we told you. Her illness is emotional, not physical. She might need to stay in a hospital for a while."

I took a long breath and held it. Not even the noisy clock stirred. Andy looked at his fingers and bit the cuticles. Saundra stared at the same spot I had focused on a moment before. Amy's stony countenance hadn't changed since we sat down, but I attributed the medication for her stillness. Moments seemed to pass without time advancing. It seemed like forever before sounds reentered the room. When I heard a watch ticking, it seemed as if minutes passed between ticks. Outside the window, a soft breeze rustled the leaves; its sibilant sound was like a sign that it was all right to breathe.

Andy took a piece of fingernail from the tip of his tongue and started to flick it onto the floor until he glanced at Saundra and set it into an ashtray. "We … uh

... we've known for some time, but didn't want to interfere," he said. "We're very sorry, but sometimes things like this happen. We'll help as much as we can."

"I know you will. I mean ... I know you want the best for Amy, and you should know that I'm doing everything I can to be sure she gets the care she needs."

"We love Amy," he said. "She means everything to us. We think the same about you and Eleni. This is going to pass. Believe me, it will. It'll take time, but it'll pass."

"I feel better having told you," I said. "I can't talk to her doctor. I—"

"Nick," said Andy. "You're right to hold back. The doctor doesn't need your opinions about what to do."

"No, what I meant was ... I want to talk to him. Maybe there are things that he should know. Things that will help Amy. I was hoping that you could—"

"He doesn't need to know everything that goes on in the family. My advice is not to tell anyone about this, especially now."

"But—"

"You'll be closing on the house in a week or so. This is not a good thing for the mortgage people to know. They don't need to know. Nobody needs to know."

"Wha ...? You think they might refuse our application?"

"People don't understand, and it's too hard to explain. Believe me; the best thing to do is to keep all of this to yourself."

CHAPTER THIRTEEN

"There are strings," said Mr. Tappertit,
"in the human heart that had better not be vibrated."

—Charles Dickens in *Barnaby Rudge*

Damn, it's nearly four. These friggin' hospital forms have become a nightmare. Taking Amy to the hospital was frightening, but I've let my imagination get the best of me. I should reread what I wrote. Maybe it wasn't as bad as I made it out to be. It's just that … Jesus; I don't want this to be happening. Please, God, make it all be a bad dream that'll just go away.

I shouldn't be so negative. Surely, some of those hospital workers are caring people, but goddamn it, I felt horrible leaving her in that place. Then coming home and trying to write down what's happened to us.… Jesus, when will it all end?

Man, I'm tired, and I have to get up early tomorrow. What am I saying? It's already tomorrow.

As I walk into Lynnwood Hospital, the lobby seems friendlier than our backdoor entry last night. Maybe I did the right thing after all.

Today was teacher checkout day at school, and no students were around. Summer vacation began when end-of-year tasks were completed, and most of those were no-brainers. Normally, I'd have been one of the last teachers to leave, but *normal* wasn't my state of mind. I ran out before three o'clock and stopped at Mom's to see that Eleni was all right before coming to the hospital … the hospital I described to Mom as a *general* hospital where Amy was having *some tests*.

Small groups have gathered in a community room near the lobby where a color TV is playing. Yesterday, people upstairs sat by a black-and-white set that no one was watching. *Are the folks down here normal people or patients who've gotten better?*

"Hello," says a woman behind a counter.

"Uh … hello, I'm here to see my wife."

I wait for her reply and realize I haven't asked anything. This place not only scares me, it makes me stupid.

"My wife is Amy Demetriou. I'm her husband, Nick."

The woman scans some papers and says, "Oh, she's not here."

"What?"

"She's not on this floor. She's on three. I'll see if you're allowed to visit her."

Allowed? Who the hell's going to stop me? Then I remember the burly guys upstairs. I set Amy's flowers down and wave my packet of yellow forms like admission tickets, explaining, "I completed these and brought them back like Nurse Thelma asked."

"Oh? Yes, I'm sorry. This'll only take a moment. You may wait here if you wish."

After several minutes, a touch on my shoulder startles me. I turn and see a man I recognize from yesterday. "Mr. Demetri?" he says. "Come with me."

I ignore his mispronunciation and say, "Hi. You're Bert, aren't you?"

"*Albert*," he says with a smile. "That's okay; most people say I look like a *Bert*."

On the third floor, the shady guy with the dangling cigarette is nowhere in sight. *Had I imagined him last night?*

"She's in thirty-two B," says Albert. "You'll have to leave by five. Next session's at six thirty."

My heart stops when I see no one in room thirty-two. Albert points toward a drawn curtain inside the room. I find Amy behind it, facing a window, and lying on her side in a child-like curl.

"Amy? It's me." She doesn't appear to hear me. I step around the bed. My throat tightens when I see her face. Dark half-circles underscore her closed eyes; a fiery red band bridges her forehead. The discoloration is stark against her pasty skin. Her puffy lips are ghostly blue and edged with dry white spittle. Amy stirs. Her eyes open like saucers, and her lips part as if to scream. A gasp is all she can manage.

"Amy, pumpkin. It's Nick. Don't be afraid. It's only me."

"Nicky?" Her voice is muffled as if her mouth is full.

"Here, these are for you." I give her the yellow forms instead of the flowers. Amy used to giggle when I made a mistake like that. This time she lunges at me, thrusting both hands from under her covers. When I try to touch her, she cowers. There are marks on her wrists—red, like the welt on her forehead. She mutters something I can't understand. She speaks rapidly and with alarm, making raspy, garbled sounds. Amy points to her open mouth to show me what's choking her.

Her tongue is swollen, and the burden slows her cadence. Her words sound robotic.

"Oh ... Nick ... it ... was ... awful. They ... strapped ... me ... and put ... rubber thing ... in my mouth. I gagged ... Couldn't spit it out. Gave me a shot. Woke up. Was raining. Open window. Made me jump. Nicky, it was raining. I ... was ... wet ... and there was ... electricity. They ... kept ... doing ... it ... in the rain ... over ... and over...."

She's asleep again. I turn to the window. Is this the one that was open to the rain? It's closed now and locked—both securities unnecessary because there is no rain and there are metal bars on the window. I see stains on the sill and immediately head for the nurses' station.

Though I want to shout, my voice is weak when I ask to see the doctor. Fear has overtaken my anger and made me feel like a prisoner pleading for mercy.

A nurse eyes me cautiously. "You're Mr. Demetriou?"

"Yes."

"Dr. Florence is here for rounds. He wants to speak with you."

She goes into a room behind her station and returns with Dr. Florence.

"Mr. Demetriou, I'm sorry you came today. We called your school to tell you not to come, but they said you had already left. Amy's not up to seeing visitors."

I feel challenged but find the strength to question him. "What are you doing to her? She looks like she's been beaten."

"No, no, you're mistaken. She hasn't been mistreated. Amy needs a few days to get accustomed to the treatments." He beckons me toward the small room from which he came. Without closing the door, he asks me to sit down. I bend my knees to sit, then straighten and stand instead. I feel like a child about to hear a lesson that's too adult to understand. I cross my arms, and then awkwardly let them hang. Nothing I do seems right.

"I'm surprised by her stamina," he says. "Her will is stronger than I expected."

"Wha ... What are you saying? A strong will isn't bad, is it?"

"Mrs. Demetriou was prepped with sodium pentathol before her treatment. She awoke while we administered ECT. Though it's unusual, we've dealt with it before. However, she became ... distressed ... and began to resist the technicians."

"Resist? You mean she fought them off?"

"Please, Mr. Demetriou. Restraints are standard for this therapy. Amy tried to take off the straps and required another injection. It didn't calm her immediately. Her struggle caused minor bruising. Nothing alarming. I don't know what she might have told you, but Amy is a bit delusional today. I'm sorry you saw her before I spoke to you."

"Why? Why am I not allowed to see what you're doing?"

Florence put a manicured hand on my shoulder. I feel like I did when my second grade teacher, Mr. Rankin, tried to calm me after I cried at school. I learned to like Mr. Rankin. Will I ever like Dr. Florence?

"Nick," says Florence, "some procedures appear unusual to the untrained. Believe me, there's nothing sinister here. Most patients benefit from ECT, and Amy will likely get relief, as well. Trust me. It's a proven technique."

I back away. "She said it rained, and she got wet during the electric shocks."

"We wouldn't allow that, I assure you. She imagined it. Give us a chance to heal her. You'll see. Amy won't remember any of it. I've prescribed bed rest and no visitors for two days. I'll assess her condition before proceeding with more treatments."

"I don't know if I want her to have them."

"Please, don't be hasty. I understand your concern, but the treatments are invaluable for relieving the ups and downs of manic depression. You and Amy have a long life ahead, but you'll jeopardize her health if you tell us to stop. I'm sure you don't want that responsibility."

Of course I don't want to be responsible for her illness; you think I'm an idiot?

"What about the men?" I ask meekly.

"The men?"

"Yes. I see a lot of men here. Is … is she in a room with a man? Is she…."

"Mr. Demetriou, your wife is not in a room with a man. She has the room to herself right now. The men are housed in another corridor."

"I want her to be all right. I want her to get well and come home."

The doctor put his hand on my shoulder again. I shudder as he squeezes gently, but my mind reaches for hope when he says, "I'll do my best to restore Amy's health. All of us want her to enjoy a normal life again. Give us two or three days. By the time you see her again, you'll notice a difference."

On the way home, I stop at a Sears store near the hospital. I need something for the new house where we'll soon move. I look through a display of decorative wall plates for electric outlets but feel like I want something else. I leave without a purchase and stop at a pay phone to call Mom. After I ask about Eleni, I make something up about Amy and tell Mom that I won't be stopping by because it'll be too late. Typically, she makes me promise to get something to eat.

The truth is, I don't give a shit about eating or anything else, but I stop by a Big Boy's anyway.

In the restaurant, I ignore the fat woman with three kids seated in the adjoining booth. Burying my face in my hands, I rub my eyes to massage my brain. It does nothing for the pain in my gut. It isn't hunger. Something's goading me to do I-don't-know-what.

"Sir, are you all right?"

A young waitress with *Trainee* written on her nametag is at my table holding a glass of water as if it's an offering she's afraid to present. I stare at the glass and watch as she absently tips it so it begins to spill.

"Here," she says, spilling more water as she sets the glass down. She wipes her hand on her skirt and pulls a menu from under her arm, presenting it upside down. Seeing her error, she moves to take it back just as I reach for it. Our hands touch, and for a moment we hold onto each other. The sensation of her touch catches me off guard. I look up and see her blush. Warmth washes over me. An ache grows in my loin. I smile. She smiles too. She's young and pretty and vibrant. My arousal from our accidental touch shocks me, and suddenly, I know what it is that I want.

CHAPTER FOURTEEN

*A man who has not passed through the inferno of
his passions has never overcome them.*

—Carl Gustav Jung

"I'm sorry," says the waitress. "This is my first time on my own."

She's about nineteen or twenty, a tall, golden-haired young woman with break-your-heart features—a girl who's easy to forgive.

"That's okay," I say, eyeing the fullness under her nametag. "Uh ... Amber, is it? I'm sure your *first time* won't be your last."

My remark is spontaneous and suggestive. That it's deliberate is another surprise.

Amber twists her mouth, tightening her red lips fiercely as if preparing to retaliate. Instead, she averts her shadowed eyes and exhales loudly, puffing her lips full again. I like the way she does that. It is, at once, forbidden and seductive.

As though signaling a countdown, she taps a painted fingernail on my table before pivoting sharply and walking away. Her hips swing enchantingly, and her shapely form bumps a message I read as an invitation. I imagine touching the soft skin and taut flesh suggested by her tight uniform. Carnal desire conquers my shame. I want a piece of that ass and don't care who sees me leering at it. Ordinarily, I'd deny the feeling. This time I savor the fantasy of screwing a girl I do not know.

I open the menu, but burgers and fries fail to steer my appetite. My mind is on Amber. Should I dazzle her with charm or play on her sympathy? *Listen, Amber. My wife is in the nut house, and I haven't had sex in....*

Hell, I don't have the nerve. What I need is a hot woman to grab me by the balls and show me stuff I only dream about. Lust is urgent and, suddenly, I want to hurt her—make her scream, be cruel and unmerciful—ravage her against her will, take her despite her protest.

A loud bang and a shriek at my left startle me. The divider separating me from the adjoining booth has crashed down. Two toddlers start to climb over the lowered bridge.

"Stop that," yells a frazzled woman. "This is not a playpen."

I force a smile and shake my head—dismayed by the children's behavior and my own folly. *Playing*, that's what I'm doing. It's a joke, and the joke is on me. No way can I bullshit this waitress or anyone else. I don't know the first thing about banter—let alone how to sweet-talk a chick like Amber.

Amber returns and says, "Sorry Mister, I'll pull up the divider to give you a little privacy." Then, as she leans on the seat opposite me, her skirt rides up, drawing my eye to her thigh. From there, my mind traces the outline of her buttocks and glides up her back to the stretched tendon on her neck. When she turns, I manage a glimpse of her cleavage, and Amber shoots me a dry-ice sneer that is hot, even as it chills my fantasy.

I have a sandwich and leave without another word, but sensual thoughts return on my drive home. Half-lit lights of a motel remind me of the first time I made love to Amy. It was our wedding night when the winter cold and power failure added to the thrill. I wanted to appear suave and in control, but I came before I undressed. Everything went wrong, but it didn't matter. We fell asleep in each other's arms and awoke eager to try again. The next day we had breakfast at four in the afternoon. Sex was good before Amy got sick. But what do I know? I've had no one to compare. I want to keep it that way but, God, what's it been—fifteen, twenty weeks? No, much longer than that. Jesus, it was before Thanksgiving when we last made love.

I flip on the radio for the Tiger game. I love baseball—love to hear Ernie Harwell call the game. At night, I play a game in my head, running through the Detroit batting order, counting Tigers instead of sheep.

"… already has fourteen roundtrippers," says Ernie on the radio.

I puzzle over who has fourteen home runs. It's another game I play: guess the player before Ernie names him.

"Tony C," I say aloud. "Tony Conigliaro's got fourteen homers."

"There's activity in the Bosox dugout," says Ernie. "If Conigliaro gets on, there might be a pinch hitter for Lonborg. The Tigers are in a jam. Their lead's been trimmed to one run here in the seventh. Two out, two on. Three-and-two's the count. The runners will go on the pitch. McLain steps off the rubber and stares the runner back to second. Denny doesn't want this one to get away. The kid's already boasted that he'll win twenty games in '66.

"Now back on the mound. Oh, it's a quick pitch, but Conigliaro lifts a fly ball deep into right field. Kaline goes back … back … back up against the fence. He leaps—"

Though I punch it myself, the sharp *snap* of the station button startles me. Static interrupted by music bursts from the radio. The reception is off. I hit another button—then another and another. It's Russian roulette with random shots. Trumpets blare on chance landings, but my station hopping mixes wails and booms with discordant squeals—conflicting sounds, sometimes low and distant, sometimes in-my-face loud.

I punch the buttons hurriedly, playing arrhythmic patterns. The faster I punch, the more cacophonous the sound—and the better I like it. Something wild and scary stirs inside me—something animal-like and untamed—a part of me I've known but refused to admit. The noise strikes back at me—strident, hard, and forceful, daring me to create more frenzy. I feel driven, glad that the dissident beat is taking me somewhere—anywhere away from where I am. It feels wrong, forbidden, lewd—and I want to go there.

"Son of a bitch," I say aloud. Eight Mile Road's ahead. I slap at the radio and break off a knob. I've gone miles too far, but I don't loop around to head back. Instead, I turn right and drive east, away from home and toward the topless bars that line the strip on Detroit's border.

Several doors are open. I slow down to look inside but see only smudge-pot darkness. Loudspeakers hurl throbbing drumbeats at passing motorists. A half dozen, side by side topless bars invite walking tours. Bubble lights and flashing neons entice me to sample the girls. Twisted tubes of inert gas glow outlines of big-busted broads. One sign boasts, "Girls. Girls. See Them All Show It All." On another, a neon babe winks, "No Cover 4 U R ME." I park directly under her out-spread legs wondering what I might see. I answer with a sharp slam of the car door and a quick step through the doorway of the strip joint.

Inside, I push into the noise and squint through a sea of whisky-soaked miasma, looking for a spot where a pretending barhopper can hide. A siren in a bikini lures me with torpedo breasts that point to a tall bar table the size of a fifty-cent piece. The waitress jerks her head, directing an eye toward the bar, but says nothing. I don't either. She does it again with gusto, and I realize too late that her gesture avoids competing with howls and whoops. She leans her boobs on my table and nearly presses her nose to mine. I look longingly at the flesh served up before me. "Two drink minimum," she screams above the din. Her breath smells of beer, bourbon, and hashish, and I want to taste it.

On the stage, a woman in a fireman's hat and a strap up her crotch is making love to a silver pole, sliding her hands up and down while the band makes fire truck noises. She toys with but never strips off a gauzy veil that fails to mask her sagging breasts. My silent disappointment echoes loudly throughout the room.

I nurse my drinks with casual sips and try to rekindle an earlier excitement. My feelings sink as my wickedness rises, and the thrill eludes me. After the fire drill, three babes taunt and titillate until they strip down to eye-patch G-strings.

When it's over, I feel guilt rather than pleasure or relief. I've been unfaithful to Amy. How dare I seek gratification when she's so miserable? I have to make up for it with penance bigger than my sin.

I find my way home, but get lost in bed when I try to sleep. Instead of running through batting lineups, my mind moves through unfamiliar rooms of our new house. Suddenly, my task becomes obvious. The house is new only to us. It needs cleaning and painting, and there's furniture to move. I vow to get it all done before Amy leaves the hospital. The house will be perfect. I'll eliminate everything that might set her off. She'll see that and know how much I love her. It's my guarantee that Amy will never be depressed again.

Andy has gone home, leaving Pop and me alone. We've finished painting and have gone to the basement to clean up. Two weeks had passed before I gave in and asked my dad and father-in-law to help. I remember the night I was sprawled on the kitchen floor, sweating like a field hand. I had worked alone without getting very far and had only this weekend before the movers arrived. Asking Andy and Pop to pitch in could've become a problem. They aren't equally privy to what's going on with Amy. I knew that there was apt to be a lot of talk while we worked, but I had to take a chance. Thankfully, it has turned out well. Andy and Pop cheered me up, and I rather enjoyed their good-natured teasing. I'm happy with what we've accomplished and glad for their love and camaraderie.

Quitting time brings Pop and me together at the basement sink to wash our brushes. There's never been a man more loving than my father, but he shows it sparingly and in subtle ways. There've been times when I yearned for more, but tonight I'm content just to have him at my side.

"Thanks, Pop," I say, with more emotion than I expected.

"You bet," he says, leaning his ample belly against the sink and stretching his short arms to the faucet. As a child, I loved him cradling me on his soft belly while wrapping me securely in his hard muscular arms. Now, as he bends forward, splashing water over a brush, Pop looks like a cuddly bear snagging a fish from a mountain stream. In his gentle but effective way, he kneads his fingers into paint-sodden bristles until the brush comes clean.

"Son," he says, still urging the paint from his brush, "how is Amy doing?"

For an instant, I'm the child I was when Pop discovered something I'd tried to hide. At once, anguish and relief wash over me. Suddenly, my shame is not in Amy's illness, but in my failure to honor my father's trust. I'm afraid to tell him everything. I want to run, but cannot turn away. Pop's question holds me fast, as surely as if he has gripped my wrists to compel an answer. I have to—I *want* to tell him the truth.

Pop looks in my eye and nudges my silence before returning his focus to his task in the sink. The brush is almost clean, and he need not press on as before.

"Pop, I haven't told you everything. Amy is very ill. Lynnwood Hospital is not a *general* hospital like I said. It's a *psychiatric* hospital. But she's ... she's going to be fine."

I hear the wooden sound of the brush handle as it clunks against the bottom of the tub. Pop looks up. When our eyes meet, I lower mine; terrified he'll detect another lie. Slowly, my gaze falls from his broad shoulders to his stout, muscular arms, down to his powerful hands—physical features that represent the emotional strength I admire. I love his hands. I remember sitting on his lap as a tot and feeling the rough calluses of his hand against my cheek. I would take his hand and run my fingers along the bumps and lines of his palm. These were mountains and rivers of my lifeline, and I measured my manhood by how nearly my hand fit into his.

Paint-stained and wet, his stubby fingers curl and his palms turn up as if he's about to reach out. In that moment, I want to put myself in my father's hands and ask him to share my burden. I want to feel his embrace and have him hold me as if I was as a toddler.

"Son, I'm sorry for you. Your mother and I were afraid it was something like this. I wish ... is there something we can do?" His hands ball into fists that are ready to fight.

"You *are* helping—Mom with the baby, and you here today. Thank you." I look again at his fists. They're poised to strike the winning blow. "Pop ... I wish, too. I wish there was something you could do."

I watch his hands open and close in vice-like grips. These hands held a bigger man's nose to the grill at Pop's diner when the drunken man harassed my mother. If anyone's hands could smite the evil that lives in Amy, his could. But we both know that her intruder can't be dealt with so simply, and Pop turns away from the sink. I wish he wouldn't hide the tears that well in his eyes. Daddy, please tell me: Is it okay to cry?

I feel the comfort of his gentle voice. I feel his love and see his sorrow. Though he says no more and veils his passion, I know he deeply feels my pain. I am thankful for this moment, grateful that he's my father. I'm glad that I have invited him into my secret, and I'm moved by the intimacy we both feel, but I wish he would touch me with his hands and make it all go away.

CHAPTER FIFTEEN

You can only predict things after they've happened.

—Eugène Ionesco

Three weeks after her admission, Amy greets me at the hospital with a kiss that sends me swooning. I try for another, but she smiles demurely and waves a naughty finger at me. It's discharge day, and I've been up since dawn tidying up the new house. I got a lot done, but had to leave a few fix-ups for another day. Before noon, I had quit working and got ready to pick her up. I had showered and shaved at the old flat, so our new home would be immaculate. It'll be Amy's first day in the new house, and I want to guarantee that she'll be happy.

She's dolled up in her sunshine dress—the yellow one with a short, pleated skirt that flares when she pirouettes. Spinning around teasingly, she shows off her figure and bobs her hair like a cheerleader. As she talks, I hear crispness in her voice and a lilt that sets my heart aflutter, reminders of another Amy—playful and impulsive, yet seductively withholding. I should've paid more attention when those endearing features began to fade. Maybe I could've prevented her breakdown.

Her hair is longer than she usually wears it, but I love the tiny curls she's combed at her temples, near her cheekbones and close to her eyes—delightfully framing her pretty face. She's wearing only a little makeup. Her lipstick is slightly uneven, and the color dotting her cheeks stands out like cherries on cream, but it's refreshing that she's less than perfect—a hopeful sign that her compulsions have eased.

But my feeling evaporates when her hand shakes in a palsy-like tremor as she fidgets with her hair, scratching and digging her nails hard into her scalp. Disgusted by what I know will come next, I look away but not before she examines and touches her tongue on a loosened particle of scalp lodged beneath her nail. When I look again, she's running her fingers through her hair and chewing something with her front teeth.

Like her fear of "white specks," Amy's preoccupation with hair is apparently not new. I had learned only last week that as a child, she hated how her mother groomed her long perfect curls. At twelve, she had defiantly cut off several ten-inch ringlets and began obsessively washing her hair—a habit that led to compulsive hand-washing and other fetishes. She got over that in a short time, and I hoped that the same would be true with her current fixations. Today, as on the last few visits, she obsesses that shock treatments have ruined her natural curl.

"Doctor says it should've curled not straightened. Sez I'm one in a million."

The phrase used to be mine when I gazed into her eyes after we made love. Now it has a different meaning. In reply, I manage only a stunted laugh that sounds like a grunt. Though Amy has reclaimed some of her charm, only part of her is back; the rest, I tell myself, will come along when she gets home—after she sees all that I've done for her.

"I wanted to look better for you," she says, "but the mirrors in here are bad. They're made of polished metal. Glass isn't allowed—in case we want to do ourselves in."

I wish to hell she wouldn't make jokes about that.

"I took a real bath this morning, but someone peeked in and said my time was up before I could sit and soak. Don't worry," she adds, "it was a woman. Men aren't allowed on this side of the chainlink fence."

"You'll be home soon," I say. "I promise to let you soak in the tub till you're *prunified*. Only, *I* won't promise not to peek."

"Yeah, well, keep your shorts on. It'll be a while before I can work up a lather." I catch my breath when she giggles. Amy's laugh and misplaced metaphor are reminders of happier times.

"Come on," she says. "Let's blow this popcorn stand. I want to see my little girl."

When first hospitalized, Amy was so medicated she barely acknowledged Eleni. As she improved, her queries became incessant. Lamenting their separation, she worries that Eleni won't remember her. Now, on our ride home, Amy speaks longingly about Eleni, and I sense her effort to bridle her grief. She asks nothing about our new home.

After I park in the driveway, Amy steps unsteadily out of the car, awkwardness I attribute to the extra medication given to help her cope. I circle my arm around her waist, but she breaks away and says, "You don't have to do that. I'm not an invalid. I'm just crazy."

"I'm the crazy one," I say. "Crazy in love with you."

I give her a peck on the cheek. She returns a weak smile. My heart, already pounding wildly, skips a beat. My love is home. Everything's going to be all right.

I laugh when I accidentally drop the house key, but Amy stands mute and stares ahead. Her elbows draw close and her hands clasp tightly at her stomach as if to ward off an unlikely chill on this warm summer day. I'm thinking that she probably thinks the house is a mess. Won't she be surprised?

I open the door, bow dramatically, and sweep my arm across the threshold. "Welcome home, sweetheart. Wait'll you see what I've done inside."

Amy enters cautiously. Her movement is cat-like, curious, but prepared to flee. She moves from room to room as if sweeping a minefield, pausing longest at Eleni's room. Her hands, clutched to her breast since entering, are locked in a white knuckled grip.

"Honey, you'll see. Everything's going to be fine once Eleni comes home."

"No, I don't want her here yet," she stammers. "The windows...."

I glance at the bare windows and then back to her worrying hands. In my gut, I feel a pang of guilt for not finishing my job, even though the window treatments were not my fault. A company I hired was to have delivered custom-made shades last week.

"I ... I want to check ...," she stammers. "To be sure of ... in case there's...."

She lets the sentence trail and exhales deeply in a tense, stuttering sigh. My heartbeat, a moment ago signaling joy, telegraphs warning. Why is she finding the things I failed to do? Goddamn her for ruining this homecoming.

"Amy," I plead, "don't do this."

I begin to stroke her hands, intending to ease her panic, but for an instant, I feel as though I could rip off her fingers. Her hands are cold, and the frost that grips them seizes me as well. Nevertheless, I say, "It's my fault about the windows. I waited too long and hired someone to do them. They'll have shades cut and put up any day now, by Friday for sure. We can do curtains ourselves next—"

"No. I can't wait till Friday. I won't have these old shades, and I can't undress with wide-open windows. The whole neighborhood will see me and know where I've been. They'll know everything about me."

"The old rods are still up. We can drape a sheet or towel when we go to bed."

"Take them down. I don't want anything old in my house. Those rods are contaminated with lead paint and germs. Don't you know how dangerous that is?"

"I didn't use lead paint, and I washed everything that I hadn't painted. Can't you see how much I've done? I tried to have everything ready so you wouldn't—"

"Wouldn't what ... go nuts?"

Suddenly, Amy's shoulders slacken, and the taut lines on her face soften. "I'm sorry," she says. "I know you worked like a coal miner to fix things up. I appreciate it. I really do. Honestly, I'm not upset. It's just that there's a lot more to a house than I thought."

"You should rest a while. How about I get some carryout burgers for lunch? There's a new place called McDonalds that...."

"No, I'm okay. I'm not hungry. You go ahead and have something. You've done a lot—too much really. I'll just see what I can do about covering the windows."

"But Dr. Florence said you should take it easy. He's—"

"He's full of shit. Believe me, I know. I saw him every day for God knows too long. He told you to keep your eye on me, didn't he? He's wrong. That ... *man* ... is a pansy. I'll bet he has lace on his shorts. Don't pay attention to him. Both you guys make me nervous. I wish you'd relax. Go out and get the burgers. I want to look around on my own."

"But—"

"Get your butt out of here. Give me a chance. I'll show you I can handle it."

When I get back with a bag of burgers and fries, there's a Shady Lane Blinds and Window Treatments truck in our driveway. Before I reach the door, I hear a woman's raised voice coming from inside the house. Amy is yelling—screaming expletives, cussing, and making threats and demands that sound like someone is threatening her life.

"Get away from there, you goddamnsonovabitch. Those shades look like shit. No way will they fit. Don'tellmeyoucanmakemright. What are you doing you stupid asshole? Stop forcing them. Whathehellsthematter with you? You've got broken glass and paint chips all over. Getouttahere! You'll contaminate everything."

Amy rants on and a woman that I recognize from the shade store meets me at the door.

"What's going on?" I ask.

"Mr. Demetriou, I don't know. There's a problem here. I guess we surprised your wife when we came by. I had called earlier, but there was no answer. I should have waited till I spoke to you, but you seemed upset last week, so I hurried the job and took a chance that you'd be home."

I hear Amy's voice in the bedroom and go there to help. When she sees me, she snarls, "Don't come in here. I'll take care of this guy. You go and talk to that ... *woman*. She wants her money or something."

I go back to the living room and ask the saleswoman to gather her workers and leave as soon as possible. "I'll pay you for your troubles," I say. "Don't worry about that. Just.... Please ... just go."

"I'm sorry," she says. "I shouldn't have hurried your order. Some items are about an eighth-inch short. We can make them fit, but your wife ... well, she ... she has a problem with it. One shade crashed down and broke a window. Mrs. Demetriou, she...."

Amy rushes into the living room. "What are you telling my husband, bitch? Nick, make her leave before she does any more damage. Make her leave or I'll kill myself. I swear it. You don't believe me, but someday you'll find out. Get these assholes out of my house, or you'll regret it for the rest of your life."

CHAPTER SIXTEEN

Let other pens dwell on guilt and misery.
I quit such odious subjects as soon as I can.

—Jane Austen

Amy made dinner tonight and insists on doing the dishes. That's a big improvement from how she was most of the summer, a sign of progress I'm glad to see because Labor Day and the start of school are fast approaching. The first few weeks after she arrived home were touch-and-go, and she would've ended up in the hospital again had she not persuaded Dr. Florence to provide outpatient shock treatments at his office. Cost-wise, I prefer the hospital because our insurance covers the treatment. Outpatient care is not covered. However, Amy is still deathly afraid of hospitalization, and my summer schedule allows me to spend the necessary time with her. I had hoped that homecare would give me a chance to help her overcome the feelings that bring on her episodes, but it hasn't worked out that way.

One day in July, about a month after Amy came home, I met with Dr. Florence, and my hope for partnership met with another setback. I remember feeling intimidated by the doctor's floor-to-ceiling bookshelves. They displayed books with embossed titles that seemed to highlight the doctor's air of superiority. I wondered what an ordinary couple like Amy and I were doing there. Florence had granted me a rare audience after seeing Amy in an adjoining room where she was sleeping after her fourth outpatient shock treatment.

"Doctor, how is Amy really doing?" I said. "I can't figure her out. After that incident with the windows, I lost any objectivity I might've had."

Dr. Florence sat at his desk with his hands together and said, "I believe that flare-up was an aberration. It was regrettable, but not alarming. Amy is quite docile when I see her."

Was he talking about *my* Amy? To me, her moods were always at extremes—sometimes passive and other times angry. The doctor spoke only of the first Amy. Did he know her? Did I know her? Have I ever really known Amy?

I looked at the doctor and wondered if he was even paying attention to me. He seemed preoccupied with the cathedral he made by placing his fingers tip to tip and extending his fingers. "The episode was uncharacteristic," he said, as if he were addressing someone within his cathedral. "This happens with patients like her. They hold in their anger until it comes out in one gigantic explosion. Since then, she's shown little emotion and has become rather submissive."

"Could that be her medication?" I said. "Amy takes Valium like cough drops."

"Yes, that is possible. You're wise to monitor her and see that she doesn't exceed my prescription. However, I'm more concerned about her reticence than her anger."

"What do you mean?"

"Are you familiar with sodium Pentothal and similar drugs?"

"Yes, *truth serum*. You've mentioned it before."

"Amy hides her willful spirit beneath her meek exterior and stubbornly refuses to reveal what's on her mind."

Not to me she doesn't. Why does she hide so much from him?

"Even after high doses of sodium Pentothal," he said, "she fights back and keeps everything to herself. Then she falls asleep before I'm able to deal with her distress."

The doctor's inability to see Amy as I did angered me and gave me courage to say, "Then why do you continue with Pentothal? She's asleep when we leave here, and she stays in bed long after we get home. I'm concerned that—"

"Don't be. Sleep is a good tonic. The drug wears off quickly, and there are no aftereffects. It's quite safe. In time, she'll learn to express herself more freely."

When Florence pushed away from his desk, he said, "Now, if you'll excuse me, I have patients to see. Amy should be able to go home soon. I'll see her again next week."

His dismissal was as sharp as a judge's ruling, leaving no room for appeal.

Since then I've been pretty much shut out of Amy's recovery, so I grab at every sign of improvement, like tonight's dinner. During dessert, I mention the idea of asking Mom to help with Eleni more often, especially when I go back to school.

Amy frowns and says, "I wish I didn't have to. I depend on your mom so much that I'm afraid she'll take Eleni away from me."

"Amy, I won't let that happen."

"Sometimes I'm not so sure. You seem to enjoy asking Mom to help."

"Honey, I don't *enjoy* it. I agree with you; I'd rather not depend on her, but what will we do in the fall? I'll be away at work most of the day."

Amy stirs her coffee with a spoon and stares at the cup as if trying to make sense of the milky swirls. "Doctor says the therapy will help. He says I'm already improving."

There's more energy in her voice than there has been in days, but she could tire before her coffee gets cold. Any strength not taken by the illness is sapped away by those damn drugs. Even the blinking of her eyes has slowed. If the Amy I remember still exists, she's locked inside this body before me—or else I'm talking to an impostor.

The truth is that I feel confined, too—isolated by Amy's strangeness and the distance that grows between me and everyone else. Friends and loved ones have become unapproachable strangers. I feel alone and without recourse except to remain alone—afraid to risk the public shame of admitting that mental illness holds my family hostage.

Amy must feel the separation more than I do. Several days ago, she acted on Dr. Florence's urgings and confronted her mother. It made matters worse. I wasn't with her when she talked to her mother, but Amy told me that she let it all out and said that she hated her. Saundra responded in her usual indifferent manner. Amy came home and burned her diary in the basement incinerator; then she slept for a day and a half.

"It's just you and me, now, isn't it, hon," I say.

"Huh?"

"Us. We're the only ones who can lick this."

"I guess so."

"You and me against the world."

"For now, it is," she says, "but how long can you keep it up?"

"I'm not a quitter. Neither are you. Remember, we signed on *forever*. We still have a long way to go. I checked it out; forever comes after two consecutive odd-numbered years."

"That's not very encouraging; I've already had at least one *odd* year. I guess it's time to get better."

"Maybe we need to do something different," I suggest. "How are you getting along with the doctor?"

Amy's reply is a stare, but her gaze isn't blank. "I think he's a fruitcake," she says, "a real pansy. Florence is a perfect name for him."

"You don't feel comfortable with him, do you? He told me how difficult it is for you to talk about your feelings. You've told me the same thing. Maybe it's him, not you."

"If he wore a skirt and combed his hair in bangs, he'd be my mother."

"You try to follow his advice, but something seems to stop you. Why is that?"

"It's like trying to please my mother—I try even though I don't want to, and it doesn't please anyone."

"I know. Underneath, you're stubborn and willful."

"I'm trying to stop that."

"Maybe that's not what needs changing. Maybe that's what'll get you out of this."

"Florence doesn't agree. He says I'm fighting him too much, resisting his questions, not letting him in, not letting his treatments work for me."

"You take his prescriptions like candy."

Amy's reaction is silent, but her stiffened body speaks volumes.

"I'm sorry," I say.

"You bastard," she says between clenched teeth. It's her first sign of emotion in days. I hate her anger—hate the way it transforms her. But this time it seems different.

"I'm sorry," I whisper. "I know you need the medication."

Amy's hands work the napkin on her lap, twisting and tearing it, rolling it into little balls, her red knuckles turning white from the effort. "You're goddamn right I need it. Do you know what it's like? Of course you don't. You don't want to know how I really feel. It's beyond anything I can tell you. I worry about crazy things that can never happen. Every day, I hope and pray that you—and Eleni—will never know, because to know is to be swallowed by it. Wanna hear how I entertain myself? I think about different ways to kill myself. Can you imagine? Thinking that death is better than life. Those pills—those friggin' electric shocks—they're my only escape before they take me away again."

I rise from my chair and kneel before her. Taking her hands in mine, I stroke them gently. Slowly her fists begin to open. Tiny balls of paper cling to her fingers like snowflakes to woolen mittens.

"Don't leave me, pumpkin," I say. "I love you. When you worry like that, just tell me. Let me carry the worry for you. I can handle it. I won't let anything take you away from me. I'll never let go. Together we can beat this ... this ... whatever it is."

"I love you too, Nicky, and I love Eleni, but I can't love you like I want to."

"Sweetheart, I've got enough love for all of us. The more I give, the more you'll have. Just let me love you. My love is strong enough to keep us together, stronger than any pain or problem. Stronger than any pill or doctor."

"Nick, you'll never leave me? You won't take Eleni away?"

"No, not ever."

"But for how long can you love me?"

"For all forevers ever to come."

Tears stream down our faces, and we touch each other's cheeks with praying hands that beg for a miracle. Suddenly, Amy points to my face and begins to laugh.

"What? What's so funny?"

"Zits," she says between giggles. "You have zits all over your face."

I turn around and look in the mirror. Tiny balls of white paper napkin are stuck to my dampened face, pasted there from Amy's hands.

Amy looks over my shoulder and circles her arms around my waist. "Leave them there," she says. "I haven't had a good laugh in a long time."

"I miss that giggle more than I dare admit."

"I don't giggle. Real women never giggle."

"And real men never cry."

"I've never giggled—or smiled, even—with Dr. Florence."

"Might be a good reason to think about a change."

"Maybe you're right, but I'm scared. I don't want to see him, but I don't know what else to do."

Visits to Dr. Florence are less frequent now, and trips to Mom's house are regular events. I drop Amy and Eleni off two or three times a week before going to my classes at Wayne State. At first, I'd return at noon and find Mom and Eleni playing in the living room while Amy slept in the den. Lately, Amy's been more focused and alert when I pick her up. Today, the Friday before Labor Day, she seems especially animated, taking over chores she used to leave for Mom and insisting on preparing lunch without Mom's help. I have a strange feeling though. It's as if Amy has choreographed her performance to make a point. Mom notices, too, and she joins me in complimenting Amy.

"Stop it, you guys," she says with a smile. "I'm flattered, but you're overdoing it."

"I'm sorry," says Mom. "It's just that the way you took charge today ... well, it's wonderful, and—"

"So unlike me, I know."

"No," I say, "not exactly *unlike you*, just different than—"

"Than the *me* you're used to seeing since last year?"

"Yes," Mom and I say in unison.

"Well, I have a confession," says Amy. "I'm tired. I could take a nap, but you know what? I'm not going to."

Mom sets down her coffee cup and touches Amy's hand. "Honey, I'm proud of you. You've made us a nice lunch, and you look so pretty, too. You did something different with your hair, didn't you? I like it."

"Oh, Mom, you'd say that if I wore an Afro. Thanks for the thanks, but don't expect this every day. Today is special because I want to tell you something."

Mom smiles and says, "I knew it. I had a feeling when you telephoned so early. I said to myself, *I bet Amy has something to tell us.*"

Mom loves it when her intuition's right, like when she knew we were expecting even before the doctor knew. I find it sappy—and annoying. What if Amy has bad news?

"Something good, I hope," I say.

"I think so," says Amy. She touches her earlobe in that endearing way she does, an indication that she's a bit uncertain. Looking first at Mom and then at me, she says, "I've decided to stop seeing my doctor. I don't want to see *anyone* anymore. I'm stopping my medication, too. I've been cutting back each day and haven't taken anything at all this week. I've turned over a new leaf and decided to quit worrying so much. Quit all that guilt crap. Quit cold turkey. I'm getting better. I promise. And I'm doing it on my own."

CHAPTER SEVENTEEN

But perhaps it is this distrust of our senses that prevents us from feeling comfortable in the universe.

—**Italo Calvino**

Though Amy calls it the power of positive thinking, I can't shake the feeling that her improvement is an act. At the same time, I'd like to believe a cure is as simple as a positive outlook, and there are signs that suggest it's true. Amy's good spirits are evident in her playfulness, like the time she stuck a silly note in my lunch bag addressed to "Pookie." I wrote one back to "Punkin-Pookie" and pretty soon, we were surprising each other with notes hidden in shoes, socks, and underwear. The silly names hark back to our dating days when everything was simpler. The other day, I telephoned from work to ask for a date on the weekend. Before saying yes, she teased and said, "Hmm, I'm not sure I remember anyone named Nick. Are you the guy who sat across from me in biology?"

This morning, we are at the park with Eleni reading aloud from a novel, a pastime we revived from the outings we used to have.

Amy takes the last bite of her sandwich and wads up the waxed paper. I'm sitting cross-legged on the blanket opposite her, and Eleni is napping in the playpen.

"Want another?" I ask, reaching into the picnic basket.

When she doesn't answer right away, I ask again, and she says, "Huh? Oh … no, I've had enough for now. Maybe later."

"You got something on your mind, hon?"

The question is one that we ask each other more casually now, and it often arises after we've read a few pages. Though reading the novels might have something to do with it, I think the ease of our conversation is more likely due to Amy's happier outlook.

"Sort of," says Amy. "I was thinking about church."

I sit up a little straighter and ask, "What about church?"

"I want to go this Sunday," she says. "I haven't been to church in months. God's probably mad at me. If I don't go, he's gonna make me sick again."

"Don't say that."

Amy smiles and says, "Oh, Nick. Stop taking everything so seriously. This is *me* again. You remember—*Amy the Kidder*. But I mean it about church. I want to go."

"What about Woodridge? You had trouble with his sermons before."

"That was *before*; this is now. I'll go alone if you don't go with me."

"Oh, great. Then *I'll* start feeling guilty."

I'm stalling and looking for a way to change her mind. Amy used to return from church crying and asking if God was punishing her because she wasn't a good Christian.

"We can try this weekend," she says. "I feel that I should."

I don't share Amy's devotion to church. Though I want to be closer to God, I see church ritual as getting in the way. I joined to please her, in spite of my doubts. To my surprise, some at Grandmont Presbyterian saw my outspokenness as an asset, and I was elected a deacon. Then again, I might just be a warm body filling a vacancy.

"Nick, I know you're not sure about this. You're wondering why I'd want to set myself up for another guilt trip."

"The thought struck my mind."

"It doesn't have to be like that. I don't have to believe all that *sin* stuff."

"You know how I feel. Like the song says, 'The things that you're liable to read in the Bible, ain't necessarily so.' It's all a matter of how you interpret it."

I'm angry at how some churches imply that solving a problem is a function of faith alone. Consequently, admitting to a serious problem invites shame. At the same time, I'm not brave enough to share Amy's story with others, and so I perpetuate the stigma of mental illness, just like the people I criticize.

"Nick, I need you to promise me something. When we're with other people, you have to stop looking at me the way you do."

"What way?"

"Like I'm a nut about to crack."

"I'm sorry. I didn't know I did that."

That's a lie. I'm very conscious about my need to check up on Amy. Her accusation tells me that I should be more discreet, so I quickly add, "I'll try to do better."

"Okay," she says. "That's settled. Now let's have dessert. Want a brownie?"

"Know what? I'm ready for a bedtime story."

"Okay, but you'll have to start 'cuz I'm having a brownie."

Amy's reading aloud is my favorite part of our picnics. I love how she takes on the personalities of the characters. We do *Gone with the Wind* often. Other novels, like *A Tree Grows in Brooklyn* and *Cass Timberline* are good, but once is enough.

I'm not as talented at voice characterization as Amy is, so I munch on dessert and wait for her. When she's done eating, she lies on her stomach, and I rest my head in the cradle of her back causing my head to bob while she reads.

Most of the books are light romantic tales, but today's tome, *Of Human Bondage,* is heavy. As Amy reads the last page, I look for something to cheer us up.

"Well, what'd you think of it?" says Amy.

"I still don't know who *Mom* is," I say.

"*Mom*? What are you talking about?"

"You said the book was about *summers at Mom's.*"

Amy rolls over, dumping my head to the ground. "*Somerset Maugham* is the author, you big dummy."

"Well, I was a little disappointed. I thought it was a detective story. Didn't Humphrey Bogart play Philip Carey in the movies?"

"That was Philip *Marlowe*, you dope. Come on, I want to be serious."

"Okay, but Bogie'd never let a dame treat him like that waitress treated Carey."

"I wonder about that, too. Philip's an intelligent, sensitive guy and Mildred's a dirty, mean bitch. Yet he can't leave her. Why does he let her abuse him like that?"

"The guy sees himself as a misfit," I say. "He doesn't believe anyone else would want him, so he's afraid to lose what he thinks he has—even if it's awful."

"He eventually loses her anyway."

"He also lost his soul because of his lust for her. I think he's ashamed of his passion—like he's ashamed of his clubfoot."

"Yeah, but he comes to his senses with Sally."

"Do you think people like that can change?" I ask.

"Caterpillars change into butterflies, don't they? Philip does the right thing with Sally. In the end, they both change."

"Uh-huh. *Why*, do you suppose?"

"Because they're meant for each other?" she asks sarcastically.

"Yeah, that could be. Just like us. And they live happily ever after."

Amy grabs a handful of grass and says, "I don't know about that. There's a lot going on between them." She tosses the grass into the air so that it flies into my face.

"Hey, stop that," I complain.

Amy kisses my forehead and says, "D'ya think we were made for each other?"

"Made in heaven, for sure."

"Is that why you stay with me? Because God wants you to?"

"We're together because we love each other."

"But I've mistreated you, too. Sometimes I'm a bitch like Mildred."

"You are not." I roll on my stomach and prop myself up on both elbows. Amy looks at me apologetically. I jump up and kiss her on the nose. "Sweetheart, sometimes *your illness* is talking, not you. I know you've always loved me."

A blackbird caws in the distance, and Amy looks up. She stares at the sky for several moments, moving her eyes from cloud to cloud as if shepherding the wispy threads. "I'm going to make it up to you, Nicky. You and Eleni. I promise. You'll see."

"Hey, cut it out. There's nothing to make up for."

"Yes, there is. Nick, I want to change. I want to do better."

"We'll both do better. We can't help but to be—"

"Do you think I can change? Do you think I can become a good person?"

"Punkin, you *are* a good person, and you're becoming who you were meant to be."

"I love you, Nicky. I love you to pieces."

I kiss her again, this time hard on the lips so that my tongue finds hers. In a moment, I'm all over her—one hand at her breast, the other circling the mound below her waist. We roll off the blanket onto the damp grass; its wetness is sun-warmed and silky like the fluid I want to touch in the V of her sex. Suddenly, Eleni wails for attention, and our passion turns comic. Still embracing, we laugh so hard that we tangle the blanket around us until we're wrapped like pupas in a woolen cocoon.

It's the first week of November, and I ought to feel pretty good about Amy's improvement since she stopped her medication and therapy nine weeks ago. Nevertheless, I still have a nagging feeling that the balanced mood I see on the outside is a fragile shell protecting an inner conflict that could break out at any time. Sometimes I feel like I'm in a Hitchcock film, constantly suspicious that something is about to happen.

Today has been especially difficult because I'm bothered by comments my car pool buddies made about Amy's weight. We had attended a teachers' Halloween party on the weekend, and this morning, the guys were talking about our costumes. Bill said something that might've been complimentary about how much weight Amy had lost, but I didn't like his later reference to the anorexic model, Twiggy.

Those thoughts, however, were pushed to the back of my mind by problems at school. After I got a surprise tenure evaluation during my worst behaving class, I discovered that I must prepare a presentation for this week's open house. By the end of the day, I'm bushed, and I'm glad that I can sit in the back seat and relax on the way home. During the ride, I'm preoccupied with thoughts about why I feel the constant need to oversee Amy's behavior, despite the fact that she's shown so much independence.

Even before school started, Amy had convinced me to return to the car pool, so she'd have the car while I'm at work. At first, I worried that she'd go to Mom's and let her take care of Eleni, but Amy had other things in mind. For several weeks, Amy and Eleni have enjoyed occasional trips to the mall where they often lunch at Hudson's Café. Other times they go to a park or do something with a church group. Church is a regular routine now, and our social life is expanding, too.

Carpooling has rekindled old friendships with the guys and brought us together for evenings out with our wives. One time, we went to a topless go-go joint. Last week, we got together with other teachers for a Halloween party, and Amy and I won first prize for best costume. We dressed as a typical '60s mod couple. Amy wore a tight miniskirt and fishnet nylons, and I wore a frilly lace shirt and high heel shoes I made by nailing blocks of wood on an old pair of Oxfords. On the way home, Amy and I commented on everyone's costume.

"How do kids dare to wear these outfits," I said. "Can you imagine? My little sister sees miniskirts like yours at her *elementary* school."

"Get real, Nicky," Amy said. "Anna dresses like this all the time."

"Come on, where do you get that idea? Why are you so critical of her?"

"The miniskirt I'm wearing is hers, you know."

"Yeah, but she's just a little kid. On her, the skirt would hang a lot lower."

"Are you blind? She's at least an inch taller than I am. I got news for you. The lipstick and the gaudy eye shadow are hers, too."

"Yeah, but Mom would never let her go to school like that."

"I'm sure she doesn't, but your sister's sneaky. I'll bet she leaves home early and slips over to someone's house to change before she gets to school."

"You think so? Jeez, maybe we should tell Mom and Dad."

"Not me, buster. I'm not saying a word. They already think I'm paranoid. Your mother will deny it and turn the whole thing around to make *me* the bad guy. Nooo thanks!"

"Come on, Amy, you're exaggerating. Sometimes I think you have it in for my mother, and I don't know why."

"See what I mean? It's starting already."

"Look, we owe my mother a lot. If it wasn't for her—"

"You're right," she said. "Your mom is a loving, caring person who'd do anything for us. That's the problem. I don't like *owing* her so much. She can be manipulative, you know."

"Mom loves you like her own daughter, and she shows it, too. Shows it more than *your* mother does."

Amy turned away. "I don't need your reminders about my mother."

"Sorry," I said, and reached for her hand. "I was out of line."

She took my hand and used the lace on my shirt to blot a tear from her eye. "I'm sorry, too. More than you know. But I'm sorrier for my mother. I should never have done that to her."

"Done what?"

"Said that I hated her. My own mother, for God's sake. I dumped on her, and she pretends that nothing happened. Nick, what if Eleni does that to me? She might, you know. She'd have a right. I haven't been a very good mother."

"Sweetheart, you've always been good with Eleni, even when you've been ill."

"Some people might not think so."

"What people?"

"Nick, I never wanted to hurt anyone, especially the ones I love, but I know that I have. Please don't let me be bad again. Promise that you'll watch out for me."

At the time she said that, I was bewildered because I was more accustomed to her anger about my constant vigilance, but it was obvious then that she didn't want to talk anymore. Now, I see why I've continued to worry. Maybe my earlier thought that she pretends to be well was correct. Bill's comments about Amy's weight simply brought my concern back into focus. What had she meant by *watch out* for her? Was her excessive weight loss a sign that should alert me?

At home, Amy greets me with a tender kiss. After an exchange about how our day went, she asks if I could change my driving schedule next week. She's aware that it's my turn to drive, but she needs the car to go shopping. Suddenly, I'm afraid to answer, and I sit down without saying anything.

Amy responds by saying, "I'm sorry, I can see you have other things on your mind." Then she lingers and touches my earlobe, lightly stroking the peach-fuzz hairs with her thumb and forefinger. It's her favorite persuasive trick, and her sensual touch usually softens my mood. This time I bristle.

Amy draws back and says, "Hey, why the worried look? Nick, if you think something's going on, you're wrong. I'm fine. Getting out has been good for Eleni and me. Think of it as a substitute for therapy. Hudson's has a special mother-daughter event at the mall—a pre-Christmas fashion show."

Suddenly, I push her hand away from my ear and say, "Amy, stop that! You always think everything's about you. Well, it isn't. I just don't want to talk about it now. Please. I'm nervous about school. Why can't you consider *my* feelings for once?"

Amy steps back. Her lip turns down and stiffens as she forces a smile. I feel sick and rise to go to her. "Amy, I'm sorry. I didn't mean that."

Gently, her hand urges me back to my chair. "No," she says. "You're right. I'm being selfish. I can wait. There'll be another time." Her response is considerate, and I should be relieved.

I work late into the night, laboring over my presentation much longer than necessary. It's an old trick of mine to get back at her, make her feel guilty by showing how hard I work. This time it backfires, and I go to bed feeling like shit.

I sleep intermittently, dreaming and awakening without resting. My dreams are vivid, and I wake up startled and frightened by the emptiness of night. Afterward, I settle into what begins as a pleasant dream of a man and child playing in a beautiful room. A young woman lies in bed in a darkened corner. There's a knock on the door, and I go to answer but find the door locked. The woman in bed stirs and reveals a key tied around her neck. I beg her to rise and unlock the door, but she continues to sleep. When I touch the key, both the key and the woman vanish. Now the door is open, and I peer through the doorway into darkness. I take a step out and suddenly feel myself falling, spiraling, and plunging until I awaken with a start.

I look to my side expecting Amy to be gone, but she's sleeping soundly beside me. Then I get up quietly and go to Eleni's room to be sure that she's okay. Though it's still early, I sit down at the kitchen table where I recall my dream and reexperience the sensation of falling.

I straighten when Amy shuffles into the kitchen. She has stepped into her slippers, flattening their backs with her heels. She's wearing a red terry robe with bright yellow roses on the pockets and stains of baby drool decorating the shoulders.

"Hi, punkin, you're up early," she says, pecking me lightly on my bristled face. She yawns and runs her fingers through her short hair, shaking her head as if to loosen the grip of last night. I've watched Amy awaken a hundred times, but I'm still caught off guard by the unintentionally sexy way she does it. As she rubs sleep from her eyes, I fall in love all over again.

"I slept like a baby," she says. "How 'bout you? Were you up late last night?"

"I'm okay," I say, trying to sound casual. "Got a lot done. Listen, I was thinking about the car. I'm sure it'll be all right. I'll talk to the guys today."

I don't explain and don't say how worried I am ... how I've become afraid to leave her alone ... how my fear has grown about her driving ... how scared I've become to arrive home and find her crying ... or unconscious ... or dead.

Those thoughts are still with me when the guys drop me off at home. When I fail to see Amy and Eleni at the front window, I go to the garage and see that the car is there, so I expect someone will greet me when I go into the house. No one does.

"Hey, pumpkins, I'm home," I say. Getting no response, I go into the kitchen, walk through the dining room, and look into the bedrooms. Every room is empty. A laundry basket with folded clothes is on the floor near the basement stairs, so I go down to the basement calling out, "Amy? Eleni?" Water dripping from a faucet into the laundry tub is the only sound I hear. My heart thumps wildly as thoughts race through my mind. It's nearly five o'clock. It'll be dark soon. Where could she have gone without a car? Damnit, it's November and it's cold outside. Why isn't she at home?

Back upstairs, I check the medicine cabinet in the bathroom. What the hell am I looking for? Suddenly, I hear the side door open. I rush toward it, but stop before I get to the kitchen. I need to calm down. I don't want to alarm her or show her that I'm worried, so I stand in the shadows of the dining room and peek into the landing at the basement stairs. Amy is unzipping Eleni's coat. They appear to be all right. Their cheeks are rosy, and they're talking to each other in those *child-sensical* words that Amy loves to make up.

"Yah-Yah, Da-Da. Let's see if Da-Da is home. Here, sweetie, bend your *belbow* so Mommy can take off your coat."

Amy and Eleni step into the kitchen at the same time I do.

"Oh, you *are* home," says Amy, a bit startled. Suddenly, her eyes widen. She stares at my hands. "Omigod, Nick, what's wrong? Your hands...."

I look at my hands. They're shaking.

"Nick, what's wrong? Sweetie, what's the matter?"

"Nothing," I say, putting my hands behind me. "I ... I was in the bathroom washing. I heard you and didn't dry my hands. I was shaking off the water, that's all."

"There's something else. You look awful. What's going on with you?"

"Nothing. When I didn't find you at home, I got a little ... concerned, I guess."

"Aww, honey, I'm sorry." She kisses me and touches her cold cheek to mine. Some obscure suspicion makes me cringe. She backs off. "Nick, what is it?"

My lips tighten. *She's trying to trick me. She acts concerned, but hasn't told me where she's been. Why not? What does she have to hide?*

"Why are you out so late with Eleni?" I ask.

"I wanted to get in before you came home, but I lost track of time. Sorry."

"Where ... where've you been?" My throat is dry, and words barely come out.

"I took Eleni to the park to take advantage of the nice weather. The swings are still up, but it won't be long before they're put away." As she talks, she gathers shoes and coats and piles them on the laundry basket. Lifting it, she peers curiously over the mound at me. "Nicky, are you sure you're okay? You're not acting right. Something's going on."

"Yes! I mean, no. Nothing's going on. I had a bad day is all. Stop pestering me."

"Well, *excuse* me. I'm sorry I care."

She starts out of the room. I raise my hand to intercept her, but step aside before saying something crazier than I've already said.

After a while, I go to the bedroom where Amy's putting away the laundry.

"I'm sorry, punkin. You know how junior high kids can get under your skin."

"I understand. Is there something I can do?"

"No, it's just one of those days. You know. Kids will be kids."

"You sure you're okay?"

"Stop asking that. I'm not a—"

"Not a nut case?" she says. "You mean not crazy like me?" She throws a T-shirt into the dresser drawer and bangs it shut. "Listen, I'm only trying to help. I can do that too, you know. You're not the only helpmate around here."

"Amy, please."

I extend my hand. She bats it away, turns, and folds her arms across her chest.

"Let's stop this," I plead. "I don't know what's happening here."

Amy sits on the bed. A moment passes before she unfolds her arms and puts her hands in her lap. When she sighs, I go to her. I feel awkward, fearful of offending her further. Again, I offer my hand. She takes it and looks directly into my eyes.

"You're right," she says. "Let's stop, but let me say one more thing. Think about how it feels to be mistrusted—to be asked over and over, 'Are you okay? Are you *sure* you're okay?' That's what you do to me. Now *you* know how *I* feel."

"Yes ... yes, I'm sorry. I know what you mean."

Amy grasps my hand in a handshake. "Let's make a deal. Unless there's something terribly wrong, you'll take my first answer when I say that I'm okay. Deal?"

"Deal."

"From now on," she says, "I'll believe that you're all right if you'll believe that I'm all right. Now, let's drop it. I need to get dinner ready."

CHAPTER EIGHTEEN

Sanity is a cozy lie.

—Susan Sontag

Amy's claim that she was doing well seemed credible for several weeks, but a snapshot of her at the Miller's Christmas Eve party raises my concern. When she posed for a picture taken by her Uncle Wilbur, I'm sure Amy hoped the photo would show a joyful person celebrating the season, but that's not who's captured on film. The Polaroid took about a minute to develop, so Wilbur set it aside and went on to other guests. Fearful that Amy would see her picture before I did, I picked it up and hid it in my pocket. The photo shows a young woman whose sunken eyes, thin body, and forced smile betray a darker mood hidden behind her makeup and party dress.

At home that night, Amy admits her masquerade. "I thought I could fool everyone a little longer," she says weakly. "But I guess you found me out."

Her confession provokes a burst of self-blame that I reject and try to steer toward a rational response. "You don't have to solve this by yourself," I tell her. "A good doctor and the right drugs can help you."

My suspicion that something was wrong arose around Thanksgiving. Before that, Amy seemed happy. The loving attention she gave to Eleni, she also extended to the house, with fewer signs of her earlier obsessions. She also showed what seemed like a reasonable approach to her appearance. Meals were well prepared, conversation was pleasant, and church and social life returned to normal. My only clue of a problem was Amy's reluctance for intimacy, which I choose to overlook because she was otherwise affectionate. I reckoned that I could overcome her reticence with time and patience.

Of course, I didn't know what went on when I wasn't around, but toward the end of November, I noticed signs that reminded me of how it was last year. Although she didn't complain, Amy seemed to slow down and tire easily. Then came periods of restless sleep and extended midday naps, which led to hurried attention to routines. Haste led to frenzy. Attentiveness led to obsession and its partner, compulsion. All these seemed to grow out of a reemergence of her old fears.

Nevertheless, Amy still insists she doesn't need professional help. "I don't want to give in," she says. "I still think I can handle it myself. This isn't the same as before. I'm sure it's because of the holidays. I'll be better once January comes around."

Amy continued to resist a doctor's care until her symptoms proved more brutal than her dread of psychotropic drugs. Finally, she agreed to outpatient care with a new psychiatrist, but even then, she demanded that I promise to keep her out of the hospital.

Since she began seeing a new doctor, Amy seems less fearful, but I'm troubled by signs of an adverse reaction to her prescriptions. She's lethargic and is sometimes so out of it that her speech is slurred. I monitor the number of pills she takes, but she resists my control and threatens to hide her medication. A moment ago, I couldn't find her prescription bottles, and when I confronted her, she stiffened and told me that she didn't want to talk about it.

"Sweetheart," I say, "I don't want things to get out of hand like they did before."

"My medication is between me and my doctor," she says.

Eyeing her suspiciously, I say, "You're not doing something you shouldn't be doing, are you?"

Amy squirms, and her eyes dart from side to side as if seeking an escape. Then she twists her mouth and begins to gnaw the inside of her cheek. Her already pale skin becomes whiter, and she says meekly, "Nick, I don't know if I did the right thing. Please try to understand." She pauses and lowers her eyes. "My doctor's always giving me new drugs. Samples that don't need a prescription. He said to stop the Valium, but I took it with the new ones."

"Amy, you can't—"

"I'm not. I'm not taking anything. I flushed them all down the toilet."

"You did what?"

Amy steps toward me—then backs away. Her eyes peer searchingly into mine. "Oh, Nick. I don't know why I did it. I threw everything away—everything, the new stuff *and* the Valium."

"Don't worry," I say. "We can get more. It was an honest mistake. You were afraid you might … afraid you might poison yourself."

"Yes, yes, that's it, but I don't want them anymore. I'm sick and tired of feeling like this. The drugs make it worse. This new doctor's a jerk. I can't talk to him about anything that matters. He just tells me to pop another pill."

My head spins and the room begins to rotate. A disaster followed the last time Amy stopped taking her prescriptions. Suddenly, I feel like I'm about to be sick, but Amy's sobs force me to get hold of myself. *Dammit, why can't she do the same?*

"Honey," I plead, "you can't go off on your own like that. We need to work with the doctor on this. Otherwise, we'll all be lost."

"I … I'm not giving up, but I'm going nowhere with this doctor. Nowhere except where I was before. I want to get well, not *numb*. Do you know how terrible it is when you can't trust anything you feel?"

I search for something to say, but nausea prevents me from focusing. I turn away, reeling, and feel my anger rising. *Maybe that's how it is with her. Maybe something physical stops her from thinking clearly.* "Sweetheart," I say impulsively, "maybe there's something wrong with you—something wrong with your system that causes these chaotic emotions."

I can feel the desperation in my voice, but my heart races at the possibility of a *physical* reason for Amy's breakdown. *What if the enemy isn't invisible? What if it's real and tangible—something that can be dealt with as an ordinary illness?*

"Think about it," I say. "You haven't had a complete physical exam. Maybe you need some diagnostic tests for—hell, there are all kinds of tests they can run."

Amy's quizzical look shows a hint of hope. "Could it be …? Nick, I'll do anything … anything to avoid this hopelessness. Do you think it's possible that … ohmigod, what if it is? What if it's different from what I thought? I've been thinking it was my fault, but maybe—"

"I have an idea," I say, grabbing hold of her. "Your Uncle Wilbur is a high-muck-a-muck at Parke-Davis. He always brags about knowing the doctors at Trent Gifford Hospital. That's a world class hospital. Maybe he can get you in."

Amy stiffens. "I don't want Uncle Wilbur to know about me."

"He doesn't need to know everything," I say. "We'll ask him to find us someone who cares about patients—someone who treats the whole person, not a specialist. We won't mention anything about psychiatrists or anything like that."

Amy and I enter Dr. Albert Hutchinson's private study with high expectations, but my heart sinks when I see a thin, aged man leaning on a massive desk. He seems unable to remain upright without its support. One hand is at the small of his back as he pushes up from the desk with the other. Seeing us, he stands ramrod straight and walks quickly toward us, extending his hand like a greeter on a cruise ship. "Mr. and Mrs. Demetriou," he says heartily. "Welcome. Forgive me for taking a moment to exercise. At my age, I limber up whenever I can."

I'm surprised by his firm handshake and gratified by his warmth. Gently, and with a gallant flare, he grasps Amy's hand with both of his and says, "Mrs. Demetriou, may I call you Amy? Yes? Good. I'm dee-lighted to see you."

We talk a while. His tone is now soft and accepting, yet just as commanding as before. His demeanor is not doctor-like, but like a chivalrous soldier proud to be called to the rescue. With a hospitable nod and sweep of his arm, Dr. Hutchinson invites us to sit down on a stuffed leather couch. For a moment, I remain standing, drawn to a picture of a magnificent flying machine behind the couch. Like the old man, this room is oddly military, rather than medical. Dominating one wall is a large painting of a vintage biplane flying upside down and straight toward us.

"The 1913 Vickers Experimental Fighting Biplane Number One," he says, obviously pleased. "British. The first aeroplane mounted with machine guns. That's an American Curtis Wasp trailing behind—appropriately so, I might add. We Brits were far ahead of you Yanks at the time. I flew a Vickers in the Great War. Been fascinated with flying ever since. I still fly. Once a week out of Willow Run. Have you ever?"

"No, I haven't, but the thought intrigues me," I say.

"Too bad. You should give it a try. It's exhilarating."

Turning to Amy, the doctor gets right down to business and captivates her with his charm. I'm drawn to him as well, and I especially like that he includes me as an equal in Amy's initial interview. Other doctors have regarded me as an intruder, but Hutchinson listens attentively and interrupts only to clarify what he's heard. Each answer seems to heighten his interest and encourage Amy to tell her story. When she begins to cry and can go no further, Dr. Hutchinson takes her hand and says, "There, there, it's going to be all right. I'm confident I can help you. I know people who'll take good care of you. I'll see to it personally."

His promise is convincing, and I can hardly contain my excitement. Much of my initial doubt has vanished. Now the doctor's aged features make him trustworthy. He speaks firmly and directly, but in such comforting tones, I can almost feel a healing begin.

"I see right off," he says, "that the psychiatric ward is *not* the place for you. I've seen those people and, believe you me, you're not one of them. First, you must have a general physical exam. This will include a stress test and require that you stretch your muscles. I'm a firm believer in exercise. Do you exercise regularly?"

Amy shakes her head. "No, I've never liked sports very much."

"Not *sport* my lady. *Exercise.* That may well be part of the problem. We'll see. How about your diet? Nutrition is very important, too. How's your appetite?"

Amy's downcast eyes show her embarrassment about the weight she's gained. Her answer's too weak to hear, so I chime in. "Amy's had a weight problem—bouncing from one extreme to another. As you can see, right now she might be eating too much of the wrong food."

"We'll check into that. You'd be surprised how good nutrition can change one's well-being. Your problem might be as simple as eating a carrot," he says with a wink.

Amy and I smile, perhaps for different reasons. A twinge of doubt returns to me.

"I also want you to have a series of thyroid tests. It might be significant that you were a premature baby. Was your mother ill prior to your birth?"

"Mother doesn't tell us much about herself, but one time I overheard her say that she had a goiter about the time I was … you know … conceived."

Hutchinson's brow rises as his eyes widen. The thought of Saundra conceiving seems bizarre to me, too, but the doctor doesn't know her. Then he throws up his fist in celebration. "Aha, now we're getting somewhere. Might be a simple thyroid deficiency."

With Dr. Hutchinson's "aha," Amy and I turn to each other and grin from ear to ear. Yes, maybe we are getting somewhere.

Unfortunately, subsequent tests fail to corroborate Hutchinson's suspicions, and each disappointment deepens Amy's depression. The failures also affect her regard for the doctor. "I tried to follow his advice about nutrition," she tells me, "but when I questioned him about the diet and exercises, he got angry."

"I doubt that he's angry," I say. "He's probably giving you a pep talk to encourage you to try harder."

"It didn't feel like that," says Amy. "It felt like he was scolding me. He said, 'Get hold of yourself, girl,' but then he said I wasn't a child but a grown woman, and that I was the only person who can make me well."

Amy says the diagnostic tests prove only that she's a failure. "There are no physical causes," she says. "It's me. I'm the one to blame. I don't have the backbone to ignore my crazy feelings."

Before seeing Hutchinson, Amy had confided to me that her symptoms had never gone away, even when she appeared to be well. Now, neither she nor I can disregard what's happening. One moment she's crying, the next she's boisterous and argumentative, threatening me with wild ultimatums. Periods of anger and argument follow periods of guilt and remorse. Hours of sleep follow spells of sleeplessness. Once again, Amy's obsession with "white specks" and cleanliness consume her thinking, and I'm constantly frustrated when she demands my attention while simultaneously demanding that I leave her alone.

Leaving Amy to her own wits seems to be precisely what Dr. Hutchinson has in mind. "He's given up on me," says Amy. "He told me there's nothing more he can do."

Amy is surprisingly matter-of-fact, and when I press her for an explanation, she says, "I told you it was my fault, and he agrees. He said there's no magical cure for something only I can control, and he grumbled that I've already taken myself out of his hands because I don't play tennis or ride a bike or do anything else he recommends."

My view is that Hutchinson feels humiliated by Amy's illness—as if her *refusal to get well* reflects upon him. I think he believes he's made a mistake by seeing her and hates to admit it. Amy says she's ashamed of this and worries about her Uncle Wilbur. "I've embarrassed him," she says. "Now everyone will know how crazy I am."

Stigmatized again, we choose to handle the episode as we've always done. We don't mention it to anyone.

Nevertheless, I plead with Amy to see Dr. Harvey Alexander, a psychiatrist recommended by Hutchinson. She refuses, claiming she has no faith in doctors. Though I want to, I dare not scream back that I can't go on without help; I'm having dire thoughts about what could happen next. In my current state of mind, I gasp at news accounts about mothers losing control and harming their children, and I'm compelled to make arrangements with Mom to watch over Eleni more often than ever. Though I know my explanations to Mom sound phony, the truth sounds even less credible because I have no idea how to explain it.

Days have passed since Hutchinson dismissed her, and Amy's condition has worsened so that simple routines like leaving for work have become major hurdles. Today, as I prepare to leave, she stands in front of me and screams, "If you leave now, you won't find me here when you get home. I'll kill myself. I'll burn the house down. I'll...."

"Amy," I plead, "control yourself. I won't leave you. I won't ever leave you, but I have to go to work. I'll be home as soon as I can."

Challenges like this have happened before. I stopped riding in the car pool months ago so that I can come home on a moment's notice. It's been weeks since I trusted her driving and some mornings, I get up early to take Eleni to be with Mom. Today, however, Mom's not available to baby sit.

Car keys in hand, I step toward the door, and Amy spreads out her arms to bar my way. I'm already late for school, but that's the furthest thing from my mind, so I set down my briefcase and go to her. She resists my touch, but I take her in my arms and fight off her struggle. I'm angry—furious at the monster that possesses her, and I tighten my grip as if I can force out the demon inside. She retaliates by screaming obscenities.

"Fuck you, you goddamn bastard! Let go, you son of a bitch, you're hurting me."

Breaking away, she flails her fists wildly, and I grab her wrists to hold them against her body. She kicks and tries to slide away. Suddenly, she jabs her knee into my groin. I let her go immediately and sink to the floor. The pain is excruciating. An eerie silence falls between us, invisible but powerful enough to keep us apart. I lie on the floor in a fetal curl while Amy gawks.

Then she kneels beside me and begins to cry. "Nicky," she whispers, "I'm so sorry. I didn't mean it. Tell me you're all right."

I stay motionless. Shock and pain warn me that Amy might strike again, but she raises her hand only to stroke my hair. Her gentle touch and wet tears dripping onto my face frighten me. With my cheek flat against the floor, I stare along the carpet surface. Oddly, my eyes focus first on the far baseboard and then zoom in on the fibers of the green carpet. Everything seems larger than life—wooly carpet that smells damp, tiny particles that cling to mangled filaments, and teardrops that rain in the forest of green treelike strands. I lie this way for several moments, examining the fibers and wondering why I see meaningless detail so easily, but can make no sense of what has just happened.

"Nick, talk to me. Are you okay? I'm sorry. I don't know why I …" As I start to rise, Amy leaps up and backs off. "Nick," she says again, "I'm sorry." Then she turns and runs into the bedroom.

I sit up and rub my eyes, afraid to touch where the pain is greatest. Getting to my feet is easier than I expect. My first thought is to check on Eleni, and I'm relieved when I see that she's asleep in her crib. I reckon that I'm okay, too, because my thoughts return to Amy when I hear sounds of slammed drawers and shoved furniture coming from the bedroom. Rushing there, I arrive just as Amy throws a hairbrush against the wall.

"Amy, stop," I say from the doorway. "Don't do this."

She spins around. "Nick. Are you all right?"

"I'm fine, but that was one well-placed knee."

"My daddy taught me," she says warily, "in case someone attacked me."

"It's a good one," I say, "but you don't need to use it on me. I'm not going to hurt you."

Cautiously, she reaches up to touch my face. Still apprehensive, I jerk my head away. "I won't hurt you either," she says.

I raise my hand to touch the side of her face and then immediately draw it back, but Amy takes my hand and presses it to her cheek, wiping away a tear as she does. Though her hands tremble, she continues to hold mine softly against her cheek. We stay that way for a long while, each wanting more from the other than we are able to give.

"Nick, don't grab me like that. Don't try to wrestle me when I'm all worked up. You can't shake it out of me. I've told you before. It makes me crazy ... crazier than I am. It's smothering, and I get more afraid. Don't ever do that again."

I step to the telephone at the side of the bed and say, "I need to make a call."

"No, Nick. Don't call the hospital."

"I'm not. I'm calling school for a sub. I'm staying home for a few days."

"Okay, that's all right. That's good. I won't need a doctor if you're at home."

"Amy, I can't always be home. You need to see someone."

We carry on like this for several minutes. Finally, Amy agrees to see a doctor, but makes me swear that I'll let her choose and won't force her to go to a hospital.

"I'll ask for some recommendations," I say. "Maybe Uncle Wilbur can help."

"No! Keep him out of it. He's still mad at us."

"Who then? Who can I talk to?"

"Maybe someone at church," she says. "Maybe Reverend Woodridge can help."

"Okay, I'll go see him today. Just promise that you'll consider his advice."

"I will, but I don't want the whole church knowing. I don't want prayer meetings and sanctimonious preaching."

"I'll tell him. I'm sure he'll understand."

I feel reasonably close to Dr. Calvin Woodridge because I served on the nominating committee that recommended hiring him, and as a deacon at the church, I've met with him regularly. He's a handsome, dramatic man who projects himself like a Shakespearean-actor whether he's speaking from the pulpit or off the cuff. A few of us have found fault with the way he flaunts his evangelical persona, but have learned to accept him. Woodridge's very appearance seems orchestrated to fit a role he envisions for himself. His long silvery hair curls fashionably over his ears, and he continually flashes a wide smile, which is brightened by perfectly straight teeth that I'm certain he whitens regularly.

Unlike most Presbyterian ministers, the reverend wears a stiff clerical collar, even when not on church business. His Sunday collar is unlike any I've ever seen. The ornate yoke, which I suspect was designed by Dr. Calvin Woodridge himself, is a cross between a seventeenth-century rebato and the dickey worn by the Quaker Oats man. Woodridge looms large in whatever he wears, whether he's in a business suit or in his jacquard frock on Sunday mornings. I overlook his ostentation because I like his persistent message of putting good works ahead of good words. With this in mind, I go to his office with confidence that he'll be eager to help Amy and our family.

Woodridge listens cordially without interrupting my jumbled account. Exhausted when I finish, I let out a weary sigh and sit back in my chair expecting the reverend to hem and haw before offering help. When he replies promptly, my heart quickens. Thank God. This man is ready with an answer for Amy and me.

"Your way is very clear," he says. "You have an infant daughter, and you alone are able to act on her behalf. You must save your daughter and yourself."

"Yes, I know that, and save Amy, too. I'm glad you see this isn't just about Amy. We're all affected."

"Yes," he says emphatically, "and you must act before it's too late. Your wife is out of the grace of God, and if you're not careful, you too will fall from his grace. You must take your child and leave your wife. Immerse yourself in the communion of saints, and raise your daughter so that, when she's of age, she will be acceptable to God."

I'm stunned beyond belief and don't know what to say.

"Nicholas," he continues, "I know this is very difficult. God's tasks are never easy. Go home and pray about it. You'll see that you must do this for the sake of your child."

I awaken the next morning wondering what Woodridge actually said. I must not have heard him correctly. My brain was scrambled when I saw him. I must have gotten it wrong. He didn't say I should leave Amy, did he? Jesus, how can a man of God say that?

Near 9:00 a.m., I dial his number and stretch the cord as far from Amy as possible. Backing into a corner, I review the question I've written on a piece of paper and then listen for Calvin Woodridge's voice. Woodridge answers, and I get right to the point.

"Reverend, this is Nick Demetriou. Listen ... about yesterday ... I ... I'm not sure I heard you correctly." I take a deep breath and read from the paper. "Is it true that you advised me that Amy is out of the Grace of God and that I should take our daughter away and ... and leave Amy?"

"Yes," he says without equivocation. "That is *exactly* what I said."

I hang up the phone.

"Well?" says Amy.

I swing around and see her standing barely ten feet away. How long has she been there?

"Wha ... What do you mean?" I stammer.

"What did the minister say? That's who you were talking to, isn't it?"

"How ... how'd you know?"

"Nick, what's going on? You told me you'd call him. Yesterday, when you got home, you said you'd talk to him today after he checked on a few things. He was going to find a doctor he could recommend for us, wasn't he? That's what you told me, isn't it?"

"Uh ... yeah. Right. He ... Reverend Woodridge ... he said he consulted with some people—other ministers and doctors that he knows. They recommended Trent Gifford."

"Well, I can't see Trent Gifford. He's dead. I need someone who can breathe."

I'm always amazed—and encouraged—by Amy's sense of humor. It comes out at the most unexpected moments. If only she could combine her wit with her will, she'd have a hell of a weapon against that goddamn depression.

"I meant Gifford Hospital. Everyone says it's the best."

"So ...? You mean the doctor works out of Gifford? What's his name?"

I say the first name that comes to mind. "Dr. Henry Alexander."

Amy frowns. "You mean *Harvey* Alexander, the one Hutchinson mentioned?"

"Yeah, *Harvey*. That's what I meant."

"Were there others? I don't want Hutchinson involved again."

"He's not. He won't even know about it. Woodridge got Alexander's name from a bunch of people. He must be very good. I say we give him a try."

"There must be other doctors and hospitals in a big city like Detroit."

"Yeah, but Gifford is one of the best, and Alexander is chief of psychiatry."

Amy fidgets with her bathrobe sash, tying and untying it. "You really think so?"

"Yes, I'm sure of it. Tell you what. Let's make an appointment. I won't insist that you stay, but I think you should see Dr. Alexander at least once."

Amy puts her hands deep into the pockets of her robe and says nothing.

"Okay if I call him and set it up?" I offer.

"No, it's not okay, but I don't know what else to do." She fusses with her robe, ties another knot, and unties it again before saying, "Yeah, go ahead. Call him. I've already lost my mind; what else can I lose?"

My feeling of being left out returns as soon as the door closes behind Amy and I'm alone in the waiting room. Since Dr. Alexander began seeing her weeks ago, he's separated me from Amy's therapy. Of course, her recovery is most important, but it seems like no one cares about me. To be fair, my isolation from friends and family is partly my fault. Just as doctors haven't confided in me, I've never opened my heart to others. Call it stigma or shame—whatever it is—I just keep mum. I certainly can't let my friends believe that I've failed in my marriage, and I can't share my worries with Amy. To complain, especially about Alexander, would undermine her fragile confidence in him.

Amy's forty-five minutes are up, but she hasn't come out. I'm pacing from corner table to end table leafing through magazines when a nurse says, "Mr. Demetriou, Doctor would like to speak with you. Come with me, please."

She leads me to an empty room and motions toward two leather chairs that face a modest desk. I look for the proverbial couch but see none. Too jittery to sit, I bide time by inspecting the sparse furnishings. Medical certificates hang on the left and right walls. A photo in a glass frame rests on the desk. Looking closely, I see my reflection in the glass covering the photo of Alexander flanked by a woman and two young men. Everyone except my reflection is smiling.

Behind the desk is a standard office chair, and on the wall behind that, an abstract painting. I look at the painting from different angles, examining it to get some perspective. Its theme eludes me. So does the reason for the long delay. I sit in silence. The ticks of my watch grow louder and louder. Countless times, I look at the watch face but don't really see it. Finally, Dr. Alexander comes in. Before I rise from my chair, he shakes my hand and sits beside me. Close up, I remember that he looks like someone I should know.

"Mr. Demetriou, Amy is a lovely young lady." As he says this, he leans forward as though he might grasp my hand again. "But," he says with a pause, "she is also very troubled, more so than I first suspected. I need to accelerate the pace of her treatment."

My heart skips a beat. "You haven't admitted her to the hospital, have you?"

"No. When I mentioned it, she became agitated, and I had to give her a seda-tive." He leans closer and puts his hand on my forearm. "Don't worry, she's rest-ing comfortably now. I promised that I wouldn't admit her today, but I can't predict what might be necessary in the future. I'd like to begin electrotherapy here in the office, and I'll need your permission. I believe you're familiar with shock therapy."

"Yes. I know what it is, but I'm not sure about.... Have you talked to Amy about it? She's had it before, and she's afraid of it."

"Not as frightened as she is of hospitalization. We've talked about it and reached a compromise. She agreed to the treatment if it might keep her from being admitted."

"Might?"

"Mr. Demetriou, you must come to grips with this. Amy's illness is serious. She now accepts the possibility of hospital confinement. Outpatient ECT will be helpful, but we can only give it once a week. I'm concerned that her depression may be more acute. In the hospital, she can have treatments almost daily. You need to be prepared."

I push against the back of my chair and look at Dr. Alexander. I study him while I absorb what he's said. He, too, leans back in his chair, leaving his arms on the armrests as if he's posing as the president of something. I think he's inviting me to look hard at him and at the meaning of his words.

He seems audacious and friendly, even familiar in a distant sort of way. He wears a white doctor's coat over a blue shirt and finely tailored brown slacks with thin stripes of blue threads that match his shirt and tie. His glasses—I believe they're called *pince-nez*—draw my attention to his eyes. They are eyes of utter confidence, almost arrogance, yet his somber facial expression shows understanding as if he were a man above it all—not because he feels no pain, but because he's risen above it in his own life. I know now who he reminds me of—FDR. In my mind, I see him giving a fireside chat, like in a photo in a history book. I look away to shake off the image, afraid my fantasy will cloud my judgment. I desperately want to believe that Dr. Alexander can help, and I've shaped him to resemble a man who is my idol.

"Doctor, I want to do what's best for Amy, but I feel forced into a corner."

"I assure you that I'll do everything I can for her. Trent Gifford Hospital is a fine facility with many excellent doctors and services."

"You talk as if she'll be admitted."

"If that's what's best."

"Yes. I want the best for Amy."

"Fine. Fine," he says. "My receptionist has the forms for you. I want you to get them ready, so I can admit Amy on a moment's notice." He offers his hand in agreement, as he stands and beckons me to stand with him. I get up and shake his hand. I let go and then regret it. In a moment, he'll be gone. "Doctor," I say, as he's about to leave. "Will Amy be all right? I mean, will she be able to live a normal life? She won't be going in and out of hospitals for the rest of her life, will she?"

After a thoughtful pause, the doctor pulls a pen and prescription pad from his pocket. On the blank side, he draws two lines—one nearly straight and the other wavy.

"You're a science teacher, aren't you?" I nod. "And you know what a sinusoidal wave looks like?" Another nod. "Look here. This *almost* straight line is what one might call 'normal.' It's what most people experience. There are ups and downs, but they are minor bumps compared to this one." He points to the wavy line. "This curved line goes up, reaches a peak, and then plunges steeply downward until it reaches a low point. From the low point, the curve climbs steeply upward again to repeat the pattern over and over again. Right now, the wavy line resembles Amy's life. Unlike the little nubs in the lives of many people, her high and low points range over a greater emotional distance. Even now, she has periods of normalcy whenever she's near the middle of these extremes. You might say that she's on the right track only when she crosses the path. My aim—the objective of our treatment—is to lift up Amy's low points and flatten down her high points." He scribbles out the peaks and valleys on his pad. "In other words, we'll try to reduce the extremes and bring balance to her life. In some cases, this isn't possible. I believe Amy's a lucky one. She'll likely respond well, but you can't expect that the waves will be eliminated entirely. Chances are she'll always have to cope with peaks and valleys, but we hope to make them more manageable."

I look from drawing to doctor and back again. "May I have this?" I ask.

"Of course. Do you have any other questions?"

"Yes. What about me, Doctor? What do *I* do?"

"I'm not sure I understand."

"People tell me not to talk about this, not to talk to anyone about Amy's illness. Sometimes ... God ... there are times when I need someone. I don't know what to do."

He looks puzzled. "Well, it's not something to talk about indiscriminately. I wouldn't broadcast it on the radio or shout it from rooftops. If you carefully choose with whom you speak, it's perfectly all right to acknowledge that she's had some emotional distress. I wouldn't go around telling *everyone*. Why would you even want to?"

The doctor removes his glasses and rubs his nose as if to wipe away his puzzlement. He closes his eyes for a moment, and when he opens them again, appears to look past me. Then he smiles, points me toward the receptionist, and bids me good day.

I don't follow him when he walks away. Instead, I remain in the room and reexamine the sketch in my hand. When I look up, I see the painting on the wall. The signature scrawled in a lower corner is illegible and resembles the curved line Dr. Alexander drew for me. The sketch, the painting, and the signature evoke many feelings, but clarity and comfort are not among them.

After school the next day, I go to Bill's classroom. We haven't talked much since I quit riding in the car pool months ago. I know I'm taking a chance, but Bill's a decent man—a Christian with an open mind and a soft spot for troubled kids. The big Oklahoma cowboy is testing a Van de Graaff generator when I walk in. His hands are on the giant spherical electrode atop the tall cylinder, and every strand of his hair is standing on end in a bizarre demonstration of electrostatic charge.

"Hey, Nick," he shouts over the noise of the machine. "I got it workin' again." He places one hand on the sphere, and his hair rises again like porcupine quills. He waves his free hand, beckoning me to take it. When I touch his hand, the hairs on both our heads spring up. We laugh, and Bill flips the off switch, causing the belt inside the cylinder to slow down.

"Five hundred thousand volts," he drawls.

"Cool," I say. "Can I borrow it one day?"

"Be my guest, pardner. Your kids'll love it. Readin' 'bout electricity bores the spurs off kids, but show 'em somethin' like the Van de Graaff and they go nuts."

Which is what I came here to talk about.

"Uh ... you got a minute, Bill? Can you and I talk ... privately I mean?"

"You bet. Lemme put this clunker away 'fore I knock it over 'gin."

Bill's Gary Cooper manner is no put-on. His friendship is genuine, too, but I'm still too uncomfortable to tell him more than I need to. When I finish my tale of woe, he puts his arm around me as if cradling a rescued calf.

"Nick, Amy's gonna be okay. Sounds like all she needs is a little rest. Call on me any time. I want to help. I'm sure Janie does, too. We'll be hurt if you don't let us do somethin'. We're here for ya, night 'r day, whenever you need us.

"But lemme warn ya," he adds. "Be mindful who you talk to 'bout this. My aunt was depressed most her life, and my uncle would never say a word about it. You'd be surprised how people get when they hear somethin' they're afraid of. She's better now, but a bit addled. A crackpot doctor nearly done her in. In those days, 'specially down in Oklahoma, they didn't know better.

"Whatever you do, Nick, don't let 'em give Amy shock ther'py. That's what messed up my aunt; I'm sure of it. Stay away from it. Don't let anyone buffalo you. It ain't right for a gal like Amy."

CHAPTER NINETEEN

In despair as in love, we are above all else, alone.

—Marita Golden

Amy's second hospitalization comes almost exactly a year after her first, and she'll miss Eleni's birthday once again. This time we expect a longer stay, a thought I'd find more comforting if school were out and I didn't have to rely on Mom to take care of Eleni. On the other hand, I'm glad to be occupied with ordinary school routines—routines that help me pretend everything is normal.

After I make copies of my students' final tests on the office ditto machine, I shoot the breeze with Betty, the school secretary. Though Betty is curt and demanding with students, she's pleasant and friendly with teachers and generally accepted as an equal. A matronly woman in her sixties, she revels in her role as mother hen for the young staff at James Junior High and offers advice freely. I've often thought about talking to her about Amy, but bad experiences with friends and clergy have taught me a lesson. Schmoozing and kibitzing is okay, but I keep my personal life hidden.

"Where's April?" I say. "Is this her wedding weekend?"

"Why the interest?" asks Betty.

The tone of her reply takes me aback. "Just wondering if that's why she's absent."

"Yes and no. The wedding's not this weekend. It's set for a week from Friday, and they're moving to Virginia the next day. At least that's the plan."

Another curious answer—one begging for another question, but as soon as I say, "What do you mean?" I have a funny feeling that I shouldn't have asked.

April Carlson is Betty Franklin's indispensable assistant. Although only a year out of high school, April is skilled at office tasks and a quick study with new duties. She's efficient, personable, and a crackerjack at getting last minute materials ready for harried teachers. It isn't just her office talent that makes everyone take notice; April is as pretty and vibrant as her spring name. Everyone likes her—even the students. Some of the pubescent boys make excuses to come in the office just to see April.

Betty removes a mimeograph from her typewriter and looks around as if to survey the office. I do, too, and discover that we're alone. "Listen, Nick, do you have a few minutes? There's something we should talk about."

"Yeah, sure. What is it?"

"Not out here. We can go in Mr. Brennan's office. He won't be back till noon." She ushers me into the principal's office and closes the door behind us. A large window allows Betty to keep an eye on the outer office. After we sit, she faces me somberly and says, "I promised April not to say anything, but she's on the verge of breaking a more important promise, so I think it's a fair trade. To be honest, I've wanted to talk to you for weeks, but didn't think you could handle it."

"Me? Handle what?"

"I'm getting to it. Listen, you've been ... well ... more at ease this week. I hope it's okay for me to bring this up now."

Though I have a feeling that I don't really want to know, I ask, "Bring what up?"

"April wants to cancel her wedding."

"Oh, my God. How sad."

"She was planning to work this week and take next week off. That was supposed to give her enough time to prepare for the wedding. Last week she talked about having cold feet, though she said she's been in a panic for much longer." Betty stops for a moment and looks me over with the scrutiny she'd give to proofreading her just-cut mimeograph. "Her beau comes home from the army tomorrow," she says. "Tony's his name. April hasn't seen him in three months. Nick, she's not sure she loves this guy."

Another pause. Another examination. *What's Betty looking for?*

"Except for a few days here and there," she continues, "April's hardly seen Tony since he joined the service four years ago. She was fifteen and madly in love ... or so she thought. Now, she's scared to death."

Betty has already told me more than I want to know, but my heart goes out to this poor girl. "Is she afraid of him?" I ask. "Has he hurt her?"

"It's nothing like that. She says he's a real sweetheart. Very gentlemanly. Not the brightest guy, but a hard worker. And as loyal as King Arthur's knight."

"I don't understand. April's so sweet herself. I can't imagine her in a jam like this. Is it some kind of career thing? Is she upset because she has to leave her job?"

"No."

Betty leans back in her chair and locks her arms across her chest. Her eyes have never left me from the time we sat down. I feel them sear into me as she says, "April doesn't want to come back to work because—"

"So what?" I interrupt, trying to stop Betty before she tells me too much. "April's young. She still lives at home. She can get another job; do whatever she wants. Why are you telling me all this? I don't really want to know." I get up and start to leave.

Betty unfolds her arms and holds up her hand. "There's more."

The heaviness of her gaze stops me. I don't know what she's about to say, yet ... *I know.*

"April doesn't want to come to work because you're here. She can't bear to see you every day. She says it breaks her heart."

"What?"

"Nick, April thinks she's in love with you."

Suddenly, I feel like the room is filling with water and I'm swirling in a whirlpool of words I don't want to hear. Betty scrutinizes me and tightens her lips as if she's trying to squeeze a response from me. I say nothing.

"Nick, don't you get it? She thinks she's in love with you. She can't marry Tony because she says she loves *you.*"

I put my hands to my face, sit back down, and sink deep into the chair. "Betty, what are you saying? You can't be serious."

"It might not be my place to say—no, that's not so. It *wasn't* my place before, but it is now. That girl is about to make a decision that might ruin her life. Maybe you haven't meant anything by how you've acted around her. Maybe you haven't even known what was going on ... but maybe you should have."

I throw my arms out and shake my head, answering Betty's glare with a look of shock. "Betty, this is me. Nick. You've got me mixed up with those other clowns ... the single guys who hover around April like dogs in heat. They're the ones who flirt. Not me. You've seen them. You've heard what they say."

"I know, but a girl like April doesn't like that. She was in tears when Gary made that crack about seeing 'a real April shower.' You were the one who came to her afterward and calmed her down. She knows you said something to Gary. You're different, all right. The charm you have on her isn't because you try. It's because you don't."

"So what are you saying? It's my fault that she's confused?"

"I don't know what I'm saying. I just think you should know what's going on ... what I saw happening between the two of you."

"*Nothing* was happening. What exactly did you see, anyway?"

"I saw it a couple of months ago. April says it started long before that. At first, I thought you were just being nice to her. I knew you were married. That was enough reason for me to forget about it. Believe me, I'd rather stay out of it, but now I can't."

"Betty, there must be some mistake."

"You're right about that. Somewhere, there's a big mistake. I think it's April who's got things messed up in her head, but you're right in the middle of it."

I twist in my chair and put my hands on the armrests, feeling like I'm going to jump out of my skin. Suddenly, I'm out of the chair and pacing back and forth. Betty's eyes follow me. "Betty, she's so young. She's just a girl."

"She's almost twenty. What're you, twenty-six? When you're that age you have hormones leaping around inside. She's been pining for her soldier-boy for a long time. Then you come along being so nice to her. At the same time, you're looking like a lost soul. You give her a lot of attention, and she figures you're just as lonely as she is."

"Didn't she know that I was married … that I *am* married?"

"Not at first, she didn't. She didn't think about it. She knew you were sad. And she saw how you'd brighten up when she talked to you."

"Betty, I'm happily married. How did she …?"

"Nick, forgive me, but I'm not telling anything out of school when I say you don't look happily married. Everyone notices, especially me because I'm the first to see how you come to work. Sad and tired. And more than a little frightened. Like I was when I broke up with my husband. April sees that you're unhappy. She doesn't just *think* that; she says she *knows* it. But even when you're down in the dumps, you find a way to cheer *her* up when she needs it. She returns the favor, and wow, you should see your face. Nick, all she has to do is say hello and you light up. I've seen you look at her when you're in here running dittos. I see how your expression changes when she smiles."

Still standing, I turn my back on Betty. It does no good. I can feel her looking through me. I sit down again and dare to face her. Suddenly, she casts her eyes downward. When she looks up again, I see sympathy.

"Nick, you can't deny that she's always able to make you smile. That's pretty clear to everyone. But here's the clincher for her. When there's something wrong—when you seem especially sad—she says she feels something inside so deeply that it makes her tremble. In those moments, she says she *knows* that she can make it better for you."

"She's an enchanting girl. Everyone likes her. I do, too. I admit it. But I don't love her. You have the wrong idea. I love my wife. I love her with all my heart.

We have a wonderful daughter. I could never betray them. Not in a million years. No way."

"It's not me that you have to convince. I don't doubt your words, but your actions ... well, they're another story. You've been either sick or sad for most of the school year. Her guess is *sad*. I don't want to get into your marriage. My concern is April. She has no one else to confide in except me, but you might be the only one who can straighten her out before she does something foolish."

"This is incredible. I can't believe she would think—"

"Nick, you should see yourself in the morning. You look like you need someone. A young woman like April can't resist taking care of a man who needs her."

"Betty, I swear to you. Never in my wildest dreams did I consider anything but a casual friendship with April. I never intended to lead her on or make her feel anything for me. You couldn't possibly believe—"

"What I believe doesn't matter. I'm doing what seems right. I've tried to convince April that she's wrong about you. I'm afraid you might have to tell her yourself."

Suddenly, I feel as if someone has yanked the chair out from under me and gravity is too surprised to act. Losing balance, I grip the armrests, and my knuckles begin to hurt. "We were invited to the wedding, my wife and I. Didn't April realize ...?"

"Maybe she sees it as a test. You said you didn't know the date of the wedding. I guess you and your wife aren't going."

"No. My ... my wife ... she can't."

For a moment that lasts too long, Betty and I sit silently facing each other. From her expression, I can see that my face is telling more than I want anyone to know.

"I'm sorry," she says. "It's probably none of my business."

This time our silence draws us together. Finally, I say, "I ... I can't talk to April."

Betty says, "I have to tell April that we spoke. She told me not to, but I think she really wanted me to say something. She'll wonder about your reaction. I'll try to explain it, but that might not work."

"Look, Betty, no offense, but why are you doing this?"

"Because April is scared out of her wits. Her folks are old-fashioned immigrants, and she says they wouldn't understand. Everyone in her family expects her to get married. It's almost an old country arranged marriage. She's too frightened to talk to anyone except me."

I hang my head and examine my hands, pressing them hard against my knees.

"If she asks," says Betty, "would you be willing to meet us, say, at my house?"

"No, not at anyone's house. If necessary, I'll meet her here at school. Late. After everyone's gone home. I'll do that, but only if you'll be here, too."

"Okay, I'll ask her. My guess is she's too scared for any meeting, but we'll see."

"Betty, tell her I'm sorry. Be sure to tell April that I'm sorry, but I had no idea what was going on all this time. I wish ... I wish that it had never happened."

Even as I say it, I know part of me wishes for something else.

CHAPTER TWENTY

Where does one go from a world of insanity?
Somewhere on the other side of despair.

—T. S. Eliot

I need help, but I don't know where to turn. It's after 3:00 in the morning, and I just did something crazy.

Eleni's safely tucked in at Mom and Pop's, Amy's resting at the hospital in a drug-induced sleep, and I'm beside myself somewhere between hell and perdition.

Earlier, I had gone to see Amy at the hospital, but she refused to see me, and I didn't understand why. I haven't seen her for days because she's had treatments during the day and I've had parent-teacher conferences at night. I had thought that she'd welcome my visit tonight, and the surprise of not seeing her set me off on an idiotic drive through Detroit's worst neighborhoods. What I did then was even more nuts.

My confusion actually started a week ago after Betty and I talked. The next day, she told me that April didn't want to see me because her mind was made up to marry Tony. She said she was just *befuddled* because he had been away so long. Betty believed that April's devotion to her church and family were too strong, and she didn't want to risk anyone finding out about her apprehension. April had made a commitment, and her obligation to obey the church surpassed her personal weakness. "Everyone gets cold feet at the last minute," she told Betty. "That's why the church teaches us to be obedient."

Though I was relieved, I was haunted by the thought that April had seen my unhappiness, and for a time at least, wanted to comfort me. Today was her wedding, and before going to the hospital, I stopped at the reception and dared to congratulate the bride and groom. Though I left immediately, I still wonder why I did such a thing. My next mistake was worse.

Now, I need to talk to someone, but I feel so alone. The last time I shared my feelings was with Bill, a couple of weeks ago. He had good intentions, I'm sure, but his advice made me feel ashamed to tell him what was really going on. I can't bring myself to talk to Pop. How could I tell him what happened? My brother, Gus, is the only one I can think of, but he and I could never talk about anything as personal as this.

A conversation between my big brother and me would be like a phone call between two deaf mutes from different countries. I've never been able to share a secret with Gus. How the hell could I confess something as ugly as tonight? Shit, he doesn't even know what's really going on with Amy. But, jeez, he's my brother, and he's really all right—a good guy, actually. It's just that Gus and I never get into personal stuff. Sports and politics are okay. Meaningless discussions and show-off arguments to prove who's smarter are easy, but not ... not anything that matters.

Back when we were kids, we had fun playing ball or joking around, but were too embarrassed to get into serious questions about girls or growing up. When I was eleven, we joined the Y because the indoor pool was open in the winter. In the locker room, we started to undress in different rows so we wouldn't see each other, but then we saw the other guys running to the pool without wearing any trunks. Without saying a word to each other, we buttoned our shirts, tied our shoes, and got the hell out of there. We never returned to the Y and never talked about it either. Had we stayed and swam bare-assed with the others, we might've learned to deal with our feelings. Maybe then I'd have the nerve to call Gus and tell him about where I was tonight.

Impulsively, I pick up the phone and start dialing Gus's number, but then I slam it down before I start the third digit. I try again and dial the first six digits—but then I stop. I stand with the phone in my hand and can't enter the last number. Goddamn it, I should talk to someone, but I feel so goddamn ashamed.

Earlier, the wedding reception, and then Amy's rejection at the hospital sent me into a spiral I can still feel. The psychiatric ward of Trent Gifford Hospital is separated from the rest of the hospital by double doors that can't be entered without permission from a receptionist that I call the "gate minder." This *guard* read me a note that said, "Mrs. Demetriou asks that she have no visitors for a day or two."

Last week, when Amy was first admitted, I was the only one she wanted to see. She was adamant that no one visit her, not even her mother and dad, but I saw her every night until this week, when my school schedule didn't allow it. My absence made Amy's refusal to see me even more upsetting.

Disoriented when I left the hospital, I missed the turn onto the Lodge Freeway and found myself at Grand Boulevard and Cass, near the GM building. Mom was taking care of Eleni again, and I didn't want to go home to an empty house, so I turned right and headed south toward my old haunts on the Wayne State campus. I figured I could do whatever I wanted—walk around campus, check out the art museum or the main library, but something else was on my mind—something not yet defined. From Cass, I made a left onto Warren and a right onto Woodward, and drove past the Vernor's bottling plant with the oak barrel and giant gnome on the roof.

I could've used some Vernor's ginger ale about then—mixed with a double shot of Canadian Club. Good thing I didn't. Might've finished what I started.

Then I made a left onto Jefferson and drove to Belle Isle. I crossed over the MacArthur Bridge and headed for Scott Fountain. I remembered taking a snooze there in the middle of the night when I was in college, and I thought about doing it again, but drove around the park instead. Around and around. I don't know how many times. The park's pretty at night. Scary, too. There was something about being scared. I liked it. I liked the danger. My heart was jumping out of my chest. It felt good—like I was really alive—but it wasn't enough.

There were people hanging around the edges of the park road. Guys were going from car to car—probably selling dope. I got out of there when a cop flashed a spotlight toward me. It was very dark when I got back to Jefferson and went west, toward downtown. I started looping around the side streets in the Cass corridor—streets in the seamiest section of town.

That's where I first saw the action. There were lots of cars. Maybe it just seemed that way because they were cruising down the street very slowly and close to the curb. Every now and then, I'd see someone come out of the shadows from a building. I thought they were dope peddlers looking to make a sale. Most of 'em were women—broads, really—with short, tight skirts, long legs, and big knockers. A few wore stiletto heels that must've been six inches high. The babes hooted whenever a car slowed, and I rolled down my window to listen. They'd first give a low whistle. Then they'd say something to the guy in the car. Something suggestive like, "Want a good time, honey?" "How about it, baby?" "Come on. I got it, 'n you want it."

The guy in front of me stopped, and I almost hit him because my eye was on a whore who leaned so low into his window her tits fell out of her blouse. Her ass was pointing right at me, and I had no doubt she wore nothing underneath her shiny skirt. I hate to admit how excited I felt watching her proposition the guy, yank on his door handle, and climb into the seat beside him. Then, when another babe approached my car and said something about 'hot licks,' I turned my wheel and gunned the engine to get out of there.

Yeah, I was a good boy. I got off Cass Avenue, but was so damned energized that I turned onto Henry Street, crossed Woodward and John R., turned left onto Brush and circled around to Beaubien. By then, I knew exactly where I wanted to go because I remembered the stories from when I was a teenager—the ones about getting your first piece of ass on Beaubien Street, right in the shadow of police headquarters.

The excitement felt good—I mean *real* good, and I wanted more. I got to thinking. Doing it wouldn't be unfaithful. Seeing someone all the time ... having a relationship with a woman I knew, someone I loved instead of my wife ... that would be wrong. Paying for it with a prostitute, that's different.

I told myself, *Nick, you love your wife; you'd never have an affair with some-one*—but I almost did. I flirted with a pretty girl that I saw every day at school. I teased her and tempted myself, and I enjoyed the feeling. Maybe my head didn't know what I was doing, but my body knew. I wanted her to excite me—to charm me out of my pants. I didn't admit it, but deep down I wanted her to keep it up until I couldn't resist. God, no, I wouldn't have seduced her on my own—not consciously—but I would have let *her* seduce me. All because the only friend I've had for two years is goddamn loneliness. The thing I remember most about my last visit with Amy is her blank stare—a familiar stare that makes me feel more alone when I'm with her than when I'm not.

What's worse is believing that it'll never get better. Nobody knows what it's like for me because I don't tell anyone. I don't dare let anyone know how bad Amy really is, because then I'd also have to admit I've had feelings for another woman. Hell, I don't admit that to myself. That's a sign of weakness, and I won't let anyone know that I'm weak. I don't need anyone to feel sorry for me. I don't need anyone. At least, that's what I thought until tonight.

At first, I tried to excuse what I was doing because it was better than the alternative. I needed to feel like a man, and what happened with that cute secretary could happen again. I had thought I was hiding my weakness pretty well, but tonight, all hell broke loose. Yet, even in my confusion, one thing seemed clear; I needed to change tactics before I did something foolish like fall in love with someone other than my wife.

That was when I told myself that I was more wacko than Amy was, and I'd better do something about it. A good piece of ass would straighten me out. Doing it with someone like April—that'd be wrong. I'm too good for that. I go to church. I love my wife. How could I face her if I committed adultery? But being with a whore is different.

I had started out the evening driving around the scummiest part of town, not knowing what I was looking for. Then, suddenly, I was sure that I had found it. I said to myself that it might be wrong, but it wasn't betrayal. It was just a step up from leering at *Playboy.*

Right then, I felt like I wasn't driving the car, and I let that old DeSoto lead me to an alley off Beaubien. Sure enough, there they were. They were like cockroaches crawling out of the corners. I stopped the car and waited with the motor running—*my* motor running. In the mirror, I saw a tight-ass chick turn around. She threw down her cigarette and walked toward me. She wore black, her silhouette outlined by the streetlight behind her. Her hands were on her hips and her handbag hung from strings at her wrist. Her flared out elbows exaggerated the bump and sway of her wide hips. When she got closer, I leaned over, rolled up the passenger-side window, and locked the door. She put both hands on the door handle. I stared at them for a long time. They looked strong, like artist's hands, and I wanted them to touch me. When she squeezed the door handle and pulled, it felt as if her hands were on my crotch.

When the door didn't open, she bent down and looked inside. I saw the skinny tubes of her breasts. "Come on, honey," she said through the glass. "Ah can't let you in unless you let me in first." Then I pulled away from the curb and turned left at the next corner. I turned left again and headed for the same street. Before I finished my turn, I saw flashing lights and heard the burst of a siren.

I knew I was busted, and I almost floored it when the cop got out of his car. Instead, I just sat there and waited. It was the smartest thing I'd done all night. A big-finned '57 DeSoto would be easy to spot in 1967.

I don't know if the cop felt sorry for me or what, but all I got was a traffic ticket for making an illegal left turn. Another thing I don't know is whether I would've gone back to that alley. All I know is that I'm glad as hell someone stopped me.

CHAPTER TWENTY-ONE

What is human life? Is it not a maimed happiness—care and weariness,
weariness and care, with the baseless expectation ... of a brighter tomorrow?

—**Ernest Renan**

Amy greets me enthusiastically the next morning in her hospital room, and tears well in my eyes when I recall how close I came to betraying her. When she asks why I'm so sad, I start to stammer and explain that I felt bad because she didn't want to see me last night.

"Honey," she says, "I called the school to tell you to take the night off. Dr. Alexander gave me a free weekend, so we have all day today and tomorrow to be together. Wait a sec; you did get the message, didn't you?"

"Well, I ... no, I didn't. It must've been put in the wrong mailbox."

The explanation is entirely possible, especially if April's substitute took the call.

"I'm so sorry," says Amy. "I wanted you to stay home and relax after your busy week. Now I bet you worried all night."

"No ... I ... yeah, for a while, but ... I ... uh ... I had plenty to keep me busy."

"I hope you didn't start another project like the last time I was in the hospital."

"No, I swear I didn't do anything like that."

Amy kisses away the tears on my cheeks and presses her lips to mine. Her tear-dampened lips taste bitter, but the softness conveys a sweetness I've almost forgotten. I melt in her arms when I feel her fingers stroking my neck in the way she used to do ages ago.

"Oh, Nick," she says, stepping back a bit. "I've put you through so much."

Her hands slide down my arms, and she takes my hands in hers. We stand silently for a moment while she searches my face. Her gaze feels soft. Her apology is genuine but not overemotional. Then her expression brightens. "But we made it through that, and you know what? I'm getting better, and I want you to stop worrying." She squeezes my hands and says, "They're good people here. It's time for you to let someone else be responsible for me. That way we'll both get well and, when the time's right, we'll be ready to make our next move."

Her buoyancy is refreshing, but I feel the need to confess at least part of my sin. "I'm sorry about yesterday," I say. "I should've known better."

"Don't be silly. I shouldn't have trusted that new secretary. She probably writes notes like me."

We laugh, each of us acknowledging Amy's frequent faux pas when hurriedly writing notes. Once she stuck a note on the front door telling a delivery crew to *please deliver next store.*

Our reminiscence isn't as funny as we make it, but the lightness of our conversation makes us laugh so hard that we slump back onto her hospital bed where I nearly roll off the edge. Amy grabs me and pulls me toward her, catching me before I fall. For the first time in a long while, I let Amy help me and hold me tighter than I hold her. It feels good.

"Hey, I have something to show you," she says, jumping off the bed. She takes a wooden plaque cut in the shape of a large pear off the wall and says, "I painted this last week. It's part of my therapy. I thought making something for our kitchen would be better than weaving a basket. Believe it or not, we do that, too."

"It's nice. Let's see … these are grapes, and these are apples and oranges."

"No, that's a tomato. This one's a peach."

"Mmm, tomatoes are my favorite, but I hope you didn't put fuzz on the peach."

"And give you goose-bumples?" she laughs. "Course not, I'm not that crazy."

"I didn't know you were such an artist."

"Don't be a dope. Rocky showed me how to do it. Turns out, he's a real artist at Wayne State. He literally held my hand as I painted. He's a big guy—kind of an all-around talent. Teaches me to play volleyball in the gym. Has hands like a masseur."

An image from the night before flashes in my mind, and I wonder if Amy sees my reaction.

"Nick, what's wrong?"

I hesitate until I think of a way to explain my shock. "Uh … these social workers … and the other *men* around here…. They don't bother you, do they?"

"What are you talking about?"

"Amy," I say as gently as I can, "you always underestimate yourself. You're a damn good-looking woman. You don't know what guys can be like if they get … well … *turned on*."

"Nick, you don't think.…"

"I do think. The trouble is that *you* don't." Though I speak softly, I feel compelled to hammer my point home. "Sweetheart," I add, "I wish you'd be a little more careful."

"Honey, this is a good hospital. I'm safe here. There are supervisors everywhere."

"Who supervises *them*?"

"Nick, I worry about a lot of crap, but fooling around never enters my mind."

"It's not *your* mind that I wonder about."

Amy laughs. "The heck you don't. That's why I'm here, remember? Nick, don't worry about somebody putting the make on me. Daddy taught me a few tricks, you know."

Amy's lighthearted answers make me realize that this time, I'm the one responding fearfully. So I smile and back off as I say, "I remember."

"Besides," she says, "this isn't a snake pit like the other joint. I'm beginning to like it here."

"So I've noticed. You seem more like your old self today."

"Thanks, I learned something that might be important. Ready for another shock?"

Before I can answer, she opens the closet door and swings her arm as if to introduce an unexpected guest. In the middle of the closet is a large bucket with a janitorial rag-mop inside. Next to it are bottles of several cleaning solutions.

"Jesus, aren't you afraid of that?"

"A little. Listen, I'm not cured, but I have an idea that might help."

"What *are* you talking about?"

"The other day, Dr. Alexander came in with all this stuff plus a small rolled up bag. He poured some ammonia on the floor over there. Then he waited a while. I just held my nose. Then he poured Mr. Clean over here and waited. I had almost no reaction. Then he poured some bleach over on the other side. When I didn't do anything, he asked me why not. I burst out laughing and told him I wasn't afraid of *liquid* detergents. I said that I was afraid of *powders*—dry stuff like Drano and Comet cleanser."

"You *laughed* at him? You mean you didn't get upset?"

"I wouldn't say that, exactly. But listen to this. When he sprinkled Ajax on the floor, I got scared, but not like I was at home. I was frightened, but I didn't panic."

"What'd you do?"

"I asked him to please clean up the mess."

"You did what?"

"Well, maybe I didn't say *please*; and I might've raised my voice a little."

"But you didn't—"

"Have a fit? No, I was frazzled but didn't scream or anything. I was nothing like I would've been at home. Reluctantly, I agreed to let him leave some stuff in the closet. The cleanser lasted only a couple of seconds, but the rest of it's been there for two days."

It's too fantastic to be true. This is a big change in just two weeks.

"You think *you're* flabbergasted?" she says. "I started thinking I was somebody else, not me. Alexander was confused, too. He asked *me* to explain it. I couldn't, but then I got to thinking. I felt better after my first night in the hospital—even before the shock treatments began—but I got upset whenever I thought about going home. So I decided that it must be the house. I think I'm afraid of our house." She pauses as if examining a thought and bites her lip before going on. "Only ... I really miss Eleni. I wish she could stay with me—here, away from home."

"Away from me, too?"

"No, no, no. I want to be *away from our house*—not from *you*. You're not going anywhere, buster—not without me you're not."

"Amy, I miss you like crazy. I want you home, but you say you hate it. How ...?"

"I shouldn't have said it like that. Don't get the wrong idea. Staying here is not permanent. The way I look at it, you and I and the doctor have circled the wagons, and I'm in a safe place where I can get strong enough to fight the war going on in my head."

Amy's resolve to beat her illness is comforting, but I don't understand what she means about our house. "You sound pretty confident," I say. "What comes after the hospital?"

"I'll get to that later, but enough about me for now. You never finished telling me what you did last night."

"I ... went home. Finished my grades ... straightened up my desk ... stuff like that."

"Oh, Nicky, I wish you'd learn to relax. That's like organizing your sock drawer."

"Did that, too."

"Hmm … did you happen to run across your acceptance letter for that summer fellowship?"

"Jeez, I forgot about it. I should tell them I'm not going. It starts in a week."

"Alexander says I can leave the hospital soon," she says almost boastfully. "When I do, I don't want to go home."

Suddenly, the good feelings I had earlier vanish, and I feel like we're back at square one where reason and reality are alien. *What in the hell is she talking about?*

"Amy," I say, trying to remain calm, "we can't just pick up and leave our house vacant while you get well. We can't afford it, and making big changes would be too risky, even if we could."

"Cool your jets," she says. "I'm only talking out loud. Oops, that's not right. I mean that I'm only *thinking* out loud while talking about it. I'm not sure about it myself, but I do want to know about the college. What's it called and where is it?"

Amy's leap to conclusions used to be part of the charm that made me fall in love with her, but the leaps that she's made over the last year or two have only made matters worse. Nevertheless, her animated talk about the future makes my heart throb with an excitement I choose to regard as hope, and I wonder if this change could possibly be the one that will make a difference.

"Michigan Tech, at Houghton in the Upper Peninsula," I say with a mix of caution and optimism.

"Is that far away? I mean, is it too far for anyone to visit us?"

"Yeah, it is. It's about eight hundred miles."

"Perfect. Let's go."

"Huh?"

"I mean it. You, Eleni, and me. You'll get paid, and we'll get to stay for free in a little apartment, right?"

"Yeah, but—"

"But, but—put-put. Let's go. You'll get your masters degree and a great vacation, at the same time. We need a fresh start to blow the stink off. A long stay away from home is just the ticket."

CHAPTER TWENTY-TWO

Home is where I was safe. Home is what I fled from.

—**Mervyn Peake**

At Michigan Tech, Amy's getaway idea looked as though it would pay off until last weekend when her parents flew in for a visit. Their arrival halted a six-week stretch of steady improvement marked by some of our happiest days since Eleni was born. However, Amy's setback was not totally unexpected, especially after I heard her response when Andy and Saundra told us about the July race riot in Detroit. Amy expressed disappointment that our house was still standing. "I don't want to go home," she said. "I'm having too much fun staying away." I might've dismissed her glib remark had her symptoms not returned with such intensity whenever I talked about leaving because my summer fellowship ended soon.

The Millers left last Sunday, and my folks came just five days later with my twelve-year-old sister, Anna. By then, Amy's depression was impossible to ignore. When Mom, Pop, and Anna left about an hour ago, Amy's mood turned nasty. She says that her anger started the second she saw them waiting for us outside our apartment. Earlier, Amy, Eleni, and I took a ride on an excursion train with other summer institute families. I had promised Amy that we'd be back long before Mom and Pop arrived, but we weren't.

"Look," I say, "they've gone home now. Why can't you forget about it?"

"Because your mother claimed they had waited here for 'hours,' and she constantly reminded me about it the rest of the weekend."

"You know how Mom exaggerates."

"Yeah, and you don't say anything to stop her."

"She's my mother. What can I say to her?"

"You can tell her to shut up. I suggest you do that before I have to. We were having a good time on Friday until we came home and found them perched on our steps like displaced Okies. You let them spoil our day, and they spoiled our weekend. I knew your mother would do that to me. Why were they waiting at the curb, anyway? Didn't you tell them we had no room in our apartment?"

"Yeah, I did, but they wanted to see us before they went to the motel."

"That's a lie. They didn't even have a reservation. Your mother just wanted to catch me off guard. What if the motel was full when they got there? There's nothing else for miles around. She knew exactly what she was doing. Despite what *I* wanted, she was guilting you into letting them stay here. I hate her for being so manipulative."

"What are you talking about? Mom's done a lot for you. I couldn't have managed without her while you were in the hospital."

"And she won't let me forget it, either."

"Amy, stop this. You're being irrational again."

"Goddamn it, I hate when you say that. What I'm telling you is real. When we showed Mom our little postage stamp apartment, she said, 'The couch opens to a bed. I can make it up for you, so you won't have to bother.' When I objected mildly, she talked to me like I was addled. 'I'll do it for you,' she said. 'I know how upsetting it is for you. Don't worry, Pop and I can sleep on the couch, and Anna can sleep on the floor. And I'll make breakfast in the morning, so you can sleep late.'"

"She was trying to be helpful," I say.

"Helpful my ass."

"Well, they didn't stay, did they? They went to the motel, and you got your way."

"But not before making us feel guilty. Admit it, Nick. Your mom plays the guilt card when things don't go her way."

"You make her sound devious and underhanded. Mom's just trying to—"

"To run our family her way. Nick, you don't see it because she's so sneaky. She's constantly making snide remarks that I can't challenge. When I object, she denies that she even said it."

"Like what?"

"Like, 'You look a little pale, honey. Are you sure you're all right? Here, let me have Eleni. She's too much for you to handle. Why don't you lie down and take a nap?'"

"But that's what you do. You set yourself up for that because you let her run things while you lie down and sleep."

"Sleep is my only refuge from her. When I confront her, she says I misunderstand. If I got angry at her, she'd say *See, I told you so.* She already *knows* I'm crazy and doesn't need any more ammunition to shoot me down. She undermines me all the time. Answer me, how often have I told her not to give Eleni peanuts to eat? It doesn't matter how often I say it, she gives Eleni peanuts and whatever else she wants. When I catch her at it, she says she didn't do it, or she acts like I'm weird for thinking a two-year-old could choke on a peanut. If I make a scene, I'm overreacting—a sure sign of my psychotic nature. Either way, she thinks I'm not a capable mother. I can't fight someone who thinks I'm dead wrong. I have no choice but to give in to her."

"Why are you carrying on about peanuts for God's sake?"

"Now *you're* doing it. It's not just peanuts. It's diapers. It's formula. It's clothes. It's naptime. It's food. Oh, yeah, especially food. I swear to God, she thinks I starve you and Eleni. I've told you before; she wants to take Eleni away from me. I know she does."

"Now, you *really* are overreacting. You know that's not true."

"Oh, she's good. She's real good. She has you convinced, too. You didn't see it, but I did. The first day they got here, she tried to take Eleni away."

"That was only for an overnight stay at the motel."

"Why should she take a baby out of a comfortable crib and put her in a con-taminated motel room that's smaller than our place? I should've put my foot down. I won't let her do that again. Just because she took care of Eleni while I was in the hospital, she thinks she can have Eleni any time she wants. Deep down, she believes *I* should ask *her* for permission to take care of my own baby. I won't let her do it."

"Good. You shouldn't let her. She can't make you do something you don't want."

"You know how she is, she doesn't take *no* for an answer. She nags at me to hold Eleni, to take her for a walk, to feed her, to change her diaper, to give her a bath. Any reason to take Eleni away."

"Amy, stop this. I think you're working yourself up."

"Maybe I have to. You won't pay attention if I don't. Nobody does. You all think I'm nuts, so nothing I say makes any difference. I have to scream to get you to notice."

"Sweetheart, I am paying attention. I won't let anyone take Eleni away from you. Okay, I'll be more watchful; just don't go off like this. I can't stand it when you do."

"I'm sorry, Nick. I don't want to scare you, and I don't want to get bad again, but you saw how I was after they came." Amy pauses. The shrillness in her voice has softened, but the intensity is still there when she says, "I try so hard to show everyone that I can be a good wife and mother, and I was doing that until we had visitors, wasn't I? I love Eleni, and I can take care of her, but no one believes me, not even you. Nicky," she pleads. "I need you to promise that you'll stay with me and let me keep my baby."

"Sweetie, I believe in you. I won't let you down, but you shouldn't be afraid of Mom. She only wants the best for all of us. She wants to believe in you, too."

"Jesus Christ," she shouts, "you still don't get it, do you?"

"I do. Yes, I do. Listen, I'm on your side. We're all on your side. No one wants to take anything away from you."

"You really believe that, don't you? You think I'm paranoid. You think I'm making this up. You think I invented the whole thing."

"No, darling. No, I don't think that. I just—"

"Your mother didn't come here for a visit or a vacation. She came to take Eleni home with her. She'd do it if you told her it was okay. Tell me she didn't talk to you about it. She did, didn't she? Oh," said Amy, mockingly imitating Mom, "she pretended to be sweet and said, 'You deserve to rest without Eleni around. Let me take her home. It'll only be a few days. Everything will be *better* when you come home, and I'll have Eleni ready for you.'"

"Amy. Amy. Please. This … this is…."

"Crazy? Yeah, that's what you all think, isn't it?"

CHAPTER TWENTY-THREE

And the end of all our exploring will be to arrive where we started
and know the place for the first time.

—**T. S. Eliot**

This morning, nearly eight weeks after returning from Michigan Tech, Amy went on a tirade that led to both of us collapsing hopelessly into a crumpled heap on the living room floor. Her wild threats went on for several minutes and eventually subsided to her present state of self-blame and emotional defeat. As I hold her in my arms, I agonize over how different we are compared to the optimism we felt the day we came home from my summer fellowship.

Nevertheless, turmoil preceded that good feeling, too. When we left the Upper Peninsula, I extended the two-day drive to four days to give Amy time to get used to the idea of going home. After a difficult first day, her disposition seemed to improve. The minute I pulled into our driveway, she rolled down her window and called out to our neighbor, Eck. The familiar sight of Eck watering his lawn, and the image of his wife Margaret, adorned in her usual juice-can hair curlers, was heartwarming. They rushed to greet us and their enthusiasm gave us all a lift. While Eck and Margaret kibitzed cheerfully with Amy and Eleni, I unpacked the car and marveled at how Amy's mood had changed after our unnerving first night on the road.

Once we settled in the house, I asked her what had brought about the change. She said she had decided that I had nothing to do with her hysterical outbreak three nights earlier, and she couldn't expect me to fix it. "It's me," she said. "It's my mind that's broken, and I'm the one who has to mend it."

I wasn't sure what she meant, but I felt defensive because of my insensitivity that first night of our trip home when Amy was all a dither after I asked her to go with me to view the northern lights. The aurora borealis was expected to be spectacular that evening, but she refused to go with me. Despite her distress, I went by myself at midnight. When I got back, she was frantic. She had worked herself into a fierce anger, and I lost my cool. I saw her outburst as more of the same old shit: when ordinary stuff happens, she's allowed to get mad, but I'm not. After all, I always have to *excuse* her because she's sick, and I can't expect her to be responsible for how she acts. I'm the one to blame, and I have to take responsibility for both of us.

After we got home, I told her again that I was sorry I had lost my cool and apologized for being inconsiderate. She told me that she had already forgiven me, and then joked, "You can't help it if you were born stupid. What happened made me see that I had to take action for myself. I decided to follow Daddy's advice to grab the bull by the horns and the cow by the udder. Only he didn't say *horns* and *udder*."

Her playful answer was encouraging but confusing, and I asked her what, exactly, she had decided.

"I made up my mind that I was through with hospitals," she said, "at least as far as staying there. I'm going back to Dr. Alexander for shock therapy, but only as an outpatient. He and I talked about it before I left in June."

"Is this ...?"

"For sure? Yes. And I don't want you to try talking me out of it. I know what you're thinking. You're right, I'm still afraid, but now I believe shock therapy helps."

"But...."

"Nick, you can't treat me like you did that night."

"I know. It was stupid of me to leave you alone in a strange place."

"It's more than that. I have to tell you something, and you have to listen. I don't understand why I'm so fearful, but I want you to know what I'm feeling."

"That's all right," I said. "I understand."

Though I said that I understood, I didn't. The phrase was a broken-record expression that had lost its meaning, like when I added, "There's no need to explain. I'll always love you, no matter what."

"I know that," she said, "but sometimes love isn't enough." She paused and took a deep breath. "I don't want you to treat me like a child. You do that all the time. I'm not a little girl. I'm a woman, and I've got to deal with this like a grown-up."

"I don't think of you as a child."

"Yes, you do."

I started to say more, but Amy put her hand to my lips and said, "Let me talk. I'm part of the problem. The way I act when I get upset—it must scare the shit out of you. Either I cry or I have a tantrum. I can't help it; I don't know what else to do. Sometimes you must think I'm just a spoiled brat trying to get my way."

"No, I—"

"Shush," she said. She was fighting back tears, and had trouble going on, but managed to say firmly that she wasn't finished. Despite her effort, she started to cry. "See what I mean? I can't help myself, and it feels like I'm getting sick again. Don't get mad at me—and don't think I'm just a little kid who wants someone to take over. I know I act that way and sometimes even beg you to take away my pain, but that's wrong. I can't demand so much from you."

Then, when I said it was okay to let me help because my love was strong enough for both of us, she backed away and told me to stop being melodramatic. At that moment, Amy seemed resolute but unsteady, and when I saw how she forced herself to go on, I thought *here it comes again.* Yet something about her expression was different.

"After the hospital, I wanted to do better," she said, "and I thought I'd be okay if we went away. Now the trip's over, and I feel the same as before. That makes me wonder about us." She raised her eyes to mine and said, "Oh, Nick, this is so hard to say because I don't want to hurt you, but I need to tell you this."

"Tell me what, sweetheart? Go ahead. I want to know."

"You think that my phobias started after Eleni was born, but they didn't. I've always been afraid. I get scared whenever I don't know what's going to happen next, and sometimes I imagine terrible things. Before we were married, we had so many plans, and I thought I'd get over my phobias. Then one the day, when I was alone, I tried on my wedding dress to fantasize about our wedding day. I should have been happy, but ... I saw something in the mirror that frightened me."

All the while she talked, Amy's eyes remained fixed on mine as though compelling me to understand. "Was ... was that the day I called?" I asked. "The day Kennedy was shot?"

"Yes. I told you not to ask about it, and you've been good, but now I have to tell you. Nick, I looked in the mirror that day and saw myself in black, and I was lying in a coffin."

"Amy—"

"The feeling never went away. Some of the time, I could ignore it, but it got worse as time went on."

"But you were so happy then. I never suspected...."

"It's a trick I learned early. Play-acting started out as a pretense for others, but it turned out to help me to feel better. That's why I thought I'd get over it. Then, after we got married, *everything* was new and scary, and I started wondering who I was."

"Yes, I know," I said. "Things have changed for me, too."

"Yeah, but only a little bit. You didn't lose your name; I did. We made a baby in one night, but I was pregnant for nine months. I lost my job and then my car. I became a mother and then got sick. Nick, my life has changed completely. I don't even dream like I used to. I don't know who I am. I feel like my life belongs to someone else."

She had gone on like this before, and I bit my tongue to quash a storm of thoughts. *Isn't belonging to someone what's supposed to happen? She belongs to me, and I belong to her. What's wrong with that?*

"Nick, I love you," she said. "To be part of someone is good for both of us, but you've gained something without losing yourself. I know I've said this before, but you don't seem to understand."

"Understand what?"

"Nick, you still have your other life—the life you started before we married. You're a teacher who's allowed to have ambition. You have a right to want something outside of our family. People know you and take your words seriously. You are somebody, and I'm nobody. I have nothing that I had before. I'm expected to be what other people want me to be, not what *I* want to be."

"Sweetie, I don't get it. What do you want to be?"

"I wish I knew, but I don't. When I think about my life, I feel like I'm drowning."

"Jesus, are you saying that I'm drowning you?"

Amy looked at me without answering and stared for a long time. Not the blank stare I saw before, this time she was biting her lip and twisting her jaw as if to shape her words before letting me hear them. Then she studied her hands and turned her wedding ring slowly—examining it in different positions as though she was wondering about its proper place.

Finally, I said, "Amy, tell me what to do. I'll do it for you if at all possible."

"Nick, I know how much you want to help, but don't you see? I don't know what I want. All I know is that I hate the thought that I have to ask you to give it to me."

"This doesn't make sense. You say I shouldn't treat you like a little girl, but you're talking non—"

"It's not *nonsense*! I can't put it into words, but I know it's not irrational."

"Then why do you get so upset?"

"Because I'm scared. I can't help how I feel. I get frightened, and then I lose control. Do you think I like it? I'd give anything to get rid of these feelings."

"Honey, I know you would. So would I, and I'm trying to understand. I want to make life better for you."

"Maybe you shouldn't try so hard, at least not in the way you do."

"Amy, I'll never give up on you."

She shook her head and grabbed hold of my arms, tightening her grip as I've done when trying to reason with her.

"Don't you see?" she said. "I've lost myself, and only *I* can find me."

"I … I'll try," I said. "I'll try to understand, but I…."

A look in her eyes made me stop. They were pleading in a way I hadn't seen before. That day, nine weeks ago, they were not the eyes of a child in need, but the eyes of a woman who wanted recognition. Suddenly, I felt as though she were a stranger asking for my attention. I did not know this stranger, but I saw that she desperately wanted me to recognize her.

Amy's resolve remained firm for several weeks, but her emotions couldn't maintain the promise of that first day back home. Shock treatments and psychotherapy have become weekly routines. When I can't take her to her appointments, Gus's wife, Janet, drives Amy to Gifford Hospital. My sister-in-law doesn't complain, but her expression tells me that the procedure frightens her even more than Amy's condition saddens her.

As for me, I've reverted to my old habit of keeping everything to myself. I appreciate Gus and Janet's kindness, but do little to cultivate a closer relationship with them. Other than arrange for Amy's rides and Eleni's care at Mom's, I hardly ever talk about Amy's illness.

Valium is still Amy's main medication. Other drugs either worsen her symptoms or create bad side effects. On days when she has ECT, she takes a heavier dose of Valium to dampen her anxiety. At his office, the doctor gives her more potent tranquilizers that he won't allow her to administer herself. For hours afterward, she appears as vacant as one of those buildings we saw in abandoned mining towns Up North. When I confront her during a lucid period, she insists on continuing the medication and battery of treatments, believing they will make her stronger.

Sometimes her spirits are elevated after a treatment, but I believe it's her willfulness, not the ECT, that gives her those periods of relative peace. Today's collapse verifies that some of her good times were acted out to fool us into believing she was getting well. The illusion she performed on stage sustained her until today when the trapdoor beneath her sprung open.

Now, Amy and I sit on the living room floor sobbing like children. A knock coming from our front porch startles me. Our entry door is open, but the door to the screened-in porch is locked. Embarrassed for someone to see us, I ignore the knock. A second and third knock go unanswered, but the caller is persistent.

"Hey, you two," a familiar voice calls. "What's going on? Come on, open up; it's Mom."

Without rising, I peer through the open door onto the porch.

"Amy? Nick? I know you're home. Open up."

Wiping my tears, I go to the door and unhook the latch.

"Oh, my God," says Mom. "Are you all right? What's happened?"

She immediately goes to Amy and spreads her arms around her like a mother dove rescuing a chick that's fallen from the nest. Together they rock back and forth—Amy crying uncontrollably, Mom whispering, almost singing, "There, there. It'll be all right. Shhhh, everything's fine. You'll be okay."

Mom works an arm free and motions for me to join them. Amy and I submit to her embrace. Sobbing, we sway to and fro to the soothing song in her voice. She cradles us as if we've awakened from a nightmare and her presence is all we need to return to normal. Slowly, calmness spreads like balm over a wound. Mom is doing what she knows how to do so well, soothing her frightened children and making it better. Though I want to believe she has the power, I sneer at her belief that her mere presence is enough to carry us through.

"Listen, kids," she says, "you can't let this beat you. You have to believe you can do better. I know you can. Other people have gotten over this, and you can, too."

"What other people, Mom?" I scoff. "This isn't as simple as you think."

"I don't want to give up," cries Amy, "but I feel so hopeless. At the hospital, I see people I've known from before. They tell me how they keep going back again and again."

"I don't want Amy to go away again," I tell her. "I can't do that anymore."

"Nick, remember what I told you when you were in school and you thought you couldn't succeed? Remember what I said?"

I twist my mouth to deride her old country simplicity and snarl, "Mom, stop. A stupid Macedonian adage doesn't help."

"Yes, it does, and you should remember it now. *Tia nema rhogoi.* It means *they don't have horns.* Those people who've accomplished something, they don't have horns growing out of their heads. They're not special. They're the same as you."

"I used to believe that when I was a kid," I say, "but look at us. We're lost. Amy ... she's.... Mom, you see her a lot, but you've never seen her as I have. You've never seen her when she's...." Even amidst the evidence before us, I stop myself from describing too much, still afraid of condemnation. "You don't know how terribly depressed she gets. We've tried everything. There's nothing else we can do."

"Yes, there is," she says, scooting around to face Amy. "Honey, you have to do something different. Maybe what you've tried isn't working, but that doesn't mean you can't get better. I've been reading something in the paper. It's from Jane Lee's advice column. She writes about depression, and people write back. They tell her about group meetings that help them get better."

Amy looks quizzically at Mom and says, "What ...?"

"Jane Lee?" I say, incredulously.

"Yes, from the newspaper. I know you make fun of me reading those things, but they're not foolish. Jane Lee, Dear Abby, and Ann Landers—all of them give down-to-earth advice and mention this group. And Jane is local. She writes for *The Detroit News.*"

"What's the name of this group?" I ask.

"It's here in my purse. I started collecting articles before you went Up North, but I didn't want to butt in. Here they are," she says, removing a rubber band from a rolled up wad of clippings. "It's called 'Recovery, Incorporated.' There are meetings all over the country, and Jane Lee printed a list for Detroit. Here are telephone numbers for five meetings on the West Side."

Like a starving child stretching for scraps of bread, Amy reaches for the newspaper clippings. Her sobs begin to sputter and stall as she looks over the articles. Early morning sunrays break over the edge of our front window and splash onto her face making her tears sparkle. Slowly, her lips form a smile. Straining against the ache of hopelessness, I pray for a miracle and yearn to believe that Mom has brought us an answer.

CHAPTER TWENTY-FOUR

Ultimately, those who are depressed have to take responsibility for their own condition and so need to understand as much about it as possible.

—Lewis Wolpert

When Dr. Alexander endorsed Recovery, Inc., Amy began attending meetings. With Recovery and the doctor's guidance, she aimed toward eliminating outpatient hospital visits and dependency on prescriptions. The motivation for independence spurred her to attend two and sometimes three Recovery meetings a week. Early on, Amy struck a deal with Alexander, and he agreed to grant her greater autonomy as she improved.

I learned that a basic Recovery mantra is *mental health through will training.* Amy's willfulness, so often the fuel that feeds the cycle of her symptoms, is harnessed in a positive way by the Recovery program. She combined that power with her doctor-patient partnership to eliminate therapy sessions within three months. Soon after that, her need for medication lessened to almost zero.

Amy's involvement with Recovery, Inc. began in October of 1967. It's now April, and she continues to show progress. For me, a baffling aspect of her improvement is that she gets better without my involvement. After feeling depended upon for so long, I now feel left out and insignificant. Amy insisted on independence from the start. She got to her first meeting by herself—claiming that it was a Recovery, Inc. policy—and has been increasingly reticent to tell me what goes on at her meetings. I should be happy with her progress but feel emptiness instead. When I try to get closer, she wards me off—not angrily like before, but insistently, nonetheless.

My anxiety has grown since March because, in previous years, Amy's condition worsened this time of year and ultimately led to hospitalization by June. Estranged from her effort in Recovery, I feel powerless to prevent the dreadful result that I believe my idleness is sure to cause. So I stand by like a reservist solder ready to act when I get the inevitable call. To justify my likely intervention, I tell myself that I have a duty to protect her because I'm certain her symptoms will escalate. Consequently, I devise devious ways to keep an eye on her. My questions about her meetings are now less direct. I listen more carefully to what she says and often eavesdrop on her conversations when she's unaware of my presence.

Amy says I *sabotage* her recovery. *Sabotage* is a Recovery, Inc. term she likes to throw at me. Another is that we're in a *temperamental deadlock*. I don't know what the hell that means either. If she'd only listen to me, she could avoid falling into the same hole she always gets herself into. She claims to use a method developed by Dr. Abraham Low, a Chicago psychiatrist who presented his teaching in the Recovery, Inc. text, *Mental Health Through Will Training*. I don't understand its method, but I must admit that it seems to help. Amy used to work herself up to a panic; now, when she gets upset, she acts confidently and counters her distress with purposeful and assertive techniques.

Still, something about tonight makes me suspicious that her depression is about to return in full force. I sense it in her sadness at dinner and her anger when Eleni spills milk on the floor. Amy seems unusually upset while watching the news on TV and reacts oddly when Walter Cronkite makes a personal plea about the war in Vietnam. "I can't stand this shit," she says, snapping off the TV. "I'm going to read my Recovery book."

After she puts Eleni to bed, I'm tempted to question her about how she's doing, but the moment seems wrong. Amy hates it when I repeatedly ask her if she's all right. At the same time, I hate that I have to plan my moves and can't act spontaneously. So we sit and read in a room that feels crowded with silence. Amy's head bobs as she begins to fall asleep. Soon she drifts off, and I feel the added burden of continuing the silence. I go on reading for a while, but am annoyed when it's time for my favorite TV show. Several minutes pass before she stirs, and I ask, "Okay if I turn on the TV?"

"Go ahead," she says, reopening her book.

On TV, Lily Tomlin's little girl character sits in an oversize rocker and goes into her comedy routine. Usually I laugh so hard I miss her lines, but tonight I hold back a little so as not to disturb Amy. Apparently, I do anyway.

"What's so funny?" says Amy.

"It's a new comedy show called *Laugh-In*. Fast paced and full of one-liners. Watch it with me. It's the nuttiest thing I've ever seen."

"Don't need any more of that. I'm going to bed."

"Come on; there's only a half-hour left. See this little girl? That's Lily Tomlin from Detroit. Went to Cass Tech, I think."

"Yeah. Interesting. Sorry, I'm too tired. I'll check on Eleni and get ready for bed."

She gets up and goes into Eleni's room, and I go back to watching *Laugh In*, trying hard to ignore my worry that Amy's lack of humor is a symptom of danger. Goldie Hawn wiggles her bikini bod, and someone chants, "Sock it to me. Sock it to me." I watch for only a minute before joining Amy in the bedroom.

"Hey, babe, you forgot to *sock it to me*. How about a kiss?"

She doesn't seem to hear me. I stifle another urge to question her, and then go back to the TV. Jeez, it's bad enough when doctors tell me that I'm intrusive, now I have to contend with Amy believing it, too.

In the last scene of *Laugh In*, an old man pedals away on a tricycle and falls over. Sometimes the show is embarrassingly silly, and I feel foolish when I watch, but I wait for the final credits in case there are more gags before I shut off the TV, and then join Amy. Seeing her in bed dabbing her eyes with a Kleenex changes my mood immediately.

"What's the matter, hon?"

"I'm okay," she says.

"Sweetie, I can tell when you're having trouble. Why don't you talk about it?"

"Why do you always think you know so much about me?"

"Because I love you. I know how you are. I can read it in your face."

"Well, I'm telling you to stop diagnosing my problems."

"Honey, it's all right to admit it. Tell me what's bothering you."

"It's *phasic, not basic*."

"What?"

"I'm *spotting*. That's Recovery lingo. I'm trying to take the *temper* out of it."

"I hear you use those Recovery terms—*temper, spotting, phasic, not basic,* and all the rest—but I don't know what they mean."

"That's the way I take care of myself. I use the Recovery method all the time."

"Why can't you tell me what goes on at your meetings? What do you talk about? What do those people say? Are they blaming me for …?"

"No, you're not the focus of attention. We spot for ourselves, not for others. And Recovery is not about blame. I can't discuss it because you don't know the method."

"Honey, I'm not challenging you. Every day, I thank God that your problems aren't so bad anymore, and our life is getting back to normal."

"It's not *normal*, it's *average*. And they're not *problems*, they're *symptoms*. Besides, you have no idea what my symptoms are. How do you know if they're better?"

"Huh?"

"You're right," she says. "I am doing better than before, but it isn't because I don't *feel* like I used to feel. I still have the same fears. I still get depressed. I still want to clean the house and get rid of the 'white stuff.' I'm still scared to death of Drano."

"But you don't seem to get—"

"Nuts about it? No, I don't get as worked up. That's because I have Recovery. I can change how I think, but I can't get rid of the symptoms ... not yet anyway."

"Honey," I say, "you're not worried about having another relapse, are you?"

"We don't have *relapses*. We have *setbacks*, and they're to be expected."

"Not if you'd let me help you. Maybe Recovery doesn't go far enough. Don't you think we could work together on this? I know you better than anybody, and I can ..."

She throws up her hands, fingers spread, palms facing me. "Stop right now. I have a lot of temper about this. Stop before I say something we'll both regret."

"But ..."

"Listen, I heard something at last week's meeting. I didn't want to tell you about it because I know how you are."

"Me? What do you mean?"

"You're a stubborn *but-in-ski*. That's my word, not Recovery's. You think you can save the world—me especially—if only I'd just listen to you."

"But ..."

"See what I mean? You always want to *but* in. I don't want you to learn too much about Recovery because I'm afraid you'll take it away from me. I can't let you do that."

"Sweetie, what are you saying?"

"Shut up and let me finish before I lose my nerve. There's this group called *Relatives, Incorporated*. It's not part of Recovery, but it uses the Recovery method—only it's for relatives of patients. Dr. Low was a founder of this group, too. He wrote a book for relatives like he did for patients. If you really want to help me, you have to leave me alone with my Recovery and go to your own group."

"It's a Recovery meeting for relatives?"

"No, it's a separate organization. The leader of the Detroit meeting knew Dr. Low personally. He was her psychiatrist when she was ill."

"She's no longer a patient? Is she a doctor or a counselor?"

"She's a *relative*. Recovery and Relatives groups don't allow professionals to be leaders. She worked with Dr. Low to develop a technique for relatives that's patterned after Recovery." Amy takes a scrap of paper from her Recovery book. "God," she says almost prayerfully, as she examines the paper, "I don't know if I should give this to you."

She closes her eyes. I study her face looking for clues to help me understand. She slides closer to me on the bed, takes my hand, and says, "Nicky, I love you ... but...." And then she lays the scrap of paper in my open palm. "Here," she says. "Here's the address. That's all I want to say about it."

"But what do they do? What kind of people ...?"

"There you go with *what kind of people* again. Believe it or not, Recovery and Relatives people are just like you and me. We're not unique. There are plenty of us *mental types* out there, and each one has at least one relative. Relatives—you in particular—are part of my *dynamic outer environment*. I can't explain what that means yet. I don't even want to. All I know is that I can't control you, and you can't control me. We're in a deadlock because you believe you can control everything—me included."

I'm stunned. I feel as if she's come closer only to slap me in the face. "Amy, that's not so. I don't feel in control at all. Since you were sick, I've always felt helpless."

"*Helplessness is not hopelessness*. I learned that Recovery phrase at my first meeting. I wouldn't be surprised if they teach that at Relatives, too."

"If ... if I go, will I learn how to help you?"

"God, I hope not. Nick, listen, do you know why Dr. Low started a Recovery group? Because he saw that the more he *helped* his patients the more they depended on him. They were in a revolving door from the hospital to him and back again. He started his groups because he wanted to break that cycle. Now I see that I've been too dependent on you, and I can't be dependent and healthy at the same time. *I* need to take care of *myself*, and *you* need to take care of *yourself.*"

I'm dumbfounded. Amy shakes her head and says, "Look, just go ... or don't go for all I care. Do what you need to do, and for God's sake, let me do what I need to do without your constant interference."

CHAPTER TWENTY-FIVE

*The impulse to control other people is ... an essential element in
obsessional neurosis. The need to control others can to some extent
be explained by a deflected drive to control parts of the self.*

—Melanie Klein

I arrive early for my first Relatives meeting held in a church basement. I am surprised to see twenty or thirty people, mostly women, already sitting at tables arranged in a large circle. Others are pulling up chairs to sit behind the tables. The lively chatter hints that many know one another, and their conviviality makes me wonder if I'm at the right meeting. Uneasy about asking, I step closer to the tables to check the title of a book some have placed in clear view. Over a shoulder, I read *Lectures to Relatives of Former Patients* by Abraham A. Low, MD.

At precisely eight o'clock—I know this by the chime of the church bell—an older woman seated at the head table says, "Can we have it quiet, please? It's time to begin our meeting." Her strong voice and firm direction fit her matriarchal appearance, but she has a quick smile and friendly eyes.

The immediate silence makes me feel conspicuous in the brightly lit room, so I drift toward the wall to be less visible. A middle-aged man holds out a folded chair and politely nods for me to sit beside him. Though I'd rather not, I accept his gesture and then awkwardly struggle to open the chair. It falls on its side. Embarrassed, I look around, but no one seems distracted by my blunder.

"This is Relatives, Incorporated," says the woman, "and I'm your leader tonight. Let's begin by giving our first names. My name is Rea." She pronounces it *Ray*.

Heads turn respectfully, and faces smile cordially as people introduce themselves. Anticipating my turn, I slump deeper in my chair and feel tightness in my throat, but the pleasant reception of the introductions eases my anxiety. The ritual is simple, yet soothing. I feel my hunched shoulders slacken as if a cord that had bound them is unwound in the circle of voices.

The man who gave me a chair is Wilfred. When everyone is introduced, he turns to me, offers his hand, and says, "Good to have you here, Nick."

His extended arm is like a lifeline, and his welcoming grip draws me into the group.

"I see we have some newcomers," says Rea. "Thank you for coming. Let me tell you about our group. Relatives, Incorporated is here to help the relatives of nervous patients gain insight into problems that come to families of the mentally ill. Relatives training helps us overcome the stigma associated with the illness and teach us ways to become more understanding and realistic. The techniques learned here help us reduce tensions in the home. We are non-profit, non-sectarian, and open to the public. There is no charge for attending meetings. Relatives is supported by voluntary contributions."

She pauses and moves a small wicker basket containing a single dollar bill in front of her. "We'll have a free will offering at the end of our meeting followed by *mutual aid* when we can relax and talk more freely. Those of you who are new should hold your comments and questions until then. It takes four to eight weeks to learn the language and techniques of Relatives, so we ask you to listen for a while until you're ready to give an *example*."

Rea opens her black book to a section marked by a piece of paper and says, "We usually begin with a reading from Dr. Low's book, *Lectures to Relatives*. Those who have a book, please share it with a neighbor. It's available for purchase, but that isn't necessary. Many libraries have copies, or you may share a book at the meeting. After the reading, we have *examples* and *spotting* on examples," she says. Then, with a smile and a wink, she shakes her finger at us like a schoolmarm and adds, "Examples and spotting are the most important times, so pay attention." Some in the crowd respond with soft laughter.

Rea's smile remains as she slides her glasses down the bridge of her nose. She tilts her head upward and trains her eyes downward to focus through the trifocals that sparkle in the light. Though she has a casual grandmotherly appearance, I detect a highly disciplined woman. Before continuing, Rea brushes her hands across the open pages as if to clear them of interference. "Tonight we'll read from Chapter Thirteen, 'The Illusion of Superiority.' I'll begin on page one-eighty-six where we left off last week."

She reads two or three paragraphs aloud before passing the task to a person on her right. Others read and pass until five or six pages are read. Some people decide not to read and simply say, "Pass." Those who volunteer demonstrate varying degrees of reading ability, and it's clear that many education levels are represented at the meeting.

Then Rea closes her book and says, "I'll give the first example." She holds up a sheet of paper and looks down the row of chairs to where I'm sitting. My heart stops.

"Wilfred," she says to the man who's befriended me, "will you read the first paragraph of the example outline?"

"I'll be glad to," he says. The outline he uses is handwritten. "Paragraph one, state the facts about a particular situation—time, place, and what happened."

Rea tells us who her patient-relative is and gives a detailed account of a trivial incident that occurred in her home. Wilfred reads the outline's second paragraph, which asks Rea to report her response and describe her feelings, impulses, sensations, and thoughts. She does so in surprising detail. As directed in paragraph three, she tells how she *spotted her temper* and controlled or did not control it. In the last phase of the example, Rea tells us how she might've handled the situation prior to Relatives training.

Following that, Rea asks the group to *spot* on her example, and several people comment on what she reported. Usually, they speak of her in the third person, saying things like "Rea did this ..." or "Rea did that...." Often these comments highlight some *spotting* that the leader demonstrated, but didn't mention. Sometimes Rea—also speaking of herself in the third person—draws out a comment by asking, "John, did you see how Rea spotted that it was *distressing, but not dangerous?*"

Others report their own examples. As before, there is *spotting* from the audience. I'm amazed by the uniformity of the reports. The range of differences in reading skills that I heard earlier is not reflected in the quality of the examples or responses. People seem to be more equally skilled at telling anecdotal stories about incidents involving nervous patients. The method seems simple, but making it work looks difficult.

The leader explains that the phrases that are repeated are part of Relatives language and technique. Although many of the words are new to me, I'm familiar with some of them. Amy uses expressions like *temper blocks insight, outer environment, trivialities,* and others when she talks about Recovery. That's not surprising, since both organizations base their techniques on the work of Dr. Abraham Low.

My optimism grows as the meeting progresses. These people truly care about a loved one and are devoted to a discipline they believe. Maybe I'll finally understand Amy's new language and be able to help her get completely well. Driving home afterward, I recall only some of what was said, but the message of hope and its emotional lift is as powerful as any spiritual experience I've ever felt.

Every Tuesday I attend a Relatives meeting and usually feel uplifted, but not tonight. Amy is in setback and refuses my help, even though I've learned some of the same spotting techniques she uses. One night she got into that Drano crap again. I tried to guide her through some spotting, according to what I've read from Dr. Low's books. She got angry and told me to mind my own business—said she knew more about it than I did. I tried to explain that I could give her another point of view. She said I was *intellectualizing*. At the meeting tonight, I'm too angry to give an example or even join the camaraderie of *mutual aid*, so I try to skip out early.

I'm about to walk to the door when Wilfred hands me a cup of coffee and says, "Hi, Nick. Black, right? No cream, no sugar. Hey, you didn't give an example tonight. Things going good at home?"

"Don't I wish."

"Ohhh?" he says, echoing Rea's favorite neutral reply. "Don't lose heart. It's average for a beginner to struggle a bit. It takes time to learn the method."

"You know, I'm getting tired of hearing that. I thought I was doing well until ..."

"You don't have to do well to give an example. Mistakes are average, too."

"Yeah, well tonight I have too many screw-ups to sort out."

"Probably just like the rest of us. You know, most new people want to work on big links and try to solve the whole crisis at once rather than deal with trivialities that happen every day."

"Seems like there's a crisis *every minute* at my house."

"Want to tell me about it—about the example you thought about giving?"

I start to shake my head, but reluctantly reconsider. "Okay, I'll tell ya. Last week I talked to Amy about working the method *as a team*—Amy with Recovery and me with Relatives. Isn't that being *group minded*?"

Wilfred nods and then shakes his head from side to side. "Depends," he says. "It could be interpreted as *domination in the guise of service*."

I curl my lip and complain, "There you go again with that *domination* stuff. I was trying to help, not take over. Cripes, can't you guys give me some credit for that?"

"Nick, when we *endorse ourselves* we don't need outside endorsement."

"What if nothing turns out right?"

"We *endorse for the effort*, remember? Not the outcome."

"Yeah, yeah, I know."

Wilfred nods again and says, "Sounds like you have temper about this."

"No. No," I insist. "I really don't have any temper. I didn't get mad or raise my voice. I always try to understand Amy. I just wish she'd try to understand me."

"Maybe she thinks you mean *stand under* instead of understand."

"Huh?"

"Sorry, those aren't Dr. Low's words," says Wilfred. "My wife said that to me a long time ago."

"Know what Amy said? Said she's afraid I'll take her recovery away from her."

"And what did you say?"

"I said she doesn't make any sense."

"That's *angry temper*. You said she was wrong."

"But…. Listen, I might've thought I was right about that, but what's the alternative—to be wrong about everything? That's the way it feels."

"That's *fearful temper*."

"Yeah, and *temper blocks insight*, and *there's no right or wrong* in most quarrels. I'm sorry, but those doggone phrases are…." I take a sip of coffee and continue. "Okay, I admit it. I can't do this right."

"Stop trying to be right. Just be average. We all make mistakes."

"My life's a mistake."

"*Helplessness is not hopelessness.*"

"I can't do that like you. I can't think of every catch phrase I'm supposed to use."

"Nick, you don't have to. None of us is perfect. Me included."

"All right, all right," I say, swirling the tepid liquid in my coffee cup. "I guess I have to try harder."

"In your case, I don't think so. Maybe you need to back off."

"How can I do that when my wife is sick and my family's in turmoil?"

"Nick, you'll learn. That's what the method teaches us."

"That takes time. How do I know I have enough time to make things right?"

"You *know that you don't know*. And you aren't going to do it all by yourself. That's not *average*. Just *spot for yourself* and deal with your *inner environment*."

"Right, and I *can't control outer environment*. Well, what am I to do, give up?"

"Some stuff, yes, but you don't want to stop trying altogether. We have to let go of some things and concentrate harder on others."

"But, Wilfred, how do I decide what to stop and what to keep doing? One minute my wife's upset and wants me to take over completely. The next minute she says I don't trust her to do things by herself."

"Nick, your wife's a nervous patient. She's improved, but she's not completely well. It takes time. Believe me, I know. My wife and I have worked on this for years."

"What you're saying is … God, you mean things might always be like this?"

Wilfred searches my face before answering. "No, it can get better, but there will be *setbacks*. As time goes on, Amy probably will depend less and less on you. You'll learn to let her have her own self-leadership. Time will come when she's in a setback and you might not even know it."

"You mean she'll always have her symptoms? They'll never go away?"

"No one knows for sure. You have to concentrate on *your* symptoms, not hers."

I don't like what I hear and wonder if I should continue the conversation, but I ask, "So what you're saying goes for me, too? This tension that I feel—this anxiety about what she's going to do next—I have to live with it?"

"Nick, remember we can't control our feelings. What we learn here is how to cope with *feelings* and *sensations*. Feelings rise and fall. Sensations come and go. We can't change them, but we can change our *thoughts* and control our *impulses*."

"So I have to be on the alert all the time. That could last forever."

Wilfred looks first at his watch and then around the room. Other members are talking in small groups, too. A few toss curious expressions our way.

"Nick, I have to go. Come outside with me. We can talk more as we walk."

I peer into my coffee cup. It's nearly empty. "Yeah, sure." I gulp down the cold dregs and immediately regret it. Tossing the cup away angrily doesn't get rid of its bitter taste. We go up the stairs silently until Wilfred asks, "How are things at work?"

"Okay. You?"

"Good. I got that promotion I told you about."

"Hey, congratulations, Wilfred."

"Thanks. I'm in an office now. Same division. Just don't pass as much gas."

He winks, and I laugh. Wilfred is a meter installer for Consolidated Gas. He says the odor permeates his clothes and he has to explain it whenever meeting new people.

In the parking lot, Wilfred says, "Hey, how about them Tigers? The way they're going, we might have a pennant this year."

I love baseball. I'm usually ready to talk about the Tigers, but not tonight. Did he call me out here to fart around and talk about baseball?

"My car's over there," he says. He surveys the lot. No one's standing nearby. Catching my elbow, he draws us to a halt. Then he looks at me as if taking a reading from one of his meters. His eyes seemed brighter during the meeting—more hopeful. Maybe it's the darkness outside, but now Wilfred's eyes appear to sag as though they've gotten heavy. He leans closer and says, "Nick, I didn't say this downstairs because it wouldn't be right in a meeting."

"What is it? I haven't offended you, have I?"

"No. It's not that. I just want to talk to you without the Relative's lingo getting in the way. Is it okay if we talk off the cuff?"

"Sure, go ahead."

After a hesitation, Wilfred says, "I'm older than you, so maybe my experience means something. Maybe not. You be the judge."

"I think it does," I say. "Whenever you spot on examples, I always listen."

"I'm not spotting right now, and I might be crossing onto private property. If I do, tell me or just ignore me."

He pauses and waits for my response. When I don't say anything, he goes on. "You remind me of me a few years ago when I first came to the meetings. I have an idea of what you're going through, what it feels like. Nick, a lot of people face tense situations in their lives, but most of the time those situations come and go. What you're dealing with is constantly with you, twenty-four hours a day, day in and day out. There's so much going through your mind, it's like a blur—you can't get a clear picture of anything. Stuff is bothering you, but you don't know how to talk about it. You expect things to happen—bad things, and you're afraid. You're afraid of what you know will happen, and—worse—you worry about the unexpected, too."

"Yeah, that's how it feels. It was worse before Relatives. Now, at least, I'm learning how to talk about it."

"Did you know I used to be a police officer? Made it to sergeant but had to quit. Too much going on at home and I didn't like having a gun in the house. Sometimes I feel like I'm still a cop prowling a dark alley looking everywhere for possible danger, hoping nothing happens, but knowing I gotta be ready when it does. You know what I mean? It's when you worry about what might cause Amy to … to do whatever she does. You feel like it's your job to make sure nothing sets her off, so you keep your eye out for anything that might startle her."

His tone frightens me. "It's better now," I counter. "Relatives has helped a lot."

"When you come to meetings like this you dare to look ahead. You see a light and you think you're walking toward it. Only, sometimes, it feels like you can never reach the light. When that happens to a cop in an alley, he can turn around and go back the way he came, or he can speed up and get out of the alley. You can't. You're stuck there. On top of that, you have a little girl to take care of and protect."

"It's much worse for Amy. Her dark alley is inside her."

"Yes, it's worse for her, but I'm talking about you right now. Downstairs you asked if it ever goes away. I said it gets better. For some people it does."

"Amy and I are both working on this. Together we can beat it … can't we?"

"Nick, I've gone to meetings for eleven years—my wife for more than that. Take it from me; you have a tough job ahead. In the beginning, you tried to do everything to prevent your wife from having symptoms. She pretty much let you do *everything*—even begged you to take care of her. In a way, that time was easier because you had no choice. Now you've learned that you can't do it all, that there's only so much you can do."

"Yeah, I really have to work on that."

"She still needs help—and you have an *excessive sense of responsibility*—so you do what's necessary. In a way, it's a sickness for you, too. Relatives meetings aim at helping you deal with *your own symptoms*, not control hers. You still want to control everything. You tell yourself it's because you want to help, but it's really because you *want* to or feel you *must* be in control."

I scratch my head and say, "I'm not sure, but is that what *domination in the guise of service* means? Look, Wilfred, I'm not pretending. I really want to help."

"I know. But sometimes she says you're interfering. Other times she demands that you do more for her. You're not sure how to react."

"You got that right. She sends different signals, and most of the time I don't read them correctly. I guess I'm damned if I do and—"

"Damned if you don't. The sad part is that it might always be like that. If you're lucky, it gets better. Little by little, she'll be doing more for herself, and you won't need to be as cautious. That takes a lot of years.…"

"Years?"

"Uh-huh. Years and years. Meantime, you'll feel like you're being stretched one way and squeezed another. You won't know when to worry and when to relax. So you never relax. Sometimes you need to clear the path so Amy won't fall—get rid of the things that bring on her symptoms. What is it with Amy? Drano and cleansers? Other times she's angry because you don't trust her. Then you blame yourself, and feel guilty."

I frown. "It's like we're on a seesaw."

"That's exactly right. It goes up and down, just like your feelings."

"But, with both of us trying, we'll be able to do it, won't we? Amy works very hard at keeping her end up. So do I."

"My wife and I are the same way. We both work on our recovery."

"That's what I mean. Amy and I are doing it like you and your wife."

"Tell me, when Amy's down, what do you do?"

"I go to her. I try harder to help her."

"You huddle close together, right?"

"Yeah, but I try not to cling to her like I used to. I need to stop doing that."

"Good. Think about that seesaw. Ever try to keep a seesaw perfectly balanced? That's what you want from your marriage—balance. If Amy is on a seesaw and her side is down, how can you make her side of the seesaw come up?"

I visualize a playground teeter-totter and say, "I see what you're saying. If I move closer to her, she stays down. I have to back off—put more distance between her and me. Otherwise, she stays down."

"Yeah, and most people can't do that. They don't even try. They go up and down and up and down until someone gets off and stops trying to do the impossible. Nick, you might decide to get off before the trouble's more than you can handle."

"You mean leave Amy? Never! I could never leave her. I love her more than life itself. I'd rather die first."

"And leave your little girl with … who?"

"What?"

"Nick," he says, putting his hand on my arm. "I never believed I could leave my wife, either."

"You and Ellen?"

"We've been separated for more than a year now. I still love her, and we're still married, but we don't live together."

"But Wilfred, she's always in the examples you give."

"We see each other two or three times a week—have dinner together, maybe catch a movie. Saw *Bullitt* the other day. Great car chase with Steve McQueen. Ellen and I held each other tight all the way through the chase. It was nice."

"Jesus, Wilfred. I didn't know. I'm sorry."

"I do things around her apartment—help her with chores, pay her rent and such. She works when she can—when she's feeling up to it. That's not very often because she started drinking again and can't stop. We still try to work it out, still hope for a … for a miracle, I guess. At least we don't have any kids to worry about."

I'm in shock. God, I can't stand the thought of being separated from Amy.

"Don't get me wrong," he offers, "without Recovery and Relatives, things would be a lot worse. Maybe someone else can do better, but I keep trying."

He looks back over his shoulder. People are leaving the meeting and heading toward the parking lot. "Listen, I'm not telling you this to sour you on what you and Amy are trying to do. Other Recovery people do it and save their marriage. You hear about that in the meetings all the time, but what you don't hear also tells a story. There are folks who just get by and manage to *bear the discomfort*. They do whatever it takes to have a little peace in their house. You might do better. With hard work, I think you can. You have Recovery and Relatives, but I guess I'm warning you that you'll need more. You'll need luck and something else. God willing, you and Amy will find it and be all right."

CHAPTER TWENTY-SIX

*Without measureless and perpetual uncertainty
the drama of human life would be destroyed.*

—Winston Churchill

"Nicky, can I ask you a question?"

"Uh-huh."

We're sitting side-by-side on a glider on the front porch, enjoying the breezes of late spring. It's a lackadaisical Saturday morning—the kind I thought I'd never know again. Things are going so well, I felt like bragging at my last Relatives meeting, but toned it down when I saw Wilfred. His attendance reminded me how fragile my marriage might be.

Right now, though, the Sunday comics are on my mind. I love the funnies, especially the gags in strips like Blondie and Beetle Bailey. Real-life types like Rex Morgan and Mary Worth tend to turn me off.

"Nick, do you think God pays much attention to unimportant people like us?"

"Mmm hmm."

"Seriously, does God *care* or are we just novelties like characters in the funnies?"

I put my paper down. "What?"

"Do you think he watches out for us—like when I'm sick, for instance?"

"Of course he does. You know I believe in a loving God."

"Remember how we used to argue about predestination? You'd say God loves everyone, and I'd say he loves only the faithful."

"Some believe even the faithful won't go to heaven unless chosen by God."

"That's what I wonder. Does God watch over people he hasn't chosen?"

"That's a loaded question," I say. "I think God watches and *we* choose."

"Well, why does he let us have so much pain?"

"We don't *choose* pain. It just happens."

"Why does he let Jews suffer so much? Does God think they're bad people?"

"Anyone who thinks that is a bigot."

"If he cares about them—if he cares about *me*—why don't I feel it?"

"Sweetheart, I don't think God ignores you."

"Maybe he's teaching me a lesson ... or maybe I'm predestined to go to hell."

"Honey, why are you talking about this now?"

"Because I can," says Amy. "Because, for the first time in a long time, I can think about it without going into a panic."

"Well, you shouldn't dwell on that now. Don't get yourself ... you know ... downhearted and depressed about—"

"About what? About something *unimportant*? You always say God's important to you. He's important to me, too. I want to figure him out. I used to accept everything I learned in church. Now, I'm more like you. Don't I get to ask questions, too?"

"I'm sorry," I say. "I never meant to undermine your faith."

"I know that. Your doubts make your faith stronger. But doubt doesn't work for me. It makes me afraid that God will punish me for being unfaithful."

"Sweetheart, stop thinking so negatively about yourself. You're a good person."

"I don't always believe that," she says.

"Well, you should. Pay no attention to preachers who harp on the 'wages of sin.'"

"It's in the Bible."

"So are murder and incest. You have to put them in the proper context."

"I worry about Eleni. What did she do wrong to deserve a mother who got sick and abandoned her on her first two birthdays?"

"Honey, stop that. You did not abandon her. You're a good mother who loves Eleni very much. You have never intentionally harmed anyone. Don't get wound up in blame and guilt. You know how you are. You start kicking yourself and end up ..."

"I'm sorry. I didn't mean to scare you. I'm okay. Believe it or not, I'm really thinking *discursively* about this."

Amy uses Recovery terms like *discursive* in everyday talk. They're substitutes for words that convey wrongfulness and blame—words that I've used to criticize her, like *irrational*.

"I couldn't talk about this before," she says. "And you know what? It feels good to be able to do it without getting emotional. I thank Recovery for that."

"And I thank God for Recovery."

"Yeah, I thank *her* for that, too. I think *she* understands."

We laugh, but despite Amy's lighthearted quip, I worry that she's working herself up. Suddenly, the comics in my hand feel weighty, and the strips seem oddly complicated. Tightness grips my throat, warning me to think before I speak. What I say could trigger her symptoms. I close my eyes to change my thoughts, but imagine scenes of Amy in the throes of hysteria. It's happened before, and I feel compelled to prevent it.

Then I remember my Relatives training. I can change my thoughts by repeating a litany of phrases: *it's distressing but not dangerous; she's not wrong and I'm not wrong, we're average.* I try to spot *my excessive sense of responsibility* and *vanity of knowing better.* Slowly, a more secure outlook replaces my forecast of certain calamity, and I spot that I could decide to *allow Amy her self-leadership.*

"Nick, I want to go to church again."

I set the newspaper down and rock gently on the glider letting it sway us to and fro several times before I say, "Are you *sure?*"

Amy does a double take and then giggles. "We used to say that to each other all the time," she says, "and we'd both get upset. This time it hit me in a different way."

I'm sorry that she pointed out my slip, but pleasantly surprised by her reaction. In the past, *are you sure* questions conveyed my mistrust and her apprehension. Now she's laughing. I haven't heard her giggle like that in years.

"To tell the truth," she says, "I don't know if it's a good idea or not. I want to go to church again, but I want to try it without an every-week commitment."

"Okay, but let's try a new church."

"You've said that before. You must have a good reason. At Grandmont you got along with almost everybody—except Reverend Woodridge. I won't ask why. There are other churches."

"All right, then," I say. "Want to go tomorrow?"

"Ask me again in the morning. I might change my mind."

"Okay." I nod, both to agree and to shake off the *here we go again* warning I hear in my head. Then I endorse myself for not acting on my insecure thought.

Amy says, "One reason I want to go to church is to make new friends. You're the only one I can depend on—you and Recovery. And Relatives, too. I'm glad we have both groups. Otherwise, we'd be alone. No one else understands."

"It's not all their fault," I offer. "We haven't been candid about your illness."

"Ha," she grins. "Nobody wants to hear the details about your *bargain* bride."

I smile and follow her cue with, "Yeah, a *half-off* wife is nothing to brag about." The joke, like Amy's improved humor, is new and surprisingly well received.

"I'm thankful I have you, Nicky. Problem is you get *me* in the bargain."

"Babe," I sing, badly imitating Sonny Bono. "I got you, babe."

Amy laughs. "We'd never make it as Sonny and Cher, but we'll make it all right. We're starting to become a team, aren't we?"

"Just you and me, babe. And baby makes three."

"Yeah, just us," she says. "Maybe that's a bad thing. Sometimes I wish our families could be part of that team, but I can't see it ever happening."

Her sudden melancholy raises another caution. "Sweetheart," I say, "they care about us—our folks especially. They all try to help us in their own way."

"Kind of, I guess. At least they don't interfere—except for your mom."

"Amy, I wish you felt better about Mom. She's a tremendous help—taking care of Eleni and being here for you all the time. Don't forget that she steered us to Recovery."

"I know, but she doesn't understand Recovery. She takes over like you do—or did—before you went to Relatives. You're better, and so am I, but we still have a lot to learn. I'm afraid Mom won't change. She means well, but I wonder if she'll ever trust me."

"Honey, give her time. Maybe I shouldn't say this, but don't you think she remembers how you depended on her in the past? She needs to see the new you."

"I try to show her, but she sabotages me. I know she's a loving person, but she smothers me with her love. That's why it's so hard to confront her. I know; it's my fault, too. I accept part of the blame, but it doesn't matter who's at fault—her or me. Either way I get too many symptoms when I'm around her. I need to see her less often—maybe even stay away."

My impulse is to take her in my arms, challenge her *unreasonable* thoughts, and talk her out of her suspicion of Mom. But I've seen what she's talking about, so I resist the urge to take over. Instead, I slide a little farther away from her on the glider and say, "Honey, I wish I had an answer for you, but I think you have to deal with this in your own way. I'll be here if you think I can help you sort it out, but I trust you to handle it the best you can."

Amy starts to rise but hesitates and draws my hand across the space that I widened between us. I'm glad for another moment together. I like being with her like this, and I want it to last forever.

"Nick?"

"Huh?"

"Thanks."

"For what?"

"For moving over to give me room, but still staying by me."

I kiss her cheek and whisper, "There's nowhere else I'd rather be."

"Are you sure?"

"Hmm," I say. "That's a hard question. Ask me again tomorrow morning."

Amy takes a wild swing at me. I whack her on the head with the comics. She jumps up and gets into an exaggerated boxing pose. For several seconds, we stand toe to toe in a mock sparring match. All the while, I'm laughing at how she tucks her thumbs into her fists and fights like a girl.

Eleni, who is playing in her room, hears our laughter and comes out to join us. Amy looks down to avoid stepping on Eleni, and, while she's distracted, I grab Amy in a bear hug until she hollers, "Time out."

I let her go and turn away, but she takes my arm, spins me around, and gives me a kiss that puts me in orbit. It's a familiar ride, but one that I haven't been on in ages.

"Thanks," she says.

"For letting you win?"

"No—for treating me like a normal person again."

CHAPTER TWENTY-SEVEN

Of all the passions, fear weakens judgment most.

—**Cardinal de Retz**

At my next Relatives meeting, Helen *spots* on my example and says, "Nick is giving up *exceptionality* and is willing to accept his *averageness.* This allows him to *act securely* and show more *spontaneity.*"

"Yes," says Rae. "Can anyone tell us what Dr. Low said about *spontaneity*?" Rae isn't guessing what the psychiatrist might have said. She knew him well for many years.

"He said patients and relatives lose spontaneity," Wilfred explains, "because we interpret feelings insecurely and can't decide how to act on them."

"What happens to us?" asks Rea.

"We're in conflict," says Harriet. "We don't know which way to turn. So we second-guess ourselves and hesitate, sometimes stopping in the middle of our tracks."

"In his example," says Rea, "Nick's inclination was to laugh, but it was checked by an *insecure thought.* In the end, he allowed himself to act on the secure impulse and his laugh came easily. Spontaneity grows out of practice. We aren't always successful, but we need to endorse for the effort. And don't forget: *humor is our best friend.*"

I'm thankful for the group's insight because I hadn't thought about spontaneity as a healthy sign for me as well as for Amy, and I don't recall giving myself credit afterward. The feeling I get is akin to a pat on the back.

Someone is spotting on another example, and I tune in on the last part of her comment. "… and we're cautioned not to romanticize our efforts," she says.

"It's common for people in Relatives to be incurable romantics, isn't it?" says Rea. "Can someone tell us why we're instructed to avoid that?"

"Because it's a sign of *exceptionality*," says Mona, "which leads to high expectations. We're taught that *high expectations often lead to disappointments*; so we learn to *expect disappointments*."

Wait a minute. This is confusing. If I expect disappointment, how can I be spontaneous?

I ask Sylvia about it during mutual aid, and she gives me the same old *be patient* stuff and tells me to *aim to be average*. Then Wilfred chimes in and says I should always be prepared for a setback. Judas Priest, can't I ever stop worrying?

As I drive home, I wonder about the people at the meeting. Compared to most of them, I'm a novice. Some have attended for ten years or more. Amy was diagnosed about three years ago, but nearly a year has past since her last hospitalization. That's a long time to me, but Sylvia says it's average to wait much longer for full recovery. Shit, according to the meeting, it's average for a patient to be ill for more than ten years. If that's what it means to be average, I don't want it.

The traffic light at Greenfield and Six Mile Road is yellow. I speed up and go through the intersection anyway. Snapping on the radio, I'm disappointed to hear a DJ announce the song, "Up, Up, and Away" by the Fifth Dimension. I'd rather listen to a ballgame, but the first-place Tigers have the night off. The upbeat song gets my attention though, and soon I'm "riding high in a beautiful balloon." I feel like singing along, but have to listen closely to learn the words so I can join in when the chorus is repeated. It's been a long time since I've sung along with the tunes on the radio.

The next tune is familiar, but the words aren't. It's a Bobby Goldsboro song called "Honey." The lyrics seem melancholy. Maybe that's why I haven't paid attention before. Still, I like the folksy style of Goldsboro's melody. I listen more attentively as he sings the phrase *Christmas Eve two years ago* ... and recall Amy as my Christmas bride.

Goldsboro's sweet voice lures me to pay closer attention to his words. Soon I find myself voicing the words aloud but wonder why he sings about his love in the past tense. My heart skips when I hear him sing how he would often find Honey crying at home, and I turn up the volume to listen more carefully. A repeated refrain—his lament over missing her and the futility of wanting to be with her—frightens me. Words like *she went away* and *the angels came* and *memories of Honey* remind me of my fear of someday coming home and finding Amy dead.

My frenzied thoughts conjure images of Amy lying motionless, a victim of her own doing, and me lying in bed where *I wake up nights and call her name.*

Suddenly, I'm on the wrong side of the road, and a car heads straight toward me. I swerve and hit the brakes at the same time. My car does a near three-sixty, ending up in the middle of the road, perpendicular to traffic. My radio drowns from blaring horns of passing cars. I turn it off but can't shut down my terror. A blur of lights streak by as if drenched by a rainstorm. The downpour is not from the sky; my eyes are flooded with tears. I blot my face with my shirtsleeve. Some-one gets out of a car and runs toward me calling, "Are you all right?"

I turn the wheel and gun the engine, nearly running down the Good Samari-tan and not stopping until I turn into a darkened parking lot where I turn off my lights and weep like a baby. Caught without a handkerchief, I wipe my tears on my already dampened shirtsleeve. The prescient song plays again in my mind, warning me that Amy has taken her life and left Eleni and me alone. Sweet Jesus, I can't let that happen.

When I turn onto our street, I grip the wheel tightly, but can't stop my hands from shaking. My panic worsens as I approach our house and see mostly dark-ness. The only light comes from the attic, a dirty and unkempt place with exposed rafters—a place that Amy would dread. I accelerate into a barely visible driveway. Everything around me is black. Suddenly, I realize that I've driven without headlights. I jump out of the car and drop my keys. They hit my shoe and skid off in some unknown direction. "Goddamn it," I say in a loud whisper. Falling to my knees, I feel around like a blind man until I find the key ring. I race to the door and discover it unlocked. *Why would Amy ...?* I step through the doorway into darkness and rush to the bedroom; no one's in our room. I check Eleni's room and find her sound asleep. I notice the door to the attic is slightly ajar and light shows from the other side. Suddenly, I see the light dim and hear a gasp, "Oh!" that startles me.

"Amy!" I scream.

"I'm up here, Nicky," she calls from the attic. "What's wrong?"

I hear Eleni stir in her bedroom, but she doesn't cry out. Thank God she's such a good baby.

"Is Eleni all right?" calls Amy with alarm. I open the door just as she comes to the top of the attic stairs and calls again, "Is everything all right?"

The moment I see her, my knees buckle as if struck from behind. "Yes," I say. "Yes, we're okay. Are you? What're you doing up there? You know the front door's unlocked? There are no lights down here. Are you sure everything's all right?"

"Honey, I'm sorry. You weren't worried, were you?" She starts down the stairs. I leapfrog two steps at a time and meet her before she takes another step.

"Nick, I'm okay. What are you so upset about?"

I put my arms around her, and we nearly fall down the stairs. She catches me and pulls me toward her. "Honey," I say, "the house was dark; I didn't know what to think."

"Oh. Well, the sun was still out when I came up, and I didn't turn on any lights downstairs. I didn't mean to scare you."

"No, no, you didn't scare me. It was just that I ... I didn't know where you were."

"Nicky, I wanted to surprise you, not frighten you. Come here and let me show you." Amy takes my hand and leads me into the attic. Two bulbs dangle from the rafters. The nearest one is burned out. In the uneven light, the unfinished attic seems less dingy.

"That bulb just went out and scared the shit out of me," she says. "But there's electricity, and the floor's in good shape. See how the two-by-fours are lined up to make a wall that separates the room from crawl space. There's plenty of stand-up room."

"Yeah, I see that. So what are you getting at?"

"Wouldn't this make a great room? Another bedroom, for instance?"

"Well, I thought about that before, but...."

"I know. I used to be afraid, but that was before, and this is now," she says, handing me a tablet and showing me pages of sketches.

"What's this all about?" I say.

"Nothing yet. I just want you to know that I'm thinking about it."

"About what?"

"Another room, silly. We might want more privacy. Or have a bigger family. Do ya think you could fix up this attic and make it livable?"

"I'm not sure, but you know I've always wanted to be a weekend carpenter. Only ... well, what about you? Are you sure you're ready for all that fuss?"

"I'm not ready yet, but I'm thinking about it. It's fun to dream about doing stuff I never did before—stuff I've been afraid to do. Whadaya think?"

God, a minute ago I thought I'd find her dead. "Honey," I sigh, "I love you."

Amy looks quizzically and says, "I love you, too, Nicky."

We embrace and kiss. Suddenly, Amy jerks her head and crinkles her nose.

"Yuck," she says. "Your sleeve's all wet."

"Oh, I ... I had my arm out the window when it started to storm."

"It stormed? I didn't notice anything here."

"Uh ... I meant *rain*. It only lasted a minute. Some kind of a freak shower passed through. Probably didn't hit here."

Amy gazes wonderingly at me, and I see a light that sparkles brighter than I can remember. "A sudden downpour, huh? Well, that's a surprise."

Sheepishly, I say, "You know how it is. You never know what to expect."

CHAPTER TWENTY-EIGHT

Self-respect—the secure feeling that no one, as yet, is suspicious.

—**H. L. Mencken**

Summer has arrived, and Amy's talked herself into our remodeling project. I'm glad to see her positive outlook and don't mind driving nails while I teach driver training in the summer. Constant Recovery practice and a strong will help her manage the inevitable symptoms produced by the project, and it's a good thing she sets a priority on being *average* rather than exceptional because my divided time means the room will take a long time to finish.

Amy takes the Recovery edict to *make a business of her mental health* very seriously and strives for gradual improvements with deliberate systematic efforts. These painstaking steps slowly build her resistance to fears that still threaten to cripple her, and allow her to tackle routines by breaking down fearsome chores into minute movements that she can *endorse* for—a process that Recovery calls *part acts.* Within the practice, Amy finds strength in humor. "*Par tax,*" she says, "is a small price to pay to get myself back on par."

Recovery people are major characters in Amy's drama. She attends meetings and practices the method like a sentry on twenty-four-hour duty. Demonstrating her effort to get through a stressful period, Amy won over her Recovery leader and earned an invitation to begin training to be an assistant leader. She accepted the invitation and seized the opportunity to repay the group that has helped her so much.

Of course, I've benefited, too. In the past, I was unable to share many concerns with Amy because they were too threatening. Now I feel confident that she can contribute to their solution as long as I'm careful not to confront her with too many problems at once.

One matter I had put off was a review of my life insurance policy. When George Daniels, an insurance agent and trusted friend of my father, called with a proposal, I took a chance and agreed to see him. Despite the implied suggestion that I might die and leave her alone, Amy handled the discussion well and even considered a policy on her life while I purchased an increase in my coverage. She wavered only slightly when her application asked about recent hospitalizations. Boldly, she admitted to her mental illness and all but challenged George to reject her. He did not, but the insurance company did—not once, but twice.

George has just informed us that the company wants more than the endorsement of Amy's personal physician, and they've asked her to submit to examinations by their own medical doctor and psychiatrist. Even then, he said, it's unlikely that they'll insure Amy without certain "waivers."

George appears uneasy when he tries to smooth things over and says, "Mrs. Demetriou, they're well-respected professionals who can give us an objective evaluation. You can see them in our offices at your convenience."

Amy neither replies nor shows a discernable reaction. I've kept my eyes on her since George began addressing her as *Mrs.* rather than *Amy*, as he did when they first met. Though she appears remarkably calm, I sense a storm brewing in that pretty head of hers. Without looking my way for guidance, she answers him directly and firmly as if her statement was rehearsed.

"Mr. Daniels, when I was released from my psychiatrist's care, I was given a letter that, in so many words, said I was *sane*. Do you have one of those? Can *you* prove that you're sane? I can. Trent Gifford Hospital certifies it. That's good enough for me. I don't care if it's not good enough for you."

As George awkwardly apologizes and packs up his valise, I sense that Amy has something to say to me as well.

"Don't ever ask me to do that again," she says after the agent leaves. "Don't tell me what a good guy George is and what a wonderful company he works for. I won't allow myself to be humiliated. I've worked too hard to get where I am and won't let some stupid insurance company take it away from me. From now on, I will lie. When someone asks about my past—I don't care who it is—I won't say anything about psychiatrists. Shock treatment? What's that? I've never heard of it. What people don't know can't hurt me."

With her refusal to comply with the insurance company, Amy has issued her rejection of societal stigma. She is fighting back, not as a frightened girl, but as a woman with self-respect. Of late, I've begun to see the rebirth of the girl I fell in love with. Now I realize that I'm also seeing the woman she's becoming. She is doing more than simply regaining the spirit I found so adorable. This *new Amy*, like the one I was smitten with in high school, loves to play. The difference is that now she has the skill to play hardball.

I'm falling in love with her all over again.

CHAPTER TWENTY-NINE

If there are obstacles, the shortest line between two points may be the crooked one.

—Bertolt Brecht

Despite Amy's improvement, mood swings continue to plague her. Fortunately, they're neither as frequent nor as extreme, and her lows haven't led to complete collapse or helplessness. When she's down, she asks me to help with chores, but her requests are clearly a purposeful plan for her recovery. Consequently, I've become accustomed to her requests to change my routines. Sometimes I do the grocery shopping and laundry or stop doing whatever it is that bothers her until she's able to get back on track.

After hauling four-by-eight panels to the attic, I'm happy to oblige when Amy offers a paper cup of lemonade and suggests a break. I set down a roll of fiberglass on the front porch and sigh. Once I wire the attic, I'll stuff the insulation between the studs and nail the panels in place.

As I take the cup, Amy steps back cautiously. "You quitting for the day?" she says.

When she scrunches her shoulders and folds her arms tightly across her chest, I get a bad feeling. "Not yet, I need to haul up some Romex cable for the outlets. I'm using that instead of the armored BX cable 'cause it's easier to handle."

"Hmm," she says, clearly not interested. "Nick? Uh … do ya think you could stop for a while … take a break from the project?"

"Yeah, I guess I could stop for the day."

"I … I want you to stop for longer than a day. Maybe remodeling was a bad idea."

"What's wrong?"

"Don't ask me to explain."

"Umm … got any idea when I can get back to it?"

"Nick, I … don't think I can do this. I don't know if I can let you finish the job."

I try to act as if it doesn't matter, but I absently crush my cup before finishing and spill some lemonade on the porch floor. "O-kay," I say, ignoring the spill, "but is it all right if I store the stuff upstairs?"

"No, I don't want you to."

"I'm gonna have a hard time returning the electrical things. I've already opened the packages. Some of the wires and outlets are hooked up."

"Electrical is okay, but not fiberglass. I don't want it in the house."

"Can't I stick it in the attic? The door at the foot of the stairs is always closed."

"No! I can't have any of it in the house."

"What if I can't return it?"

"Then give it away. Or dump it. Don't argue with me. Just get it out of here."

"Sweetheart, I'm not arguing. I just don't see why—"

"Stop asking *why*."

"I'm sorry. I just want to understand."

"Understand what—that your wife is crazy? That she's an irrational nut."

"I didn't say that."

"You're thinking it. It's your favorite expression. *Amy, you're so irrational.*"

"I wish you'd give me some credit. I haven't said that for a long time."

"Maybe, but you've thought it. I know you have."

"You *know that you don't know*, remember?"

Amy's crossed arm grip on herself tightens, and she shudders as if struck by a sudden chill. "So now you're telling me how to use my Recovery," she says. "I don't need you for that. I don't need you for anything."

"The hell you don't."

"What?"

"Nothing. I didn't mean it. I'll do as you say. I'll get rid of the damn fiberglass."

"Nick, I don't want you to be mad at me."

"Mad at you? Ha! I'm not mad at you. I'm never mad at you."

She turns away. Her fingertips press deeply into the flesh of her upper arms.

"Sweetheart, I'm sorry," I say. Then I add, "I'm not angry," knowing damn well that I don't mean it. Then I start to second-guess myself. I can't hold her responsible for what she can't control. I shake my head slowly and say, "It's hard to know how to react to you. I don't know when to—"

"When to treat me like a normal person instead of a loony?"

"No. Damnit; stop putting words in my mouth."

"Maybe you'd like it if I wasn't here anymore."

Her words take me aback, but I step toward her and cautiously say, "Amy, don't say that. I promise to get rid of whatever upsets you."

"Maybe you should get rid of me. I hate myself when this happens."

"Nothing's happening. It's average to worry about some of these things. I need a break anyway. I'm tired. Driver's Ed is starting to drive me ... Hey, a few days off will do us both some good. I'll get the fiberglass outa here so you won't be bothered."

"Can you vacuum downstairs—and the porch, too? That pink stuff gets all over."

"Sure. I'll do whatever you say. Want me to throw my clothes away afterward?"

"Don't make fun of me! I feel bad enough as it is. Just throw out the vacuum bag—not just the insert, the outer bag, too."

"The entire bag?" I ask.

"Yes! Take it off outside, away from the house. And don't hate me for asking."

"Okay. Okay. Punkin, honest, I don't hate you. I will never hate you."

When she turns away, I clench my teeth and feel my lips form an ugly sneer.

Still turned away, she says, "You're always looking for explanations from *outer environment*. Stop trying to explain it. It's not that easy to pin down."

I sigh in resignation and say, "Is there something else you want me to do?"

"No, just what I said. I hate that you feel you have to ask that all the time. I know that I need to get through this my own way. All the doctors—including Dr. Low—say that a setback is *phasic*. It'll pass. I know it isn't easy for you, but we have our meetings to help us."

"How can you be sure it'll go away?" I say cautiously.

"It has in the past," she answers. "And it will again."

"You haven't had setbacks like this one," I say.

"Yes, I have. Lots of them."

"Why didn't you tell me?"

"Because I know how you are, and I didn't want to bother you."

"Well, maybe it's different this time," I say. "Honey, I'm worried that it'll get—"

Amy spins around and draws her fist up like a cornered fighter. "Don't say any more. I refuse to believe that I'll end up in the hospital again."

"Sweetie, I'm only saying that maybe you should see a doctor."

"No. I'll get over it without a damn doctor. They keep telling me, 'mental illness is a mystery,' but they talk to me as if I've committed a crime. Okay, I'm guilty. I *shouldn't* feel this way, but I do. So what am I supposed to do about it? Doctors have lots of questions but no answers."

"That's not completely true. You've gotten some answers."

"Yeah, mostly psychobabble. Like the guy who said I should tell my mother that I hate her. I tried it, remember? A lot a good that did."

"It's not always like that."

"No. Sometimes they dope me up and stick my head in an electric socket."

"Amy, I know you mistrust doctors, but we're smarter now. With a little effort, we can find a doctor you can respect."

"It's *their* respect for me that I need. I don't like being talked to like a child. For a long time, you did that, too. Don't start again."

"Honey, I understand, but please don't let this go too far. Remember, Recovery doesn't replace the physician. Promise me you'll see a doctor if it gets too bad."

"Look, I'm not an idiot. I won't be foolish. I'll see someone if I feel I need it, but you'd better believe that seeing a psychiatrist is up to me, not you or someone else."

"You know," I said, shaking my head, "sometimes you are your own worst enemy. You're just too damn stubborn."

She folds her arms across her chest again and hunches her shoulders defiantly. "It's lucky that I am," she says, "because that's what'll get me through this."

CHAPTER THIRTY

Comedy is medicine.

—**Trevor Griffiths**

Amy's progress of two-steps-forward-and-one-step-back is tough to deal with, but it's better than being stuck where we were a year ago. Within a couple of days after I halted the remodeling project, she asked for other changes to our routines. She explained the changes were part of her effort to find balance by eliminating situations that brought on her symptoms. Recovery, Inc., calls these situations *dynamic outer environment.* They include whatever she can't control by any means other than avoidance. Because of her fear of chemicals, she's eliminated contact with certain cleaning products, has made me switch to organics for yard care, and has become extra diligent about our intake of food additives. Amy also restricts her contact with friends and relatives she finds particularly troublesome. Oddly, this evasion doesn't apply to chance meetings away from home.

One activity I'm glad she hasn't stopped is her outings with Eleni to the mall. Weekly shopping trips have proven to be as therapeutic as any medicine. Early on, she had to plan every activity to avoid triggering her symptoms. Starting with short visits, outings soon extended to visiting the bakery for breakfast goodies, browsing through the mall, and lunching at Hudson's Café.

Each excursion has given her another measure of joy, and her reports about them have become standard fare at dinnertime. For me, the extent of animation and detail included in her review hints at how well she's doing. To Eleni's delight, Amy's tales have become more whimsical and entertaining with each passing week.

I look forward to the stories, and little Eleni gets twice the pleasure I get because she experiences the events firsthand and then relives them with me as we play audience to her mother's theatrics, which include exaggerated voice charac-terizations and funny faces. Tonight at dinner, Eleni urges her mom to tell about what happened on today's visit to the mall, and, as usual, Amy begins as if she's introducing a radio skit.

"Hudson's Café," says Amy, "is busy when Eleni and I get in line. The hostess tells us that we'll get faster service if we're willing to share a table with a stranger. That's pretty common at lunchtime, so we're prepared. When we get to the front of the line, Eleni spots a big woman wearing a feathered hat. She's eating alone at a table for four. *I wanna sit by that bird lady,* sez Eleni. *I don't know about her,* sez I. *She looks unhappy. I think her hat's on too tight.* We look around and see no other place to sit, so we scurry over like chipmunks to ask the fat-hat lady if we can sit with her. The woman has just taken a bite of her Waldorf salad and nods as though gesturing toward the empty chairs. I read it as a *Yes,* although it occurs to me that she might mean *No, go away.*

"*Hi, I'm Amy and this is my daughter, Eleni,* I say, showing off my best curtsy.

"The woman crunches a walnut and winces. I figure the nut must have hurt her teeth because she makes another face when she introduces herself as Mrs. Prendergast. *How do you do, little girl?* she says to Eleni, sounding every bit like Mrs. PrenderSnoot. *And how old are you?*

"Eleni looks up to me, and I give an approving wink. *Three,* she says in perfect English. *Almost four.* Good thing she didn't have to say *linoleum,* I say to myself."

(Eleni laughs at her mother's aside, knowing how she butchers the word.)

"*Oh, and you are so well mannered and speak so well for a three-year-old, says Mrs. Prendergoogoo, cocking her head like an old hen and adding to me, You know how terrible it is when children pronounce 'three' as 'free' and their mothers don't correct them? I believe a child should be corrected, especially when in public. Eating habits for example. Some children are disgusting when they eat at a restaurant.*

"Well, I get it right away," says Amy with an exaggerated accent. "I din't jes fall off a turned up truck, ya know. The woman's warning me to watch Eleni's p's and q's—and a, b, c's, too.

"Right on cue, Eleni opens the menu and sez, *I want spishgitti.*

"*You can have spishgitti,* I say, *but don't talk with your mouth open.*

"Mrs. Prendergosh flinches, but goes on prying into our business. She is clearly looking for gossip when she sez, *Tell me, Eleni, did you go to Sunday school yesterday?*

"When Eleni sez *No,* Prendergulp grunts, *Humph,* like a hippopotamusturd. I figured she was startled by Eleni's answer or she just swallowed a peppercorn."

(Eleni giggles and says, *Hip-potamust.*)

"*Well,* I said to the Hippotamust, *Eleni sat next to her father with the grownups. It's a new church, and she's a little shy with children she doesn't know.*

"*Oh, how wonderful,* says Frienderless. Her smile stretches her thin lips so that the wrinkles under her makeup show through, making her look like a prune dipped in powdered sugar. Then she sez, *I'm so glad you're church people. You can't always be certain nowadays, if you know what I mean.*

"The waitress comes by, but I need another minute to decide. I'm in the mood for something different. Meanwhile, Mrs. Prendergump leans forward and whispers, *I wasn't so sure at first, but now I'm glad you came to my table. I was sitting here alone and feeling very angry about what happened to me in the jewelry department downstairs.*

"*What happened?* I ask, imitating her whisper.

"The old battle-ax sits back again and says, *Oh, it was nothing really.*

"*You seem very upset about it,* I sez, coaxing her along. *You might feel better if you tell someone. I can keep a secret. I promise not to tell a soul.*

"*Me too,* sez Eleni, mimicking our whispers.

"*Oh, very well,* sez Pretendtogush, leaning forward again. *You seem the type I can confide in. And you're young. Perhaps my experience will be a lesson for you.*

"Rendergosip lowers her voice until it's barely audible. Now we're all leaning forward, and Eleni's eyes are Frisbees when she sez real loud, *Oh boy, a secret.*

"Prendertattle eyes Eleni and me suspiciously, but goes on. *You see,* she sez, *I was waiting for a clerk at the counter to show me a brooch I admired. I'd been waiting for quite some time but the girl was busy with another customer. I am <u>always</u> polite, you see. Suddenly, a gaudy woman with a crook-nose barged up to the counter and—at the top of her voice—demanded that the clerk attend to her. When she got no attention, she crowded to the counter and <u>pushed</u> me out of the way. The woman had the gall to look directly at me, fling her pink boa in my face, and announce, 'I'm next.'*

"*I'm sooooo sorry,* I say to Prendergoof. *I can see why you're angry.*

"*Yes, but don't you see?* Pretendtogasp sez, *I should've been wary. I knew there was trouble as soon as I saw what she was. It happens all the time with those people.*

"*Who?* I sez.

"*The Jews,* she hisses. *They're all like that. I could tell she was a Jewess the minute I saw her nose. The way she talked and behaved. Those people should be with their own kind. Especially shopping for jewelry. Jews own all the small jewelry stores. She need not be shopping at Hudson's. Mr. Hudson was a Christian man. I'm sure of it.*

"Just then the waitress returns. *Yes,* sez I. *My daughter will have <u>spishgitti</u>, chips, and chocolate milk. I'll have a lettuce and tomato sandwich and a Coke.*

"*You mean a bacon, lettuce, and tomato sandwich?* asks the waitress.

"*No,* I say. *Lettuce and tomato, only. No bacon.* Then I turn to Mrs. Prenderblast and say in a hissing whisper, *I can't eat ham or bacon, you see. I'm Jewish.*"

Eleni's part in episodes like this indicates the significance she plays in her mom's improvement. While I'm glad to see Amy's happiness, I wonder if the role of comforter was thrust on Eleni at too early an age. Amy has relied on the bond between them to bring peace into her chaotic world, and Eleni's importance to her mother might prove to be too great a burden. I'm hopeful that Eleni's role in Amy's crises will lessen as Amy gets better, but right now Eleni is a key player.

Mother and daughter clearly have fun together. They learn each other's likes and dislikes and share special moments, but their friendship goes beyond the ordinary parent-child relationship. Amy has said that she worries about Eleni taking on too much responsibility and vows there is nothing she wants more than for Eleni to grow up well adjusted. Though I envy the closeness of their relationship, I also wonder how our daughter deals with the emotional suggestion that it is her job to make her mom feel better.

CHAPTER THIRTY-ONE

Humor is emotional chaos remembered in tranquility.

—James Thurber

They say that time has a way of putting things into perspective, and my memory of the summer of 1969 might be a case in point because what happened that year has changed the course of our lives.

It started on an afternoon in May when I was puttering around the yard itching for school to end, and hoping this would be the first summer in three years that didn't focus on Amy's illness. Amy had complained of the cold weather and stayed inside, but just as I was about to go in, she called to me from the edge of the lawn.

"Hey, hotshot," she said. "What are you doing in just a T-shirt? It's cold and windy out here." She was wearing a winter coat and zipping it up higher as she stepped closer.

"No problem for me," I said. "I like it this way."

"Oh, that's right. Your furnace is always cooking. Whatcha thinking about?"

"Summer days without school. How 'bout you?"

"Going on vacation's on my mind," she said. "Someplace warm."

"Oh?" I said, a bit startled. "I thought we decided our DeSoto's too old for a trip."

"Yeah, well we're getting old, too. Now that I'm hitting on all cylinders, I think we oughta get some new wheels and live it up."

Though I suggested keeping the old car and taking a short trip close to home this year, I knew Amy wouldn't hear of it. She obviously came out to talk because she had something bigger in mind.

"One of these days," she said, "we're gonna buy a car, right? Why not now? Only, I think we should buy a van instead."

"A van? You mean a truck?"

"No, I mean a family van with seats up front and room in the back to stretch out."

"A van is a truck, seats or no seats. How about a station wagon instead?"

"A van would be better for a camping trip out West."

"Wait a second. A camping trip? What about the remodeling project?"

"I'm putting that on hold."

"Again? What is it this time?"

"Don't ask," she said.

"But, Amy, a camping trip? Where'd that idea come from?"

"Ever since we went west in sixty-four, we've wanted to go again. Why not now?"

"For one thing," I said, "I don't think we can afford a trip like that."

"We can if we go camping instead of moteling," she said with a smile.

"Uh … sweetheart, I've never gone camping. Have you?"

"No, but that makes it an adventure. We'll be like pioneers on a Conestoga wagon."

"Sounds like a slow trip. We'll be lucky to get as far as Iowa."

"Not if we take a month," she said.

"Whoa, Nelly. You forgetting something? I've got a summer job, remember?"

"You can work the last half," she said. "Six weeks of Driver's Ed is enough torture."

"But Eleni's too little, and you'll miss your Recovery meetings."

"Eleni's gonna be four, and we need a break from meetings. We'll take our books with us, so we'll have something to throw at each other if we can't work out a problem."

"Yeah, but Amy, let's face it … camping? You and dirt don't get along."

"I'm tired of being neat and tidy," she said. "I never wanted that. Tidy was my mother's idea, remember? I want to make a change and get the stink blown off."

"Amy, people can't change overnight—not something as basic as that. Are you sure you want to get into all that … dirt?"

"I think I can tolerate dirt. It's cleansers and chemicals I can't stand. I don't know what they use in motels, but I can control what's in our van and our own little campsite."

"Son of a pup," I said, shaking my head. "You're one surprise after another. I love you for it, but sometimes.…"

"I like to keep you guessing," she said. "You'll get over it someday."

"Gosh, I hope not," I said, giving her a hug. "Life would be too boring."

Three weeks later, after we bought a van, I was at the kitchen table mapping an itinerary when Amy put her hand on my shoulder and said, "You're working awfully hard organizing this trip. Need any help?"

"Yeah," I said, "how many hours can you stand sitting in the van?"

"I don't know," she said, "I never stand while I'm sitting."

"Very funny. Come on, you know what I mean."

"I can't think about it right now," she said.

"How about five or six hours?" I offered. "An early stop will give us time to enjoy the campsite."

The hesitation that followed, and then the tremor in her voice caught me off guard. "Nick, I've been thinking that maybe ..."

A second earlier she'd been joking, but her surprisingly fearful tone made me wince, and I answered with a sharp "What?" that gave away my own fear of *here-we-go-again*. Amy stepped back and folded her arms across her chest. Doubt darkened her eyes. I looked down at the maps spread on the table and saw her shadow dulling the highlighted line I'd drawn over Interstate 80.

"I'm not saying I will," she said, "but would you be mad if I changed my mind?"

I threw down my pencil and tore a hole in Wyoming. Amy tightened her arms around her chest and begged me not to be angry.

I remember picking up the pencil and spinning it horizontally at the ends of my fingers. Then I closed my eyes and counted the pencil's edges that I felt without seeing. It was my way of retreating to mathematical certainty to restore my confidence.

"Sweetheart," I pleaded, "what are you worried about? Here ... let me show you how carefully I've planned. You'll feel better if you see—"

"Nick," she interrupted. "I know how much you want to go."

"Yes, but you do, too, and I've worked out a way to help you do it."

"If we have to be so restricted," she said, "why bother going? Part of me wants to *kick out the jams* and be free, but I'm scared. What if I get afraid when we're in the middle of nowhere?"

I invited her to look at how I had listed roads to take, hours to drive, places to stop, food we'd need, storage space, even how we'd clean up, eat and use the toilet.

"What if I can't stay at those places?" she said. "What if I don't like camping?"

"Got that covered," I said. "I have reservations at motels near the camps. We'll keep them till the last minute. My idea is to give us options. We can be free as birds or be canaries in a motel room. And we can always turn around and come home."

"You'll hate me if I make you turn back."

What I hated was how I felt when she asked me *not* to do what we had already agreed to do. Nevertheless, I told her that it was all part of our adventure. "We can do all of it, some of it, or none of it," I said. "It's up to us according to how we feel."

Though Amy seemed comforted by my explanation, she remained hesitant. All of a sudden, she shook her fists above her head as if to free herself from an unseen snare, and said, "God, I want to do this. I want it so badly I can taste it."

Then, as if suggesting that I was the one holding us back, she declared, "What are we waiting for? Let's get our thumb out of our bum and our mind out of neutral. It's time we blew this popcorn stand."

Her quips were pet phrases she often invoked to give herself a kick in the ass and spur me to believe that she could do the impossible. I was skeptical, but hated to waste the time and money we'd already put into the trip. More importantly, I didn't want to waste the opportunity to take a chance that life might someday be normal again.

We left home the afternoon of my last school day with a plan to return in a month. Our resolve was tested on the first night when a rainstorm hit us just as we pitched our tent. That night I saw bats overhead, and in the morning, I awoke to see creepy-crawly insects covering the outside of the tent. My fear of bugs and bats made a curious mix with Amy's anxieties and Eleni's chronic carsickness. In Iowa, however, we proved our mettle for surviving the West when we overcame an upheaval not even Calamity Jane would've imagined.

We had three "rooms" in our camp. The van, where we slept, the outdoors, where we cooked and played, and a five-by-five umbrella tent that was barely tall enough to stand in and just wide enough to allow us to sit on our crude toilet, which was a simple folding stool with a potty seat, to which we attached a plastic bag to catch the droppings. The bag and its contents were disposed of after each use. Amy favored the inconvenience in order to avoid public toilets. She shunned portable flush toilets and pit outhouses because of chemicals used. The only chemical we used was Lysol spray. We set the tent on a heavy tarpaulin and lined the floor of the tent with another tarp. In addition, we put plastic sheeting on top of the inside tarp to catch spills and splashes. The toilet sat on the layered plastic, and we tossed out the top sheet when we broke camp.

One day, at our third campsite, Eleni was outside spooning dirt into an empty coffee can (her favorite pastime), I was in the van blowing up air mattresses, and Amy was on the potty inside the tent. We were in the middle of an Iowa plain, and the nearest camper was two hundred yards away. Suddenly, I heard Amy cry out, "Niiiick. Oh, Nick, come quick."

I ran to the tent and quickly learned that the toilet had caved in under Amy.

"Don't come in," she said.

"What happened? Are you hurt?" I said. Though I was concerned about the immediate problem, I was also worried about the hysterical fit that Amy was certain to have at any moment.

"No," she whimpered, "I don't think so. I sat on the potty and it collapsed."

"I'm coming in to help you."

"NO!" she screamed.

"Amy, don't be silly. I've seen your bare ass before."

"Not this way. The toilet wasn't empty."

"Oh, shit."

"You got that right."

"I don't care. I'm coming in."

"No, not yet! No sense contaminating both of us. Get some rags from the car … and all the paper toweling we got. And start hauling water, but leave the buckets outside the flap. Put some water to heat up on the gas stove … and on the campfire, too."

"Right," I said. Her rapid-fire directives suggested she was calm, but I asked, "Are you sure you're okay?"

"I'll tell you after I get cleaned up," she said. "Just do *exactly* what I say. No arguments. Whatever I tell you to throw away, do it. No questions asked. Pitch everything—my clothes, buckets, even the tent if I say so. Promise me!"

"I promise," I said.

"Good thing you put down some plastic," she said. "It might save the tent."

"I don't care about the tent, for God's sake. Just make sure you're all right."

"Let me do this my way," she said. "When I'm done in here, I'll come outside and wash again. Run two ropes from here to the van and hang sleeping bags and blankets so nobody can see me come out."

"Okay, but—"

"I'll take care of my *butt*," she said. "Just do what I ask."

I found it amazing that Amy had always insisted I take Eleni into public restrooms because she was afraid to use them herself, yet she handled the collapsed toilet with relative calmness.

We survived that event and more, including monsoon rains at Mount Rushmore, extraterrestrial thunder at Devil's Tower, Rocky Mountain fever at Estes Park, sand storms at Cheyenne, rockslides at Dinosaur Monument, lake-size mud puddles at Jackson Hole, and twelve inches of snow on July 2 at Yellowstone. Amy burned the soles off her moccasins on a campfire in Shoshone Forest, but couldn't melt the artificial cheese for grilled cheese sandwiches. Eleni cried when she saw Yogi Bear (whom she called "Loki") at Jelleystone Campground and cried again when she *didn't* see Smokey Bear in Yellowstone.

We traveled through eight states and unanimously picked Wyoming as most memorable after I earned the nickname *Sundance Kid* when I nearly choked to death inhaling a toast crumb in Sundance, Wyoming. In Gillette, I quit shaving and declared a new identity by starting a Buffalo Bill style mustache and goatee. Amy bought me a cowboy hat in Laramie and promptly flattened it when she accidentally sat on it.

At the Red Bandanna Café in Cody, Eleni was certain she spotted Buffalo Bill Cody in full Wild West regalia. I made the mistake of saying "that's impossible" and battled Amy when she agreed with Eleni. The matter was settled when Amy confronted the look-alike. Turned out that he was Cody's grandson, and he ran a dude ranch/river raft business. When Eleni asked him for a pony, she got a laugh and an invitation for the family to be his guest for a buckboard barbecue at his ranch.

Although I did most of the planning and many of the set-up chores, Amy was responsible for the spirit of fun and adventure in our trip. Before we started out, she decorated our new van with colorful stick-on flowers. The huge fluorescent dots of every imaginable color turned our '69 Dodge van into a real hippie-mobile. It was our home for thirty days, and we treated it as one of the family. We loved it so much that Amy and Eleni christened it "Fluto the Bus," naming it after Eleni's favorite dog, Pluto.

Fluto—as faithful as a puppy—quickly became our best friend. We slept in Fluto almost every night, crawling into sleeping bags laid on manually inflated air mattresses. While we drove, the reception on our radio was poor, so we carried on with our own sing-alongs, including our version of John Denver's *Rocky Mountain High*.

Although the broken toilet almost dis-assed her, Amy became the happiest camper of all, and our mobile lodging inspired her to make up a travel song about

Fluto. Every day we bounced along the highway with Fluto's windows rolled down and our voices turned up singing:

Fluto the Bus is our house in a rush, and he's very important to us. (BeepBeep)

We travel and we eat, and we even sleep in our own little Fluto the Bus. (Beep-Beep)

We're Nick, Amy, and Eleni, 'n we're all very zany in our own little Fluto the Bus. (BeepBeep)

So we travel along and we all sing our song 'bout our own little Fluto the Bus. (BeepBeep)

CHAPTER THIRTY-TWO

TRANSITIONS

A journey is like a marriage. The certain way to be wrong
is to think you can control it.

—John Steinbeck

Nearly six years have passed since our road trip in 1969, and I feel like we've finally arrived at a place called normal. Actually, the place is our new home in Thompsonville, a small town forty miles northwest of Detroit and an easy freeway drive to my suburban Detroit school. Its nearness, however, isn't the main reason we moved here in 1973. What drew us when we first explored the area was the town's independent character. What sold sold us was the sense of community we felt after we visited several times. Thompsonville is only about a mile long and a mile wide, but it's the county seat and has a distinctive center with a historic courthouse, Carnegie library, churches, and locally-owned businesses within a quarter-mile of the four-corner intersection at Main Street and Michigan Avenue. Our home on Main is only a half-mile away from, well, everything. From the very start, we felt a sense of belonging that made us feel like we had lived here for ages. For me, a standout feature of the town is the integrity of its general appearance, a quality that seems reflected in its people as well.

Amy and I started talking about moving to a small town while we were on our trip in '69 when auto travel stirred our spirit of adventure and gave us hope for the future. Responding to the freedom of the road, we took risks that proved our resistance was stronger than our vulnerability. We learned that, by controlling aspects of our routines, we could be less fearful of everyday life and allow ourselves to tackle challenging projects. (A short while after we got back, Amy gave her okay to finish the attic bedroom, which became a plus when we sold the home.) Other camping trips followed, and soon we purchased our second Fluto the Bus, a versatile VW camper-van.

Fluto II provided regular transportation as well as a nearly self-contained *house in a rush* for vacations. Its portable units included a sink with a pump-faucet, an icebox refrigerator, and a genuine Porta-Potti chemical toilet. The interior converted to two six-foot foldout beds—one extending to the rear of the van and one on the overhead pop-top. We also had an attachable ten-by-ten tent that could be divided into two sections with a tieback drape. The tent-van combo turned our campsite into a five-room cabin. We had everything we needed within the enclosure and could roam freely with less fear of unwanted elements. In this way, our travel arrangements mirrored our passage through life. We took risks by inventing ways to enjoy our adventure within limits that permitted retreat when Amy's needs demanded it.

Though I continued to accommodate her requests, my role in Amy's journey lessened with each new experience. When Eleni turned five, we went on a circle tour of Lake Superior, and Amy surprised us by insisting on a fourth passenger—a Dalmatian puppy. Never in my wildest dreams did I think that Amy would allow a dog into the family, let alone on a camping trip. When she first mentioned getting a dog, I dismissed it as an impulse sparked by the movie *One Hundred and One Dalmatians*, but she and Eleni adored the cartoon puppies and saw no reason why we shouldn't have one. Though I offered a hundred and one objections, they went ahead and chose the breeder's most energetic and mischievous pup, which Amy named *Daisy* after L'il Abner's *Daisy Mae*, whose black-dotted white blouse matched Daisy's perfect markings. Daisy was easy to love despite her penchant for trouble, like her habit of eating pebbles and other objects. On one ocassion she swallowed a live toad in one gulp. Though I began to feel like it was *my turn* for the loony bin, Amy merely laughed and enjoyed Daisy's antics.

One day, soon after that trip, Amy and I were relaxing on the porch when our conversation turned to love notes we used to write to one another, mushy ones addressed to *Pumpkin* and *Pookey and Minch*. I laughed and recalled that we had sometimes referred to Eleni as *Pumpkin-Pookey* when she was first born, but Amy had an earlier time on her mind. She was remembering a time before we were married when we spent an afternoon at the park writing and exchanging notes across a picnic table—notes that turned into wish lists for our future.

"You called 'em *dream catchers*," I said, "and I called 'em *Amy Wants* and *Nicky Wants* lists. I still have yours tucked in my drawer."

"Me, too," said Amy, "but it was a long time ago—long before I knew anything about life. I think I need a new one."

"What ... a new life?"

"No, silly, a new list ... but I'm working on a new life, too."

Though our conversation had been light up to that point, the exercise of writing lists became more meaningful as we put pen to paper. First, we wrote about our personal ambitions and hopes, and then Amy wrote what she believed I wanted, and I listed what I believed she wanted. Oddly, the list I made for myself was harder to write than the one I wrote for Amy. When we compared our lists, we laughed at how wrong we were about some things, and we sighed at how often we had written similar notions. Finally, we compared our notes with what we had written before we were married. Not surprisingly, our expressions as naïve lovebirds were quite different from those we wrote twelve years later. However, the most heartwarming thing about the old and new lists was their similarity in optimism for the future.

We refer to those lists from time to time, but one thing Amy said only once was that I had omitted mentioning her desire to lose weight. The truth was that I had avoided that issue because it made her angry. It still does, and part of her anger comes from her parents' criticism, which often takes the form of snide remarks about fat people. Nevertheless, I think the shame she feels about obesity is largely her own because she readily joins her parents in those comments. I stay away from the topic because I'm afraid my judgment might add to her self-condemnation and trigger another bout of who-knows-what.

Whether I say anything or not, I can't help noticing that Amy's weight goes up and down like stock exchange gains and losses. Her response has varied from accepting herself as pleasantly plump to joining diet fads that result in a greater loss of money than weight. The worst aspect of her ever changing diet, however, is the trouble caused to her digestion, though one incident might have been providential because it led to the diagnosis of something more serious. After trying an herbal diet, Amy complained of stomach distress and immediately stopped the program, but her discomfort continued. When the annoyance turned into pain that extended to her back, she consulted a doctor, who promptly insisted on removing her gallbladder.

Amy's emergency surgery took place on Eleni's first day of kindergarten, which was sad for them and worrisome for me. I was not only alarmed about Amy's operation, but worried about her emotional state as well. Nevertheless, she was brave and good-natured throughout the ordeal. With Amy's calm assurance, Eleni took her

Mom's absence on the first day of school without complaint—perhaps because she'd become accustomed to coping with angst surrounding her mother. Daisy pitched in by showing exceptional devotion to mother and daughter. While Amy was in the hospital, the frisky pup entertained Eleni with playful clowning. When Amy came home, Daisy seemed to sense her delicate condition and calmed down without losing any of her cheerful spirit. Amy improved quickly and made up for lost time by inviting Eleni's kindergarten class to walk the block-and-a-half from school to our house for a show-and-tell performance of Daisy running circles in the backyard.

Meanwhile, I was relieved when Amy regained her strength and began to resume household chores. Then, about a month after her surgery, I received a letter from Amy delivered to my school by the post office. I immediately tore it open, thinking it was one of her gags—maybe an invitation for a private evening. It wasn't that at all.

Dear Nick, the letter began. *I've been thinking about this since my surgery last month. With Eleni at school and me physically laid up, I had plenty of time to cogitate. It might seem strange to you, but I was glad to have physical problems instead of something else. I can tell you that being physically sick is a whole lot different from being mentally sick.*

This note might sound too dramatic, but I mean every word, and I'm writing it out so you can't interrupt me.

I'm sorry to have caused you so much pain and worry over the years. I love you more than I can ever say—you are the dream of my life. Without you, I'd have no chance to give to others and fully live. Now I want to give something to you. One of the things I want to accomplish is to fulfill your expectations and be the wife I should be. But I'm still hampered by too many fears. You and Recovery help me overcome many of those worries, but there's one in particular that I can't get over.

What I'm most afraid of is that you'll run out of patience and decide that you can no longer love someone who drains your strength and gives so little in return. I want to give you more, but I either don't know how or I lack the courage to do it. If I could learn new ways to live without being so scared, I could enjoy life, not just cope with it. I'd do anything for that.

Nick, you're doing all you can, too much, really, and maybe that's my fault. Up to now, I haven't done my part, so I've been thinking that I need to go somewhere to learn how to do what I don't know how to do. I've read about places I could go—retreats that teach you different ways to be a better person. I don't want to go away without you, but if I could come back and love you as I know I <u>want</u> <u>to</u> love you—I will go. I want to give my whole self to you, but right now I can't find myself *to give. I want to give you more babies and love them to pieces. Most of all, I want to find out who I really am.*

There was a time when I thought I was better off being dead, but I know now that I won't ever quit living—I can't, because I want to live for you and Eleni—and for the new babies I want us to make.

I know I have a lot to do before I can really live without fear, and I'm trying like hell to get there, but I hate it when I work so hard and get nowhere. When I look back at my life, I sometimes feel like that desert lily we read about ... the one that lies dormant for years and years before it blooms. Is that me? Have I been buried all these years? Do I dare expect to grow into something better? One of the programs I read about said they prepare you for the rest of your life. Nick, I have so much to do, and I keep asking myself if I will be there when my life begins.

Then I tell myself that, with your love and the help of God, I will! No matter what, I will make it.

And I will Forever be your loving wife, Amy.

I had put the letter in my briefcase at school, but stuck it in my shirt pocket before I got home, so that it showed when Amy greeted me. She frowned when she saw the envelope, but said nothing. I gave her a kiss and asked about Eleni. "Where's my little minch?" I said.

Amy seemed glad that I hadn't mentioned the letter and said, "She's taking a nap. You can peek in, but don't wake her up."

"Okay, I'll only be a minute. Got any coffee? I need a pick-me-up before dinner."

"How about herbal tea?" she offered. "I'm cutting back on caffeine. Would you like a snack? Gayelord Hauser says an apple with a little peanut butter is a good source of quick energy."

Hauser was her latest nutritionist guru, and I went along with some of his advice, particularly his enthusiasm for yogurt. I was raised on a diet that regularly included homemade yogurt, so I said, "Apple's okay, but I'll have yogurt instead of peanut butter."

When I returned to the kitchen, I saw my yogurt and a sliced apple on a plate. Some slices were dabbed with peanut butter, and a mouth watering scent of cinnamon-apple was in the air. "Mmm," I said, "did you bake an apple pie?"

"It's the tea," she said. "I thought it'd go well with our snack."

Amy's ability to engage in small talk was one of the signs of her health, and I hoped that her pleasantry signaled another good mood. Touching my hand to my shirt pocket, I said, "Got your letter today."

She sipped her tea and said, "Yeah, I see. I'm sorry. I shouldn't have sent it."

"No, I'm glad you did. I think it took courage ... only—"

"I know," she said before I finished. "The part about going away is confusing."

"Can we talk about it?"

"Maybe, but not right now."

"It sounds important. You can't expect me to ignore your note."

"I wrote it as much for me as for you. It's not a request; it's more of a promise to myself. I'm not very proud of what I've done with my life so far."

"Honey, you have nothing to feel guilty about. I know how hard you work."

Amy set down her teacup and looked into it as if searching for something. "You've done more for me than I deserve," she said.

"Stop that," I said. "None of it is your fault."

"That's not the point. I want to make it up to you ... and to me. I need to take charge of my life and make something of myself."

"You're already doing that. Give yourself credit for how much you've done."

"It doesn't seem like enough."

"Honey, you've improved a lot. It takes time to make those changes, but it'll all happen, and I'll be here no matter what. Believe me, I'm not going anywhere."

"I know you're not," she said. "But maybe *I* need to go someplace."

"Without me?"

"Maybe."

"Why do you say that?" My tone was angrier than I had wanted, so I added more gently, "Amy, I don't want you going away. What's behind all this?"

"I'm not sure," she said. "Not sure what I mean and not sure what I want either, but I have to figure it out without you. Don't worry; I won't leave you or do anything stupid. Maybe it's a girl thing ... a *woman* thing. I have to learn how to be the woman I should be."

I clenched my jaw to stop my thoughts from becoming words I'd regret. *How about being a wife and mother instead of focusing on yourself all the time?* I waited another moment before saying, "How can I stay out of it when you talk about going away? You can't draw lines and tell me not to cross them. I don't put a boundary around myself, and I don't put a limit on how much I love you."

"That's part of it," she said. "You're already too involved. You, your mother, your sister, my family ... everyone. All of you are part of what I have to sort out."

"Sweetheart, I know you feel judged by the family, but—"

"Look at me! I'm fat and unhealthy and...." She fingered an apple slice, picked it up and then set it back. "I need to unscramble my head without you holding my hand."

Then she scooped up the apple, popped it in her mouth, and licked a dab of peanut butter from her finger. I started to drum my fingers on the table—a habit of mine since I was a boy. I drummed slowly and arrhythmically, then rapidly until the sound resembled galloping horses, thundering hoofs like I used to hear on the radio—The Lone Ranger rides again.

I stopped drumming and without looking directly at Amy, I said, "All right. I don't know what's going on, but I guess I have to trust you." Then I looked up suddenly and said, "I do ... I *do* trust you." Our eyes met, and I reached for her hand before adding, "Just promise that you'll never go away from me—I mean, never *really* go away."

"Nicky," she said, caressing my hand, "that will never happen. I promise."

A year passed without Amy going anywhere, but I never quite put the matter out of my mind. Although I was comforted by her wish to improve, I was also apprehensive about her wish to do something different. Months before receiving her letter, I had enthusiastically endorsed her effort to become a Recovery leader because I saw how she had become a mentor to others. Indeed, her dedication inspired me so much that, soon thereafter, I began training as a leader for a Relatives group. Our groups meant a lot to us, and the comradery they gave us was worth the time and effort we spent with them. Even so, I saw that the security we gained from like-minded people was double-edged.

Amy was most at ease with those who understood her effort to get well, and she was increasingly sensitive to sabotage she felt from those who didn't understand. Unfortunately, she felt the harshest sting from our family, and therefore, began to separate herself from them. Though they were sometimes sympathetic, Amy felt that many people didn't respect her need to rely on Recovery practice. I tended to support her view because, in earlier days, I was unintentionally one of her saboteurs. Until Relatives, Inc., guided me to be a partner instead of a partisan, I was alienated from much of Amy's progress. Nevertheless, I felt some resentment when Amy insisted on distancing from our families. It was an accommodation I made to assure peace, but not without regret. To Amy, there was nothing more important than her mental health, and she was determined to protect it at all cost. Though I was glad for her victories, I sometimes wondered what I lost by trying so hard to please her.

Summer travel was both a getaway and a bonding experience for Ami, Eleni, and me. A few weeks away from the rest of the family provided a tonic that sometimes produced memorable moments. On June 29, 1971, we were in

Montana when twelve inches of snow fell, but that wasn't what made it a red-let-ter day.

The snow had forced us to take a room at Glacier National Park's MacDonald Lake Lodge, and we left Daisy to camp out in the van by herself. While we waited for the dining room to open, Amy modeled a reversible parka from the gift shop and asked if I liked it.

"Too expensive," I said. It also made her look fat, but I shut my mouth about that.

"Oh, please, Nicky," she said. "It's perfect for days like this. You don't want me to freeze my butt off, do you?"

"No, we've already spent way more than we budgeted," I said, avoiding an urge to say that freezing her butt off might be a good way to trim a few pounds.

"Come on, Daddy," Eleni said, "Mommy looks nice in the *parker*."

"The answer is no!" I said. "And that's final."

"Nicky, I'll do anything for you if you let me buy it."

"Listen, we're staying here an extra night and spending more money than—"

"Look," said Amy, holding out a wad of bills. "I've got money that I saved from the grocery budget. I can buy *you* something, too."

Amy had been doing the shopping for several months. Before that, she had been afraid of stores because she believed dangerous substances contaminated their shelves.

Six-year-old Eleni pulled a handful of pennies from her pocket and showed them to me. "Here, Daddy. I got seventy-forty cents."

Then Amy stretched her arm under my coat and rubbed my back. Nuzzling me, she cooed, "I said I'll give you *anything* you want, and I meant it."

I looked around the store and said, "There's nothing here that I want."

Stealthily, Amy slipped her hand under my belt and said, "Yeah? Well, there's something in *here* that *I* want."

"Hey, cut that out," I complained.

"Eleni, honey," she said, "go look at the teddy bears. I'll bet you can find a Smokey Bear if you look real hard."

"I don't want to."

"Yes, you do. Now go along and behave."

"I'm being haved," she said.

"Well, behave over by the stuffed animals. Daddy and I have some business to transact."

Eleni went off to the toy display, and I tried to wiggle away from Amy. "Sweetie," I said without a hint of sweetness, "you're wasting your time."

Not to be thwarted, Amy stretched her free hand up to my ear. With the tip of her icy finger, she began playing with the bottom edge of my earlobe, teasing it in that way that drove me crazy.

"Amy, stop that. We're in a public place."

"I don't care. I can't control myself. I've got cabin fever and can't resist a husky, hairy mountain man like you."

"Look, you're not playing fair."

She fluttered her eyes and said, "All's fair in love and sex, big boy."

Then she opened the huge leather bag she called a purse, dug around, and pulled out a plastic disk that contained her birth control pills. Clicking the box like Carmen's castanets, she whispered, "Tell you what. Let me buy this parka, and I'll toss these. Tonight, we can start making that son you've always wanted. How's that for—"

"Deal!" I said before she could add another word.

Another surprise snowstorm, this one in April of the following year, didn't chill the welcome we had for Timothy Nicholas's arrival to our family. I was delighted and only slightly amazed that Amy's promise came true. After all, surprises had always been her stock and trade. Still, her good health hadn't happened by chance; it was the result of her willful determination to overcome the emotional chaos she felt for so long. In a sense, Tim's birth came after a seven year labor—a span after Eleni's birth that demanded more of Amy than she had bargained for.

Despite Amy's happiness, Tim's start in life wasn't as pleasant as his sister's early months. When a pediatrician suspected that a painful malformed hip caused Tim's irritable moods, he prescribed a cumbersome brace for him to wear. The brace seemed to relieve some of his and our discomfort, but it made the rest of the family uncomfortable. Though Amy followed the doctor's instructions responsibly, she felt that others in the family saw her zeal as another of her obsessive compulsions.

When Tim developed chronic diarrhea, Amy stopped breast-feeding, but bottled milk worsened his stomach distress and moodiness. I began to think he was the type of child who was naturally cantankerous, but Amy thought differently and took him to another doctor. When he found no physical cause for Tim's problems, I privately told him about Amy's emotional history. After that, he dismissed her as an overanxious mother and implied that *she* was the cause of Tim's ill temper and resultant nervous stomach.

Amy was livid, but too focused on Timothy's health to challenge the doctor. Resolved to find a better answer, she sought other opinions, even as Tim's problems continued. His bowl movements emitted the foulest odors imaginable, making diaper changes nearly unbearable. Hospital tests for disease, toxicity, and parasites were inconclusive. Doctors looked at the clinical results and tried to assure us that nothing was seriously wrong with our son. Indeed, it seemed that everyone—doctors, nurses, and family members—spent more time trying to convince Amy that she was wrong than they did in finding what troubled Tim.

As a last resort, Amy called on a Dr. Giesh, a pediatrician with an office nearby who we later discovered was a distant cousin on Amy's side of the family. When family members learned of this, they admitted to have lost touch with him, but offered that his eccentric ways had made him a bit of a black sheep in the family. He was also a man well into his eighties. Neighbors who recommended him from experience, however, said he was an old-fashioned physician who believed in listening to mothers and trusting their intuition.

In Giesh's office, Amy and I apologized when six-month-old Tim, who was naked on the examination table, had an offensive bowl movement.

"Don't be silly," said the old doctor. "What better luck could you ask for than the chance to show me exactly what you're talking about?"

After examining the feces, he went to the door and called loudly to his nurse, "Doris, bring me that issue of the *New England Journal* that I was telling you about. I want to check something."

After flipping to the article he wanted, he scanned it and muttered *hmm* and *aha* at regular intervals. "I think I've got it," he said, handing the magazine to Amy. "Here, read this section and tell me what you think."

As Amy began to read the two paragraphs the doctor pointed out to her, her eyes widened. Then she smiled broadly and said, "It's the milk, isn't it?"

"Yep," says Giesh. "I think Tim's problem is lactose intolerance. His little body doesn't make enough lactase enzymes to digest milk products. A salesman came by a month or so ago and left a sample of a milk substitute you can try—soy, I think it is. Use it for a week. If it works, Tim's troubles are over."

When Dr. Giesh left the room to look for a case of the product he mentioned, we cheerfully attended to Tim. Amy's joy changed to anger, however, as she recalled the many delays that preceded our discovery.

"Those other frickin' doctors never listened to me," she said. "All they did was blame me for being overly worried. We should've had this settled long ago."

"Maybe you're right," I said. "That Dr. Janiki was especially rude even after I talked to him."

"You talked to him? What did you say?"

"Nothing much. I was upset about how he spoke to you, so I told him to lay off. I said you were sensitive to criticism."

"Meaning what?"

Uh-oh. I don't like where this is going. "I didn't go into detail," I said. "I just mentioned your ... uh ... history."

Amy was furious. "Why did you tell him that?"

More forcefully than I should have, I said, "Hey, I'm sorry. I didn't think he'd blame you. I thought he'd be more understanding."

"You don't get it, do you? No one in the family gets it. People—even so-called smart people—are prejudiced against anyone who's been to a psychiatrist."

"Amy, get over it. It's nineteen-seventy-two. Educated people don't think like that anymore."

"Tell that to Tom Eagleton. How long did he last as McGovern's running mate?"

She was right. In 1972, presidential candidate George McGovern picked Missouri Senator Thomas Eagleton to run with him for vice-president, but rescinded his choice after learning of Eagleton's earlier psychiatric problems.

Amy was relieved and proud that her persistence had paid off, yet she was not surprised when the family continued to second-guess her. They often questioned Tim's dairy-free diet and sometimes offered him ice cream behind Amy's back. In her mind, the rest of the family would always treat her as a potential mental patient. For her, the only solution was to move away.

Another problem that gnawed at our relationship was Amy's mistrust of my teenage sister, Anna. Though I hated choosing between my wife and my sister, I had to agree that Amy had good reason to be cautious. Anna's questionable habits began with childhood lying and led to pre-teen experimentation with suggestive makeup and provocative dress before moving on to marijuana and eventual addiction to hard drugs. To Amy, the worst part was that my parents denied the seriousness of Anna's actions until it was too late. Certain that her mental health and our children's safety were in jeopardy, Amy chose to move as far from danger as possible.

Our move to Thompsonville was a compromise after months of considering states like Wyoming and Colorado. For me, its nearness allowed me to teach at the same school and retain my salary level. For Amy, our new home was far enough from family to avoid their suspicion and criticism. Another plus was the availability of Recovery meetings at a nearby town where the first national president of Recovery, Inc., led a weekly meeting.

Just days before our July move-in day, Amy learned that she was pregnant. My immediate reaction was to worry about how she would respond to the anxiety of pregnancy when she had to deal with concerns about Tim and the uncertainty of moving into an unfamiliar town. However, Amy handled it all without a whimper—until, that is, the day she dropped the bombshell that we had to find Daisy another home. It was a change that nearly devastated Eleni and me.

I was hurt and angry. For all her talk about recognizing that *outer environment* was beyond her control, Amy conveyed a strong message that we should try—especially for matters that affected *her*. What that meant to me was that I couldn't show how I really felt, because I still had a responsibility to look out for her mental health.

Nevertheless, the ease of adapting to a new home in a new town and a new daughter named Erin six months later indicated that I was wrong. Soon, my optimism rekindled. Once I decided to view the changes as signals that we were starting fresh, I felt a new vitality. Today, I serve on a city commission, and Amy and I are active in the local church while continuing our volunteer work as Recovery and Relatives leaders. Above all, we've drawn closer to each other and to our children even as we've pulled away from the rest of our family.

Last weekend, Amy and Eleni took their usual Saturday walk to the library, while I stayed home with Tim and Erin. A couple of hours later, I watched them skip home the last few yards, despite the burden of armloads of books. They entered the house giggling noisily, and the first thing Eleni did was present a book she had selected for me. The joy I remember from those moments make me realize how far we've traveled to get here. Despite bumps in the road, I think we've finally moved on.

CHAPTER THIRTY-THREE

Merely innocent flirtation,
Not quite adultery, but adulteration.

—From *Don Juan* by Lord Byron

Karen's briefcase closes with a *thud*, and I look up just as she jerks her hand to her lips and says, "Ouch, this darn lid won't stay open."

Then she touches her tongue to a tiny red drop that oozes from the tip of her finger, licks away the spot, and holds her finger to her mouth while making soft sucking sounds. "One of these days that lid will chop off my hand," she says.

Karen Vessee is my partner teacher, and she's at my house to work on a school project. Our relationship is professional, but at this instant, I see her as a pretty young woman whose hurt feelings need attention. Embarrassed when Karen catches me eyeing her, I, nevertheless, enjoy the rush.

Twenty-three-year-old Karen started teaching two years ago as my student teacher. Now, I'm her department chairman and tenure coach/mentor. I take those jobs seriously and enjoy helping new teachers, though I'm sometimes forced to recommend dismissal. Karen, however, is a keeper. Though she works hard, she never loses that fresh and lively spirit that draws me toward her. When we first met, I thought she'd find me boring because I'm more than ten years older than she is, but she and I hit it off when we discovered that we shared similar interests in new teaching methods. As a result, we became partner-teachers for individualized math classes I had set up at the junior high. Our ambitious project requires frequent head-to-head conferences and after-school meetings that often keep me at school an extra hour or two. This week, we're working on plans to revamp the program, and when I told Amy that I'd be working later than usual, she insisted on inviting Karen for dinner so I could work at home. It's the first time they've met.

Though it's almost ten o'clock, we still have things to go over before calling it quits. I've retreated to my easy chair to review an outline of our plan, and Karen is standing across from me at the dining room table where several papers lay strewn about. Her finger is still at her mouth when she turns her back to me and reopens her briefcase with one hand to arrange folders inside. Undetected by her, I let my eyes wander over her body. Karen is especially fetching under the light of the dining room chandelier. The frosted streaks in her blond hair are aglow like corn silks in a morning light. Her tiny ears appear even more petite, and her large teardrop earrings wiggle with the slightest bob of her head. If I were single, Karen would be a sweet chick to date. Then I think about Amy and sigh. Amy's ears are still small, and so are her hands and feet, but the rest of her body doesn't begin to compare to Karen's slim figure.

Karen continues to nurse her finger as she tilts her head to peer into her briefcase, and I follow the line of a slender tendon that runs along her neck and curves away at her shoulder where it disappears under the scoop-neck sweater that hugs her body like a second skin. Though my thoughts warn me of danger, the same thoughts trigger another rush that stirs my imagination. I want to see Karen purse her lips again and, suddenly, want to risk detection, daring to admit I want her to know that I'm undressing her with my eyes.

She turns, and her smile evolves like predawn light haloing the horizon. The moment stretches beyond an instant, and I long to extend it. Her lips spread without parting; their cranberry hue, faded after a long day, is the color of new autumn leaves. When her lips part to show a hint of tongue, she says "What?" in a way that I'm afraid to answer.

"Thud!" shouts the briefcase lid as it suddenly slams shut again.

Then Amy's voice comes from the edge of our gaze. "Oh, leaving already?" she says.

Karen turns sharply and stammers, "Uh ...? Well ... I...." She glances at me and then at Amy. "No. Um ... I guess it's up to Nick. We got a lot done, but we still—"

"It's too bad you have to go," interrupts Amy. "You two have been *sooo* busy that you and I barely had a chance to get acquainted. Shall we try again? Next time bring a friend. Make it a night out."

"Yes," says Karen. "I ... that might be nice." She snaps the briefcase latch shut hurriedly, leaving her folders on the table. Quickly moving to the door, she fumbles with her coat, but I don't dare get up to help her. "Thank you," she says to no one in particular.

Closing the door behind Karen, Amy shoots dagger-eyes at me and in a throaty voice, says, "Don't ever do that again. Not in front of me or behind my back either. How often does *that* happen? And don't tell me this is the first time."

"What?"

"That's what I want to know," says Amy. "What do you do, meet her in the parking lot early in the morning? Or do you wait until she comes inside, so she can put on her act like she did tonight."

"Sweetheart, I'm—"

"She is so *sly*. Must have practiced for hours to perfect her *charming* expression. Thinks she's got it down pat, but she can't put one over on me. You were looking at her all night and had no idea what she was doing, but I saw through her the minute she came in the door."

"Honey...."

"Oh, *Nick*," says Amy, mocking Karen's voice and mannerisms. "'Oh, *Nick*, can you help me with this?' she says to you. How the hell does *she* get to purr *Nick* like that?"

"Jesus, what's ...?"

"Then at dinner, when she batted her eyes like Mata Hari and cooed, 'Oh, *Nick*, I forgot my briefcase outside in my car.'"

"Amy, what are you ...?"

"I'm trying to be a cordial host, but my mouth drops open at this phony *lady in distress*. *You*, my shy Prince Charming, drop everything, jump up, and volunteer to get her briefcase. Flash—you're out the door and back before I can close my mouth."

I'm at a loss for words, but it doesn't matter because Amy isn't listening when I plead, "But, honey, I—"

"Damn good thing you asked for her car keys," she sneers. "If you had them in your pocket, I'd have flung my knife into your groin."

Startled, I wonder if that was all that Amy saw.

She turns on her heel, stomps to the bedroom, and slams the door. Too stunned to follow, I try to calm myself by clearing the table, taking more time than necessary to avoid another confrontation. Still too rattled to go to Amy, I move the chairs aside and vacuum the dining room floor. The kids won't hear the noise because they're asleep upstairs, but Amy's nearby, and I want her to know that I'm tidying up. I know that it's *domination in the guise of service*—a Recovery and Relatives no-no—but I'm thinking that it might ward off Amy's anger.

After more procrastinating, I finally knock on the bedroom door and say from the outside, "Honey, I'm sorry. I didn't mean anything by it. I was trying to be a gentleman when I went for her briefcase. You wouldn't want me to be any different, would you?"

There's no response, so I try again. "Sweetie, can I open the door?"

"Go ahead, I don't care."

Amy is lying in bed with the covers pulled up high.

"Sweetie," I say, tasting sourness in my tone. "I'm sorry. I didn't mean anything by it. I was—"

"I heard you," she says, pulling the covers higher. My back stiffens as Amy goes on. "You tell me you're sorry, but I know you think I'm a bad wife. You think you're so good because you tolerate me and stay with me despite how horrible I am. What you really think is that *I* should be the one to apologize."

"For what?" I say, relieved that her tone seems less angry.

She answers by pulling the covers over her chin.

"Amy, I've never been unfaithful to you."

"I know you haven't," she whispers in a trembling voice. Then she turns on her side to face the wall away from me. For a long while, neither of us moves or speaks, but suddenly, she turns around again. Her face is barely out of the covers when she says, "You'd *better not* cheat on me. I don't believe in divorce. Murder, maybe—but never divorce." Her voice is harsh, but forced and theatrical, like Alice on *The Honeymooners*. For a moment, I wonder if she's over her anger and trying to be funny, but then I see a tear run down her cheek.

"Darling," I say moving toward her. "What's wrong?"

"Nothing," she says, scooting to the edge of the bed to stop me from sitting beside her. Dabbing her eyes with the coversheet, she pulls it almost over her head.

After a moment, I go to the closet to get ready for bed and notice that Amy's nightgown is still on the hook, but I wait until I slide under the sheet on my side of the bed before saying, "Amy, aren't you gonna put on your nightgown?"

"Don't worry, I'm not naked."

"Huh?"

"I put on pajamas so you wouldn't see my fat ugly body."

"Amy...."

"I know you hate me—hate the way I look."

It's an expression she uses whenever she feels threatened, and one I've grown to despise. What I want to say is *not half as much as you hate yourself.* Instead, I attempt to deny it with a feeble, "Don't say that. I don't hate you."

"Yes, you do," she snaps. "You said so. You said you didn't want to see me naked."

"I didn't say that. I said women—*you*—you look sexier with a suggestive gown than with a cheap thing that shows everything."

"Yeah, especially when you're fat like me."

"You're not fat. And you've never been ugly. I wish you'd get over that. It's not me who hates fat; it's you and your parents, remember? I love you the way you are right now. I wouldn't want to be with anyone else. Not in a million years."

"Nick, you're so naïve. Someday you'll admit you have impulses like everybody else. You're not Superman. A man can't control all his urges. It scares me that I haven't been all you've wanted me to be, but *you* scare me even more."

"What are you talking about?"

"Hiding your feelings from me is one thing. What's worse is hiding them from yourself. You deny it, but I can see it—and so can other women. Women like Karen pick up those vibes. You say you couldn't be attracted to anyone—not Karen or anyone else—but you know what? You set yourself up for a woman like her—someone who sees how vulnerable you are. Right now, I'm so fat and ugly, a Karen or any pair of boobs and a tight ass could take you away from me. You're so trusting you'd be in bed before you knew what was happening."

"Amy, I love you. I would never do anything like that. I swear I wouldn't. I hate it when you do that. Hate it when you accuse me of being like other men."

"You *are* like other men, only you don't admit it."

"Don't get started on that kick of ridiculing men and then lump me with the worst of them. I'm not an adulterous brute. If that's women's lib talking, then you read too damn many magazines. I'm not like that. I'm as loyal as they come. I will never leave you or betray you or do anything to harm you. I *have* not, and I *will* not."

"I know you haven't. Not yet, you haven't. I just hope you hold on a while longer. I want to be thinner. I'm working on it. You'll see. I'll be skinny again, and you'll be proud of me. You won't be ashamed to show me off to your friends."

I start to say that I'm never ashamed, but don't because I'm afraid my defense will prove that her accusation has hit home.

"If you left me," she goes on, "I'd get skinny right away—I know I would. Then it wouldn't matter, but I'd do it to spite you—to show you that I can do whatever I make up my mind to do."

"Sweetheart, let's stop fighting. I want you the way you are, not like when you were sick."

"Maybe I'm still sick; maybe I'm not. Not *as* sick is probably right, but I'm working on it. Nicky, I promise, someday I'll get it all together and won't have to worry about losing you to someone else. By then, I hope you'll still care."

CHAPTER THIRTY-FOUR

Teach me to feel another's woe,
To hide the fault I see;
That mercy I to others show,
That mercy show to me.

—Alexander Pope

On a gray morning in 1976, as my family and I watched my sister's coffin disappear into the ground, I felt the weight of competing emotions descend on us. Though the ceremony commemorated Anna's burial, nothing could bury the anger that so many of us felt. Anger, however, was never expressed. Only an overwhelming sadness poured from our hearts at graveside because we knew that the worst of our venom would eventually be aimed at ourselves.

The sealed, brass-handled casket contained more than just the body of my sister. It also hid the secrets of her troubled life and tragic death. She was twenty-one when she died in Los Angeles, where she had lived for about a year. The family had last seen her on her visit home during the Christmas holiday. At that time, Mom's excitement to have Anna at home had prevented her from acknowledging what the rest of us saw through Anna's veil of puffy, long-sleeved blouses and full-length skirts. Anna's thin, pasty appearance and needle-marked arms suggested that she still used the drugs that had separated her from the family for five years, and her words during overheard telephone calls indicated she was still involved with the wrong crowd. Our worst fears were confirmed three months later when LA police found Anna's body at a construction site. Uncounted wounds and fresh needle marks led police to investigate foul play. The coroner confirmed that she had been beaten, and shot up with enough heroin to kill ten of her street friends.

A few years before that, my parents' inability to deal with Anna's drug habits and repulsive friends had given us reason to move away, but I know that my estrangement began years earlier. Though I was always concerned about her rebellious behavior, I had claimed to be too busy caring for a daughter and ailing wife to do anything about it. The truth was that I also lacked the courage to get involved when Mom and Pop bickered about Anna. Amy was afraid of Anna's influence on Eleni, and we both worried that family turmoil would harm our children. When forced to choose between mother, father, sister, or wife, siding with Amy was no contest. At the time, I rationalized that I had no choice, but I wonder now if it was only an excuse to run away.

Amy and I have often quarreled about how to steer away from mistakes made by my parents in raising Anna. Our early disagreements shook our marriage and affected all our relationships, but it wasn't until our anger was spent in the process of bereavement that we finally realized the foolishness of blame.

Mom and Pop were good parents who had successfully reared my brother Gus and me. They had come to America as poor immigrants from Greece and carved out a life by adapting to new ways while blending traditional Orthodox values with patriotic American citizenship. When Gus and I were fourteen and thirteen, Anna was born amid optimism and high expectations. Mom and Pop nurtured her with the same loving care and offered the same instruction and guidance they'd offered Gus and me, but Anna came of age in the sixties, an era very different from our time in the fifties. Although I had judged them harshly before, I now know that Mom and Pop did the best they could, and didn't deserve the cruelty of events that led to their horrific loss.

Humbled by this crisis, Amy and I have become more accepting and willing to acknowledge that external circumstances shape people's lives despite the best efforts of those who love them. In addition to the Recovery maxim that *we can't control outer environment*, we often recall our need to *give up the fallacy of knowing better*. Tragic as it was, Anna's death has led us to greater insight into our faulty indictments against both sets of parents. In recognizing Mom and Pop's innocence in Anna's fate, I had to admit that I was also guilty of unfairly blaming Andy and Saundra for Amy's illness. Now, when I see how Saundra mitigates Andy's moods, I see myself doing the same with Amy. The difference is that Amy and I have guidance from Dr. Low's Recovery and Relatives techniques. Andy and Saundra do not.

The causes of human behavior are countless, however, and I know that exceptional effort alone cannot control the ultimate outcome of life. Anna's death has taught me to accept human nature as a mystery and reminds me that *there, but for the grace of God, go I*.

CHAPTER THIRTY-FIVE

A minute's success pays the failure of years.

—**Robert Browning**

Amy's at the sink scrubbing a pan with a brush and plain soap and water. Her preference for elbow grease over gritty cleansers is a reminder that some of her old symptoms still linger, though they're not as crushing as before. Four years after Anna's death, we've settled into a family life that I'm happy to call routine.

Most of our time revolves around the kids, but once a week Amy and I take turns preparing a romantic dinner exclusively for us. Enjoying each other and our children is our primary focus, and protecting our kids from undesired influence is next. We're involved at school, church, scouts, and an increasing number of unplanned activities. Our vacations have included trips to California, Kentucky, Ontario, and Up North, Michigan.

On the long drive to San Francisco, Amy entertained us with her animated *Nicky the Stunk* and *Fartsack Jones* stories, and they've become favorites of every trip. Even Eleni, who at fifteen has developed into a typical, sometimes-charming, sometimes-moody teen, demands to hear Amy's made-up tales. Eight-year-old Timothy has overcome his early frailty, and plays so enthusiastically that he's often rolling on the floor with laughter. Seven-year-old Erin seems content and amused by it all, and is a sweet reminder of the blessings of unexpected events. On a trip to Pigeon Forge, Tennessee, Amy and I bought three ceramic bears whose individual expressions reminded us of each child. Eleni's bear is most stately and appears to have everything under control. Tim's bear is laughing and rolling on its back. Erin's bear, the smallest, appears to be aloof and puzzled over what to do with her siblings.

Amy and I keep busy with non-family activities, too. I'm a vice-president in Relatives, Inc., and a deacon at church. And I'm considering a run for the Thompsonville City Council. I've also queried publishers with a book proposal based on my classroom teaching, though my hope is fading. Amy has even more to crow about. Despite elusive health problems (this time physical), she is active in the church and a member of the choir. In addition, she continues to lead a local Recovery meeting and has become the head of Recovery's Mid-Southeast Michigan Area, a volunteer position with administrative and financial duties as well as responsibility to train future leaders. Her success, reflected in many ways, includes increased attention to her appearance. Amy says she's happy to think of the Recovery post as her calling for now, but she has other plans—like getting a college degree for a career with real earning power.

Meanwhile, back at the sink, Amy rinses a pan and says, "Honey, did you see the mail I put on your desk?"

"Hmm?" I reply with feigned disinterest. I know the letter she's asking about, but I'm avoiding the rejection that I'm sure it contains. The company has already said no to an earlier query.

"Isn't there one from a publisher? So-and-so and Bacon, I think it was."

"Uh-huh," I say, picking up the newspaper I've already read.

"Well?" she says expectantly.

"Well, *what?*" I snap. "You don't even know the name of the company. Maybe it's not a publisher."

Amy wipes her hands and then faces me directly. "Well, I know it wasn't Eggs and Bacon," she says, "but it was *something* and Bacon. Come on, what's in the envelope?"

"I donno. Same ole same ole, I guess."

"You didn't read it yet?"

"No."

"Well, Mr. Fartsack Jones, don't you think you should at least open it?"

"What for? It's probably like the hundred other rejections I've already gotten."

"Eleni says one hundred and one is good luck."

I frown at her reference. Eleni has tons of *101 Dalmatians* mementos to go with pictures of Daisy—reminders of a dog she loved but lost. Odd that she thinks *a hundred and one* is good luck. To me, it suggests disappointment and proves my cynicism.

"Come on," says Amy. "Open it. I've got a feeling about this one."

What *I* have is a *God-awful feeling*—the one I get when I wish for something I can never have. Each rejection makes me more depressed; each one proves that writing a book is hopeless. I'll never have time to do it, anyway. I'm too busy taking care of shit that Amy can't handle. If I have a free moment, I feel guilty and worry about something I should be doing around the house. I was crazy to send those letters, and nuts to work so damn hard trying to be creative at school. Nobody appreciates it.

"Nicky, are you listening? I said I've got a really strong feeling about this letter."

"Take an antacid," I say. Amy chews Maalox like candy for a discomfort her doctor says is heartburn and she thinks is a heart attack.

"Nick, don't be like that. This could be it. I can feel it in my bones."

"You always have a gut feeling about something. I wish you'd quit it."

"If you don't open it, I will."

Amy's intuition is a quality I both scoff at and admire. Often, I enjoy her hunches but find it irritating when she brags about her accuracy. When she was ill, her intuition was prompted by paranoia. Lately, she's been consistently positive, a sign I'd like to take as an indication of her good health, but I'm afraid to believe it. Although she's doing well, I don't expect the sassy, shoot-from-the-hip girl I fell in love with will ever totally return.

"You're beginning to annoy me," I say. "I'll open the damn letter when I feel like it."

Amy makes a face and then steps away. My sneer is uglier, and I give her the finger when she walks outside to her garden. My irritation surprises me. Why am I so disagreeable? One more rejection won't kill me. After a while, I give in and go to my den to open the envelope. When I read the first line, I shout "YIP YIP YAPOO!" at the top of my lungs.

Eleni is the first to hear me. "Yip, yip, yapoo," she yells from her bedroom. Even without seeing her, I know she's dropped everything and is running to find out what's happening. *Yip, yip, yapoo* is the cheer she invented when we went camping back in '69. It has become a combination distress call, cheer, and summons for celebration. No matter how surprised we might be, no one is caught flatfooted when the alert is sounded. We all respond by echoing the call and rushing to whoever sent the signal.

Tim's "*Yip*" comes on the heels of Eleni's second "*yapoo*." Erin, who's usually content to watch our antics, runs in ahead of Tim. Though she has no idea why, she jumps up and down, timing each jump with a "*yip*" followed by a screeching "*yapoo*" that's loud enough for Amy to hear out in the backyard. She, too, runs into the house, *yip, yipping* all the way. When she gets to my desk, I slap the acceptance letter into her dirt-caked hands. Then, even before she reads all of it, she exclaims, "You're starting right away. No more driver training or summer jobs for you."

"Whoa, hold on," I say. "We need that money. This book will take a couple of years. There's no paycheck—only royalties after it's published. And the money doesn't start until printing expenses are paid."

"You take care of that, and I'll take care of the home expenses," she says. "I'm getting a job."

Taken aback, I cautiously say, "But you said...."

Amy has talked about working part-time before, but I've tried to discourage it. I'm still afraid that a job outside the home would be too much for her.

"Amy, wait a minute, just yesterday you were complaining about that stomach pain again. Are you sure you can handle it?"

"I can deal with a little indigestion," she says. "You think you're the only tough guy around here? Haven't you noticed? I do my share now. Just cause you're too stubborn to ask for help doesn't mean I can't give it. I'm gonna help you whether you ask for it or not, and I'll make damn sure you get to write your book. When it's published, I'm throwing a big party. I refuse to be sick for that."

It's true that the local doctor said her ache is only stomach distress, but habit tells me that Amy's old symptoms have a way of cropping up when least expected. "Amy," I say, "you can't ... I mean ... well ... there are things around the house—projects we talked about. How will they get done?"

"Got that covered. I'm starting the bathroom next week. Gonna wallpaper and paint, and I'm doing it myself. You shut up and sit down on that typewriter. This summer you have only one job—to write a book. The tables are turned, buster. From now until I say so, *I'm* taking care of *you*. Now, be a good boy and say *Yes, dear*."

I laugh and say, "Okay, but I'm confused. Do I sit *behind* the typewriter or *on* it?"

Amy punches me and says, "Don't make fun of my words. I mean what I mean, not what I say. Perch on the damn typewriter like a mother hen for all I care. Just write the frickin' book and don't worry about me. I want to do this, and if you don't let me I'll beat the shit outta ya."

"Whoa," I say. "I guess I can't say no. How can I resist such friendly persuasion?"

I reread the letter several times over the weekend and thought about all that needs done before I can start work on the book. The publishers, Allyn and Bacon, want it to be part of their series called "Guidebooks for Teachers," and I need to become acquainted with their style. Even before that, I'll need to agree to a contract that spells out the details of ownership and how they will pay my royalties.

As I leave for work on Monday morning, I spot something on the kitchen table—a bud vase I haven't seen before. Instead of a flower, the vase contains a rolled up sheet of Amy's notepaper that shows a flower etched on the script "A" of her stationary. *Oh great. Here we go again, another mysterious note from Amy.*

I pull the note from the vase and read:

Dear Nick,

Since I have no flowers to give you today, I offer this note to cheer you up and tell you how much I love you. It might be silly to write a note to your husband—but today I wanted you to really know how much you mean to me, and I don't think I could say this correctly face-to-face.

Nicky, a house means nothing without you in it. Money has no importance without your happiness. Day has no end without you coming home. And night has no softness without you being near. All that I treasure has greater value because I can share it with you.

I know that you, as a man and head of the family, feel that you must bear the greater burdens—but they're not yours to bear alone. Our Love binds all our troubles together just as it binds us together. It's time that I do my part, too. I claim my title as Helpmate with full knowledge of what it means. I do this now because for the first time in my life I truly believe that I can.

Nick, you have helped me so much, so often—including these last weeks with my small problems. And I know you have overlooked yours to come to my aid. Please let me in to help you with yours. I want you to know that NO MATTER WHAT HAPPENS IN THE FUTURE—WE CAN DEAL WITH IT. The love of our tightly knit family can beat any problem you try to solve alone. You are not alone. Together, we will take care of worries about your job, money, school, book, and life in general. As long as we're together, we can't be beat. Please know that I'm here to help.

When I was ill, you had the weight of the world on your shoulders. Move over, Love, and let me carry my share.

So these words are my "love gift"—so seldom spoken, but always here whenever you need them. Never fear, my love, we are together—and that's enough to make all the difference in the world.

All my love——Always and Forever and a Day,

Amy

CHAPTER THIRTY-SIX

She has walked through an invisible screen
Into the fire of every change.

—**Peter Porter**

On the morning before Memorial Day in 1979, Amy shook me awake and said, "Nick, did you hear that noise last night?"

When I blinked my eyes and looked at the bedside clock, I discovered it was only six a.m. It was too early to be up, but Amy was wide-awake when she added, "I hardly slept a wink. As soon as I dozed off, I woke up again. After a while I couldn't sleep at all."

I sat up beside her, and, through a yawn, said, "Was it that humming sound?"

"Not 'was,' *is*," she said. "It's still going on right now. A hum with a beat. It pulsates, and there's a regular pattern. If you listen carefully, I'm sure you can hear it."

"Um, hush for a second, and let me see."

The little town of Thompsonville was usually quiet on a holiday weekend. Most of the businesses closed, including the Patriots Insurance offices across the street. When we bought our house, we wondered why the two-story office building was in the middle of a residential area, but we learned later that being the town's biggest employer allowed them certain privileges. They had been good neighbors until a few weeks earlier when plans for expansion had intruded on us.

"Yeah," I said. "I hear it. HMMMmmmmm. HMMMmmmmm HMMMmmmmm. You're right. It *is* annoying."

"It hurts my ears," said Amy. "There's something about that sound that's different. I tried all night but couldn't ignore it, even with a pillow over my head."

"Now that you've called it to my attention," I said, "I see what you mean. During the night, I was vaguely aware of some annoyance, but thought it was worry about getting Aunt Gertrude settled." Gertrude West is Amy's elderly aunt who moved next door so that we could look after her.

Amy sat up and said, "You're not saying it isn't there, are you? You don't think I'm making it up?"

"Heck, no. I hear it too. Might not bother me as much as you, but I hear it."

"Well, I hope it stops soon."

Her complaint was one among many that started soon after Patriots began construction. That morning, I believed our concerns were legitimate and could be remedied by talking to one of the Patriots executives I knew. The president and several other officers attended the same church as Amy and I, and I thought that church people would be especially cooperative with a family who shared the same faith. On the other hand, I also wondered if my activism in the community would be a detriment. As president of a citizens group that supported restrictions on new and old businesses, I was considered a thorn in Patriots' side. Amy warned me that the company might suspect I had political ambitions and wanted to advance a personal agenda. I shrugged off her caveat, but was concerned about her fearful reaction. I didn't want her to have a setback because of a simple problem I could easily solve.

Company President Vernon Castle was Timothy's Sunday school teacher, so I asked him about the noise while enjoying a cup of coffee in the fellowship hall that morning. He said he'd look into the situation. We quickly learned that the noise came from air-conditioning units on the roof, hardly a hundred yards from our house and directly facing us. The units kept data processors cool and dry, and the condensers had to stay on twenty-four hours a day, every day of the year.

Our polite request that the company muffle the noise was met with ambivalence. Initial calls resulted in ambiguous messages that implied our request was frivolous. When people ignored our subsequent calls, we realized that the company wouldn't cooperate. Meanwhile, Amy's anxiety increased as the annoyance continued, and so did my worry about her emotional state. My suggestion that we put the house up for sale only compounded her discomfort. She countered that we loved our century-old house and had invested a lot of money in remodeling. She also pointed out that we had convinced Aunt Gertrude to move next door by promising her and the rest of the family that we'd remain near so we could watch over her.

What started as a simple concern had turned into an adversarial deadlock. Patriots believed we wanted a victory that would result in driving the business out of town. The company made the bizarre accusation after I had won a city council election, though I never mentioned the issue during my campaign. Perhaps the owners were miffed because I had defeated incumbent Otto Stroegger, an executive attorney at Patriots, who had been on the council for eight years. For my part, I left our complaint out of the council chambers and pursued a solution through personal persuasion rather than coercion.

Even after Patriots refused our offer to help pay for necessary changes, I still believed we could prevail *if only the owners understood the problem*. So we hired acoustical engineer Hank Thurston from Grand Rapids to prove our case with scientific evidence. Patriots responded by spending more money to fight us than they would have spent had they installed the quieter condensers that Thurston had recommended. We could only conclude that they preferred to stall us until we quit in exhaustion. Our strategy had backfired, and we had placed ourselves in a Catch 22 situation because our own data showed that the noise was so damaging that we'd have to sell our home at a loss if we chose to move away.

Amy was beside herself and suggested that we camp out in the country until the problem was fixed. Though she appeared rational and controlled in other ways, I wondered if her reaction was a warning that excessive fears had resurfaced. To ease our stress as the problem dragged on, we shared our dispute with those we thought were sympathetic. Our families, however, showed little compassion and responded as if we were acting on another of Amy's phobias. Only a small circle of friends seemed to care. We soon became *persona non grata* among many because we had challenged the town's largest revenue producer. Even at church, people turned away from us, and the minister was evasive.

Reverend Tyson Smith had been pastor of Highlands Presbyterian for nearly twenty-five years. On his twentieth anniversary, I helped organize a tribute to him and was master of ceremonies at a dinner in his honor. Ty was a friendly guy, and he and I got along well. Because he was especially chummy with people from Patriots, I asked him to speak to someone on our behalf.

"You don't need to take sides," I said. "Just tell them you trust Amy and me and believe we're telling the truth. They seem to think we have ulterior motives."

Reluctantly, Ty sent Patriots a friendly letter vouching for our good intentions, no more and no less. The following Sunday, I saw Ty in the church hallway schmoozing with several people, a ritual he conducted regularly before getting down to the serious business of sermonizing. Ty's back was to me as I walked toward the group where everyone was laughing. *The Rev* loved to entertain with jokes and long-winded stories, so I thought it was a good time to talk to him. As I neared the group, those facing me lost their smile, and one of the men caught Ty's attention to warn him of my approach.

Ty turned to me, then to the others, and back again to me as if he were following a tennis match. His crimson befuddlement alerted me and warned the others to disperse into the throng of parishioners, leaving the two of us spotlighted in the hallway.

"Oh, Nick, you … uh … surprised me," he stammered. "I … didn't expect you."

A bead of sweat formed on his upper lip as he forced a smile and said, "Listen, I have to get ready for the service."

"Ty," I said as he stepped quickly down the hall, "can I walk with you? I want to ask you about the—"

"You better get into church," he said, walking faster. "It's late."

When I tried to catch up, he stopped and said, "No, don't come with me."

We were at the deacon's door, which led to the wrong side of the altar. Ty's eyes darted up and down the hall and then to the far door, the one reserved for him to enter the sanctuary. Surprisingly, he opened the deacon's door, grabbed my arm, and pulled me into the stairwell. The door closed from behind, leaving us in the dark.

"Nick," he whispered. "I wash my hands of this whole thing."

"What?"

"You're on your own. You have to understand. Patriots' people are big contributors here. I can't do anything to jeopardize that."

"Ty, I—"

"Don't. I don't want to hear any more. The less I know the better."

Then Reverend Smith scurried up the short flight of stairs toward the dimly lit sanctuary, his black robe masking his disappearance as he blended into the shadows.

During church service, I held Amy's hand so tight that she gave me an angry look, but she must have seen something in my eyes because her icy stare melted almost at once. Then she searched my face with an expression that asked, "What is it?"

No one paid us attention when we left in the middle of the opening prayer. Presbyterians are good at pretending that nothing's amiss.

At home, Amy wrung her hands and moaned that everyone would know about the neighborhood noise problem and we'd never be able to sell our house. Nevertheless, we felt we had to finish what we had started, so, the following week, we hired Dennis Cantrell, a highly respected local attorney to represent us. Our hopes fell again, however, after the attorney met with company representatives and reported astonishment at their cavalier stance.

With fees for Hank and retainers for Dennis, our expenses mounted, but we paid our advocates as we went along and decided that we'd quit our fight when we ran out of money rather than ask them to work with only a promise of what might come.

While the company dragged its feet, we spent thousands of dollars insulating our house with sound-deadening foam material and installing triple pane windows to block the noise. Because I was still working on my book, our only supplemental income was Amy's minimum wage salary as secretary at the local cancer society. Things got so bad that we ate oatmeal for dinner two and three times a week, got haircuts at the local beauty college, and bought some of our clothes at the Salvation Army Thrift Store.

I felt like a bolt that got started in the wrong hole. I had forced myself to go on because my direction seemed right and the end seemed so near. Backing off meant stripping our power and leaving us vulnerable. Either way we were screwed.

After a year of fruitless negotiations, we decided to file suit. As we prepared to go to court, I was griped with fear that Amy's emotional scars would open under the attack of courtroom cross-examination. Then, during a pretrial conference in his office, Dennis, our attorney, asked Amy if there was anything he should know about her past that the opposition might use to discredit her.

Amy and I looked at each other with eyes that asked if we should say something about her hospitalization. Then I turned back to Dennis and said, "Like what?"

"Well, suppose they ask—"

Amy interrupted. "I was hospitalized twice for a nervous breakdown."

Though he already knew of Amy's illness and her volunteer work in Recovery, Inc., our attorney was unaware of the specifics. Nevertheless, he seemed unaffected by her sudden disclosure.

"Fourteen years ago," Amy went on, "I was treated for depression and obsessive-compulsive behavior with medication and shock therapy. What do you think they'll make of that?"

With a nonjudgmental expression, Dennis said, "Shock treatments are ...?"

Amy laughed. "Jolts of electricity to the brain. That's why my hair's curly."

Dennis chuckled but remained serious. "That's clever," he said, "but it won't work in court. Answer truthfully, but don't try to be cute. You should be prepared to answer a question about your mental health. I don't think they'll go that way unless they're backed into a corner and afraid of losing. If they do, I'll counter with examples of your volunteer work." Dennis gave us an encouraging smile and went on. "You need to tell me all about your work, especially at Recovery, Inc., so I can show them how healthy you are right now."

We arrive for the hearing at Circuit Court on September 17, 1980, fifteen months after we first complained. The Patriots attorney is a high-powered barrister from Bloomfield Hills named Wendell Phillips, a hired gun and former circuit judge brought in from the outside to lead the cast that includes Otto Stroegger, the man I defeated for the city council seat. Judge Clarance Drexler presided. Before his election to the bench, Drexler was chief corporate attorney for Patriots Insurance Company.

Hank Thurston is first to testify for us. With convincing charts and graphs, he tells about readings he took from various locations both in and out of our home. As suggested by our attorney, he's careful not to report readings taken on Patriots' property. Although Patriots gave Hank permission to take those readings, there is no written proof of that permission. Nonetheless, that data might come out later when Dennis cross-examines the insurance company's acoustical consultants.

The most important part of Hank's testimony is that the problem we're experiencing is due not so much to the decibel level or loudness of the noise, but to the quality of the tone. Initially phrasing his testimony in scientific language and elaborate substantiation of his findings, Hank ends with commonsense examples.

"It's a *pure tone*," he says. "The ring of your telephone is a *pure tone*. So is an alarm or a siren. All are impossible to ignore. The phone company designs the bell so you feel compelled to answer it. The loudness is not as important as the fact that the tone is pure. The repeated drone of the condenser units is a pure tone. It has the same irritating affect on the Demetriou household as a repeated ring of a telephone or blare of a siren."

The judge gives equal time to the acoustical company hired by Patriots, and Dennis expertly shows that their testimony supports our position.

As I take the stand, I feel confident that we're doing well, and Dennis guides me in presenting evidence of how we've been injured monetarily and emotionally by the sound emanating from the air condition condensers. Upon cross-examination, I feel a surge of confidence and continue to answer without faltering, but then Otto Stroegger throws me a curve.

"Isn't it true," he says, "that, in your consumer's guidebook, you wrote about how the IRS allows a tax deduction for home improvements that are related to energy conservation?"

A bit bewildered, I say, "Uh ... it's actually a math book." Then I suddenly realize where he's going, and I add, "But, yes, I wrote about it because it's an opportunity to save money on taxes."

As I watch Stroegger shape a *gotcha* smile, I sit back in the witness chair, waiting to give my next answer as a cat might wait for a mouse. "I submit, Mr. Demetriou," he says, "that you replaced the windows and insulated your home in order to get a tax write-off—NOT to stop any alleged noise problem. Isn't that true? Please answer yes or no."

"No, absolutely not."

"Absolutely? Be certain of your answer now. Remember you are under oath. Did you take a tax credit for window replacement and insulation—a credit you brag about in your book and exhort because it yields such a grand saving?"

"No, sir, I did not."

"Wha …?" Stroegger clears his throat and walks back to the defendant's table where he shuffles some papers, apparently pretending to have proof that I lied. "Are you sure of your answer? Perhaps you've forgotten. Be careful, you are under—"

"I did not take a tax deduction nor claim a tax credit for the cost of replacing windows or insulating my home. And I do not intend to do so."

"Ah. I see. You refused it in order to win your case against Patriots Insurance."

"No, sir, I did not."

"Come now," he laughs. "Why else would you refuse a credit or deduction?"

"Because I already took the allowable lifetime maximum the year before when I replaced my furnace with a new energy efficient model," I say with self-assurance. "By law, I can't take any more deductions,"

Then, in a moment of bluster, I add, "I try to make it a point to obey the law."

The attorney looks toward his colleagues at the Patriots table. Though I recognize no visible signal, I imagine one of them drawing a finger quickly across his throat because Stroegger says, "No further questions."

Dennis must feel the same leap of elation that I feel because he seems eager to strike one more crushing blow to Patriots. He jumps to his feet and says, "Mr. Demetriou, tell us in your own words what you feel *emotionally* when you hear that sound—that pure tone from atop the Patriots building across the street from your home."

Before I answer, I look toward Amy and see her not as the poised woman she is now, but as the frightened girl she had been and could easily become again. Suddenly, my bravado is gone, and fear strikes me. I look away from my attorney and stall to think, but the air of expectancy in the court is too urgent to ignore.

"I.... It … it sounds like a … like a B-29 flying overhead," I say. "I … can't sleep. None of us can. My wife, she … no one can concentrate. It's impossible. I worry ... what it might do to us ... might do to my ... my family. I worry about Amy ... that she'll...."

Thank God, I'm crying too hard to be understood—sobbing so much that I can hardly breathe. I cannot go on, so I stop—or Dennis—or the judge stops me.

I could alibi that my pathetic response was triggered by the way Dennis couched the question, or because I had let my guard down, but I know better. I broke down on the witness stand because I realized that we were winning, and Patriots, with their back against the wall, would attack Amy when she testified next. Patriots will strike hard with all they have. Amy will be vulnerable to their merciless questioning about her unstable past, and I'm too broken up to ask Dennis not to put Amy on the stand.

Before I know it, she's up there in her salmon-colored blouse and wearing the gray-lilac suit she bought special for this day. She looks so pretty—all dolled up but still so businesslike. Her color is back. Her face glows bright. Her eyes sparkle. And I love her hair. It's cut short again, the way I like it. It's been years, but Amy's hair is vibrant again. Like it was before. And I can see its reddish glow showing in the sunlight coming through the window. How long has she looked like this? Where have I been that I haven't seen her?

Oh God, she's already answering a question. I haven't heard what Dennis has asked, but Amy has started talking. I want to shout, but the same fright that urges my shout strikes me dumb. As she speaks, I try to get her attention so that I might guide her and help her as I've always done. *Amy! Wait. Let Dennis lead you through the hard spots. Be careful. They're sitting back now, but they're preparing for the strike, like sharks stalking their prey. Amy, they're losing. They're desperate. They'll do anything to discredit you. I've already proven that I'm not okay. Were they surprised? Maybe. But they know about you, and they know how to get to you. Dennis, please stop. Get her off the stand. Make up something—you know the tricks. Don't let them attack my Amy.*

Incredibly, Amy is as placid and unruffled as the Queen Mother on a Sunday stroll. Dennis looks pleased as he struts across the courtroom like Sir Laurence Olivier across a stage, and Amy is so poised that he extends his questioning well beyond the three minutes he had suggested in his office. When he finishes, he walks back to the table and winks at me before he sits down.

Wendell Phillips starts in on Amy without a preliminary soft glove gesture.

"Mrs. Demetriou," he says with the haughtiness of Police Inspector Javert, "how do you feel today after not sleeping for fifteen months?"

The judge sustains Dennis's objection, but Amy has already calmly answered, "Oh, I'm a little tired." A smile spreads across her face and, suddenly, I realize that Amy is ready. It's as though she has worked for fifteen years to get to this point where she will show everyone that she can stand up for herself.

Phillips counters by rephrasing Dennis's question to me. "Mrs. Demetriou, tell the court how a woman *in your condition* feels when hearing the alleged noise."

Dennis is on his feet objecting before Phillips finishes his sentence, but Otto Stroegger is up, too. He whispers something into Phillip's ear and then asks the judge for permission to approach the bench. All three attorneys stand looking up to the judge like schoolboys asking for a teacher's favor. I can barely hear them. Stroegger is saying something about the company's president needing to be somewhere. He's already two hours late. Could he give his testimony now so as not to further disrupt his schedule?

The judge excuses Amy but tells her she'll still be under oath when she returns to the stand.

He then calls Vernon Castle, president of Patriots, to the stand. The judge apologizes for keeping him and expresses hope that the rest of his day will be unencumbered by nuisances. Whether the judge's tone is fraternal or patronizing is unclear to me.

I'm too jittery to understand all that President Castle says, but as his testimony continues, I sense that he finds the whole matter to be a bothersome bore. Like a racehorse eager to burst from the gate and run the race he's certain he'll win, his tail is up, and he slaps at Dennis's questions as if swatting at flies.

"What is the bulk of the business conducted at Patriots Insurance?" asks Dennis.

"We handle the majority of the Workman's Compensation Claims in Michigan."

"Can you tell me the exact dollar amount of the transactions carried out by Patriots on a day when those checks are printed by your data processing machines?"

Castle's grin could make a Cheshire cat cringe. A dark spot appears between his upper front teeth. Is it a gap or something left behind from breakfast? "I wouldn't know," he says. "I don't pay attention to those matters. Millions. Tens of millions. Perhaps more."

"The condenser units referred to in this grievance—is it their function to maintain temperature and humidity for data processing machines that print those checks?"

"That's what I'm told, yes."

"What would it cost to install quieter units, like those advocated by Mr. Thurston?"

"Who?"

"Mr. Hank Thurston. He's the acoustical engineer who gave today's first testimony."

"Oh, yes."

"Well, sir," says Dennis, "what is your answer?"

"I'm sorry. I forgot the question."

"What would it cost to replace the condensers on roof with quieter ones, like those advocated by Mr. Thurston?"

"I have no idea. The gentlemen at the far table could answer that better than I."

"Oh, but surely you have some notion, don't you?"

"Well, yes and no."

"Let me ask the question this way. How does the cost of those condenser replacements compare to the cost of a single day's business at Patriots Insurance?"

Castle smiles. The gap reappears. "It's a pittance," he says. "A mere pittance."

Unexpectedly, Judge Drexler raps his gavel and motions the attorneys to the bench. A few words that I can't hear are exchanged, and then Castle is quickly whisked away. Then the judge calls the attorneys into his chambers. Exhausted, I manage a feeble apology to Amy for losing my composure on the stand. Suddenly, Dennis returns from the judge's chamber and cuffs me on the back.

"You both did a fine job," he says. "It's over. It's all over except for the details. I'll meet with them in a week or two to iron out the final settlement."

"I knew it," says Amy. "What happened in there?"

"At first, I didn't know what to make of it," says Dennis. "The judge practically grabbed Otto by the ear when he took him aside. I couldn't hear it all, but he said something like, *Otto, you'd better settle this right now. If it goes to full trial, you're going to lose a bundle. Today, these folks want only their expenses. If you deny them, I might persuade them to go for the jackpot. Settle with Dennis, and pay the man his due.*"

Though the consent judgment was not entered until May 4, 1981, Amy and I are satisfied. Patriots agreed to replace the units with quieter ones, and the entire process from selection to final installation is subject to review and approval by our attorney and engineer. We have also received an anonymous letter that we suspect came from a dear friend who just retired as the private secretary to a Patriots vice-president. The letter is a copy of a claim sent by Patriots to a company that insured them for construction failure and liability. In it, Patriots used Hank

Thurston's data to substantiate their demand for reimbursement by their insurer for the cost of the newly installed condensers.

Most gratifying to us is the line that reads, "We, in good faith, believe that the demands made by the Plaintiffs are reasonable."

CHAPTER THIRTY-SEVEN

The purpose of life is to live it, to taste experience to the utmost, to reach out eagerly and without fear for newer and richer experience.

—Eleanor Roosevelt

After finishing a chapter of *The Screwtape Letters*, I pause for a moment before starting a crossword puzzle I selected from the pile next to me. Amy has a stack of library books at her feet, but she's reading her own well-worn copy of *Claudia and David*. The kids are in their rooms, and we're taking advantage of their unusually quiet behavior.

We're at our cottage a hundred and thirty miles from Thompsonville. After paying what we owed in engineer and attorney fees, ten thousand dollars was left over from the settlement. That money was like cashing in on forced savings because it represented what we had already spent, so we used it for a down payment on peace and quiet.

The three-hour drive to the cottage is short enough for a quick trip, but far enough to provide the seclusion we want. Although it's primarily a summer retreat, the small bungalow has a furnace and fireplace for winter comfort as well. However, we have no television or telephone and rarely turn on a radio, but that's by design. Scarcity of people, things, and demands helps us see what's really essential: our love, our children, our loyalty to each other, and our strength against adversity. Most of all, the Spartan lifestyle gives us more of what we can't buy or save for the future—*time*.

Amy sighs and says, "Holy shit, I've been sitting for hours without worrying about anything. I feel like jumping up and shouting *hallelujah*."

"Hmm," I say, glancing at my puzzle. "Good word, but it doesn't fit."

"Hey, I'm serious. I think we should be thankful."

"I'll say *Amen* if you don't say *Praise the Lord*."

"Why? Afraid I'll turn into a zealot?" She pronounces it *zee-lot*.

"Y'might, if you keep watching *The 700 Club*. I'm glad there's no TV up here."

"*The700 Club*'s not so bad. Sometimes I like the way they make right and wrong so black and white. 'Course, there are other times when they make me really mad."

"Yeahhh …? Like when?"

"You know *when*. I hate when they imply that all you have to do is believe and everything will be all right. I tried like hell to believe—I thought I *did* believe. It did me no good. Maybe I didn't do it right—didn't pray right and have enough faith."

"That's nonsense. Your doubts came *after* you got sick. They didn't cause it."

"I'm never sure about that. Maybe I should've believed more. I'm glad I'm better now, but I still don't like having doubts. I don't want to be sick again."

"God doesn't punish a skeptic. Even Jesus had doubts."

"Uh-huh. Look what happened to him."

"That's not why he was crucified."

"Sez you."

"Me and C. S. Lewis. Read *Mere Christianity* again. He explains it … sorta."

"Well, I still don't want people—God, especially—to think that I don't believe."

"Is that why you memorize Bible verses?" I say.

"You memorize them, too," she says. "What are you, a hypocrite?"

During our dispute over the noisy air conditioners, we turned to prayer and Bible study for spiritual strength. When some of our regular church friends shunned us, we found new ones and joined a more conservative church. I'm still uneasy with some Bible thumpers and wonder why I go along with them—and why they tolerate me, as well.

"The difference," I say, "is that I admit I'm a skeptic."

"You're so proud of it and act like it's a good thing. Not me. I'm afraid of doubt."

I frown and say, "I know. I'm sorry I bother you with my arguments."

"Oh, it's all right. You sound kind of sexy when you get that professorial tone."

"Oh, yeah? Well, the kids don't like it. They say I sound like a teacher."

"'Cuz you explain too much. That's why I needle you when you get preachy. Anyway, I decided it's okay for you to be wrong."

"Thanks … I think … but why won't you let yourself be wrong?"

"God might punish me and make me ill again. Maybe he's like that."

"Vengeful? I doubt it."

"Ha! You say *doubt* when you disagree, and use it just to win an argument."

"No, I also doubt some things that I agree with. It means that I don't know for sure. Sometimes I take a leap of faith anyway."

"How can *doubting* be a leap of *faith*?"

"Because I believe the *process* of my search is part of my faith."

"I don't like that. How can you be sure you're doing what God wants? Didn't I get well because you—and I—had faith? And isn't that why we beat Patriots?"

"Payback isn't a sign of righteousness. There are believers at Patriots, too."

"What if it hadn't turned out as it did? Would you have given up on God?"

"If my faith depended on things turning out, I wouldn't believe in God at all."

"Yeah, even that kosher guy doesn't know why bad things happen to good people."

"*Kushner*," I say, correcting the author's name.

"I'm sure he is," she says. "He's a rabbi, you know. What do you pray for, anyway? Do you ask for more doubt?"

"Sometimes, yes."

"Not me. I pray for more faith and less doubt. I always wonder, though, if what *I think* is right is the same as what *God thinks*. Isn't that what humility is?"

"I think you're proving my point, aren't you?"

"That's stupid. I don't like doubting. I hate it."

"That's the difference between us. I'm comfortable with doubt and you aren't."

"You make it too complicated. I wish I had my Ernie Ford album. I'd play his hymns to drown you out. I need a little 'Almost Persuaded' and 'Blessed Assurance.'"

"Hold it right there. Our rule is no TV and no records or tapes while we're Up North. Besides, you own ten or twelve Neil Diamond records and only one Ernie Ford."

"What's wrong with Neil Diamond's 'Holly Holy'?" she asks.

"Jeez, what's with you? One minute it's 'Rock of Ages,' the next it's rock 'n' roll."

"Maybe I've been saved at 'Brother Love's Traveling Salvation Show.'"

I laugh. "Can you imagine singing that at our church on Sunday morning?"

"It'd make *my* day," she says.

I shake my head. "How do you change so fast from prudish to outrageous?"

"Can't I be that way and still be a good Christian?"

"Sure, but you go from cold to hot quicker than … than I don't know what."

"I love it when I get you tongue-tied. It's so sexy. Come on, let's go to bed."

"See what I mean?"

"Yeah, baby, I'm sizzlin'. Better get me before I burn to a crisp."

"Amy, we have kids in every room of the house."

"Okay," she says, "let's go outside and get naked in the woods."

Autumn has arrived, and I'm ready for another romp Up North, but just as we prepare to leave home, Amy tells me she's not going. When I complain about corralling the kids by myself she smiles and jokingly says, "They'll be good 'cuz they know I'll beat the crap out of 'em if they aren't."

Despite her good humor, anxious thoughts race through my mind. *Is she feeling all right? Maybe she's staying home because of that stomach pain she complains about. Or is it something worse? Something at the cottage that she's afraid of? Have I missed the signs of an approaching setback? God, I wish I didn't have to worry about that all the time.*

But when I look into Amy's brown eyes, I see nothing that resembles those terrible years. Her face is smooth and bright even without makeup. A pink glow shows through her fading summer tan. Her lips shape a smile that pushes two tiny dimples into her cheeks that beg to be touched. When I ask her to explain, she gives me an envelope with a prominent letter "P" encircled in laurel and "Palmer House" beneath the logo—stationary from the hotel in Chicago where she goes for annual meetings of Recovery, Inc. Her handwritten message on the envelope says, "Nick, read this later tonight. Love, A." Somehow, I know it's all right and I shouldn't ask questions lest I spoil something delicate that she's conjured in her mind.

At the cottage, I open the envelope and find another Palmer House envelope folded to fit the first. On the outside of the second envelope I read:

Dear Nick,

I love you for letting me stay home this weekend. It's a gift that couldn't be bought. Sometimes I get smothered with all the kids' problems. I want to think about our future this weekend and what I can contribute by going to school or working. I know I'll miss you, and by the time you read this I'll be sorry that I didn't go—but I still need to stay home. I have a lot of duality about this but, Nick, this is important to me.

So, I love you tonight a little more than last night—that seems impossible, but it's true because my love gets bigger every day.

See you Sunday after dark. All my love,

Amy.

Within that envelope is another note:

Nick,

I was thinking about you so much all through the night, I had to write you a note to tell you. We have to get some time (as in <u>hours</u>) by ourselves—and before this week-end is over, I plan to work on this problem. I know you'll ask why I didn't come this weekend. Yes, we need time together—but that doesn't always work with the kids around. You and the kids going away makes sense because you need a time <u>without taking care of me</u>—a habit you have that I'm trying to change.

I really need to touch you & hold you without the bright light of the clock beside the bed & knowing you'll be tired in the morning if we take time on a work night. I need to feel there's time and space for US. I'm working on this and have some unconventional ideas that I'm sure you'll go for. So please be careful and come home to me well rested and feeling a bit freer.

Before we were married, I never wanted you to have a good time without me. Now I want you to feel free as the wind (no women, of course) for forty hours or so. Eat out. Eat in. Do what you want. Enjoy yourself!

& come back home to your hot tamale.

Love, Amy

The kids and I get home Sunday evening and, like a pied piper, Amy leads them to the kitchen with a plateful of brownies. Exhausted, I let her take my hand and pull me into the bedroom. She puts her arms around me and kisses me hard and long while deftly kicking the door shut. My eyes nearly pop out when she presses against me and winds her tongue around mine. Taking a breath, I scan the room for clues of what's next. The bedcovers are thrown back, a tall candle is lit on the nightstand next to another plateful of brownies, and the stereo is playing Neil Diamond's "All I Really Need Is You."

Sometime later, I wake up alone in bed. Confused, I look at the nightstand to check the clock radio. It isn't there. Instead, I see the flicker of a flame on the tiny stub of a candle. A tall glass of milk is next to a plate of untouched chocolate squares. Suddenly, I remember a most exquisite dream and close my eyes to recall it. A smile spreads across my face as a recognizable ache stirs in my groin. I hear the door crack open and see a quick sliver of golden-yellow light cut across the bed and shoot up the opposite wall. Then the bright streak is filled with shadow, and Amy says from the doorway, "Wow, Mr. Lumberjack, the great outdoors sure makes you hungry."

I sit up and beckon Amy to join me in bed. She slides in and rests her head on my shoulder. Crinkling her nose, she backs off a bit. I sit up and start stuffing brownies in my mouth and gulping down the milk.

After a while, Amy says, "Well, how was it?"

"The dessert deserves an *A*, but the main course was an *A-plus*." ·

"No, silly. I mean how was your weekend?"

"My *end*? *Weak*? Jeez, I didn't think my end was weak at all." I feel around under the sheets and add, "Well, now it is."

Amy laughs. "Look, Fartsack, I want to know if you had fun Up North."

"Uh, yes and no. The girls were okay. So was Tim until we went fishing."

"Did he do that drifting away thing again?"

"Yeah. I don't know what gets into him. He kept asking why you didn't come along. It's as if he's mad at me for separating him from you."

"That's partly my fault," she says. "He knows I love him, but sometimes he makes me angry, and then you feel obligated to step in to keep me from braining him."

"Tell me about it. You two are too much alike—like you were with your dad."

"But we clash on silly things and get into arguments over nothing."

"It doesn't look like nothing. You're both too stubborn to let the other one win."

"He's always been a handful for me," says Amy. "I don't want it to be like Daddy and me. We had a love-hate relationship that was pretty confusing."

"Sometimes it's like that between Tim and me, too," I say. "Only, with me, he doesn't say anything. We went fishing on Saturday and got into it. You know how much I hate fishing, but I thought, what the hey? Anyway, he's good at it. He's a natural at casting—much better than I am. I complimented him and joked about my clumsiness. He seemed to be having fun, and he caught a fish that we took back to the cottage. I think it's a rainbow trout. It's just a little thing, but he wanted to cook it. I said I didn't know how to clean a fish, so I put it on ice and told him we'd do something after we got home—maybe even mount it."

"Yuck. Is he gonna hang a stinky fish on his bedroom wall?"

"I don't know. He wouldn't talk when I asked what was wrong. I don't remember doing anything to make him mad. I can't figure him out, and his silence doesn't help."

"He'll get over it. He's almost ten now and starting to think he knows more than you know. What happened with the girls?"

"You know how Eleni is always trying to please and never complains? Well, we went to Iva's for chicken dinner, and they had a clown going from table to table making animals out of balloons. Eleni hates clowns, so I said let's come back when he's not around. When Tim and Erin grumbled, Eleni insisted it was okay to stay. We did, but I could see she was uncomfortable."

"She didn't say anything about it to me."

"Of course not. You know how she hides her feelings. Later, Erin asked to go to the park just as I was about to take Eleni out to practice her driving. Erin cried, and Eleni gave in to her. I love Erin, but she always wants to do what *she* wants to do."

"She's only seven. Kids are more self-centered at that age."

"But I'm trying to get Eleni to stand up for herself. Anyway, at the park—"

"Erin told me. She sat on a bouncing ducky and stirred up a bee's nest."

"Yeah, they came out with a vengeance and scared the hell out of her. She got only a couple bites but wouldn't go outside the rest of the weekend. On top of that, Eleni didn't go out either. She said she didn't feel right with Erin as upset as she was."

Amy frowns and touches my face as she says, "You have a real 'tale of three kiddies,' Mr. Dickens. I have a lot to do to make things better for you. I'm sorry I put you through all of that."

"Goes with the territory, I guess. I hope it was worthwhile for you. I read your letter. Didn't understand all of it, though. How'd it go for you?"

"Great. Thanks for the time alone. I got a lot done, but have tons to do and lots of changes to make."

"Changes?" I say.

"Yeah, starting with us and the kids. You still have a habit of stepping in when they get on my nerves. You gotta stop that. I need to smooth things out myself, especially with Timothy. He's always butting heads with me, pulling in and then pushing away, and Eleni is almost too close to me. We kinda grew up together. She needs to see that I'm gonna be okay without her. She shouldn't be trying so hard to please me. Poor little Erin—she's so adorable, but I haven't spent the time with her that I did with Eleni. We've got some catching up to do."

"Whoa, wait up. You're going a mile a minute, and I can't follow you. Why are you making all these pronouncements?"

"'Cause I have things to do—mountains to climb—and not much time to do it."

"What's come over you? Have you been listening to motivational tapes?"

"No tapes. I've been thinking about the time I've wasted. I'm almost forty-one, and for the first time in my life, I can make long-range plans. I've focused too much on one part of me for too long. I need to do other things. It's time I found out who I am. I feel like my real life hasn't begun yet."

"You're my wife and the mother of our kids. You're a respected Recovery leader. You help a lot of people at the cancer society. Isn't that enough?"

"No. It's a start, but I want more out of life."

"Like what?"

"I'm not sure yet. I told you; I have a long way to go."

"So you're just talking in general terms right now?"

"No. I have specifics. I'm gonna stop complaining about aches and pains that don't matter. I won't let a bellyache stop me from kick-starting a new life. I want to quit my job at the cancer society and begin classes at Lansing Community College. I've saved some money, so it should be okay. By next July, I'll quit Recovery leadership and eventually cut back on meetings, too. I'll always have the method, and you can bet I'll use it. After fifteen years, it's become an instinct."

"Man, you've really thought this out, haven't you?"

"There's more," she says. "I want to do something for you, too."

"You don't need to do that," I say.

"Shuddup. You never let me do anything for you. Once upon a time I couldn't, but now I can. You still fight me whenever I try to take over one of your jobs. I wish you'd let me do more. I can handle it now. You don't have to be in charge all the time."

"But you've already helped me finish my book. There's nothing—"

"Hey, I'm proud of you. And the kids should be, too. Your book will be in print early next year, right? I know you don't want a 'signing party,' or whatever they call it, but I'm having the family over to celebrate. After that, I want to take you and the kids with me to Recovery's meeting in Chicago. It'll be my last, so it's my treat."

"What do you mean *your treat?*"

"Well, my way will be paid because I'm still Area Leader. I'm going to pay the extra charges for you and the kids to stay with me at the Palmer House. I've saved enough for that, too. Nick, I want to do this. It'll give me a chance to show off the family and do a little bragging myself. Next to you and the kids, Recovery has been the most important thing in my life. It's my last hurrah before I retire. Our children should know that other people think their mom and dad are pretty damn good."

"Helen Reddy," I say. "That's what it is. It's that Helen Reddy thing."

"What?"

"Of course," I say, striking a Eureka pose. "It's not a motivational tape. You've been listening to Helen Reddy. I'll bet you sang "I Am Woman" all the time I was gone."

"Nick, please don't patronize me. This is important."

"I know it is. I'm not putting you down. I want to put a star on your forehead."

"Dammit, I'm not your child."

"What the hell …?"

"You're like all men. Everything's fine as long as *your woman* stays in her place, which is a little bit lower than you, so you can pat her on the head and say 'good girl.'"

"Amy, I hate when you start into—"

"You should see how those doctors—males, of course—how they treat me at the cancer society. They can barely stand it when I take charge. I have to pussy-foot around and make them feel like my *good* idea was their *great* idea. I get along fine if I let them flirt with me. They love it when I flutter my eyelashes and blush. Anything else and I'm a bitch, and bitches ought to shave their heads and drive trucks with their lesbian friends."

"Amy, I'm not like that, and you know it. I've always encouraged you. Sure, some guys are pigs. Your beef is with them and with the system that keeps women down—not with me. Dammit, I'm glad you're all fired up. Maybe you need to build up steam to get your engine going, but don't take it out on me. I'm on your side, remember?"

"You can't treat me like a little girl anymore."

"Little girl? I … I never meant…." I stumble over the denial. When Amy was ill, she was so helpless and vulnerable I did treat her like a child, but haven't I changed? Still uncertain, I say, "Sweetheart, I thought it was you and me against the world."

Amy takes my hand and sighs. "Nick, it'll always be you and me. I still need you, but not the same as before. I'm not asking you to let me go; I'm asking you to let me *grow*."

We sit up in bed and hold each other. Amy's body is soft and pliable like potter's clay until she senses my tension. She sits back and studies my face. Then she twitches her nose the way Elizabeth Montgomery does on Bewitched and says, "I know you're upset. I'm sorry. I shouldn't have gone on like that. As usual, I should have quit while I was ahead."

"No, no," I say. "It's all right. I guess I haven't changed as much as I thought."

"Nick, I love you, and I appreciate all that you do. I'm not saying it very well, but I want you to be free, too. You don't have to take care of everything anymore."

"Uh-huh." I nod to show my agreement, but inside, I'm not so sure.

"You were right about Helen Reddy," she says, "but I listened to another one of her songs, too. It was 'You and Me Against the World' that triggered my thoughts about you and the kids. The song is about always being there for a child. There were times when I was like a child and I knew I could count on you. Now, I'm no longer like that, and we have to be there for our kids. Just as I had to learn to be strong without you, we have to give our kids confidence that they can take care of themselves without us. Remember the line *And one of us is left to carry on … our memories alone will get us through?* There'll be a time when our kids will need to be on their own. I want them to feel confident they can do it *because* of us, not in spite of us. Our Eleni is almost at that point, now."

"And you're already there," I say.

She nods her head and says, "Way past it, I think."

"I guess I understand."

I feel a tear trickle down my cheek. Amy brushes it away and giggles.

"There you go again," I say. "Honestly, I'll never *really* understand you. I think you're being serious, and all of a sudden, you giggle. What are you laughing at?"

"I can't help it. Your face is so dirty that tear carved a path down to your chin."

"It's Up-North dirt, and I'll never wash it off."

"You'd better, unless you want to be a hermit. I gotta tell ya, I like how your animal instincts are aroused when you come home from the cottage, but I wish you'd leave the wild stink in the woods where the deer and the antelope play."

CHAPTER THIRTY-EIGHT

CLOV: Do you believe in the life to come?
HAMM: Mine was always that.

—From *Endgame* by Samuel Beckett

Amy's work in Recovery had paid dividends for her and the organization, so I was surprised that she'd decided to quit. In addition to weekly meetings, she chaired monthly gatherings of other leaders, oversaw a regional budget, wrote a newsletter, and conducted instructional programs for current and prospective leaders. She made regular contacts with newspapers and presented Recovery panels to professional and university groups. As spokesperson for an organization she loved, she had trimmed her weight and reclaimed her flair for fashion, presenting herself attractively and posing confidently for publicity photos. For all this, she got high praise but no pay. However, she earned invaluable satisfaction from helping others and boosting her self-esteem.

Amy kept her promise. When my book was published she threw a party for the family, where she surprised me with a new briefcase stuffed with briefs—tighty-whitey Jockey briefs. Later that spring, she commemorated the start of her new life with a celebratory farewell to the old one at the site of Recovery's Annual Meeting. Eleni had already started college and didn't join us in Chicago, but our trip to the Palmer House went well on several counts. Tim and Erin got a glimpse of their mom's prominence in Recovery and a taste of big-city high life. A downside was that they discovered steaks and wanted them whenever we went out, including on our visit to Grand Rapids, where we stopped to see Eleni on the way home.

When Amy began classes in Lansing, her routine proved to be less disruptive than I had anticipated. She started slowly, taking only one class in each of the first two terms. That allowed us to spend time at the cottage during the school year as well as the summer. All and all, Amy's changes brought back happiness reminiscent of the blissful years of our courtship and early marriage. Best of all was our good feeling about the future. We grew to believe that the strength we gained from the past would allow us to defeat any obstacle that came our way.

Amy's second year class schedule put her on track for an associate's degree in medical and dental office management, a program designed to teach her how to run the business end of a heath provider's office. It was her first step toward a career in health management where her Recovery experience would be an asset. Her classes met in the evening at the main campus of Lansing Community College, about forty miles away. When a problem with night blindness made it hard for her to drive, I offered to take her. Amy accepted my assistance only after I suggested we get a babysitter and turn her school night into a night out we could share.

Amy ate her dinner while I drove, and I ate in the college cafeteria while she was in class. The long drive gave me an opportunity to mention that I admired her focus on school, but was concerned that she no longer complained about certain physical problems. When she replied that she had vowed to stop whining about her health, I told her that she wasn't very good at hiding her discomfort. At that time, I was concerned about her stomach distress, and she passed it off as indigestion. I didn't know about the soreness she felt in her breast until one night when she winced at my touch when we cuddled in bed. Though she passed it off for several weeks, I finally insisted that she take time from her studies to check with her doctor. The local doctor dismissed her indigestion as a minor result of eating hurriedly in the car, but he recommended that she see Dr. Jordan Hosler, a breast cancer specialist, to check out the tenderness on her breast.

On the way to her appointment in Glen Acre, a town thirty-five miles away, I masked my concern as best I could, but my calm exterior had little resemblance to how I felt inside. I was terrified of the *big C*—so scared that I was unable to assess how Amy felt. It used to be that she would talk about her fear obsessively or show it in her strained voice or in fidgety, compulsive mannerisms, but Amy had mastered the tools of Recovery training to short circuit her fearful thoughts before they got the best of her. Sitting next to me in the car, she appeared resolute. During the ride, she calmly read from her latest textbook, *Taber's Cyclopedic Medical Dictionary*, but as we got closer to the medical center, she began twisting her mouth to one side and sucking the inside of her cheek—old habits that were signs she was upset.

"I hope I don't miss any classes," she said, "but the doctor might have to do an *aspiration*."

"Uh … what's that?" I asked.

"*Aspiration*? I just read about it here in my book. It's '... the withdrawal of fluid from a cavity by means of suction,'" she read. "We've talked about it in class. They stick a needle in my boob and suck out some guck." Amy screwed up her mouth, slammed the book shut, and loudly declared, "I'm not getting cancer! I don't have time for it, and I won't allow it!"

The word *cancer* came at me like an airbag bursting in my face. I reacted by pushing my hands hard against the steering wheel but managed to say, "Nobody said it has to be ... *that*."

"Be realistic," she said. "That's what they're looking for. They run a biopsy and see what's in the fluid. If they suspect cancer, I lose my left boob."

I cringed as racing thoughts darted through my mind, and I was afraid that Amy would see my alarm. I searched for words to counter my anxiety but could only reach over to touch her hand. Characteristically, Amy had no trouble finding cuss words. "That son of a bitch better not say I have cancer," she said. "I hate the bastard already."

There was comic relief in her anger. She was mad as hell at a doctor she hadn't met for saying something he hadn't said about something that he had no control over.

"You don't have cancer," I said, as if I had anything to do with it.

"I damn well better not."

"The chances are that it's nothing but a ... I don't know. A cyst or something. Right?" I glanced at the medical book still in her lap, hoping she'd find an assuring phrase.

"My mother had cancer," she said. "Had a breast and a lung removed."

"But you're more like your father."

"Oh, great," she said with a nervous laugh. "I can look forward to a stroke, too."

"They're both doing fine now," I said. "They're as healthy as you and—"

"Thanks, I feel better already."

"All I'm saying is that it does no good to worry."

"I'm not worried. I'm mad."

"Good," I said, feeling encouraged. "Stay mad. Mad will give you a better chance to beat *whatever* it is."

Over the years, I learned that I could tolerate Amy's anger more than her fear and depression. Anger told me that she was fighting. If I knew anything about Amy, it was that she was a fighter. When combined with her sense of humor, she was unbeatable.

We had a long ride ahead—too long for her to stay angry. I could only hope that the cancer threat went away as easily. After a while, she spoke up again. This time her voice sounded regretful. "Nicky," she said, "will you still love me if I lose both breasts?"

"Sure," I said. "I'm basically a leg and thigh man."

"Bullshit. I know better."

"Look, I love you no matter what body you're in."

"What if ...?"

"I don't want to hear it. You're gonna be fine."

"God wouldn't let it happen like that, would he? Not after all we've been through. We've won before; we can win again. Right?"

"Absolutely."

"Okay, I won't say anymore. Let's wait and see what *Hose-ler* has to say."

"I think his name is pronounced *HASS-ler*."

Amy smiled and said, "I'll call him something else if he says the wrong thing, but I'll wait until I see him before deciding."

My first impression of Dr. Hosler was negative when I heard him gruffly tell his nurse to take me to the room where Amy had been for an hour and a half. The tone of his sharp directive shocked me, and I hoped he wasn't like that with Amy.

A man in his mid-forties greeted me in the examination room. His thin frame surprised me, as did the rest of his appearance. He wore a gray T-shirt under his partially buttoned white smock, and had a dark five o'clock shadow that accentuated his expression of fatigue. To me he didn't look like a doctor; he looked like ... something else.

His lean appearance didn't fit the harsh authority in his voice either, but his manners did. He hardly said hello to me before he started explaining his examination technique and the aspiration procedure. I didn't understand half the technical jargon he used. Feeling lectured at, I let my head hang like a chided schoolboy. That was when I noticed his New Balance running shoes. They were the kind that serious runners wore, but his were badly scuffed and worn. When the doctor raised his voice, I thought it was because he caught me looking for blood on his shoes. It wasn't that at all. He simply came across harshly when he described the laboratory process with such an authoritative tone. In the end, he told me more about procedures than I wanted to know but not enough about Amy.

"How's Amy?" I asked when he took a breath. "Is she going to be okay?"

Hosler said, "Huh?" as if I had awakened him. Then he pushed his glasses up onto his high forehead and rubbed his eyes with both hands, making his mostly bald egg-shaped head appear more prominent than it already was. With his hands covering his face and his black-rimmed glasses resting on his smooth, bare scalp, he looked like an incomplete Mr. Potato Head.

"I'm sorry," he said. "Amy and I already talked about this. I thought I told you. Yes, of course, she's fine." When he said Amy's name he looked her way. As he spoke directly to her, his tone change and his expression become gentler. When I looked at Amy, I saw in her smile that she liked him.

"It didn't hurt," she said. "I hardly felt a thing, and it was over in a few seconds."

Dr. Hosler faced Amy and took her hand before he continued. "Forgive me," he said. "I've just come from marathon surgery. An emergency that took...." He checked his watch without letting go of Amy. "... twelve hours. I'm used to explaining procedures to med students, and I played my lecture tape to your husband."

As he talked to us, he turned to me, then back to Amy, and nodded to emphasize his sincerity. "Amy's going to be okay," he said. "There's no cancer. I've seen enough of these lumps to tell the difference even before I draw the fluid. We'll still check with the lab, of course. I'll have my girls call you as soon as we get the report, but don't worry about it. We don't know what causes these cysts to spring up, but some women seem more susceptible than others do. Amy, stay away from coffee and chocolate. They both have caffeine, and caffeine seems to exacerbate the problem." He checked his watch again before going on. "See me here in a month. Don't be alarmed if this happens again. It's likely to, but trust me, you're at no greater risk for breast cancer than any other woman. I don't want you to be afraid. Come see me anytime you notice anything unusual."

Amy and I bobbed our heads like happy marionettes. Dr. Hosler rose and unbuttoned his smock, then stopped to ask if we had any questions, but we were overwhelmed and begged off until we had time to digest the news.

"All right then. Young lady, if you don't mind," he said while undoing the remaining buttons of his coat, "I want to get home to my lovely wife." When his white coat opened, I read *Boston Marathon, 1982* and the number *592* on his T-shirt. His worn-out shoes and slender, reedy appearance suddenly fit the "something else" that had eluded me earlier; he looked like a long-distance runner. I wanted to ask if he ran in last year's race, the one identified on his shirt, but his hand on the doorknob meant he was eager to leave.

Just before he opened the door, he paused and tapped the ring on his left hand against the steel knob, rhythmically as one might tap their foot while waiting for something. Then he glanced back at us. In that quick turn, his mouth changed from anxious frown to struggling smile. It was genuine but, oddly, it seemed forced as he said, "Take good care of each other. When it finally comes down to it, *each other* is the best thing you've got."

Our initial worries calmed, but they rose again when additional aspirations were required. Amy's visits to Dr. Hosler became such a routine that she stopped counting. "Counting is a form of temper," she said, quoting a Recovery mantra. Through repeated visits over the next several months, our anxiety was kept in check by confidence in our Recovery experience and our faith in Dr. Hosler.

"He reminds me of my daddy," said Amy. "Hard as nails on the outside, but soft and mushy inside. I trust him, and he trusts me. He believes me and doesn't talk down to me like other doctors. I wish he didn't specialize in just one thing, though. He's the only doctor I'm comfortable with."

Amy took the ailments in stride and didn't let frequent trips to Glen Acre interfere with her studies. Her plan was to have a degree and a job by December of 1984, and she was right on schedule. Early in the year her symptoms subsided, and she began her practicum assignment at a dental office in Perry. She had to work eight hours each day, four days a week, and attend a seminar on the fifth day. It was a taxing schedule, but Amy did it happily because her goal was in sight. She got *A's* in all categories of the internship, and the dentist offered her a paid position as soon as she obtained her certificate. I was proud of her and more enthusiastic than ever about her career.

She was close to completing all requirements for her degree when the discomfort she'd been treating as indigestion for ten years grew into a more debilitating stomach pain. My concern rose when she told me about being late to her dental office assignment three days in a row. I was alarmed because I remembered that the abdominal pain she had twenty years before was diagnosed as colitis, or *nervous colon*, and it turned out to be a prelude to her nervous breakdown. I had to be careful to avoid a suggestion that her emotions caused her problem, because that was what doctors often said when they knew of Amy's past mental health history.

"Is it a sharp pain or a dull ache?" I said.

"Both, but not at the same time. Sometimes I feel a little nauseated, too."

"Ever had anything like it before?"

"No. I get a little indigestion once in a while, but that's after I've cheated and had something I shouldn't have—like chocolate. Usually, a cup of yogurt makes it better."

Amy was convinced that nutrition was the key to maintaining good health. Reading all she could about the value of organic products and nutritional supplements, she shunned artificial additives and preservatives as if they were pesticides. Two foods were constants in her diet. One was yogurt, which she lauded as the near-perfect food for everyone. Her other favorite was chocolate—something she knew was not good for her, but she found impossible to resist. Consequently, Amy blamed her ailments on the decadent allure of chocolate, and treated those ailments with a dose of plain, low-fat yogurt.

"Did it work this time?"

"Yes and no. I had some yogurt before I left in the morning and then again at work for lunch. I didn't feel better until I got home, nine hours after it started."

"Is this stomach pain anything like you had … uh, maybe a while ago?"

"Like when?"

"I don't know. Anytime. Last year? Several years ago?"

Amy eyed me critically. "You're thinking about *colitis*, aren't you?"

"Oh, I don't know. Anything that has to do with your stomach."

"No. This is entirely different. It's up higher in my tummy, near my ribs. It's not gallbladder either because I don't have one anymore. Maybe it's too much stress, but don't worry. It's not like before, and I'm not going crazy again. I'll get over it."

CHAPTER THIRTY-NINE

But bombs are unbelievable until they actually fall.

—Patrick White

Through half-open eyes, I see an empty spot next to me where Amy ought to be and immediately jump out of bed. The *Wreck of the Hesperus* stares at me from the dresser mirror and jolts me into remembering that Amy is in the hospital for tests. I sneer at my mirror image and then smile. *Wreck of the Hesperus* is a favorite expression of Amy's and apropos for my appearance. I look like a shipwrecked sailor and feel a seasick nausea from a throbbing migraine that began last night. My bed's a disaster of wound-up sheets and mangled pillows, and I remember a frightening dream that had me thrashing throughout the night. A house. Big rooms. Odors that gagged me. The partially recalled images stir waves of terrifying feelings and stop me from remembering more.

Suddenly, I feel a need to draw my children close and protect them, so I hurry to the kitchen to prepare breakfast for Tim and Erin before they go off to school. After they leave, I have an urge to call Eleni, who's away at college, but talk myself out of it because I'm afraid she'll sense my anxiety. A God-awful feeling grips my stomach, and painful tension spreads from the back of my neck to the top of my head. Oddly, a cartoon sketch of our family that I drew when our future looked bright flashes through my mind and vanishes just as suddenly.

Doctors kept Amy at College Park hospital last night. It's November, and since June, we've been scrambling from doctor to doctor trying to figure out the cause of Amy's stomach pain. I try to calm myself with the notion that waiting for an accurate diagnosis is probably worse than the ailment. Some doctors still think her complaint is a nervous problem rather than a physical illness. I wonder about that, too, and worry that Amy's nerves might sink her into depression again.

Meanwhile, I've not told Amy that my own health is suffering. My migraines got so bad that doctors suspected a stroke and nearly hospitalized me. The cause of my headaches is unknown, but the God-awful feeling I get in my chest has been diagnosed as acid reflux disease. Both problems have worsened because of anxiety—and anger—over Amy's complaint. She doesn't need this. She's starting a new career. The elusive identity she had been looking for is just emerging.

It's been hectic since June when a heart specialist ordered more tests for Amy, and we entered the bureaucratic maze of hospital care. Lack of personal attention and miscommunication compound our confusion in a megalopolis of departments. Specialists focus only on one organ and don't regard Amy as a whole person. Though we welcomed a report that her heart was fine, we were unnerved when our insurance refused to pay for the tests because Amy didn't have a proper referral. Still, delays and bewilderment over the diagnosis are far worse problems than the insurance hassle. By the time Amy saw a gastroenterologist, her symptoms temporarily disappeared, but yesterday she was admitted to the hospital anyway. This time, I made sure the insurance would cover the bill.

I arrive at the hospital and discover that Amy is no longer in the same room. A woman at the information desk says Amy has completed several procedures and is now resting. I figure I can take her home in an hour or so. I must appear confused because the attendant escorts me to the correct hall and smiles kindly as she points to the door I should enter.

Her pleasant helpfulness comforts me until I step through the double doors and am surprised to see that Amy's *room* is a large ward with several other patients, some of whom appear seriously ill. The vastness of the room and the mingled odors of antiseptic, gauze, and bathroom stench, remind me of a charity ward. Is that why Amy's insurance coverage was so readily approved?

I don't see Amy until I locate the source of a garbled voice calling my name. When I go to her she rasps, "Oh, Nick, I'm glad that's over. I want to get outa here. My school exam is in ten days, and I've got some serious studying to do."

The sound of her rough voice concerns me, but I'm relieved by her desire to leave. "Don't sweat it," I say. "It's not official, but I think I can take you home before dinner. We'll stop on the way and get fried chicken or pizza for the kids and—"

"Not for me," says Amy. "I have to stay away from fatty foods. Besides, my appetite was spoiled by castor oil and a concoction that tasted like Lemon Pledge."

"Lemonade and oil, huh? That's a good sign. You can go home *oily*."

"Don't joke, Fartsack. What they did to me I wouldn't wish on a serial killer. That stuff ran through me like a bulldozer, but one dump wasn't enough. So they reamed me out with a Roto-Rooter and washed me out with soap. Then—get this—they pumped *air* up my butt along with a rectal camera that took snapshots of the scenery."

"I thought they were checking the upper tract—the esophagus and stomach."

"They did that yesterday—stuck a camera *down* my throat that time."

"Glad that end was first."

"Not funny, McGee. That's why I'm hoarse—my vocal chords got stretched."

"I hope it's worth it and we get some answers. I don't like all this mystery."

"Me neither. I hate it here. These tests are a walk in the park for them because they do it all the time, but I'd like to see what they'd do with a hose up their ass."

I smile at the humor she injects in her derision but look anxiously at the surrounding beds. A nurse passes through drawn curtains holding an odoriferous triangular pan at arm's length.

"I see what you mean," I say. "There's no privacy in this gymnasium."

"How can it be private when committees of doctors treat me like a guinea pig?" she says. "I'm just a lab specimen to be discussed by tight-ass guys with *rectalitis*."

Her expression makes me smile again. "I know," I say. "Their eyeballs are crossed with their hind ends and they have a shitty outlook on life."

"*Ass holes*, not hind ends," she corrects. "They don't deserve euphemisms."

I laugh. Joking about unpleasant situations has helped Amy through hard times before. Her remarks are a cross between Don-Rickles-nasty and Joan-Rivers-spite. Like her father, Amy uses wisecracks to expel her fears. I can almost feel her anxiety escape as she lets off steam. *Psst off* is how she describes it.

"What the heck's your doctor's name?" I ask. "Guyan? Gryten?"

"*Gryden*. Must be a guru around here. He always comes with an entourage—sometimes as many as six. So I call them 'Dr. Gry's Guys.' I hate every one of 'em. I wish Dr. Hosler were here. He and I can talk man-to-man."

In the distance, I hear voices talking about Kirk Gibson's homer in the Tigers' World Series win and then see a group of three men wearing white coats gathered at the entrance to the ward. When a portly gray-haired man steps through the double doors, they stop talking and assume sober expressions. The older man is much shorter than the first three, but projects a commanding presence the others try to emulate. They march directly toward Amy, who looks up when I nod in their direction and ask, "Are these Dr. Gry's Guys?"

The four men stop before reaching Amy's bed. "Hello, Mrs. Demetriou," says the portly one. He smiles and removes his hand from his pocket. I get up and step toward him. "Hello, I'm Dr. Gryden," he says, "Chief of Endocrinology. These are my associates. Are you Mr. Demetriou?"

Endocrinology?

"Yes," I say, extending my hand. "My name's Nick." Gryden's hand slips through mine like a fish in a cold stream. I immediately feel it's my fault and blame myself for not offering a firm handshake.

Gryden flips open a clipboard and, without regard for Amy or me, begins his litany: *stomach and lower chest pain, nausea ... heart ... esophageal ... colon ... ruled out*. Words like *pancreatalgia, pancreathelcosis*, and *pancreatemphraxis* get my attention. I don't like what I hear and want to change the subject. *Hey guys, how about those Tigers? That was some World Series win, huh?*

"Doctor," says an intern, "what led to your diagnosis of possible malign ...?

Dr. Gryden clears his throat, and the younger man stops immediately. Then all the interns hunch their shoulders and turn toward Amy and me. I've seen penguins with more expression than these four characters.

Gryden steps forward as if to deliver a message. His nameless associates move aside and then flank him like an emperor's guard—standing a respectful half step back. Their military-like precision arouses my suspicion. The one whose question went unasked sports a Vandyke style mustache and goatee. If the facial hair was meant to show maturity, it failed. The men stand ramrod straight, and almost in unison, jam their hands into their pockets bulging them out with balled up fists. I want to ask when Amy can go home, but their synchronized stand-at-attention gives me pause. Gryden appears to hide something on his clipboard—something he is about to dump at the foot of Amy's bed.

"I've reviewed the results of several tests," says Gryden, "and I'm afraid I have some ... news." I hear a rustle behind the men and look up to see a tall woman approaching us. Dr. Gryden glances back and nods as if to acknowledge her before going on. "Mrs. Demetriou, I hesitate to say that it's *bad news* because we aren't certain, but you'll remain in the hospital so that we can do a proper biopsy at another site."

The floor beneath me feels as if it suddenly gives way, and I put my hand on Amy's bed for support. I glance at her, carefully moving only my eyes so she won't sense my alarm. From the expression on her face, I believe that she, too, felt the earth move.

Dr. Gryden is talking again, but his generalizations seem to skirt a hidden agenda. I feel off-balance—as a ballplayer caught unaware by a curve ball—while Gryden tosses words like a pitcher offering nothing and hoping to avoid a full count. I hear the word *cancer*. Images blur and sounds fade. Amy begins to cry. I try to comfort her, and at the same time nod to the doctor and say, "Of course. Yes, I want Amy to get the proper treatment. Yes, it's best to act immediately and avoid delay. Certainly, we'll cooperate." *Tell us, sir, what to do, and we'll march in line just like your students.*

Gryden says, "Nurse," in a commanding voice, and the tall woman steps forward. The doctors leave when the nurse attends to Amy. Despite her effort to stop, Amy continues to cry. A dark-skinned woman with blonde Dolly Parton hair appears and takes over from the first woman. The black nurse prepares an injection and whispers instructions that send the tall one off on an errand. The sight of a hypodermic needle startles Amy. She draws a stuttered breath and struggles to regain control as she asks, "Who are you?"

"My name's Rose and I'll be here most of the night if you need me. Let's see," she says examining the hospital bracelet, "you're Amy, aren't you? Hello, Amy."

"What's that?"

"Doctor ordered a mild sedative."

"I don't want it. I don't want to stay here tonight. I want to go home."

"That'll be up to Doctor."

"But I have to go to my class. I need it to get my certificate."

"Oh, congratulations," says Rose sweetly. "I'm happy for you, and I'm sure your husband's proud of you." She winks at me. I take it as a signal to help cheer Amy.

"You bet," I say a little too proudly. "That's not all. You wouldn't believe what she's overcome in her life. She's fought some tough battles and won every one of them."

"What good is it to win," Amy stammers, "if you lose when it matters most? Nobody wins against the *big C*."

"We haven't lost yet," I say. "They said they *suspect* cancer. They won't know for sure without a proper biopsy. They might be wrong."

Amy tries to rally. "Do you really think so?"

"Sure," I say. "It's possible, and even if it is cancer, it's early and you can beat it. If anybody can beat it, you can. You're the best fighter I know."

"But it's pancreatic cancer. Do you realize how bad that is?"

"I don't know. It doesn't matter. Nothing's as *bad* as you are *good*—and good always wins. Just ask Dudley Do-Right."

"Nick, don't joke. I wish Dr. Hosler was here instead of Napoleon Gryden."

"Honey," I say, "Hosler's field is breast cancer. Gryden's is the pancreas. Besides, Hosler doesn't work at this hospital. He's at St. Michael."

"I know, but I trust Hosler more than anybody."

I look at Rose hoping she might help me, but she's busy preparing Amy's injection. I watch her insert a needle into a tiny vial and pull back on the syringe to withdraw the liquid. There's a slight squeak when she pulls the needle out. Then, holding the syringe to the light, she taps it with her index finger while squirting out bubbles and excess liquid. Rose smiles as she swabs Amy's arm with antiseptic and says, "There, there, hon, let me give you this to help you settle down."

Amy pulls her arm away. "I don't want to calm down. I want to get out of here. God, I hate this place. I don't like being an experiment. I want my own doctor!"

Rose gently but firmly takes Amy's arm again. She is about to give her the injection but stops. Straightening, Rose draws one hand to her breast and holds the other so the needle points upward. She looks at Amy sympathetically, tilting her right ear dangerously close to the sharp point of the syringe in her hand.

"Hon," she says. "Are you talkin' about Dr. *Jordan* Hosler?"

"Yes," we say together.

"Well, darlin', I can understand why you'd want him. I work at his office from time to time. He's a crotchety bear to work for, but he's a sweetheart to his patients."

Amy's lower lip quivers making a round knob appear and disappear on her trembling chin. "Yes," she says, in a bird-like trill.

Nurse Rose gives Amy the injection and says, "There you are, hon, that'll help you get some rest. You'll be having a big day tomorrow."

"Rose," says Amy. "Do you think Dr. Hosler will come to see me if I ask him?"

"Doctors don't usually do that, darlin'. They especially don't when it comes to visiting hospitals where they're not working. They're busy people." Rose peers squarely into Amy's face, and Amy stares back. Neither moves for a moment as if searching each other's mind.

"You know," whispers Rose, "you're right about him being at St. Mike's, but you're wrong about his practice. He's a cancer surgeon. One of the best. He treats all kinds of cancer—pancreatic included. If I were you, I'd give him a call."

The tall nurse returns with a plastic bag and an IV kit. "Lunch and dinner," she says cheerfully. Amy falls asleep before the nurses finish setting up the apparatus. I'm already thinking about how to get Amy out of here and into Dr. Hosler's care.

From the hospital lobby, I call Hosler's office and leave my home number with his answering service. Driving home, thoughts about the seriousness of

Amy's condition ricochet in my head like laser shots on mirrored walls. I make mental notes to ask about diagnosis, treatment, and aftercare. As I near home, I try to calm down. The kids will ask about their mom. What should I say? How should I act in front of them? Eleni is away at school; should I call her or wait until I have news that is more definitive?

I get off the expressway at Michigan and head up to Main Street. Just seconds away from home, I wait in the left turn lane for traffic to clear and realize that I need some answers before I see the children. I can call the local cancer society where Amy used to work, but I might learn more from an organization devoted to pancreatic cancer. It's ten minutes to five, near closing time for most offices—and a Friday to boot. I can't call from home because the kids might hear, but the Four Corners Drugstore has an old-fashioned phone booth where I can talk in private.

Swerving out of the left turn lane, I dart across Main Street and park the car in the drugstore's loading zone. I run inside and find the booth vacant. Dialing information, I ask for the number of a pancreatic cancer group and pay the extra money to be immediately connected. It's four minutes to five. I count the rings. Twelve to a minute. Forty-seven to go. After forty-one rings, still no answer. I wait. Finally, someone says, "cancer society." The female voice sounds annoyed and hurried. All my questions bunch on my tongue like flies on dead meat. "Hello?" says the voice again. "Hello? I'm sorry, but we close at five and if...."

I'm crying, sobbing like a baby, but I force myself to spit out my question. "My wife has pancreatic cancer. Can you tell me how long she will live?"

The silence on the phone frightens me—a silent alarm that I hear too clearly.

"Hello," I say. "Please talk to me."

The woman at the other end turns her voice back on, but speaks to me like I've gone postal. Gradually, sympathetic words blend with her professional tone to help me compose myself. I think of all the times that Amy responded to panic calls for Recovery, and more recently, crisis calls at the cancer society. Then it hits me. Oh, God. Amy knows. She had dispensed cancer information for two-and-a-half years and has probably read every brochure there is.

"You should discuss this with your doctor," says the voice on the phone. "I can send you a brochure if you'll give me your address."

"Tell me what it says," I plead. "I have to know right now."

"Sir, I can't do that. I know you're upset, but only your doctor can give you—"

"What is the survival rate? What can we expect? Please read it to me."

"I'm sorry, but that wouldn't be—"

"Read it too me!" I scream.

Another silence. Then the muffled sound of a hand covering the mouthpiece followed by someone taking a deep breath. "Sir, I can help you if you tell me where you are right now," she says very slowly. "I can give you a crisis number that you can call in your area. Please tell me your city and state."

I slam down the phone.

I'm wasting my time. Amy kept some cancer pamphlets at home. Why didn't I think of it? She must've saved something about pancreatic cancer.

When I get home, Tim and Erin are watching TV.

"How's Mom?" asks Tim.

"Is Mommy-poo all right?" says Erin.

"She's okay. She's resting now. They gave her a lot of tests—X-rays and stuff—so she's pretty tired. Uh ... did anyone call while I was out?"

"Unh, uh," says Erin.

"When will she be home?" says Tim.

"Uh ... I'm not sure. They couldn't do one important test because the machine broke down. I'll know more when I see her tomorrow."

"Can I go, too?" asks Erin.

"I'm sorry, sweetie. Mom would like to see you, but the hospital says *no*. You have to be thirteen. I'll get Linda to stay here with you."

"I'm almost thirteen," says Tim.

"Tell you what. If Mom has to stay past the weekend, I'll sneak you guys in. Till then, Tim, I need you to stay home with your little sister."

"I'm not little," says Erin. "I'm ten. And I'm smarter than Tim."

"You mean *farter*," says Tim.

"You're the *fart*. You're always smelling up the place."

They continue bickering back and forth until I raise my voice.

"Look, you're smart enough, just not old enough. And you're proving that right now. Stop fighting. I'm tired and need you guys to help me out, not drive me crazy."

"When do we eat?" they say.

I sigh loudly. "Listen, I can't make dinner right now. I need to check something upstairs. You two stay here. I won't be long. After that, I'll make spaghetti."

"You sure you got the right ingredients?" asks Tim with a smirk.

"Yeah, Daddy Dude. We don't want that stuff you made Up North with a can of chili."

I force a laugh. "Hey, that was because we had nothing else in the cupboard. Besides, I thought you liked Mexican spaghetti with chili beans."

"Yuck," they say, finally agreeing on something.

Upstairs in Amy's file cabinet, I find a folder containing two different pamphlets about pancreatic cancer: a short one prepared for the public, and a longer report labeled *Physician Statement: Pancreatic Cancer.* Neither pamphlet skirts the issue of severity. Almost every line is alarming: "25,000 new cases each year … 26,500 expected deaths … Warning signs: Usually none until disease is advanced … Five year survival rates at or near the lowest of all cancers.…"

The *Physician Statement* is even blunter. "… rarely curable … for 85 percent of patients … survival rate is less than 1 percent at five years *with most patients dying within one year.*"

The reports grow heavy in my hand. I set them down and begin to arrange the desktop, wiping dust and setting everything neatly in place. My obsession with order only temporarily blocks my grief. In a moment, my tears spill onto the desk and chaos returns.

I weep for Amy because she will die, and for myself because I will lose her. But I also weep because I will lose myself. Amy's death sentence is my life sentence. I must again take control of my emotions and not allow my feelings to rise above Amy's needs or the needs of my children. It's the role I assumed twenty years ago—a hated role that I've only recently learned to discard, but now cannot escape.

I want to scream *goddamn you, God,* but I whisper it so the children won't hear. From now on, I must be strong. I can't show anyone how I feel—how angry I am that God would allow Amy to win her battle over depression and snatch away her victory just as she is about to celebrate it.

I go downstairs and make spaghetti. My homemade sauce is light on pepper and heavy on salt. Tim and Erin don't care; they just want it fast. Erin has a second helping and Tim has a third, dashing my hope that there'd be leftovers for another meal. The kids eat, as though they're famished. Amy would say, "Like there's no tomorrow." I overeat, too, probably for the same reason.

A Dr. Kerrington calls to say that Dr. Hosler is unavailable until Monday, but he's certain that Hosler would want to know about Amy. Yes, it's possible to have him as Amy's physician, but she has to go to St. Michael's Hospital. Kerrington explains that Amy should request a transfer of records. She must do that herself; a physician can't do it for her. Oddly, he adds, "Tread softly in those hallowed halls. It's not good to step on toes at competing hospitals. They don't take kindly to transfer requests. Good luck."

On Saturday, I find Amy eating a light lunch of thin broth and soft food. She seems depressed. When I ask her about it, she explains that late Friday she had more tests, including a procedure where she was partially conscious. Apparently, doctors performed a needle biopsy. Guided by X-rays taken earlier and by real-time ultrasound, they took a sample of a tumor in her pancreas.

"It hurt like hell," she says.

I try to cheer her with the news about Hosler. She's glad but wishes she didn't have to wait until Monday. I promise to get the necessary forms right away.

However, there is no *right away* when it comes to hospital procedures, and the usual red tape is even worse because it's Saturday. People I need aren't around, and next week is iffy because of Thanksgiving. After hours of running from department to department, I'm no closer to getting Amy home than when I started. Exhausted, I go back to Amy with a made-up excuse. She's not fooled by my phony optimism.

"Amy," I finally admit, "it's almost as if they're purposely trying to block us."

"Maybe it's the money," she says. "They figure they've made an investment in me and don't like someone else using what they bought."

"We'll get those test results. We have to. Otherwise—"

"Otherwise, I'll have them done again," she says. "I don't care. I want Dr. Hosler, no matter what—even if it means repeating every one of those stinking procedures."

At home, I try to unwind by watching television, but I'm preoccupied and can't follow the storyline of *Magnum, P.I.* Judging by today's standstill, Dr. Gryden is sure to resist Amy's transfer, and he's out of town and unavailable till Wednesday. At ten o'clock, the telephone rings. I immediately go to answer it, but then hesitate. *What if it's Eleni? What will I tell her about her mom?*

It's Dr. Hosler. He says he wants to see Amy, but it'll have to be on Monday. In the meantime, he advises I should get the forms for Amy's release and have the hospital forward her medical records to him. I tell him that seems impossible. He groans and then barks, "Those bastards! The sons-of-bitches are trying to lock us out."

After a moment, he says, "They don't like to admit that a patient might prefer another hospital. I'll do what I can, but my hands are tied until Monday. Don't worry. I know how to deal with those arrogant bastards."

I feel better knowing that Hosler is on our side, but I don't like the battle lines drawn around Amy. She shouldn't be subjected to that. This is 1984, for crying out loud. Doesn't a patient have any rights? I have to do something before they start some procedure that can't be interrupted. Jesus, I hate to think how Amy might react if Hosler can't be her doctor. My mind is made up to take action tomorrow, so I go upstairs and tell the kids to sleep in and forget about Sunday school. Downstairs, I snap off the TV, but don't fall asleep until I work out a scheme to get Amy out of that damn hospital.

I'm in the hospital at seven a.m. with Amy's sweat suit and winter coat. In the empty lobby, I commandeer a wheelchair. Tossing the clothes onto the seat, I push my way to the elevators, past signs marked "Restricted, Staff Only" and "Visitor Hours Strictly Enforced." I think about wearing a surgical mask, but settle for the mask of determination that I shaped last night. Then I walk briskly past a uniformed guard. Taking a cue from the swaggering tactics of Tom Selleck, I pretend to belong here and know exactly what I'm doing. A female guard looks sternly at me. I look first in her eyes and then through her in the direction of Amy's room.

Amy is lying in bed and facing the windows when I come through the double doors of her ward. I figure she's asleep. Sheets and blankets are tucked tightly around her, outlining the fetal position of her small body. This is how she lies when she's in pain, and it must be bad because she's tucked her knees up to her chest.

I shake her gently and whisper so others aren't disturbed. "Amy, wake up."

She looks up with a start and says, "Thank God you're here. They came early this morning and told me I can't leave. They said I have to have surgery as soon as possible."

"That's not likely," I say. "Gryden's away until Wednesday, and Thursday's Thanksgiving, but none of that matters. We'll be long gone before they know it."

"What are you talking about?"

"Come on. Put on these clothes, and keep real quiet. I'm taking you outa here."

"Are we going to St. Mike's?"

"Not yet. I haven't cleared it with Hosler, but we're working on it. First step is to break out of this prison camp."

"You mean escape like Steve McQueen?"

"You got it, babe."

"Nicky, I love you."

"I love you, too. Now quit gabbin' and hurry up. Time's a wastin'."

I kiss her gently and assume my tough-guy persona before I lose my nerve. As I help Amy dress, I glance toward the double doors. They seem farther away than before. Some of the patients are awake now. The woman at the end of the row nearest the door coughs loudly twice and then adds a third bark. It sounds like a signal.

"Don't worry," says Amy. "She always does that when she wakes up."

Suddenly, both doors burst open and in walk Gryden's three interns. Amy fills a pant leg of her sweat suit, but stops dressing when she sees them.

"Keep going," I say. "Just ignore these guys."

"Mr. Demetriou. Mrs. Demetriou. What are you doing?" asks the surly one.

I swallow hard. This one is tougher than the Vandyke kid that I expected would take charge. I decide not to argue. They already know my plan but might not be sure what to do about it. I pretend they aren't there and Amy and I have authority to do as we please.

"Mr. Demetriou, your wife is very ill and should not leave. If she does, we can't be responsible for what happens. She should be in the care of a competent doctor."

Amy and I are in our own little bubble now. We're used to that. We've fought and won most of our battles when we've felt most alone. Amy slips on her things and sits down in the wheelchair. "I don't know where they took the clothes I wore when you brought me in," she says. "Should we look around?"

"No time for that. You got your wedding ring?"

"Yeah. You took my diamond and my watch home already, right?"

"Right. Forget the rest. Our donation for their five-star accommodations."

The three doctors-to-be continue to object. "Mrs. Demetriou, we must insist...."

We pay no attention. Amy adjusts the footrests on the wheelchair and sets her feet firmly in place. "Okay, dude," she says, "let's blow this popcorn stand."

The trio steps forward just as we start to roll.

"Mr. Demetriou," someone says, "we can't let you do this."

I clench my jaw and feel my temple throb. Moving only my lips, I say—or think I say—"Oh, no? Just watch me." On cue, Amy flips one footrest out of her way and pedals her foot against the floor, propelling the chair forward. I wait long enough for her to lift her foot to safety before I bull the two of us headlong toward the center of the three men. They step aside, narrowly escaping the imaginary horns of the wheelchair. Hemingway would have cheered our bullish action even while mourning the defeated matadors.

CHAPTER FORTY

He had surrendered all reality, all dread and fear,
to the doctor beside him, as people do.

—William Faulkner

"We took another biopsy to be sure we got it all," says Dr. Hosler.

The surgeon has come out to see me several times during the long night. Each time he visits, I want to hear that it's over and Amy's all right. Instead, I hear about another wait and get only the barest details.

"I'm sorry it takes so long," he says, "but we're waiting for the analysis. I want to be sure we get all the cancer without cutting away more than necessary."

I search his face for clues about what's really going on. Even on his slim face, his jowls sag like the surgical mask that droops from his neck, hinting at fatigue and despair. "How's she doing?" I say, as if Amy's effort is as important as the doctor's is.

"She's taking it like a trooper. Amy's a fighter with the will of a saint. That's going to help her when...." He pauses. The sound of "win" quickens my pulse until he adds, "... when this is all over."

Earlier, Hosler told Amy and me to expect weeks of hospitalization and months of home convalescence. He's never mentioned winning. Neither has he said how Amy might react to radiation or chemotherapy; that's someone else's department. No one tells us how Amy will die; that's nobody's department.

"Her heart's okay?" I ask, remembering Amy's experience with arrhythmia.

"Ticking like a Swiss watch," he says without changing expression. "Her heart's been fine throughout the night. If it hasn't acted up, after what she's been through, her heart won't ever give her trouble."

"Thank ... thank God for that," I manage to say.

The name of God sticks in my throat, and I have to force it out. Then I regret my hesitation and hope God won't see my doubt and anger. My pleas to an almighty started with invocations of faithfulness, beseeching him to heal Amy completely. As the night wore on, I begged for intervention despite my unworthiness, and I fortified my prayer with promises to be forever obedient—stacking my petitions like barricades against my increasing apprehension that maybe God doesn't give a shit about Amy and me.

"I need to go back and scrub," Dr. Hosler says. A spot of blood on the surgeon's cap stares at me, and I stare back, not knowing what to ask. When he offers, "It won't be much longer," I hear a double meaning. He sees my alarm and squeezes my shoulder as he says, "You'll have some time together. She'll be coming home before you know it."

I look into his eyes. Even at one a.m., after ten hours in surgery, they are caring eyes. I wonder if God shows his love through servants like Dr. Hosler. Or are God's servants merely vassals who show their love to ward off his wrath?

Hosler presses a disk on the wall. Huge doors open with a hiss, and the doctor passes through the doorway. I want to follow him and do, I-don't-know-what, but the passage is quickly sealed. I'm alone again, just as I've been since Andy and Saundra left the hospital when a long wait became apparent. Without hesitation, I had told them I could wait by myself. Perhaps my suggestion came too early, but Amy's parents are not well and can't bear the strain. I assured them that I'd be all right and promised to call often. Before that, I said the same to my family. At the time, I thought I had made the best decision. The waiting room was crowded then, and I had to walk to another hall to find an available phone. Since ten o'clock, I've had the room to myself. Occasionally, I hear a distant voice, but mostly I hear the rickety clatter of a broken-down pop machine. The noise is like the chatter of an ascending roller coaster. The imaginary car never reaches its pinnacle, but I anticipate its plunge at any moment. No one is with me to share this ride, but that's the way I want it. Being the only one to hear the news delays its reality until others confirm it. Good news will be reinforced by repeating it often. Bad news might fade away if there's no one else to hear it.

Ten-year-old Erin and twelve-year-old Tim are staying with the Landons, the parents of their favorite babysitter. Eleni's been away at college since I drove her back to Grand Rapids on the Saturday after Thanksgiving. Like her younger brother and sister, nineteen-year-old Eleni doesn't know the seriousness of Amy's surgery. I thought it not fair to burden her with too much worry because she'd feel responsible to take care of Tim and Erin. The last thing that Amy and I want is for Eleni to quit school and become a substitute mother.

It's up to me to shepherd everyone and keep things as normal as possible. Four days ago, Amy, the kids, and I spent Thanksgiving with my folks and visited Amy's family in the evening. Mum was the word regarding Amy's diagnosis.

When I took Eleni back to Calvin College, Amy stayed home, pretending she had to prepare for a "diagnostic procedure" scheduled for Monday. Eleni suspects something, but, long ago, she learned not to say anything that might frighten her mother. I don't like being the control master again, but see no other way. I know the dangers of micromanaging everyone's conduct, but I also know that my present responsibility doesn't compare to the detailed supervision that'll be necessary in the months ahead.

I look up at the clock and count the seconds as I hear them tick away. Counting has always comforted me. It's something I understand in an unfathomable world. Opening my briefcase, I count the computer grade sheets that are due in the principal's office tomorrow. An advantage of my solitary sentence is that I've completed my schoolwork. I'm proud of that, just as I am of my regular attendance at work. Amy is due to come home at Christmas, and I can't take any time off until then because I'll need lots of days off later to handle homecare, chemo and radiation therapies, and who knows what else. In the meantime, I'll need to manage driving between work, hospital, and home. Every day, I'll connect corners of a triangular route, traveling more than thirty-five miles along each leg like an itinerate circuit rider.

Satisfied that I've recorded my grades, I sort through my briefcase and start a detailed list of what I'll need to do to balance my tasks. Numbered lists provide a cognitive defense against the emotional chaos I'm feeling. Among my papers, I discover To Do lists that I had forgotten and a diagram labeled "Whipple Procedure" that Hosler made at his office to explain the surgery. Then my heart sinks when I come across two letters that I got weeks ago and ignored without telling Amy.

One is from my principal, a form letter generated from a computer analysis of grades I issued last card marking. I know I can justify my grades, but I'm annoyed that I have to. The principal accuses me of using grades to control troublemakers and implies that my retaliation is because I'm under stress, yet he knows nothing of Amy's condition.

The other letter is an IRS audit alleging I owe $2,141 plus interest and penalties for my 1982 tax returns. The notice is the latest of repeated denials of my requests for a postponement. I have no time to search shoe boxes of receipts related to writing my book, but the IRS doesn't believe my excuse that I'm facing life-threatening matters at home. The thought of putting into words that my wife is dying of cancer makes me cringe.

The *swish* of the automatic door startles me, but Dr. Hosler's smile is a welcome sight. "Good news," he says. "Amy's come through okay." He's still wearing his stained surgical cap, but he has the look of a man who's proud of what he's done. "She's in intensive care," he says, "and we'll watch her closely. I don't expect any problems."

"Oh, God. I'm so relieved. Thank you, Doctor. When can I see her?"

"Not tonight I'm afraid. She's in a sterile environment. It's a normal precaution against infection. Her incision is extensive, and we had to keep it open for a long time. Once I cut out the main tumor—it was a big sucker more than ten centimeters long—then I removed small sections of tissue around it. I took only a little at a time until I got a clear biopsy. I'm confident I got it all, but I took samples of lymph nodes as well."

"How much did you have to take out?"

The surgeon takes a pen and prescription pad from his pocket and answers me by drawing the same diagram I have in my briefcase. As he describes what he did during surgery, he marks incision lines and blacks out sections until he has obliterated the entire sketch. He has removed Amy's entire pancreas, spleen, and bile duct, part of her stomach, nearly all lymph nodes in the area, her duodenum, and portions of her small intestine.

"Fortunately," he says with a sigh, "I found no cancer in Amy's liver or lungs."

There is no triumph in Hosler's endnote. Rather, he seems hesitant to claim any consolation. Though he leaves a door open to doubt, I choose to accept Hosler's report as entirely positive. Denial and acceptance go hand-in-hand when you're desperate. Amy will be home in a month or so, but learning that she has survived in this damaged way is like salvaging a rare flower that's been stepped on. Nevertheless, I can't afford melancholy; I need to cheer the children with news that their mother is still alive.

"Nick," says Amy, "can you help me ask my questions when I see Hosler?"

"Sure," I say, drawing closer as Amy leans to brace herself against the bathroom sink. "I'll be right beside you."

"Hand me another square of gauze," she orders, "and then wrap the roll around a couple more times—but not as tight as last time. I'm not a mummy, you know. I still gotta breathe."

Since Amy came home, our dialogue has been constantly interrupted by medical needs, so we hold two or more conversations simultaneously—one always bumping against the other like we do now as we struggle with bandages in our tiny bathroom.

"I have so many questions," she says with a grunt, "I'm afraid I'll forget some of 'em. Reach over here and do this spot."

I squeeze between her and the toilet to unravel a roll of gauze and press it in place. "Oops, sorry," I say when I brush a tender spot. "How about a list to help you remember?"

"Okay, stop. I'll hold it right here," she says, pointing to a section of gauze. "Go ahead and cut it. No, not there. Up about six inches—and tape it down on my back. I don't want you pressing any spots up front where it hurts so much."

Amy is naked except for the huge bandage across her midsection. I move awkwardly in our crowded bathroom to avoid unnecessary touching. It's hard to be alert at 5 a.m., but we have to start early. I don't sleep much because I keep waking up from a dream that leaves me frightened but with no memory of its images. Good thing we don't sleep in the same bed.

It's December 28, 1984, our twenty-first wedding anniversary. We'll celebrate by visiting Dr. Hosler at his Glen Acre office. One of the things we'll discuss is Amy's home nursing care. My Christmas vacation started the day Amy was released from St. Mike's, but I'll have to return to work on Wednesday, January 2. The thought of Amy at home without me is terrifying. We talked to a visiting nurse this week and will make plans after we iron out the details. Hopefully, Hosler will help us decide. Meanwhile, we've gotten used to everyday routines like changing a dressing.

I see a wet spot on the gauze and say, "Uh-oh, you're seeping through. Should we do it all over again?"

Amy, who's gone through this for five weeks now, says, "Don't worry about it. That always happens. We'll just follow the schedule. I'm due for a change at eleven. Then Hosler will change the next one in his office at four."

"Sweetheart, how will you get by next week? You can't do this by yourself."

"I'll learn by then. Some of it I can already handle. Oh … could you write out the questions for me? My eyes keep crossing when I try to write, and I can't control the pen. I feel like a drunken sailor."

"It's the narcotic pain killers," I say. "No problem. I'll be your *sexitary*."

"That's one of my questions," she says.

"What is? Here, let me help you put your arm through." I guide her into a gown that's ten sizes too big. She hates anything binding because her skin is so sensitive.

"Sex," she says. "Ouch! Watch what you're doing. The thing is, I don't know if I want to talk about it. Not with him, anyway."

"You don't want to have sex with Hosler? Jeez, I'm relieved."

"No, silly. With you. I mean I do, but I can't."

Like a teenager whose secret wish is about to be discovered, I deny having such thoughts and say, "Of course not. It'd be too painful. Don't even think about it."

"I wasn't thinking anything until the visiting nurse brought it up when we talked privately. She said there were *ways*—other ways to have sex—and she has a book and video to help us. She said it's a common concern when recovering from major surgery."

"She's nuts. You can hardly get in and out of a hospital gown without assistance."

"She means later, after I've healed a little."

"Yeah, but you'll be laid up ... I mean ... it'll be weeks—months maybe."

"That's her point. It'll be a long time before we have normal sex, and that can be a problem. Some people lose the will to live because they don't feel loved. The nurse said that could lead to stress and screw things up between us."

"Great choice of words. I guess Freud was right."

"Nick, don't make fun. What she said worries me. You'll be unhappy and—"

"*And nothing.* I'll never leave you. I don't care if we never have sex."

"You'll want to see another woman."

"Bullshit! I've never been unfaithful and never will be. Stop worrying about it, for God's sake." *Why am I yelling? What am I mad about?*

"Please don't be angry," says Amy. "I've thought about it since she brought it up. Nicky, I love you, but sex is the last thing on my mind. I want to be with you, but—"

"What did she tell you ... that you were a bad wife because you can't have sex? That's nonsense." Then I lower my voice and say, "Honey, of course I want to make love to you. I love you very much, but I don't need physical love to express that. I know you love me, too. You show me in other ways besides sex. That nurse is an idiot."

I talk as if I'm angry with the nurse, but I know better—and knowing that I feel so lonely makes me feel selfish and hateful. I hate myself ... I hate the whole damn situation, and I'm ashamed that I sometimes hate Amy. But goddamn it, I need to feel loved, too!

"I like it that we hold hands and hug as much as we do," says Amy. "I miss cuddling, though. I'm okay with that, but what about you? The nurse thought—"

"Whatever she told you means nothing to us. It's for other people—shallow people who don't have the kind of love we have."

"She said that I had to think about you. I had to consider your needs, too."

"My need is to take care of you and make sure you get healthy again."

"Are you sure? Nick, she wanted to talk about oral sex and … touching … and other things. She said we could learn different positions. When I think about that, I get scared. I don't think I can do those things. I have got so much pain, and there are tubes still hanging out of my body. And my period starts and stops and starts up again without warning."

"Honey, I know how difficult it is for you. Put the whole thing out of your mind."

"Nicky, are you sure that it's all right with you?"

"Look, let's stop this right now. I love you, and you love me—and we don't need sex. Besides, abstinence makes the heart grow harder … er, I mean fonder."

"You're making jokes, but do you mean it? Maybe a little advice will help us."

"Amy, when the time's right, we'll have a really good time. End of discussion."

Amy sighs and says, "We're not done yet. We still have two things to do. First, give me a big kiss. Then we need to make that list for Dr. Hosler."

The list has to wait. Amy is exhausted after changing her dressing, but she still has to check her blood sugar and give herself the proper dosage of insulin. I'm surprised at how adept she has become at pricking her finger for a blood sample, measuring her insulin, and injecting a hypodermic into her thigh. She's always been squeamish about shots, and her fear of needles and pins ranks high among her phobias. Yet, she does the life-giving ritual four times a day, knowing that she'll be insulin dependent for the rest of her life.

She follows her injection with in-bed stretches and breathing exercises, while I set out her fifteen medications and prepare her breakfast. I measure and record everything that enters or leaves her body. She eats small, calibrated portions six times a day. Since Amy's come home, I've worked out a routine to prepare what I can ahead of time—a task that'll be more important when I'm away at work.

After her regimen, Amy takes her morning nap on the La-Z-Boy in the sun-room. When I walk in later with a tray of her midmorning medicines and a snack of one-third cup frozen yogurt, she looks startled and asks, "Where are the kids?"

"Upstairs, playing Monopoly," I say. "Honey, what's wrong?"

"I had a bad dream."

I set down the tray and take her hand. "I'm sorry. You want to talk about it?"

"Nick, I want to tell you something, and I don't want you to take it the wrong way. I have to say this because you're so strong and I'm a scared-ass chicken."

"Sweetheart, you're the bravest woman I know. No one could have—"

"Shut up and let me finish." The weakness of her voice negates her chiding. Lines of tears roll from each eye and stop at high points of her cheeks, remaining balanced until more tears cause them to drop from her face. I try to look in Amy's eyes, but she turns to stare out the windows. She seems to look past the gnarled two-hundred-year-old pine in our front yard, over the privet hedge we started from seedlings, across the busy street that runs in front of our house, and beyond all else that limits her sight.

Amy's hand beckons mine. She takes it and says, "Nick, I'm glad it's me who's dying instead of you."

"Sweetheart, you've got a long way to go before—"

She ignores my interruption. "I could never do what you're doing now or what you'll have to do when I'm gone. I'm sorry to leave you with so much to do—the children, the house, everything. You're strong and can manage it. I couldn't."

"Honey, please. Don't talk like that. Together we can lick this. We've done it before. We've beaten every setback we've had, and I know we can do it again."

"Nick, remember when you had an epididymal cyst? You thought you had cancer. So did I, and I was scared—so scared that I couldn't take care of you without getting angry."

"That was my fault," I say. "I was too stubborn to let you. You know how I get. I want to do it my way, and I don't take advice very well. I can be a mean bastard."

"Maybe, but you also were afraid that you couldn't rely on me. I always get scared when you're sick. Even the flu makes me think awful things, and when I get scared...."

"You get angry," I say. "I know."

"I turn into a bitch because I'm frightened that you won't always be there to take care of me."

"You're long past that now. You're a lot tougher than you used to be."

"I don't know. I'm really worried now. I might not be able to do my share."

"Amy, don't belittle yourself. You have more guts than any woman I know."

"Maybe, but my guts are all hanging out right now. If this incision doesn't heal, I might lose the whole nine yards or nine feet—whatever it is."

"See what I mean? You still have a sense of humor, even when you're scared. You can make it if anybody can. Like Hosler said, you're one in a million."

"Thanks, but what if I can't live up to that? Nick, I love you, and I'm not giving up yet. I'm going to fight as long as I can, but I know there will be a time ... oh shit, I wish I were a poet. I wish I could say it like Shakespeare or Keats, but the simple truth is that my time is short. Please don't hate me for dying. And don't let the kids hate me for being a bad mother and leaving them."

"Amy, sweetheart ... I...."

"I can't talk anymore. Just promise that you'll forgive me and try not to hate me."

"I'll never hate you, and there's nothing to forgive."

"Just say it, dammit. Just say that you forgive me."

"Amy," I say through my tears. "My darling Amy. Please...."

"Say it!"

"Okay. Okay. I forgive you."

I want to ask her to forgive me, too, but I have less courage than she does. Amy is confronting death and admitting weakness—something I'm afraid to do. I dare not ask her for what my heart begs to hear ... that she forgive me for letting her die.

Our list of questions for Hosler has to wait again because Amy needs her dressing changed. I put some bread, lunchmeat, and cheese on the kitchen table and tell the kids to help themselves while I attend to Amy. We finish with the bandages just as the children finish eating, so Amy sits down at the kitchen table right after she comes out of the bathroom. I make sure the kids are out of earshot before I join her.

Pencil in hand, I say, "All right, you talk, and I'll write it down."

"Okay, but once I get started, I can't stop. Sort of like diarrhea of the mouth."

"Blast away. It'll do you good to blow the shit out. I won't say a word."

"Remember," she begins, "when they inserted a tube to drain my liver? It was torturous. I thought I was going to die. Will it always be like that? Can they put me out cold to avoid the pain? I need to have hope that the pain is worth it. Will it be so terrible that I'll *want* to die? If that's how it'll be, wouldn't I be better off dying right away?"

Amy's words convey a fury that belies her helplessness. Like someone leaping across an abyss, she's uses all her energy to make the jump, and, while in midair, wonders if she'll reach the other side. Unable to comfort her, I can only nod and write as fast as I can. I am her mute scribe, catching her words before they fall with her into nonexistence.

"We have to ask Hosler how we'll handle this when you go back to work. What about everyday routines? How will you drive me to chemo and radiation? What about side effects? Will it hurt? What good will it do? How sick will I be? Who will be my doctor? Do I have any choice? Should we look for help at other places like the Mayo Clinic?"

"Wait a sec," I say. "Slow down, I can't write that fast. How can you rattle off so many things all at once?"

Amy pauses before going on and then says, "Sorry, but I feel like I have to hurry because I don't have much time." She tries to straighten in her chair but groans and then gives up and slumps into what must be an uncomfortable position. I apologize, too, and then she continues, this time speaking more slowly. "Sometimes I wonder if we know what we're getting into. What kind of life can we expect from now on? What will it be like with more treatments and procedures? What about afterward when nothing else can be done? Will we have time to enjoy our last days together? Can we take a vacation? Will we need special equipment at home?"

Amy's exasperation increases as her words conjure more thoughts. "Don't get me wrong," she says, "I want to live, but maybe more treatments are a waste of time. It might be better to forget about it—just wait for the surgery to heal and then go out and have a good time. And what about my diabetes? At the hospital, Dr. Bashur talked to me like I was an *ordinary* diabetic. I'm not. I've got cancer, too. He wants me to be a *good diabetic patient*. I want to hit him when he says that I'll need to do this or that for the rest of my life. What *rest of my life*? I could kill myself by taking too much insulin ... or by stopping it altogether. What'll kill me first, cancer, or diabetes? And what difference does it make anyway?"

I stop writing and nearly push the pad off the table when I say, "Amy, please. I wish you wouldn't talk like that. This is hard on me, too."

Amy reaches across the table to take my hand. For an instant, I want to draw away, but I turn my palm up to accept her touch when she says, "I'm sorry. I don't mean to take it out on you. Sometimes I just get angry at everybody."

In a pleading tone that is also accusing, I say, "Well, turn that anger on your illness. Make it work *for* you, not *against* you." I want to say that I need her to extend her life as long as possible. *Is that selfish of me?*

"Amy," I say, "don't let anger destroy you. As you damn well know, your willfulness has worked against you sometimes, but the strength of your will has also meant the difference between getting well or staying sick. All of us—me and the kids—we need to know that you want to go on living."

"I do. Damnit, I do. And I will get better. For you and for Eleni, and Tim, and Erin. I'm going to do my best. I promise you."

"And for yourself, too," I say. "You have your degree now, and a career to look forward to."

"I owe that to my teacher," she admits. "She let me pass without taking the final."

"What do you mean, *let you*? You had all A's. You deserved it."

"Damn right I did. And I deserve to live too, don't I?"

"You bet you do, baby. You and I have a lot of living to do."

Later, at his office, Dr. Hosler answers our questions patiently and reassures Amy that she has a good chance to get better. When she expresses concern about a visiting nurse, he recommends a new home-nursing group headed by his friend, Mary Lindstrom, and he immediately sets up an appointment for us to meet her on Monday evening.

Amy insisted that we spend the early part of Monday putting the house in order so that Mary will have no reason to turn us down. Snow begins to fall in the morning with a predicted accumulation of several inches by nightfall. Once upon a time, Amy and I loved snowstorms—storybook intervals when nature took complete control—but tonight it makes me wonder what would happen if a storm trapped me at work and I couldn't get home, and what if the visiting nurse couldn't reach Amy when she was most in need?

I hide my concern from Amy while we sit in the sunroom watching a rerun of *MASH* until the nurse arrives. The sunroom has nine windows along three walls, allowing sun to come in most of the day. It's our small but cozy family room where a hide-a-bed couch doubles as my bed in the evening while Amy sleeps alone in the bedroom.

Comedy shows like *MASH* are all that Amy watches. In this familiar episode, Hawkeye discovers that his new nurse is a married woman he was in love with years earlier. I try to follow the storyline, but I have one eye on the TV and the other on the snow falling outside. The fluffy white stuff is mesmerizing and leads my thoughts elsewhere. Eleni will soon be back in college—something Amy and I insisted on, though Eleni had asked to stay to take care of her mother. I worry about returning to work and leaving Amy alone, but putting Eleni in the position of nursemaid and not graduating on time is out of the question. That's why Mary's coming tonight. Still, I'm not convinced that it's okay to trust strangers to care for Amy.

Amy directs my thoughts back to the TV when she says, "I'm glad you're more like BJ than Hawkeye."

"What?" I say.

"Hawkeye has no qualms about chasing married women. BJ would never do that."

"Hmm," I utter. "I guess you're right."

"*Guess*? You'd better be sure, buster. What if my new nurse flirts with you?"

"Huh? What are you talking about? It's a TV show, for crying out loud. Hawkeye's a make-believe character who lives like there's no tomorrow."

"For some of us, there *is* no tomorrow."

"Bull crap, I'm counting on having you around to keep me straight."

Unexpectedly, the doorbell rings. It's twenty minutes before the nurse is due. At the door, I see a tall, thin woman wearing a parka with the hood pulled up protectively. In her right hand, she carries a small black satchel that looks like an old-fashioned doctor's bag. "Hello, I'm Mary Lindstrom from Personalized Care Services," she says. Her accent shows a trace of British, and her early arrival in bad weather indicates her reliability.

It doesn't take long for Mary to win us over. By the way she responds to Amy's questions, I can tell that she's caring and sensitive to the needs of the entire family.

"Mary," says Amy, "I worry about Nick. He thinks everything is on his shoulders. I'm afraid he'll worry all day long when he's at work and drive home every night like a bat out of hell."

I cringe when Amy says that. The truth is that, after receiving an alarming report from the hospital, I raced the entire thirty-five miles at speeds well over eighty miles per hour, often zigzagging through traffic and passing slower cars by tearing along the shoulder or the median.

"Oh, Nick, I'm sorry," says Mary. "I know how you must feel sometime. I cannot promise that emergencies won't occur, but I can promise that our nurses will respond so you won't have to act with such urgency. You can trust us to handle it for you."

I ask if other nurses besides her will be coming on a regular basis.

"Yes," she says. "I work with Kristyn, Margritt, and another Mary. They are all excellent nurses. I'm sure you'll like them. Two of us will come together until we're accustomed to the routine. Then at least one of us will come three times a week, probably Monday, Wednesday, and Friday or Saturday. How would it be if we plan to be here when you're at school? That'll provide assistance for a good part of those days. You'll be back at work on Wednesday, won't you? Well, Kristyn and I can be here by midmorning and stay for two hours. Does that suit you and Amy?"

Instead of answering, I make a statement that is harsher than I intend. "I still want to be the one who takes Amy to chemotherapy," I declare.

"All right then, we'll plan for that. Dr. Hosler tells me that those treatments won't begin until February. He seems very confident that Amy will need very few chemo treatments. The good news is that no radiation is required at this time."

The remainder of the visit is devoted to finalizing our agreement to employ Mary's company. Her repeated mention of Dr. Hosler reminds me of their friendship and prompts me to ask her a question, out of Amy's earshot, as she prepares to leave.

"Mary," I whisper, "I'm concerned about how I talked to Dr. Hosler after he did a procedure that hurt Amy terribly. I worried that the cancer had spread and was frightened out of my mind after trying to reach him for two days. When I caught up with him, I accused him of not keeping me informed. I'm afraid I said things I shouldn't have said. He was very angry. I never heard a doctor talk like that."

Mary stops buttoning her coat and touches my shoulder. "Don't worry about it, Nick. He's heard it all—and he's said it all, too. Jordan Hosler is a dear friend. I know he can be a holy terror, but that's because he's so dedicated to his patients. He gets very angry if someone questions his commitment. Many surgeons get mad—or go mad—but it's ego-driven for most of them. It's not like that with Jordan. With him, it's because he tries so hard to do the right thing. His nurses have heard his roar—believe me, I know because I've been his nurse—but he never bites. He expects his staff to have the same devotion to patients that he has."

Though her words are helpful, I need to confess more. "I'm afraid I might have offended him beyond repair."

"Since the incident, has he said anything to make you feel that way?"

"No. He hasn't brought it up at all, but I was such a fool."

"I assure you that he does not think you're a fool. Trust me; he knows how difficult it is for family members, especially husbands and wives."

"That's why I feel so bad. He told me about his wife. He said she has breast cancer and that he worries about her like I worry about Amy."

"You didn't know that at the time, and now you do. Let it be a reminder that he understands the pain you feel and he'll do all he can to make things better for you and Amy."

After Mary leaves and I tuck Amy in bed, I pick up the brochure from Personalized Care Services. In one section I read, "PCS is a pioneer in the field of home nursing and offers hospice care to those in need. Ask us about hospice. We are proud to pioneer this service in Michigan."

Later, as I'm falling asleep in bed, I wonder: what the hell is *hospice care*?

During February and March, I took time off from work to drive Amy to Hosler's office and to the hospital for her chemotherapy sessions. She responded so well to the chemo that Hosler canceled her final treatment. She was elated and used the free day to answer a letter from an old friend who was planning a reunion with twenty-six others who went through elementary and high school together. Amy celebrated her good news by accepting the invitation for us to attend the two-day party in April at a Glen Acre hotel.

CHAPTER FORTY-ONE

Hope is the worst of evils, for it prolongs the torments of man.

—Friedrich Nietzsche

Amy is stunning, modeling her dress in our hotel room. She's as beautiful as the day we were married. Turning before a full-length mirror, she spins and lets the gossamer layers of her magenta gown flow like Salome's veils. Two weeks ago, when she bought the petite size eight dress and talked about attending her class reunion, I allowed myself to imagine our own intimate reunion. Last week she wore the dress to church—her first visit in six months—and received a round of applause from parishioners eager to acknowledge God's work and proud that their prayers brought about her apparent recovery. I teased her about our upcoming tryst, igniting anticipation of being alone after the lights go out at the hotel reception. Now her tantalizing dance stokes that fire.

Suddenly, Amy stops in mid-twirl and shoots her hand to her midsection. She twists her mouth and makes an ugly face while tugging at her dress to adjust the hidden waistband that lies beneath the bloused layers of delicate nylon mesh. Drawing a breath, she winces then exhales with a sigh and frowns at her image in the mirror.

Startled, I say, "Honey? What's wrong?"

"It's getting worse," she says. "I might not be able to stay through dinner."

"Maybe if you let out the elastic some more."

"I've done that." She smoothes the bodice of her dress and screws up her face. "My stomach's puffed up, and it hurts up higher under the ribcage, like it did before."

It's nearly five months after Amy's surgery. In March, Dr. Hosler gave us hope for full recovery. Amy's spirits rose as she primped and preened like a lovebird. At Easter, we dared to believe in her renewal, but held off our celebration to coincide with tonight's reunion. Then the ache returned. For me, it was sudden, but God knows how long Amy had sensed it. Now, I stand by helplessly imagining the ghastly tumor growing exponentially as she wreathes in agony. A bad feeling washes over me, and I'm reminded that coincidental with the recurrence of her pain was the return of my dreadful nightmare that I can only vaguely remember.

"Honey, it would be a shame if no one saw you. You're as pretty as a bride."

"Yeah? Well, I haven't been much of a bride for you. It would have been better if nothing had ever happened between us. You'd have saved yourself a lot of—"

"Stop that. I love you. I loved you then, and I love you now more than ever. I have no regrets. I'd do it all again in a New York minute."

"Nick, you're such a romantic. I love you for that and thank you for loving me, but...."

"Hey, it's been my pleasure, Scarlett. Now, how about it? A little celebrating will do you a lot of good."

"I don't know if I can. It hurts too much, and I never knew physical pain could make me so incredibly tired. It's as though all my energy is used to grow more cancer."

"Amy, don't give up. It's not quite five, and dinner's not until eight. You've looked forward to seeing your friends. Let's go down for the cocktail hour just to say hello. Then we'll leave early so you can rest before dinner."

"Hmm, maybe you're right. I would like to see who's here before I get too tired."

"And I'd like them to see how beautiful you are."

"You really think so?" she says, glancing at the mirror. "Okay, I'll give it a try."

I step closer to kiss her, and she gives me a soft peck on the lips.

"Don't mess my lipstick," she says. "I want to save myself for my husband."

With my head still angled for a kiss, I send her a question with my eyes.

"Don't get excited on your first cruise," she warns. "I can't promise anything."

Amy is bright and effusive talking to friends as we sip soft drinks and cocktails. I don't think anyone suspects anything when we slip out early, but she takes her strongest painkillers as soon as we get back to our room. Flopping onto the bed, she flips through TV channels and stops at a scene with Audrey Hepburn in *Breakfast at Tiffany's*. Amy seems spellbound by Holly Golightly but soon falls asleep.

An hour or so passes, and I consider waking her for dinner. Suddenly, she awakens with a start, looks about the room, and says she'll be ready in fifteen minutes.

The rest of the evening goes much like the first part. Amy is charming, and she listens attentively to other people's stories, laughs at their jokes, and giggles when someone teases her about how little she's changed in all these years. Her repartees remind me of how I saw her when I was a teen believing I was doomed to watch her from a distance. Like tonight, everyone in school seemed to like her. Yet I know that wasn't quite true. Some resented her good humor, believing she was too shallow to worry about important things. Today, they'd be surprised to learn of Amy's depression, yet I wonder.... At a party like this, who knows how many people pretend to have a good time? How many have experienced problems as Amy has, or worse? Perhaps Amy, too, senses that because she seems genuinely interested in their stories. She hasn't seen any of these people in years, so I'm surprised when she talks at length about her cancer surgery to a woman who was never her intimate friend.

Back in the privacy of our room before the party breaks up, Amy is quiet and contemplative. Resting on the bed, she lies on her back and closes her eyes. She used to lie like that and invite me to lie crossways while she cradled my head on her tummy. Then she'd stroke my hair and play with my earlobe in that bewitching way she did before we made love. Now my heart quickens when she pats the spot beside her and says, "If you prop yourself up so your weight's not on my tummy, you can lie here like we used to."

I lie awkwardly on my stomach with my arms folded across my chest to support myself. Gingerly, I put my head down so that my ear brushes her breastbone, touching but not pressing onto her chest. The familiar sound of Amy's heartbeat transports me to another time, and I forget my discomfort. Amy's heart is pounding strongly—drumming a beat as if it had years of marching to look forward to.

After a moment, she says, "Nicky, I feel so sad that no one knows who I really am."

"Honey, you haven't seen this gang in years. They don't know about the real you. The people who know you are the ones in Recovery, especially the ones you've helped. They know you as a caring person who's worked hard to get well."

"No, they don't know me either. Not as a whole person. No one does—not even you—and no one ever will because the part that's still inside me is gonna die. I'm just a desert lily that never fully bloomed. Our kids will remember me through children's eyes. School friends will remember me as happy-go-lucky. Your family will know me as sad and fearful or angry and mean. I wish people saw more than that, but no one will know the *Me* whose life has never begun. After I die, they'll remember the wrong person and misjudge me like the *Break-*

fast at Tiffany's girl. 'Amy GoBrightly' is only a piece of who I was, but who I *was* is all I'll ever *be*."

Her sorrow breaks my heart, and I try to quiet her sadness. "Hush, my darling," is all I can offer. "Don't think about that now. Shhhh. Shhhh." Over and over, I repeat quieting words. Yet for all my sibilant hushing, I secretly want her to go on talking. Her toes curl around the edge of life, and when she dares to look, she can see the other side. How strange it must be to see the end when it is so near. Does God give special wisdom to those who know that death is imminent? My heart says yes. Why else would he be so cruel?

The notion that Amy's death might have meaning is not comforting because I don't want to believe she will die. I refuse to accept it even now after another week of hospitalization. I'm waiting for the results of Amy's latest tests in a visitor's area at St. Mike's. The room, with windows along the north, east, and south walls, reminds me of our sunroom at home, but is much larger. The sun, my companion for several hours, now hides behind gathering storm clouds. It's late in the day, now. Earlier, sunlight allowed me to direct my thoughts to daydreaming and planning the conversion of our sunroom into Amy's convalescent room. I'll move the couch upstairs and set up a hospital bed in its place. In my mind, I imagine how a warm, sunshine-soaked room will aid her recovery. Yet the idea frightens me in a way I have felt before. It's the same terror I feel when waking from that God-awful dream whose details I can't remember.

"Nick, did you hear me? Do you understand what I'm telling you?"

It's Dr. Hosler. Yes, of course. He must have come in when I was napping.

"Nick, the tests verify it. There are no uncertainties. I'm afraid another tumor—"

"What?"

"There's new growth in the same region as before."

I rub my eyes and stare at the doctor. *Snap out of it Nick! Don't lose control now.* "What have you told Amy? How is she? I want to see her." I get up from my chair and start toward the hallway. Dr. Hosler rises part way and gently holds me back.

"Not yet. I gave her something to help her rest. She's had a grueling three days."

He waits till I sit again before going on. "Yes, I've talked with Amy. She took it very well. I think she already knew. Amy's been very brave through all of this."

"Hold on. What are you saying? I have to see her. Where is she?"

"She's back in her room and sleeping comfortably."

"But why? Is she in danger?"

Hosler peers at me quizzically. "No, not now, and not for a while yet, but, Nick, you need to understand that Amy's condition has become very grave."

"But surely you can do something."

"I'm afraid not. The tumor is in the same cavity as the other one. Three weeks ago, there was nothing. Now it's nearly the size of the one we removed in November."

"Then operate at once. You've already scheduled it, haven't you? If it's growing that fast shouldn't you...." I leave the sentence unfinished and get up to leave again.

The doctor puts his hand on my shoulder and urges me back into my chair. The racing thoughts I had earlier have stopped. My mind is suddenly blank, and where my heart is supposed to be I sense a widening hole whose size mirrors the tumor growing inside Amy's body.

Hosler leans forward and looks deep into my eyes as if to be sure he has my attention. I turn away. He grabs my shoulders and jerks me toward him. I feel manhandled, forced into a box I can't escape.

"Nick. Listen to me. You need to know this. It's *inoperable*."

My head spins. I feel a jolt and a shove, like at the start of a roller coaster. Then another jolt and a change of direction—as if I've been switched onto another track. I grab the armrest of my chair but can't stop plummeting down a long railway. Suddenly, I'm obsessed with knowing the precise moment of the end of the line.

"When?"

"No one can tell for sure. It depends on whether Amy can accept chemo and radiation treatments. I'm sorry to say that none of those treatments hold much promise. They might extend her life long enough to give you and the family time to—"

"Time? That's what I'm asking. How much time?"

"Nick, no one can be sure. Don't be fooled by what you see on television. Most often, doctors can't put a time frame on this kind of thing—especially at Amy's young age. There are too many factors. We just don't—"

"Will she make it through the summer?"

Dr. Hosler shakes his head and frowns. "Nick ... I'm sorry. I don't think so."

I search his eyes for more explanation and see only my own frightened image staring back. I look away, shocked by how tiny I appear in the doctor's eyes and afraid of the reality that I'm an insignificant observer of approaching death.

Dr. Hosler stands and offers his hand. "Thank you, Doctor," tumbles from my mouth, and I lurch forward as if to catch the words before they reach him, strategizing that if I show no gratitude the messenger will retract the message.

Hosler's lips move, but I can hardly discern his words. I hear something about priest or minister. "No, not for me," I reply, "but maybe for Amy." *Yes, ask her. When she wakes up. By the way, when will that be? Oh, that's right. You don't know for sure. Yes, of course, I'll want to see her. I don't want to let her out of my sight for the rest of….*

In a flash, my role has become clear. I must be with Amy every moment. I must take care of her. I must be sure her last days are as comfortable as possible. I can't allow someone else to do what I am fated to do. By God, if I can't control the hour she dies, I'll make damn certain to control every second of our time together.

The doctor leaves. I glance around the waiting area and find myself alone. Visiting hours must be over. *Hey, Jesus,* I say to a Catholic crucifix on a wall, *what are your visiting hours? Were you there when they put my Amy on the cross?* A poster catches my eye. It shows a tiny lamb walking in a valley that's darkened by the shadow of a menacing cloud. In the distance, a shard of light breaks through. Beneath the scene is the familiar verse … *Lo, though I walk through the valley of the shadow of death….* I turn away only to face another crucifix. Everywhere there is proof that God is dead.

Then, from the chapel down the hall, I hear singing and remember Amy's voice blending with Ernie Ford's: "Be not dismayed what e're betide, God will take care of you …". *Starting when, God? We've begged you to take care of us. Haven't we prayed hard enough? Or did we pray the wrong way? What do you prefer—Greek Orthodox, Presbyterian, Baptist … how about agnostic? I've said your prayer every way I know—Pater imon …, Our Father …, Ayous a Theos…. Jesus Christ, God, what do I have to do to get your goddamn attention?*

I sob uncontrollably. Ashamed, I look about. At the door, a habited nun spies me. I turn toward a window just as the sun breaks through a cloud and shines into my eyes. When I squint, I see a million suns in my tears. The fireballs stab my eyes, but I stand in place, arrogantly absorbing the pain as if to do so would eliminate suffering everywhere.

"Excuse me, sir," says the nun. "Are you all right? Can I be of any help?"

Sister, I need help, but not from you.

I avoid the woman and walk into the corridor, stumbling to the grip rail at the wall realizing I need someone, *but who? Who will be the first person I tell that Amy is about to die?*

With a sudden urgency, I phone Dan Donaldson, our church pastor. He's a dear friend who knows God. When he answers, I don't say hello but sob, "Dan, she's going to die. Amy is going to die. Where the hell is God?"

CHAPTER FORTY-TWO

Ah, "all things come to those who wait,"
(I say these words to make me glad),
But something answers soft and sad,
"They come, but often come too late."

—From *Tout vient à qui sait attendre* by Violet Fane

The Home Medic people are here with equipment Amy will need when she comes home from the hospital. Earlier, Tim and I moved furniture out of the sunroom to make space for a bed, a toilet disguised as a chair, and a table that'll cantilever over the bed like a bridge to nowhere. Tim helped with the heavy lifting and showed surprising strength for a thirteen-year-old, but Erin stayed in her room with the door closed. Though only eleven, she has picked up clues from my dark mood and avoids me while I prepare the room for her mom's homecoming. Thankfully, Eleni's away at college. Amy's illness has forced our kids to grow up too fast and turned Eleni into a worrywart. Amy and I used to enjoy imagining what our children would be like in a few years. It breaks my heart to realize that she will never know.

Tim, Erin, and I shoot baskets outside while the agency's crew puts the bed together. Erin hangs in like a trouper in a game of *horse*, and refuses to let us give her a break, exhibiting willfulness like her mom used to have. I made a pitcher of Kool-Aid and set it on the picnic table with some chips, so we wouldn't go in the house and see our family room change into a hospital room. I'm glad Eleni's away. Though she is much older, she is more sensitive to her mom's needs than the younger kids. As for me, I'm not shocked by the room makeover because I've been picturing the layout for several weeks, but I am disturbed by an odd sensation that I've experienced all this preparation before, even though I know it is impossible.

Dave from the agency steps outside and says, "Mr. Demetriou, we're all set. If you'll come in, I'll show you how to adjust the bed."

As I start for the door, Tim gets nothing but net on a long jump shot. "Come on, Dad, one more. If you miss, I win." He tosses me the ball. I dribble to the same spot, stop, bounce the ball twice, and let it fly. It bangs off the backboard, hits the rim, spins, almost teeters off the front edge, and then rolls around the iron before falling through.

"Arrrgh," grumbles Tim.

"My turn," says Erin.

"No way, you already spelled *horse*."

"Did not, donkey breath."

"Did, too, buttface."

"Play nice, you guys." I laugh and hop up the steps into the house. Sweat rolls into my eye and its sting brings me back to reality. I pull up my Disney T-shirt and wipe sweat off my face with Mickey Mouse's gloved hand. *When this is over*, I think, *I'm taking the kids to Disney World.* Mentally, I slap myself, but excuse the crass thought as another one of the crazy tricks my mind keeps playing on me.

Suddenly, I stop in my tracks. The sight and smell of the sunroom-turned-convalescent-chamber raises a feeling of déjà vu. When Dave shows me the crank at the end of the bed and says, "Use the lever like a jack and let the mechanism do the work," I sense feelings of familiarity and fear. "I've oiled the bearing, so you won't break your back," he says. "Go ahead and give it a try." As I bend down, I feel dizzy and nearly fall forward. "Easy," he says. The crank turns freely, but I gasp as if overwhelmed by the task. "You all right?" asks the agent. I stand up and touch my face when I feel a rush to my head. My face is warm, my hand is cold, and the odd feeling I got when I came into the room is still with me.

"Yeah," I say. "Just winded from playing hoops. I didn't get much sleep and...."

Then it hits me. I know this feeling. It's how I feel when I wake up from that God-awful nightmare whose details I can't remember.

Hours have passed since the kids and I put up inspirational posters to brighten the paneled walls of Amy's new room. They selected the posters and helped me tack them up when I got a call from the hospital verifying that their mom would be home tomorrow afternoon. Right after the call, Tim said he had something else to do and Erin went to her room, slamming the door hard enough to shake the dining room chandelier. I was tired then, but now, three hours later, I can't sleep. So I sit up in bed and start another diagramless crossword, my third. Usually, I only need one to relax. Not tonight. Tonight, I'm afraid I'll dream that horrible dream and wake up remembering it.

My head nods—then bobs back with a start. Somewhere around 34-across, I fall asleep, but feel another part of me get up and wander from the bed. In a dream state, I see myself sleepwalking and sense my movement. Part of me tries to wake up, but the dream pulls me toward a French door with glass panes extending its length—a door like the one on the dining room side of our sunroom. The door is open, but I see nothing on the other side—like a doorway into nowhere. Although I sense danger, I push forward and enter the room. I'm unafraid until I detect an odor, an oddly recognizable mixture of fresh linen, antiseptic lotion, and ... oiled metal. In the dark, I make out the shape of a crouching figure at the end of a bed with one arm turning in a circular motion. In the bed is another figure—an old woman I don't recognize. The man at the end of the bed is no stranger; the crouching figure is me.

I'm frightened and want to run, but can only thrash about without going anywhere. Reason tells me that that's how it is in a dream; you fall into emptiness and grasp at nothing. Like in all my dreams, I feel as if I'm watching myself act on a stage, but even though I am the writer and director of my fantasy, I cannot order it to end.

The old woman stirs and breathes hoarsely, making sounds like air forced through paper bellows. Though her panting breath is offensive, my sleepwalk-self is drawn to her. Part of me objects, but I see my hand reach for hers and feel a ghostlike spirit move within the me that I'm watching. My dream-self is possessed by that essence, and it advances despite my reluctance. It's more powerful than I am, and I remain an observer, letting the nightmare play out until I'm strong enough to wake.

The old woman's hands feel like stones and sticks delicately dangling from the ends of cord-like arms. Her body is thin and bony, matching the gaunt features of her hundred-year-old face. Yet the palm of her tiny hand is warm, and the skin is soft and pink and smooth—not wrinkled like the skin drawn tightly over the fleshless skull on the pillow. I slide my upturned hand under hers, opening my palm fully. She offers no resistance or aid—her only labor, the breath she takes without will. Sweet Jesus! What are those tubes stuck into the back of her hand and running along her wrist and up her arm to that grotesque machine? Those needle insertions must hurt terribly. Why would someone do such a thing to such a frail old creature? The machine answers with a *whir*, and liquid races through a transparent tube toward the lifeless woman. I want to ask if her pain is unbearable, but I don't. Haven't we already talked about that? Yes, in other dreams there were long one-sided discussions. She did not answer then and cannot answer now. Dear God, I hope she heard me tell her that I will always love her.

I move my hand so that the heels of our palms are together. In what seems to be a game I've played before, I smile at the match and mismatch—thumb at thumb and finger at finger—the tips of her fingers barely reaching my first knuckles. Her hand is like a child's hand. Tiny, like Amy's hand.

Amy should be here. I want her with me. I need her comfort. *Amy! Amy!* I shout from my director's chair. But the dream-me whispers, *Amy*, and she does not come.

The old woman's breathing quickens, momentarily subsides, and quickens again. She breathes with her mouth open, and spittle runs from the corner of her mouth to her chin. I turn her head so the gurgling fluid won't wash down her throat. I dab it as gently as I can, but thickened drool collects at the edges of her lips. I use a sponge-tipped stick to moisten her mouth and nose with water and ointment, painting like an artist trying to restore a wisp of her beauty. Though I fail, I continue attending her—skillfully, as if I've done it a thousand times before. Traces of salt-like encrustation remain in her nose and mouth, like deposits on walls of caves. I reach for salves and lotions on the patient's table, confident that they are there because I have memory of them being there. How strange it is to remember details of a dream only while dreaming.

Taut skin pulls the old woman's lips back beyond the gum line, making her mouth gape and exposing her teeth in a hideous smile. The teeth seem monstrous and out of place in what remains of the woman's shrunken head. They are straight and white and healthy looking—a young woman's pearls strung for an aged stranger.

Suddenly, the old woman stops breathing and opens her eyes. She stares at me as if to beg me to give her breath, but I am like stone, unable to move. Closing her eyes, she opens her mouth wide and juts out her tongue as if to lap a final taste of air. Her chest heaves and shudders. The sight is repulsive, and I tell my dream-self to avert my eyes and pray to awaken, but the sleep spirit is too strong, and the dream continues.

I cannot turn away from the gasping woman, and when her motion stops, my heart crumbles like shattered rock. Ashamed, I thank God she cannot see my weakness. Her eyes shut tight—as if her last breath has been painful. Her eyelids fold upon themselves, making layers of skin that resembles tightened edges of drawstring purses. She has no eyelashes. At her brow, there are only wrinkles and memory lines. Vaguely, I remember that her eyebrows—and some of her hair, as well—have vanished in the course of torturous efforts toward unfulfilled healing.

My dream hand touches the dead woman's hair. Though fearful, I don't stop myself. The dark full hair I saw a moment ago now feels more like straw than hair. I'm shocked when I join the me I am watching and feel myself drawn to lie with the dead woman in intimate embrace. *No!* I shout. *Stop this madness.* I call out to Amy, begging her to stop me. Amy has the will to halt this incubus. *Amy, where are you? Amy, please come help me.*

Appalled, I watch as I embrace the old woman and brush my face against a cheek that isn't there. Suddenly, I sense my *dream-self* lying with the woman, and feel my *voyeur-self* rising above the scene where I look around the room like a spider dangling on a thread suspended from the ceiling. What I survey is an unknown place but not unfamiliar. The old woman is dressed in a hospital gown and lies in a hospital bed. Though I smell the scents of hospital care, this is no hospital room. The walls are paneled, and windows line three sides. Drawn yellow shades appear golden-brown as outside darkness passes through. Posters on the walls reveal pastoral scenes and frolicking dolphins and baby pandas watched over by their mama. Biblical verses cover the sky and landscape of these scenes—verses Amy and I memorized years ago. The words speak triumphantly as if God were responsible for only goodness. *God gave us eternal life ... Ask and you will receive ... Trust in the Lord ... God is faithful ... and ... will provide a way of escape.* A plaque sits directly in the sightline of the woman who can no longer see. On it, I notice a lacquered page from an old hymnal. Its edges appear tattered, but the title of the hymn, "Blessed Assurance," sings loudly from the page.

I look about, hopelessly aware that my nightmare is happening in our family gathering room, where drawn shades and the pall of death shroud light—a dying-room in the living room of my house.

I begin to pray—not for the soul of the dead woman, but for Amy to take me out of here. I repeat Bible verses and utter the Lord's Prayer in phonetic Greek: *Pater imon ...* I stammer and halt for I have forgotten it, and I beg forgiveness when I see Christ on the wall. *Nicholas,* ask the eyes of Jesus, *will you let me take her now?* I shake my head, *No,* and make the Orthodox sign of the cross, awkwardly invoking the words in Greek: *Ayous a Theos, Ayous a Sheerous, Ayous a Thanatos, E laysonimas.*

Suddenly, Amy appears, but, when I take her in my arms, her body is limp and cold. I look into her face and see the old woman. Though her raspy breathing has stopped, the nightmare goes on until I awake and everything fades except my feeling of horror.

CHAPTER FORTY-THREE

A body seriously out of equilibrium, either with itself or with its environment, perishes outright. Not so a mind. Madness and suffering can set themselves no limit.

—**George Santayana**

Amy and I prepare for another visit to her oncologist, Dr. John Agnew. I accompany Amy to all procedures and am near enough to hear her curses and screams as doctors manipulate devices that will only extend her misery. Shortly after Amy's last hospitalization, I told my superintendent that I could no longer continue teaching because I felt compelled to stay home to care for my wife. Graciously, the school board granted me an indefinite leave, and I've been with Amy every moment since then.

Amy accepts the oncology visits with a mix of gratitude and realistic resignation. "I wonder," she says, "how a gentle man like Dr. Agnew stays so kind and upbeat despite his *failures*. Think about it. Most of his patients are getting ready to die."

Like so often these days, Amy's comment goes without a reply, despite its ominous thought. Her dark mood can no longer be soothed, for physical features reflect it. Black circles around her eyes and tiny threads of blue veins exposed by thinning skin accent the hepatic complexion caused by repeated bouts with jaundice. Her hair has stopped falling out, but not before leaving her skull looking like a battered doll's head. Often, she tries to force a smile for the children or me, but cannot fully remove the perpetual scowl because her facial muscles, like other parts of her body, don't work as they used to. In the weeks since her school reunion, Amy has aged fifty years.

"Can you help me with this lipstick?" she says. "Shit, I can't hold my hand up and hardly have enough energy to talk." Her voice is weak. Her thin words come slowly as if strained through a sieve. "I hate for the kids see me like this," she says. "They must think I look like a scarecrow. One day I asked Tim to sit with me.

He said he had homework to do, and I accused him of ignoring me on purpose. He snarled at me, and I said he'd be sorry when I'm not around anymore. I felt awful. I would've gone to him, but he ran upstairs. He knows I can't do the stairs."

"I heard the exchange," I say, "and we talked about it. He said he understood."

Actually, I did all the talking. Tim said nothing. At thirteen, he can't verbalize how he feels. He and I haven't communicated well for quite a while. When I talk to him, he doesn't respond. I don't know if he's tongue-tied or if he just chooses to stonewall me.

Amy stands as still as she can while I try to apply her lipstick. After a couple of quick swipes, I give up, and she says, "I hope you've prepared Eleni for coming home. She hasn't seen me like this."

"I know," I say. "I try to give her a clue when I visit her at school, but she doesn't know the whole story. I'm concerned about how she'd feel; she's always thinking she has some responsibility to care for you. She'd quit school in a second, if we let her. Tim and Erin don't know everything either, but they see you every day."

"I'm worried, Nick. Eleni's going to feel she has to be the mother. Don't let her. She'll be twenty soon, and she has to start living her own life. She's going to give you a tough time about that, but you have to let her go so she can pursue her own dreams."

"I know, but she's really attached to you, even more than Tim and Erin are."

"Poor little, Erin. I wonder how she's handling it. She's so young and sweet. I'm proud of how well she did at Four-H. That dress she made is adorable."

"She's a cutie all right. I'm glad all the kids will be here for … for the summer."

"I'm so sorry. I don't envy you the job of telling them. I know how I'd feel if I were you. I get so sad when I think about how you and the kids will get through this."

"That's for later. Right now, let's finish this list of questions for Agnew."

"Okay, here's one. What about the auto-syringe Mary mentioned?"

"Got it covered," I reply.

Mary Lindstrom's PCS people want us to consider around-the-clock nursing care after Dr. Agnew prescribes a continuous dose of morphine using an automatic syringe. Up to now, they've been here for two eight-hour shifts each day. "Mary also said to remind Agnew about swelling and puffiness," I add. "She made a distinction between two kinds of swelling, but I don't—"

"One's called *edema*," says Amy, "and the other is *ascites*. I learned that in my medical terminology class last year. A lotta good that did me. I pissed away all that money on an education I'll never use."

Amy giggles and adds, "Speaking of piss—I can't, and I'm worried about constipation, too." Her giggle isn't the one I remember from before, but the sound of it still makes my heart flutter. "I guess you could tell him that I don't give a shit anymore," she laughs. "Trouble is, that's no joke." Her frown returns, this time heavier and darker. "I don't want them going up my ass with spoons like they did the last time."

I can't help but make a face when I nod, "Uh-huh."

"Oh, Nick, I'm so embarrassing to you and the kids. How can I do this without losing my self-respect? I'm not allowed any modesty. All this crap—and for what?"

"It might get better."

"Ha. When figs cry."

I smile. "Pigs fly," I say.

"I knew that. And you know what I meant."

I know also that Amy has agreed to an aggressive sequence of radiation and chemo with the prospect of only temporary improvement at best. After several procedures, our hope that she might gain enough strength to enjoy a month or so with the children seems unlikely. Other efforts seem just as futile.

Amy wanted time to prepare a gift for the children, so they would remember her in pleasanter ways, but changes have come too fast. Now, the kids are frightened by her appearance, and she agonizes that the only memory they'll have of her will be the deteriorating invalid she's become.

Amy gazes out the window like a passenger on a train. "Everything's going by so fast," she says, "and I'm just sitting here getting meaner."

"We both know what that means."

"It means I'm scared. It means I'm frightened that I can't do this. Nick, for a long time I couldn't live like a normal person. Now, I can't die the right way either."

"Sweetheart, there is no *right way*."

"I'm afraid of everything—big things like death and going to hell. Little things, too. I worry that everyone will be mad at me. I *know* God is angry. He won't forgive me for having so little faith. I've made such a mess of things."

"Honey, that's not true."

"Yes, it is. I was wrong to make you buy this old house. I put us all in danger—with the traffic and the noise and the worry about asbestos and lead and formaldehyde. I was the one who insisted on insulation to stop the noise. That stuff probably gave me cancer. This house has cancer everywhere, and it's my fault that you have to live here."

"Stop that. No one ever suggested that you got sick because of this house."

"Nighttime is the worst. I'm afraid to be alone because I think of all the bad things I've done. The nurses say I should leave something for all of you—something you and the kids will keep as a reminder of me—but I can't do it. I try, but I can't make myself do it. I must be a bad person. I should be able to write or say something in a recorder, but I can't. I'm just a selfish, selfish person."

"Sweetie, stop that. You're not selfish. You have no energy to do these things. What you're asking yourself to do is heroic. You don't have to be a hero."

"I know. All I have to do is die, but I can't do that right because I'm too much of a coward. God, yes, I'm scared. They tell me I can be comfortable—that they can control the pain. Yeah, when they pump me full of embalming fluid. Why do they call it *pain control*? It's not. I feel like shit, and it'll only get worse. It's a trip to hell, and they pretend it's a … a goddamn *journey* of some sort."

"Everybody's trying, sweetheart. They're looking for a combination that works."

"I know. I know. I should be grateful. They're good people. Saints, really. I couldn't do what they do—or what you do, either."

"Hon, we don't know what it's like for them either."

Amy looks at her hands and then raises her eyes to mine and says, "I'm sorry. I shouldn't complain. You've given so much to me, and I have nothing for you."

"Don't think like that. You've already given me everything I've wanted."

"It doesn't matter, does it? I can't do a thing about it except worry. I worry so much my brain hurts—even my hair hurts. You know what I think about most? The end. It sounds so simple to say *The End* like my life's a movie. *Okay, guys, roll the credits.*" Amy closes her eyes. Her eyelids, nearly absent of lashes, flutter along their edges as if unable to close all the way. "I ask myself what it'll be like in the end and what I'll do when the pain is unbearable. Oh, sure. I'll have that automatic syringe, but what about insulin? I'm already shaky; how will I give myself a shot when I'm doped up?"

"I'll give it to you. I'm here to take care of you—always will be."

"Nick, I demand so much from you. You'll hate me before this is over."

"Never. I will never hate you."

"I already hate myself. The worst of it is that I can feel myself getting to be like I was before."

I wince at her admission because of what I did a few days ago. In a weak moment, I let my own fears get the best of me and threw them in her face. One evening, when I thought she was asleep, I decided to catch up on chores. At about two in the morning, I went upstairs to clean the tub in the kids' bathroom. It's an old worn-out tub, and I can't make it come clean with the liquid cleaners that Amy wants me to use. For the first time in twenty years, I bought a can of powdered cleanser that Amy is afraid of. I knew I was taking a chance but thought Amy wouldn't know because she can't easily get up the stairs. Believing she was fast asleep, I brushed the dry abrasive onto the dark bathtub ring. The noise of my scrubbing blocked the sound of Amy's slow climb up the stairs and entry into the hallway leading to the bathroom. When she confronted me, I got defensive and then frightened when I recognized her old obsessive-compulsive mania. She wouldn't accept my explanation and became furious, accusing me of lying and deceiving her about other matters because I didn't trust her.

"Amy, I'm sorry," I said. "But, for God's sake, do you think I like doing this in the middle of the night? I hate it. I hate all of it. I wish to Christ this would all end."

She shook and backed away into the hall.

"Honey," I begged, "forgive me. I didn't mean that."

"I know. Just ... please ... don't leave this room until you've cleaned it all up." Her tone was more pathetic than demanding, but she kept it up. "Make sure there's no cleanser anywhere. I don't want any white stuff to worry about."

At that moment, I hated her and wanted her out of my life.

"Jesus, Amy," I said, not quite under my breath. "I wish you weren't so goddam crazy. What difference does it make? You'll never see this room again anyway."

I remember how vile I felt when I said it. I also remember other incidents—like arguing with her because she wants to sell the house before she dies. Every day, some new anxiety links with a resurgence of fearful thoughts that plagued her for years. I hate having to be a controlling person, but tell myself that Amy's needs demand it, yet I spend most of my time trying to control minutiae that surround the real chaos. I want to believe that I'm doing the best I can—that I don't make that many mistakes, but memories of my oversights rise above everything else I do. Like the scum on the bathtub, my blunders build one upon the other while the good I accomplish just washes away.

Eleni is home now, and I'm sad that I haven't spent much time with her. She's the apple of my eye and will always have a special place in my heart, but I'm afraid to go to that spot because it aches so much. Since coming home for the summer, she's had a tough time getting used to her mom's worsened condition. It's especially difficult for her because Amy looked so well the last time they were together at Easter. Nevertheless, she puts on a good front and tries to blend into the new routines around the house.

"What's that?" she asks when I walk into the kitchen with a Glucoscan meter.

"This? Oh, it's the thing I use to check your mom's sugar level, so I know how much insulin she needs. You've seen it before, haven't you?"

"Yeah, but you've never shown me how to use it."

"No, because it's my job to take care of those things. What are you filling out?"

"A form for my job at the title company. I start tomorrow."

"Just for the summer, remember. You're definitely returning to school in the fall."

"Uh-huh."

I put the glucose meter away and sit down with Eleni. "So, how's my Eleni Poo?"

"Okay, Daddy Dude," she says without looking up. After a moment, she sets down her pen and says, "Dad, can I talk to you?"

"Sure, what's on your mind?"

"Remember last Thanksgiving when Mom went into the hospital? I know you kept everything from me because you didn't want me to worry. I appreciate that but—"

"Yeah, Mom and I wanted you to finish the term before we said too much."

"I understand, but … it made me feel … funny. When I found out later, I.…"

"I'm sorry, sweetie, but we thought it was best not to tell you."

"I know. You're right, I would have had trouble finishing if I had known. Still.…"

"I'm glad you understand. We want you to know that we love you and it's okay for you to be away while your mom's sick. We can take care of things without you."

Eleni winces and looks away. I sense her discomfort. What is it? Is she angry? I doubt it; Eleni's always so cooperative. I don't think she *can* get angry—not for long, anyway. Still, she does have a hard time expressing herself, and maybe I should listen better.

"And then this Easter," she says, "I wish … well, I would've liked to have known more about Mom. I could've helped. Maybe you wouldn't have had to quit your job."

Her hand trembles. I take it in mine and pat it gently. "Hold on, I won't hear any of that. Sweetie, I love your mom like crazy, and you're on a pedestal right beside her. Quitting work was easy. I did it for all of us—me included. I wouldn't have it any other way. I don't want you to be responsible for taking care of your mom."

"But … I … I felt like you didn't trust me."

"No, no, that's not it at all. When you were home at Easter, we didn't even know the cancer had come back. We didn't find out until after we went to the reunion. There was nothing to tell you on Easter day. Honest, we didn't lie to you."

Eleni starts crying now, sobbing, but fighting to gain control as she usually does. "I know, and I'm sorry. It's just that … oh, never mind. I'm sorry I brought it up."

I'm confused about what she means, but she has difficulty coming to the point. At the same time, I think that she must understand why I have to take charge. The rigid schedule I kept in December is nothing compared to how I'm needed now. On the family ship, I'm the captain, the ensign, and the seaman. I organize, direct, and carry out the jobs that keep us afloat, and I'm so obsessed with control that I use my newly acquired computer to create guide sheets that list medications, menus, and schedules for Amy, as well as chores for the kids to do around the house.

Then again, I suppose the computer is a symbol of my delusion that I'm in control. I know that I've become almost maniacal, but I need something to prove that I'm doing all I can to care for Amy. I accept the nurses' assistance, but I'm reluctant to ask friends to help because I feel so compelled to be in charge of as much as possible.

This plays havoc on how I treat the children. Believing they shouldn't be their mother's caretakers, I don't ask them to do a lot. I'm especially concerned that Eleni doesn't take on the emotional responsibility she assumed as a child when Amy was deep in depression. Neither Amy nor I want our children to suffer more than is necessary, so I make myself responsible for practically everything—from every pill she takes to nearly every spoken word and every conceivable need. I take my role as a father seriously, and try to help the children understand what's happening, yet it's impossible to set aside enough time to be with each of them. Casual one-on-one huddles are best, but opportunities for spontaneity rarely occur. Though I believe my insistence on order is necessary, I wonder what the kids believe, and I worry that I can't be all they need me to be.

It's Tim's turn to do dishes, and he's at the sink scraping burned spots off the roaster. I'm at the table recording Amy's latest statistics: glucose reading, insulin dosage, medication, type, and measured amount of food she's eaten, and on and on ...

"Dad, this dumb plastic pad doesn't clean anything. Why can't I use cleanser like Shane's mom uses?"

"Quit griping. Cleanser wears out the pan, and you know Mom doesn't like it."

"Arrrgh." He grumbles and squirts more Palmolive onto the pan.

We do the dishes by hand because Amy's afraid of the soap that has crystallized in the dishwasher. I go to the Laundromat to do the clothes for the same reason and because Amy worries about what might be crawling around the basement laundry area.

After Tim finishes the pan and sets it down to drain, he wipes his hands on his jeans and says, "Dad, can I ask you something?"

"Shoot."

"Remember at Easter when you ... you said Mom might go to the cottage this summer?"

I push the tally sheet aside and sigh. Jeez-O-Pete, why's he asking that *now*? "Well, Tim ... I ... uh ... some things don't always work out."

Tim stands slump-shouldered and leans his gangly frame on the kitchen counter. I'm surprised how tall he is. Every time I look, he seems to have grown another inch. His hair seems darker, too, and he's beginning to look like me. I wonder how much of Amy he'll retain as he gets older. Searching for a meaning behind his question, my eyes focus on the fuzzy beginnings of hair above his upper lip. Will he ever grow a mustache like mine?

"You didn't actually promise or anything," he says, "but you said we'd go when it got warm. It was hot yesterday, and the weather's going to be good from now on, isn't it?"

Is this an accusation or a roundabout way of asking if his mom will ever get well? God, should I tell him? Or is he just a kid asking to go Up North to have fun? I wish we could go. Tim seems so disappointed, but I'm afraid he'll be that way even if we go.

"I'll try to work something out," I say. "Maybe we'll go a little later."

"But not with Mom?"

"I don't know, Tim. I don't think so. Maybe just us. If I can get someone to stay with Mom, I might be able to manage a day or two."

"Uh-huh."

He starts to walk away, then turns and raises his eyes to meet mine. It's unlike Tim to do that. He usually avoids eye contact, hanging his head to match his droop-shouldered stance. Not this time. The hangdog expression is in his body but not on his face. It's the face of a boy forced to grow up too fast.

"Dad?" he says. Tim's eyes momentarily look away, and then return to mine. "Dad, are you sure you're doing everything you can?"

His question is like a punch in the stomach. I stiffen and draw a breath. "Yes, son. I'm sure. We have the best doctors looking after your mom."

"What about places like the Mayo Clinic? Maybe *they* can do something."

"Tim, we're trying everything. If the Mayo Clinic or anywhere else will help, believe me, I'll take your mom there. I'm not sparing any expenses."

"I just thought ... I hope ... you know?"

"Yes, Tim," I say, trying to sound as comforting as I can. "I know that you love your mom very much, and you want what's best for her. I'll tell her that, and you should tell her, too."

All Amy's doctors—surgeon, endocrinologist, oncologist, and radiologist—are located in Glen Acre. We make the seventy mile round trip three times a week, not including occasional trips like the two needed to remove new cysts from Amy's breast. On the long drive, we try to keep our talk light, but sometimes we deal with a problem or two. Often, we sit in silence and hold hands—a simple way to say I love you without uttering a word.

Dr. Agnew says today's chemotherapy treatment is Amy's last because she hasn't responded well to either radiation or chemo. He kept her in the hospital for two days last week to give her a massive dose and monitor her reaction. It proved futile. While she was there, Amy got a visit from a team of Wayne State University Medical School researchers who asked her to participate in an experimental pancreatic cancer investigation. She's still troubled by her answer.

Recalling the visit, Amy says, "Nick, don't be mad at me. I can't do it. I got angry and told them to get out. I feel terrible, but they want to experiment on me—like I'm a laboratory rat. They said it might help someone years from now—that someday my participation might save a life. They ... oh, God, they made me feel guilty—like I'm being selfish to turn them down."

"Sweetheart, you're not selfish, and I'm not mad at you. You've already been through enough. No one has a right to ask you to do more."

"They said, 'Wouldn't it be a wonderful gift for your husband and children if you could be well, even for a short time?' But when I questioned them, they said I might get worse—that the treatment might kill me before the cancer. Then I asked them how I would die, and they didn't answer me. They just kept coming back to giving my family a *wonderful* gift—that everyone will remember my example. Nick, when I die, will you remember that I said no? Will you hate me for not trying harder?"

"Amy, there's no way I could hate you. Stop thinking that."

"I might have thrown away my last chance."

"Honey, how much of a chance is there? They said it's a long shot. No one's ever survived the experiment. What you'd have to endure is almost criminal. The only thing they're certain of is how torturous the treatments would be."

"I'll do it if you want me to. If you think I should, I will."

"Punkin, I've seen you hurt by some treatments. I've been there when you've screamed bloody murder. Honest to God, I swear I could feel the pain with you. I couldn't stand that now … not without more assurance."

"You know that I *am* thinking about you, too, don't you? Wayne State is in downtown Detroit, fifty miles from home. You'd be driving back and forth in all that traffic, and I'd hardly ever see the kids. They're already so frightened because I look like a monster to them. Those doctors said I'd get sicker for a while. What's *a while* mean? I don't have any more *whiles* left. I'll be so ugly no one will want to look at me."

"Bullshit. I'll always remember you as my beauty queen. Now, let's put this talk of more tests and treatments off limits. I want you at home with me and the kids."

"I wish.… Oh, Nick, I wanted you to be proud of me. I wish.…"

"Hey, knock it off. I *am* proud of you. You've done all you could."

An empty space around my heart suddenly felt emptier. A year ago, we were on the verge of fulfilling our lives—not just with things that we lost, but also with dreams of our future. Now, none of those wishes will come true. The best I can hope for is someone's assurance that I, too, have done all that I could.

CHAPTER FORTY-FOUR

Life is a great surprise. I do not see why
death should not be an even greater one.

—Vladimir Nabokov

The nurses are making plans for Amy's around-the-clock care, and Mary's here on her regular shift. She's given Amy a bath and is coming out of the bathroom with Amy leaning heavily on her for support. I hurry to finish making the bed and pull the top sheets back just in time for Amy to lie down.

"Phew," she says, "that was exhausting. I'm so tired; I think I'll sleep forever."

Amy forces a strained smile. That is all she can manage nowadays, and I wince at her effort. Despite her increased discomfort, she's tried very hard to be cheerful.

"Don't worry," she says. "I don't mean *forever* forever. I just need a long nap." She gives a soft giggle and winks, lending a bittersweet touch to her pitiable effort.

"Here," says Mary, "let me help you get settled under these crisp new sheets. Next time, I'll bathe you right here in your cozy bed." She guides Amy gently, but I know the strength it takes to lift and position her just so. Amy's body is a collection of mismatched parts. Her thighs and hips are puffy, and her arms and legs are slender and getting thinner. At the same time, her midsection has ballooned to twice its normal size.

"I'll go in the kitchen and bring back a glass of juice," says Mary.

"And Maalox, too," Amy whispers roughly.

Mary returns and suddenly trips, spilling juice onto Amy's lap. Alarmed, Mary and I scurry to clean up the mess. After an initial startle, Amy is surprisingly less troubled about it than we are. While Mary removes Amy's soiled clothes and peels away the sheets, Amy smiles and jokes weakly, "I think you did it on purpose, just so you could prove you can bathe me in bed."

Her reaction shows a turnaround since she rejected further treatment. She's calmer and more at peace, and she's more apt to ignore trivial matters that she used to fret about. Although she struggles with her fate, she seems more accepting of it, and, oddly, I'm saddened by her restfulness. It breaks my heart to see her abandon the willfulness that has been a hallmark of her life. Over the last several months, her anger helped fuel her will to live. Sometimes, she fought on *because* of what was happening to her, not in spite of it. Yet, her anger was often aimed not only at her situation, but at herself as well. That self-judgment created anxiety. Now acceptance has reduced her panic, but hasn't completely cured her dysphoria.

Several Recovery phrases express her surrender more agreeably, and I find comfort in repeating them. Amy is practicing *patient waiting* and trying to be *a partner* to the process *rather than a partisan*. She is waiting as one might wait expectantly for a train to take her home, but I'm not as courageous. To me, watching Amy give up her will is like watching Joan of Arc lay down her sword.

Later, after Mary leaves, I hear a noise in the front closet and find Amy in her bare feet rummaging through a box of odds and ends. Her quest is almost comical. As she bends down awkwardly, her oversized nightgown rides up to expose her dimpled fanny.

"Honey, what are you looking for? You shouldn't be up by yourself."

"Remember that wooden plaque I picked up at a garage sale a couple years ago?"

"You kidding? Am I supposed to remember every piece of junk you collected?"

Without straightening, she starts on another box. "The one with the page from an old hymnal pasted on. It was "Blessed Assurance," and it was lacquered over to protect it."

"You probably threw it out."

"Not me, and I hope *you* didn't either."

"Come on, you'll never find it. Why don't you forget about it?"

Amy stands and rubs her hand across her midsection, groaning. I don't like the redness of her face and the frantic look in her eyes. She is sweating profusely and appears exhausted when she says, "You don't understand. I *have* to have it. I *need* it *right now*. It's ... oh, there it is. Up on the shelf on the right." I reach up toward a slender box, but she says, "No, over there," and points to a plaque about the size of a book. Amy's eyes light up when I take it down. "That's it," she says. "Hang it on the wall opposite my bed. I want it where I'll always be able to see it."

The old hymn is one that Amy enjoyed singing while listening to her favorite Ernie Ford album. When I see the line *Perfect submission, all is at rest,* I know why it's so important. Amy has begun her submission and preparation for the end, and she needs assurance that it's what God wants for her. Still troubled by thoughts that she's failed in life, she hopes to win God's approval in death. The words she prays for, the ones with promises she hopes to earn before it's too late, are those in another verse:

Perfect submission, perfect delight/Visions of rapture now burst on my sight; Angels descending, bring from above/Echoes of mercy, whispers of love.

While Amy seems more cooperative, I'm not as comfortable as she is with changes Mary Lindstrom has made, particularly her decision to add another nursing service to augment her own. The new nurses are drawn from Duffy Services Temporary Nursing and come "as needed" during a trial period. The group is a healthcare branch of an organization known for interim office help. I'm concerned that my authority will be reduced, and suspicious that another service will be less conscientious than Mary's will. Nevertheless, I was pleased after one particular Duffy nurse stayed for an eight-hour shift, and I asked that she be called whenever PCS was shorthanded.

Later, when I was assured that Amy wasn't in danger and wouldn't need twenty-four-hour care for a while, I asked Amy if she'd mind if I took the kids to the cottage for a day or two. She agreed and suggested that her mother stay with her while I was gone. The nurses would be with Amy for sixteen hours, and Eleni, who insisted on staying home, would be available, too. This gave Saundra plenty of help, and I felt free to ask Andy to come to the cottage with Tim, Erin, and me.

I think I understand Saundra better than I did before, and now, when I see how controlling she is around Andy, I get a little sad. She serves as protector for Andy in much the same way that I do for Amy. Saundra and I believe our job is to be a buffer between our mates and any danger we perceive to their psychological health, but, while Amy and I learned effective techniques in Recovery and Relatives, Saundra's only methods are denial and suppression of her feelings. I know now that my anger at Saundra is partly because I see myself as controlling as she is. Though I learned to loosen that control after years in Relatives, Amy's current illness requires me to be as vigilant as I ever was. Perhaps because I know better, I hate having to be that way.

Before leaving for the cottage, I make a computer printout of Amy's typical day and list her meals, medications, and other routines. Eleni rolls her eyes at my excessive planning, but Saundra thanks me for the directions. She makes it clear that she'll rely on Eleni and the nurses for most of the tasks. I hope this will free her up to be a companion to Amy and give them time to reconnect. Though Saundra doesn't express her feelings well, maybe she and Amy will find a way to communicate. I wonder if Amy hopes for that as well.

I back out of the driveway with apprehension. It's the first time in more than two months that I've left Amy in someone else's care. I've tried to tell myself I'm doing the right thing for the kids and for Amy and her mother as well, but I won't be convinced until I return home.

Meanwhile, Tim and Erin seem happy to be off on a trip. They love Andy's spirited nature and seem glad he's coming with us. I hope the three-hour drive will allow Andy and me to share some things with each other, but I'm not sure how he'll be when we're Up North. He's not only very close to Amy, but also very much like her. I'm afraid he's more likely to be melancholy than cheerful.

Sixty minutes have passed since we waved goodbye to Amy, and my hands just stopped shaking. Driving on the open road usually relaxes me, but not today. Crossing over the Zilwaukee Bridge, our halfway point to the cottage, feels like I've passed the point of no return. Andy has noticed my nervousness, and I'm glad the kids distract him while I concentrate on the road. Then a truck with an odd cargo enters the freeway ahead of me. I try to make out the load as I get closer. Before I know it, I'm stuck in traffic and am unable to pass the truck. My hands start to shake again when I draw close behind and see what it's carrying.

The truck is hauling cemetery coffin vaults, and I'm worried Tim and Erin will recognize what they are. I slow down and let other cars go between the gruesome truck cargo and us. After a few miles, I'm relieved when the truck turns off at an exit. As I watch the truck go up the ramp, I say a silent prayer that Tim and Erin won't see the cargo, but the large concrete boxes are odd enough to draw their attention.

"Grandpa," says Tim, "what's on that truck?"

Andy starts to cough. My stomach wrenches and sends the acidic taste of bile up my throat. Erin answers first. "Cement blocks, you dumb stinkbutt. What do you think they are, marshmallows?"

"Shut up, Erin," says Tim. "I'm asking Grandpa. You don't know nuthin'."

"Uh," says Andy, "I don't know for sure, Tim, but I think they might be *septic tanks*. Like the one underground at your cottage."

"See, Erin," says Tim. "You were wrong."

"Gross," says Erin.

The weekend doesn't go well. Mostly, it rains, and we stay inside. Though the cottage is small, we manage to avoid sharing our feelings. We're afraid to step into anyone's private space because we are protective of our own space.

When we return home from the cottage, Saundra signals that Amy's asleep, so Saundra and Andy leave right away. Later, Amy asks me, "How was it?"

"Uh ... okay," I say. "Thanks for letting us go."

"I'm glad I could do it," she says. "You needed to get away from me for a while."

I offer a weak smile and say, "Maybe so." Then I add, "How about you? Did you and your mom ... uh, talk or anything?"

Amy's smile was always a delight to see, but this time her gaunt features make it appear sinister. "Well," she says, taking my hand. "I know you hoped for something special between Mother and me, but it didn't happen. Don't worry; I resolved the thing with Mother long ago. I don't know all the reasons she can't express herself, but Daddy makes up for it, which is funny because he's part of why she keeps herself so controlled. He *always* shows that he loves me. I know Mother loves me, too, but mostly because Daddy loves her. Now tell me; what's the story about the truck?"

"Truck?"

"Yeah, Erin told Eleni about seeing *septic tanks*. Tim says they were something else but won't say what. When I asked him, he clammed up and went upstairs."

All of a sudden, it dawned on me that Tim regularly rides his bike through the Thompsonville cemetery on his way to the city park. He's seen those burial vaults before. Ruefully, I tell Amy what happened on the highway.

When I finish, she labors to draw a deep breath and says, "We should tell the kids what to expect."

"Yeah. I think tomorrow night might be good," I say, swallowing hard on the word *good*.

Amy takes my hand again, this time clasping it with both of hers. Before going on, she kisses the back of my hand sweetly and continues to hold it. "I need to talk to them, too," she says, "but I'll wait for you. Better do it soon, though, before it's too late. I get tired easily and can hardly talk." Though she could barely complete her last sentence, she manages to add, "There's something I want to tell you, too."

Oh God, what now? Frankly, I'm all talked out. What else is there to say?

"Nicky, I want you to get married again."

Though caught off guard, I reply quickly. "We've already had this discussion, remember? I'm not gonna. I'll never love anyone but you."

"Yes, you will. You have a lot of love to give. I want you to get married. You deserve to be with someone nicer than I am."

"There's no one like that. Never will be. I won't even consider it."

I start to pull my hand away, but Amy hangs on.

"What if I demand it on my deathbed?"

"Don't say *deathbed*."

"What else do you call the thing I'm in right now?"

"Look, I let you order me around all these years. I'm not going to let you tell me what to do when you're gone, too."

"I love you, Nick, and loving someone means being able to let him go."

"That works for kids, not husbands like me."

"I'd argue some more, but I'm too tired. Just remember what I said."

I don't answer her. There are some things I don't want to talk about, and there are a million things I don't want to remember. Most of them are happening right now.

The next day after dinner, I ask the kids to stay at the table. I don't call for a *family meeting* as I often do because that'll scare them away. I also don't want my message to come across as a coldhearted speech, so I turn to each one and softly say, "Eleni … Tim … Erin, I need to talk to you about something that's really hard for you to hear, but just as hard for me to say. Please try to understand."

"Uh-huh," says Eleni, nervously. At twenty, she must know what's on my mind, but that doesn't make it easier. Eleni is the child that Amy most relies upon. Now Eleni needs her mother to guide her as she enters womanhood, but she'll suddenly be left without her. I know Eleni can do it, but I wonder if her best asset—her willingness to put others before herself—might not also be her Achilles' heel.

"Hmm," says Tim, almost moaning. He's the one I worry about most because he has locked horns with his mom so often. Now, at thirteen, he resists her authority with adolescent ire. It's a difficult age for any boy, but Tim's natural instinct to rebel coincides with the unnatural loss of his mother.

"Is it about Mom?" says eleven-year-old Erin. Because of her age, she doesn't understand as much and is often more forthright with her questions, yet her inexperience also makes her more vulnerable. Erin has known her mother for the shortest time, and for that same reason, she might have the most to lose.

"Yes," I say, "it's about Mom. She loves each of you very, very much, and I know you love her more than anything in the world. I'm sure you don't like to see her so sick, but it's been good for her to be with you here at home instead of in the hospital. This way, she's always nearby, and we can show her that we love her."

"Is she going back in the hospital?"

Tim grunts. "Erin, let him finish," he says gruffly.

"Tim," says Eleni, "don't pick on her." Eleni's tears have already begun, and her reprimand is hardly challenging.

"Eleni," I say tenderly. "It's all right. You don't have to take charge of the kids. That's my job." I pan around the table. "Listen, I'd like all of you to feel free to say what's on your mind, but please wait until I finish."

They nod in unison. Tim looks at tearful Eleni and makes a face. Erin kicks him with her stocking feet. I clear my throat and start again. "No, Mom's not going back to the hospital, but it's not because she's getting better." My voice cracks. I close my eyes to compose myself, but my mind sees Amy's degenerating body. When tears well in my eyes, I bury my face in my hands and feel as if I'm eerily separating from my body—like I'm at the edge of consciousness and entering a world that's between the eternal one Amy is near and the real one where my children are. Like trains on parallel tracks, those three worlds run side by side, but only I can pass into all three.

I press my hands to my eyes and try to wipe away my trance. When I look up, Tim and Erin look away. Eleni covers her face and weeps. Clasping my hands tightly together, I press them hard on the table as if to keep them from separating. Staring at my hands, I say, "She won't ever go back to the hospital." Then I look up to see three expressions grow from puzzled frowns to stunned awareness. *God, please spare me this task. I don't want to say straight-out that their mother is going to die.* Then, as if she has heard my thought, Eleni's face contorts as she tries to hold back her grief.

With convulsive sobs, I say, "Your mom's a very brave lady who's won a lot of battles before, but ... this fight's too big for her. Her cancer is back stronger than before. The doctors can't help her anymore."

Eleni hides behind a wrinkled handkerchief. Tim's eyes redden, but he doesn't cry. Erin suddenly bolts from the table and runs to her room. I go after her. She slams her door in my face. I try to open it, but she resists with surprising strength. Through my pleas, she screams, "Don't come in."

Finally, I let go of the doorknob, step back and say, "It's okay, sweetie. We can talk later."

"No!" she shouts. "I don't want to talk anymore."

Reluctantly, I return to the kitchen. Tim and Eleni are standing side-by-side holding each other. Eleni is crying loudly, and Tim, already taller than she, pats her shoulder while they both rock back and forth. Tim's eyes glaze over, and puffy sacs appear beneath them, but he doesn't allow a tear to fall.

Sobbing, I draw them into my arms and say, "It's all right to cry. All we can do now is cry and pray for a miracle, pray that God gives us strength to get through this."

Tim wrenches from my grasp and steps back from our huddle. I search for words to petition God's help, but no elegant prayer comes to me. Tim stays off to the side, keeping his own silent vigil. I urge him closer, but he stands his ground. "I'm sure you have a lot of questions," I say. "I want you to feel free to tell me anything that's on your mind. We can talk as a family, or I can talk to each of you alone. Maybe alone is better. Whatever you want. Just remember that I'll always be here to talk with you."

"Why do you always want to *talk*?" says Tim, abruptly. "What good is it? Shouldn't you do something for Mom, instead?" He turns on his heel to leave but stops at the archway. His fists ball up, and his body stiffens. For a moment, it seems he might spin around and strike me.

"Tim, I love you," I say.

"Yeah," he says derisively. Then he walks upstairs to his room, carefully avoiding any glance into the sunroom where his mother lies sleeping.

I turn to Eleni and say, "Sweetie, what about you? Do you want to …?"

She answers before I finish. "Yes … I … I will," she whimpers. It's a pitiful reply, like a child promising to be good from now on. Then she forces another *I will* and quickly adds, "But not now. Can we talk later? Is that okay?"

I recognize Eleni's obedience. She sounds sincere, but I feel she's responding out of obligation to me rather expressing her own need. It's typical of Eleni to consent to another's wishes and not express hers. Down deep, she doesn't want to talk any more than I do.

I step closer to embrace her, but she backs off and shakes her head, *no*. As she walks away, I say, "I love you Eleni. It's okay. We're gonna get through this; I promise."

Suddenly, I'm aware of darkness in the house. It's August, and the sun sets earlier each night. There was plenty of light when we first got together tonight, and I never turned on a light. How can time pass so slowly and be gone so swiftly?

CHAPTER FORTY-FIVE

No, it is not only our fate but our business to lose innocence,
and once we have lost that, it is futile to attempt a picnic in Eden.

—Elizabeth Bowen

Amy appears noticeably pleased when we survey the new posters the kids have put up in her room, but I'm surprised that the new scenes take me aback. Though I haven't selected them, the new pictures seem familiar. With Bible verses inscribed on scenes of frolicking dolphins and playful pandas, the images should brighten the atmosphere, but, oddly, the room's appearance triggers an ominous feeling in me. The new items, posters and a Greek Orthodox icon of Jesus my mother gave me, decorate the paneling on either side of an archway on the west wall, the only wall without windows. I've already placed a tension rod in the archway and hung an opaque curtain we can draw when Amy's modesty demands it. Privacy shades cover the single French door and nine windows on adjacent walls. I've selected them to maintain the yellow-gold hue that Amy favors.

Though Amy has responded cheerfully to the children's efforts, her condition worsens as time passes, and other attempts to make things better only intensify our Sisyphean task. Our church group built a ramp to allow her to go outside in a wheelchair, but she used it only once on the same afternoon they built it. Resigned to dependency, she stoically tolerates my intrusion as I assist her with basic bodily functions, but she shuns other visitors.

One day, Dan, the church pastor, waited in another room while a nurse helped Amy finish a particularly difficult time on the toilet. Though the French door was closed and the curtain drawn, unmistakable sounds carried into the kitchen where I sat chatting with the pastor. When Reverend Donaldson and I finally stepped in to see Amy, she greeted him coldly and hardly spoke. Though he was a treasured friend as well our pastor, Dan appeared embarrassed and ill at ease. Amy closed her eyes shortly after the pastor stepped in, and he left after offering a short prayer. At the door, he seemed to apologize to me because it was so difficult for him to see how much Amy had "changed" in such a short time.

Amy spoke to me immediately after Dan left the house. "I wasn't sleeping," she said, "I was angry and embarrassed. I don't want any more visitors, and I don't mean just for today. I don't want anyone to see how ugly I am. It's hard enough for me to be like I am, but I can't stand watching someone else's pain when they see what I go through. I won't put anyone through that ordeal again."

Before I could respond, the automatic syringe connected to Amy sounded an alarm. The dosage had run out, and I had to insert a new ampoule to maintain the flow of morphine.

Pain management is both a blessing and a curse. The syringe that Amy controls with the touch of a finger allows us to monitor her pain. Several times a day, she increases the dosage. These increases are not signs of progress, but are marks of advancement toward destruction, and I wonder what goes through Amy's mind as she watches the plunger move more rapidly each day. Amy can measure the decreasing time she has left by the increasing rate of morphine dripping into her body. As I silently loath the futility of my effort and loss of her dignity, I can only hope that she is able to see her weakness as an ally that will lead to ultimate escape. My prayer is that she has found some inner defense for the invasion she endures. Otherwise, there can be no justification for allowing her body to shut down and her spirit to leave her.

Earlier, I associated the signs—hair loss, skin discoloration, puffy joints, limp muscles—as necessary battle scars in the war against cancer. They gave us hope for a respite from the disease, if not a cure. Now, the changes are irreversible. Amy's face, limbs, and upper body continue to shrivel, while her abdomen swells enormously. Dry, colorless skin crawls over her once-beautiful face, spreads like cracking mud drying in the wind. Wrinkles sag and translucent skin stretches over bony features. I have no right to stand by like a voyeur, but I can do nothing about it. I feel as though I am bound, gagged, and forced to observe a grotesque murder.

I don't dare presume to understand how Amy feels, but I try to picture what our children experience. When deciding to care for Amy at home, I had hoped they would benefit from daily contact with their mother, but I've yet to realize that benefit. Every day, the children experience new drama and make fewer and fewer visits to her bedside because Amy is barely aware of them. Though Amy's fate is sealed, theirs is uncertain. Ahead are endless miles of unexplored roads, and, as they prepare to begin their journey, I wonder what lessons they learn by seeing their mother come to the end of hers.

Mary's here today for her afternoon shift and will stay until nine. Taking advantage of a break, I sip iced tea on the patio and catch up on yesterday's newspaper. The screen door slams shut, and Erin comes out with a curious look on her face.

"Daddy Dude?" she says. The inflection in her voice hints of a question.

I look up from the comics and say, "Yeah, what's up?"

"Uh ... I think I started something."

"You're always starting something. What is it this time?"

"My ... uh ... *exclamation point.*"

I set down the paper. Amy often used that expression to joke about her monthly period. For her, *period* was a punctuation mark that was much too mild for the end of a menstrual cycle. I know Erin enjoys imitating her mother, and she might be kidding me, so I tilt my head and squint through one eye to ask if she's fooling me before I say, "You mean your *period?*"

She smiles and sheepishly says, "Yeah."

"Are you sure?"

She rolls her eyes and twists her mouth to the side—just like her mom used to do. "Daaad," she says, drawing out her reply, "this isn't something that you're not sure of."

"Are you okay?"

"Yeah, I guess so."

"Feelin' all right?"

"Why? Am I supposed to be sick?"

"No. I just wondered." I smile and get up from the patio table. "Well, congratulations, young lady," I say, hugging her tenderly. "I'm very proud of you."

"Dad!"

"Hey, I can be happy for you. Today you've grown from eleven to eleventeen."

"I don't feel happy. I feel yucky."

"I don't know about those things. You should talk to M ... eh, you'll have to talk to your sister about that. Or you can ask the nurse."

Erin shrugs.

"You know what this means?" I ask. "It means you're on your way to being a little lady."

"I don't want to be a lady. I like being a kid."

"Do you know what to do? I mean, do you know how—"

"Yeah, yeah. Mom talked to me about this a long time ago. She said she started when she was eleven, so I should … you know, watch for it."

"Well, how about we go and tell Mom right now?"

She scrunches up her shoulders and cocks her head to one side. "Yeah, I guess so." A tiny smile, like a rosebud poking out from behind a leaf, bursts onto her lips.

We're both smiling as we near Amy's bed. I'm proud of my little girl and hope Amy's cheered, as well. The nurse gets up and starts to leave.

"Amy's awake and comfortable," she says. "I'll leave you alone with her."

"No, please stay," I insist, "Erin has news for her mom that I'd like you to hear."

Amy doesn't notice us until we stand directly in front of her. Her eyelids sit halfway over her eyes, motionless and drawn like the half-closed window shades in her room. She opens her mouth slightly and forces an uncurled line that resembles a smile.

"Hi," she chirps. Her voice is more bird-like than it was yesterday.

"Hi, Mom," I say. "Guess what? Erin's got something to tell you."

I nudge Erin. Her eyes dart to the nurse and back to me. Her face shows an *oh-Dad-what-are-you-doing?* expression. Turning to Amy, she takes a deep breath and says, "Mom … I started my period today." Her face lights up with a grin.

"Oh," squeaks Amy. She tries to match Erin's broad smile but manages only a grimace. "That's wonderful. You're a big girl now. Did you—?"

"I took care of it just like you said. I remembered about the you-know-what."

Amy sounds breathless when she says, "Good. How do you feel?"

"Yucky."

"You can talk to Mary about it," Amy says, nodding slowly toward the nurse. The simple motion seems difficult. "Or to Eleni. Or Dad. He's not as big a dummy as you might think." Already fatigued, she takes a breath but is unable to form another smile.

Then Amy closes her eyes, and Erin looks as if she's about to cry.

More loudly than necessary, I say, "Well, dummy or not, I'm taking this little lady to the movies." Amy's eyelids flash open, but her eyes stare blankly. I turn to Erin and ask, "What do you say, kid? Okay to go to the movies with your old man?"

"Dad, it's no big deal."

"Why don't you two go ahead?" says Mary. "I'll stay right here with Amy."

"How about *Back To The Future*?" I say. "I hear Michael J. Fox fires up a time machine and meets his parents before he's born. Sounds pretty scary, huh?"

As we leave, Erin turns mournfully toward her sleeping mother. She wants something from her mom—something I'm afraid I will never be able to give her.

Amy's behavior seems strange this morning. I checked her at five o'clock and found her slumped over, and she didn't stir or wake up when I tried to make her more comfortable. Now, an hour later, I can't tell whether she's sleeping or unconscious. I shake her to ask if she feels okay. She opens her eyes and answers incoherently, and then falls asleep again. Could she be in a coma? I check another blood sample in the Glucoscan. It's 112. The book says that's normal before a meal, but Amy's eating erratically now, and maybe she should be on intravenous feeding. Wouldn't the Glucoscan show a dangerous reading if the insulin were wrong? I remember the same thing happened once when Kristyn was here. Amy was all right then, but I can't tell if this is the same thing. Maybe the automatic syringe is pumping too much morphine. A nurse is scheduled to be here at 8:00—a substitute for Kristyn, and I hope she's on time. What if she doesn't show up? These signs have occurred before, but not when I was alone. Jesus, what will I do?

I can't tell if I've given her the wrong insulin dose, so I take another test. It's 89. Ordinarily that's not alarming, but I need more assurance. The book says she might go into a hypoglycemic coma if I gave her too much. Too little will bring on a diabetic coma. God, I could kill her with the wrong dosage! Her breathing pattern seems all right, and I don't detect a sweet smell or scent of acetone—signs the doctor said to look for. Her pulse and blood pressure are normal, but, Jesus, Amy's life hangs in the balance of my judgment. Where's that friggin' nurse?

Frustrated, I call Amy's endocrinologist. At first the sound of his calm voice eases my anxiety, but I panic when he doesn't answer as I expect.

"My God, doctor," I cry into the phone. "Have I killed her?"

"No. No. No," he says in his Middle Eastern accent. "You say she appears unconscious, but all of her vitals are normal. I think she is only sleeping."

"But, doctor, she gets worse every day. I could kill her if I make a mistake. Are you sure she's all right? Should I call 911?"

Another long pause precedes his answer. "Mr. Demetriou, I am sorry. Has no one told you? Her surgeon? Or the nurses coming to the house? Surely, the oncologist has explained what to expect."

"Expect? What do you mean?"

"At the end," he says. "Surely, someone has told you that your wife ... that Amy will not survive, no matter what you do. A coma is likely at the end. She will simply lose consciousness and then gradually cease functioning. That is what you and Amy decided when you chose to remain at home. If you brought her to the hospital, we would use any method available to resuscitate her. In Amy's case, a coma is far better. It is nature's way. She will die by God's grace. Be thankful for it, Nick. Cancer is a horrible disease. Right now, for your wife, death is a gift."

"God," I whisper. The word I utter is my prayer, its bitter tone my blasphemy.

When I become silent, the doctor nearly shouts "Mr. Demetriou" in a way to command my attention. "You can't be thinking she will go on indefinitely," he demands. "I must admit that, somehow … I thought that somehow you would have already known."

Another long pause before I say, "Yes, I guess I should've figured it out."

I hang up and go to Amy's bedside. She's sleeping peacefully. An insulin syringe lies nearby like an assassin's dagger. I pick it up and consider ending Amy's misery before it becomes more torturous than I can bear.

Then a knock on the front door startles me. I examine the syringe once more before setting it down. When I open the door, a middle-aged woman says, "Hi, I'm Pat … the substitute nurse from Duffy. Sorry I'm late."

Though it wasn't a crisis, it was alarming, so Mary Lindstrom promises to set up twenty-four hour care as soon as possible. Because the regular PCS staff is already overburdened, Mary has to schedule a nurse from Duffy for one eight-hour shift every day. Amy goes in and out of consciousness in what the nurses call a *semi-coma*, a condition that Mary says often precedes a full comatose state.

Nurse Sharon from Duffy has been arriving at midnight. When everything is going well, I catch a few hours of sleep while she's here. *Going well* is a euphemism for *death doesn't seem imminent*, but I know this is the beginning of the end and dread it more than I fear my own death. Amy seems to rest comfortably, but only by monitoring her vital signs can we tell for sure. Some bodily functions, like menstruation, stopped long ago. As other failures occur, I sense my own functions wane and feel more and more as if I'm sleepwalking.

Kristyn left the house tonight at eleven to assist Mary in an emergency. I wait for Sharon's arrival at midnight, but 1:00 a.m. comes and passes without Sharon and without a word from anyone. I call Duffy Services. A gentleman tells me he'll notify the night coordinator at Duffy and I can expect a call shortly. Another hour passes. I ring the Duffy number again and get the same reply. Twenty-five minutes later and nearing 3:00 a.m., the night coordinator from Duffy finally calls.

"Mr. Demeter, what seems to be the problem?"

"It's *Demetriou*, and I already explained to someone that my nurse—my *wife's* nurse hasn't shown up."

"What is her name, please?"

"Sharon. Sharon Crandell. She was to be here at midnight."

"Hmm. Why did you wait so long to call us?"

"I didn't. I called at one o'clock."

"Well, even *that's* a little late," she says. "I got your message only a moment ago. Are you sure you called the correct number? To whom did you speak?"

Like a chastised schoolboy, I answer, "I didn't get his name." Then, angered by my timidity, I shout, "Why are you making this my mistake? It's yours, not—"

"Actually, sir," she interrupts forcefully, "I believe it's *Ms. Crandell's* error. She's the one who didn't show—"

"That's right, so, what are you going to do about it?"

"I've checked my roster, and I'm afraid I don't have anyone available."

"But ... listen, don't you understand? My wife ... she's ... wait. You haven't even asked about her. You don't know if this is an emergency or—"

"Emergencies are handled by calling 911," she says impassively. "I can't—"

"No, I guess you can't!" I scream. "What good are you, anyway? If you can't send someone now, don't come at all. I don't ever want to deal with any of you people again!"

I carry on without a nurse until 8:00 a.m. when Mary Lindstrom comes and promises not to use Duffy Services again. Though she pledges to fill the void as soon as possible, she admits it'll be hard to get another nurse, so I warn myself to expect the unexpected. The makeshift arrangement is confusing, and when Virginia arrives for the next midnight shift, she says that no one is available for the next morning. Mary has to juggle the roster, trading Kristyn's slot with hers and the other Mary's. I have trouble following Virginia's explanation and don't catch the other Mary's last name, but I prepare to be alone from 8:00 the next morning until the following midnight. In the interim, while Virginia is here, I catch up on my sleep and get up at 6:00 a.m. to get her report. She says there is no change in Amy's vitals and she seems comfortable.

With no word of a substitute nurse, I carry on. Shortly after 2:00 in the afternoon, Amy begins a pattern of labored breathing. When her pulse weakens, I call PCS for advice and learn that neither Mary is available. The woman who has answered says she'll page someone immediately. Around 5:00, Amy's pulse is barely detectable, and I telephone Amy's mother and father and tell them they should come right away to say their good-byes. When I call the nursing service again, a woman assures me that she has summoned a nurse. Nearing 6:00 at night no one has arrived, so I speak to the children in the kitchen, and then ask them to make their own dinner. Andy and Saundra arrive at 7:00 and sit with Amy while I try to comfort the kids—a task I find impossible.

The Millers stay beside Amy for about two hours while I open the hide-a-bed and prepare the spare room upstairs. There is no way of telling if our vigil will last a single night or several days, so I suggest that Amy's folks sleep upstairs and stay as long as they can. They agree, and I promise to rouse them if it becomes necessary.

Feeling fatigued, I go into the bathroom to splash cold water on my face, and catch a glimpse of myself in the mirror. Wearily, I recall a poem titled *Fall* by Hans W. Cohn.

> *One morning*
> *his face fell out of the mirror*
> *into his hands:*
>
> *he let it fall.*

This isn't the way I thought it was going to be. There was a time when I had fantasized the end coming peacefully, as in a Frank Capra movie scene, where I held Amy's hand as she drifted into a quiet slumber and passed serenely into the next life. Consciously, that visualization is all that I've allowed myself to anticipate, but now the cloak my mind threw over my subconscious has dissolved, and I find myself living the nightmare I once refused to picture.

It's the middle of the night, and, as I sit alone with Amy, I'm alarmed by her breathing pattern. I dare not leave her because it sometimes becomes wild and frenzied. As her chaotic episodes intensify, my own breathing becomes frenetic, and I feel as if I'm mimicking her behavior.

I've left the front door partially open, and when the other Mary finally arrives, she comes directly to us and seems startled to see that Amy is barely breathing. Within minutes, she urges Amy to seek the "warm white light" that beckons her, implying that that will ease her transition. But I'm not persuaded by her intonations, and while Mary leads her toward the light, I cling to Amy as if I can pull her back toward life, whispering remembrances of joyful moments with me and the children.

Then Amy's breathing slows and becomes barely perceptible, and I feel her leaving me. Sliding in beside her, I take her in my arms and gently rock her back and forth. Mary suddenly stops her incantation, and, in the silence, I think I hear

Amy sigh. I listen for another sound all the while longing for our embrace to last forever, but Amy transcends forever and passes to eternity before I take another breath.

Nevertheless, I continue to hold her and pray for a sign that she is truly at peace. Alas, the only sign I sense is the amazingly short while it takes for me to feel the coolness of her body.

Andy and Saundra leave before the mortician arrives, but Mary stays to offer comfort to me and the children. I'm so grateful for her compassion and commitment to our care that I have all but forgotten her earlier absence and my confusion about the two Marys.

"Nick," she says, "how did you do it? It must have been agonizing to watch her go on like that. You shouldn't have had to do that alone. Why didn't you call us?"

"I did. Didn't Mary Lindstrom tell you? Didn't you get my messages?"

Mary Noname looks dumbfounded. She did not receive a message. Frantically, she examines her pager and punches and shakes it. Then she snaps open the lid and inserts a new battery, but nothing brings it back to life.

From beyond the draped figure lying on the bed, an Orthodox icon of Jesus—my mother's promise of healing—stares at me over Mary's shoulder. He, too, appears to have no life.

A soft knock on the partially open front door is followed by someone's entrance. "Nick, it's Brian O'Donnell," says the young man from the funeral home. He and I got acquainted weeks ago when we made what he called "the necessary arrangements."

I raise my eyes and see Brian step toward the sunroom. Two assistants wheeling a stretcher that bears something resembling a black laundry bag follow him. From my vantage point in the dining room, I can see the mortuary men, the nurse, the bed with a motionless body, and the icon of Jesus.

I say nothing aloud, but in my mind, I hear myself say to all of them, *Yes, of course. Come in. I know what you want, but don't take her away. I'm going to wake up from this dream soon and have no memory of any of it.*

CHAPTER FORTY-SIX

Life must go on
... I forget just why.

—Amy Lowell

Amy died three weeks ago. Three weeks—and still I tell myself, this is only a bad dream. But what will I find when I wake?

School began for the kids only a week after their mother's funeral, and they stuck with it for two more weeks before I decided that we needed ... what? A retreat? A rest? A vacation?

I asked for an extension of leave from teaching, so my time is flexible, but Eleni, a college senior, can only spare a week away from the university. After I take her back to her dorm, I'll return to the cottage with Tim and Erin for another week. My notes to their teachers say they'll be away for about ten days. I thought the kids would welcome the idea. Now I'm not so sure. I can't imagine them eager to return to live again in the house where death came to visit.

Here at the cottage, outside on the deck, I try to relax doing crosswords while the kids play inside—if I can call it play. They spend most of the time squabbling, and their squabbling scatters my thoughts. I brought us Up North to draw us together, to start again. But start where?

We arrived on Saturday, and so did a cold and rainy spell that's lingered for three days. I want to make the most of the two days left before driving Eleni back to school, but I don't see anyone going along with what I've planned. Part of me wishes I had no plan, and I'm proud that I haven't spent a lot of time talking about what's happened. Oh, I bring it up, but I don't get philosophical, and I try to avoid being a *teacher* in the way my children hate. I'm sure that surprises them.

This morning, they were crabby when I made what I thought was a great breakfast. I slammed down their plates of poached eggs on whole-wheat toast and scowled at them. Then I stormed out for a walk in the woods. Along the way, I picked up a stick and snapped it angrily. It felt good, so I did it again and again.

After a while, I remembered a story about how individual sticks can easily break if handled one-by-one, but are almost impossible to break when bound together. It seemed like a good object lesson for the family, but I decided not to teach it when I got back. The only thing worse than being too *teachy* is to be too *preachy*. That's when I realized why we were here. We went Up North to eat junk food and have fun.

I've thought a lot about how to do that—have fun. The problem is, I'm not much in the mood.

Back on the deck, I hear the screen door creak open and sense that someone is easing it back slowly because I don't hear it bang shut. Then I hear Tim and Eleni whispering in undertones that seem anxious and quarrelsome. I cock my ear and recognize a few *don'ts* and *okays* that sound like trouble, but their hush suggests they don't want me to know about it. Just as I'm about to pass off their chatter as kid stuff, Tim says, "He's gonna be mad." When I look around curiously, I hear a not-so-hushed "Shh!"

Stillness follows Eleni's caution. In a second, she and Tim step around the corner and saunter toward the picnic table where I sit. Tim's head-down shuffle shows a reticent defiance that I've seen before. Eleni, however, has her arms folded across her chest and wears an expression that's different from her usual shy and submissive self.

"Dad," she says, "can Tim and I talk to you?" Her voice has an edge that I don't recognize. Twisting her mouth, she begins chewing on the inside of her cheek like her mom used to do when she was nervous.

"Yeah, of course you can. What is it?"

"Not *talk* really—not about … you know."

Since Amy died, the word *talk* brings on symptoms resembling lockjaw.

"Sweetie," I say, "we don't always have to be serious."

"You won't get mad?"

"About what?"

Eleni tightens her folded arms and raises them higher. Looking down, she squints as if to peer through the space between the slats of the deck floor. Then she shifts her feet and lifts her eyes to meet mine before saying, "Uh … can we go home early? Tonight, maybe?"

I hesitate too long because they start to cower away. I try to smile, but can't force my mouth to turn upward. Suddenly, the taste of bitter bile makes me grimace as my stomach sends stinging acid to my throat. It's called *acid reflux*, and it's officially why I'm on leave. I learned from Amy's experience never to say that I'm depressed.

"Why?" I ask.

Eleni looks to Tim for help and struggles to say, "Tim and I.... Well, we just—"

"Yeah," says Tim, nodding his head but offering no information.

"What about Erin?" I ask. "Does she want to go home, too?"

Eleni shrugs. "She didn't say. She just ... scrunched her shoulders and kept drawing stupid cartoons."

"Well, let's talk about it. Can you tell me what's wrong? Want to do something different? Go canoeing? Or catch a movie in town?"

"No, it's not that. Dad ... I don't know." Eleni lowers her head and raises her eyes. "You're mad at us, aren't you?"

"No," I snap. Then, more softly, I add, "No, I'm not. I'm only asking what you guys want. What's on your mind? I'll try to—"

"Dad, please don't analyze. It's nothing we can explain. We just want to get back to school. We don't want to talk about Mom all the time."

"I didn't think we ... I only thought I could—"

Eleni interrupts again. "Dad, please don't.... You're always trying to *explain*. Couldn't we just ...?" She shakes her head and runs into the cottage.

"Tim? What about you?"

Tim has retreated to the corner of the deck and stands under my homemade "Nick's Place" sign hanging from the edge of the roof. The sign is a cutout caricature of a cowboy in a ten-gallon hat. It was Amy's idea that I carve and paint it to resemble me.

"I dunno," he mutters.

"Well, do you want to go home, too?"

"Y-y-yeah, I guess so."

A breeze picks up and blows my puzzle into the yard. Damnit! Nobody asks what *I* want to do.

Unable to face them yet, I take another walk in the woods. Eleni's right. I shouldn't analyze so much. I thought our retreat would give us a new start, but it's ... man, what a waste. We haven't done half the things I planned.

Thirty yards from the cottage, I hear the kids bickering again. When I walk inside, I see the Monopoly board askew on the kitchen table. Someone's tossed money into the air, and several slips float to the floor. Tokens and title cards lie scattered about the room, and several of the cards are torn in half.

"What happened?" I say.

"Nuthin'," everyone answers.

"Well," I bark, "we're not going anywhere until this place is cleaned up."

"We're putting it away now," says Eleni. "No one wants to play anymore."

I glare at them and then go to my bedroom, but it's not a place of comfort any more. On the wall, hangs a *Gone with the Wind* poster, and Clark Gable and Vivien Leigh hover over the bed where Amy and I once made love. I turn my back and sit on the edge of the bed to think about what's happening. That's all I do: think and worry—and plan what to do next. *God, will I ever be able to just let go?*

Things need buttoning down before we leave, but procrastination seems like a legitimate option. I have no packing to do because most of my Up North clothes are old things I keep at the cottage. I should go outside and put the outdoor stuff in the garage, but I stay in and rifle through my dresser, looking for I-don't-know-what, until I come across my old Bermuda shorts. Suddenly, an idea pops into my head.

I put on an outfit my kids love to hate—orange shirt, red-plaid Bermuda's, black knee socks, and brown moccasins. I top it off with a crushed cowboy hat flattened when Amy sat on it in Laramie, Wyoming. My face in the full-length mirror shows a growing smile. The spectacle I've created is a family joke that has always made us laugh. Sparked by Amy's flint-edged tongue, the friendly ridicule often turned a boring day into whimsical fun. Then I frown and shake my head. Can I pull this off without Amy?

After a deep breath, I call through the bedroom door, "Hey, guys, can we negotiate?"

Together, Tim and Eleni say, "What?"

"He said," answers Erin, "'can we *go-see-eight*?'"

"What's he talking about?" says Tim.

Assured of their attention, I step out in my full regalia. Everyone is wide-eyed. Erin begins to snicker but stops when Eleni and Tim look askance. After a moment, Eleni says, "Dad, we know what you're trying to do, but—"

"Come on," I say. "You guys used to laugh when I joked around and—"

"It's not the same without ...," mutters Tim.

"Dad, we love you," says Eleni. "We want to laugh, but we...."

They're all looking away now, but I can see their sadness. "Listen," I say as gently as I can, "I want us to have fun again. Can't we try one more day? Remember when your mom used to say 'Let's do something to blow the stink off'? I think we need that before we go home. Can we compromise?"

After a moment, Eleni and Tim exchange glances and offer a reluctant nod. Erin shrugs and says, "What do you mean?"

My getup didn't get the reaction I hoped for, but at least we're able to talk. In the end, they agree to stay for another day if I let them spend it at the outrageous tourist traps nearby. Our spirits lift a little by the time we pig out at the sweet shop, which energizes us to play a round or two of Michigan Rummy when we return to the cottage.

The following day, I try to refresh our spirit by proposing a "farewell" breakfast after letting everyone sleep till noon, but the kids react with strident cries of *pancakes, scrambled eggs, French toast* and *bacon*—individual demands that lead to new arguments.

When Erin says *snausages* in the way her mom used to say it, everyone stops yelling momentarily, and I say, "Okay, okay, but I'm not taking orders. Nick's Place is not a restaurant."

"We'll eat whatever you make, Dad," says Eleni.

"Just make lots of it," says Tim.

"Yeah," says Erin.

Then they immediately scatter.

"Hold on. You aren't going anywhere. Everyone has to help."

They look at me as if I've asked them to forage for silage.

"Kids, let's get a few things straight. I'm the only parent now, and I need your help."

"Just tell us what to do," says Eleni. "Please don't make a speech."

"I'm not speechifying."

They look up as if they were puppies made to sit obediently before allowed to eat.

"Look, we're all having a hard time because we have too many memories."

Eleni looks at me defiantly and says, "I don't want to forget. You can't make me."

"No, no, of course not, but I want us to remember that Mom loved us so much that she wouldn't want us to be sad forever."

Tim's lower lip trembles, and he says, "Dad, please … don't.…"

A tear appears on Eleni's cheek, and I begin to cry. Erin seems bewildered and reaches out to take my hand.

Between sobs, I manage to burble, "I need to say one more thing."

They stand silently, but I can't go on.

Then little Erin pipes *I love you* in a voice that's barely heard. In a moment, we all repeat it in a way that feels like *amen* as we turn away from each other.

A shrill call of a blue jay animates us, and we start making breakfast. I let Tim help me make French toast, as long as he doesn't use the popup toaster as he did the last time. Erin can brew coffee in her mom's antique coffee pot if she washes it and rinses out the soap. (On one occasion, the pot percolated coffee-flavored soap bubbles.) Eleni volunteers to make the beds after gathering last night's poker chips. I think she wants to escape before having to referee the inevitable fight when Tim and Erin bump into each other in the tiny kitchen.

After breakfast, I pat my belly and say, "Man oh man, that was great. Thanks for helping. Now, let's get the place in order before we blow this popcorn stand."
"Smelly's turn to wash," says Erin, crinkling her nose at Timothy.
"Unh, uh, buttface. It's *yours.*"
"Shut up, doggie breath."
"Dad, did you hear that? Tell him it's *his* turn."
"Cry baby. What's the matter, can't fight your own battles?"
"Stop arguing," says Eleni. "*I'll* do the dishes."
"We'll *all* pitch in," I say. "Tim, you clear the table. Eleni washes. Erin dries. I'll take care of the trash and do the vacuuming. When you're done, I want everyone packed, pottied, and ready to go." I clap my hands sharply to emphasize my commands. They respond by making faces at each other. When they finally get started, it's with the enthusiasm of slugs.

I guess it'll always be this way—with our moods ebbing like the waves that lap our shore and recede to the lake. Discord will follow harmony. Argument will follow agreement. Hopefully, happiness will follow gloom.

Anger creeps in as we prepare to go home. Teasing banter turns into sarcastic taunt, and my pleas for cooperation become shouts. The children rail at each other to the brink of outright battle until we stop talking altogether. Silence and the rapid approach of nightfall accentuate my sense of urgency.
The kids are startled when I snap on the room light. They peer outside, and their faces show anguish that I wish I could relieve. But there is nothing I can do about the passage of time. We'll be traveling in twilight and arriving home in darkness. In that moment, I know that my children must be my primary focus until they're grown, and I'll have to wait to start a new life.
But I wonder: *will I be there when my life begins?*

AFTERWORD

Most men discover when they look back on their life that they have been living ad interim, and are surprised to see that which they let go by so unregarded and unenjoyed was precisely their life.

—**Arthur Schopenhauer**

Lydia and I are sipping coffee at the kitchen table. She is knitting, and I'm reading the comics. I'm struck by how little has changed in the funnies while so much has happened in the world. Here it is 2007, and I still find Blondie and Dagwood amusing, and Charlie Brown and Lucy charming. Looking up from the paper, I gaze at Lydia and feel a sense of comfort that's beyond anything I can say. Suddenly, she catches my admiring glance, but I don't look away.

"What?" says Lydia. Then her lips stretch into a smile.

"Oh, I was just thinking about the story I wrote."

"Not surprising," she says, flicking another stitch. "You've been working on it for a long time."

"Yeah," I say, "but it never really felt like work. Parts of it were hard to tell, but I never looked on it as a task—except for the last line. I had trouble figuring out how to end it."

"You mean the question about your life beginning? Well," she says, putting down her needles, "I don't know how hard it was to end the story, but I do know the answer to the question. You *were* there when your life began."

Suddenly, tears well in my eyes and without hesitation I say, "And I'm so happy that you were there, too."

More than twenty years have passed since Amy died, and many more have gone by since I first thought about writing our story. Now that it's done, I'm grateful that our children will know the tale from my perspective, and hopeful they might be able to recall their own memories as they lived them.

It was not out of sadness that I wrote our story, but out of joy. And though there are several sources of my joy, I will speak of only two.

First is the totality of my experience with Amy. Ours was a love cast in the mold of innocence and burnished by our labors. In the end, even the fire of hell made our love stronger. Horrible as some periods were, I believe they prepared me, not only to endure the pain of Amy's death, but also to be there when my life began again. I'm grateful to Amy for the years we had together and the joys we shared. Without them, I would never have been able to find the gladness I feel today.

One of Amy's last requests was that I find someone to love after she was gone. It took me eight years to break out of the shell where I hid, and it took an extraordinary woman to draw me out, but now, after fourteen years of a new marriage, I can declare that I love today as I have never loved before.

So my story does not end; it continues because I'm here with Lydia, whose love is the wellspring of a joy I once feared I would never feel again.

APPENDIX

The self-help mental health program, Recovery, Inc., can be contacted at its international headquarters at 802 N. Dearborn Street, Chicago, Illinois 60610,
Telephone: 312-337-5661, Fax: 312-337-5756,
Email: inquiries@recovery-inc.org.
It's Web site is http://www.recovery-inc.com/.

The self-help mental health program, Relatives, Inc., is now called The Relatives Project, and can be contacted at The Abraham A. Low Institute, 550 Frontage Road, Suite 2797, Northfield, Illinois 60093,
Telephone: 847-441-0045, Fax: 847-441-0046,
Email: lowinstitute@aol.com.
It's Web site is http://www.lowinstitute.org/Relatives.html.

978-0-595-44120-4
0-595-44120-3

Printed in the United States
93408LV00004B/1-84/A